PENGUIN CLASSICS

THE COMPLETE STORIES

TRUMAN CAPOTE was born in New Orleans in 1924 and was raised in various parts of the South, his family spending winters in New Orleans and summers in Alabama and New Georgia. He left school when he was fifteen and subsequently worked for the *New Yorker* which provided his first – and last – regular job. In 1948 his first novel, *Other Voices, Other Rooms,* was published to international critical acclaim, assuring Capote a place among the prominent postwar American writers. His other works include *The Grass Harp* (1951), *Breakfast at Tiffany's* (1958), *In Cold Blood* (1965), which immediately became the centre of a storm of controversy on its publication, *Music for Chameleons* (1980) and *Answered Prayers* (1986). *Summer Crossing,* Capote's first novel, was sold at Sotheby's, New York, in 2004, and published for the first time in the UK by Penguin Classics in 2005. Truman Capote died in August 1984.

REYNOLDS PRICE is the James B. Duke Professor of English at Duke University and the distinguished author of more than twenty-five books of fiction, poetry, drama and essays. He lives in North Carolina.

The Complete Stories of Truman Capote

with an Introduction by REYNOLDS PRICE

PENGUIN BOOKS

PENGUIN BOOKS

Published by the Penguin Group
Penguin Books Ltd, 80 Strand, London WC2R 0RL, England
Penguin Group (USA) Inc., 375 Hudson Street, New York, New York 10014, USA
Penguin Group (Canada), 90 Eglinton Avenue East, Suite 700, Toronto,
Ontario, Canada M4P 3YZ (a division of Pearson Penguin Canada Inc.)
Penguin Ireland, 25 St Stephen's Green, Dublin 2, Ireland
(a division of Penguin Books Ltd)
Penguin Group (Australia), 250 Camberwell Road,
Camberwell, Victoria 3124, Australia (a division of Pearson Australia Group Pty Ltd)
Penguin Books India Pvt Ltd, 11 Community Centre,
Panchsheel Park, New Delhi – 110 017, India
Penguin Group (NZ), cnr Airborne and Rosedale Roads, Albany,
Auckland 1310, New Zealand (a division of Pearson New Zealand Ltd)
Penguin Books (South Africa) (Pty) Ltd, 24 Sturdee Avenue,
Rosebank 2196, South Africa

Penguin Books Ltd, Registered Offices: 80 Strand, London WC2R 0RL, England

www.penguin.com

First published in the United States of America by Random House 2004
First published in Great Britain in Penguin Classics 2005

6

Compilation copyright © Truman Capote Literary Trust, 2004
Introduction copyright © Reynolds Price, 2004
All rights reserved

The moral right of the author has been asserted

Printed in England by Clays Ltd, St Ives plc

Except in the United States of America, this book is sold subject
to the condition that it shall not, by way of trade or otherwise, be lent,
re-sold, hired out, or otherwise circulated without the publisher's
prior consent in any form of binding or cover other than that in
which it is published and without a similar condition including this
condition being imposed on the subsequent purchaser

ISBN-13: 978–0–141–18808–9

CONTENTS

Contents

INTRODUCTION

Usable Answers

Reynolds Price

America has never been a land of readers, not of what's called literary fiction in any case. And in the twentieth century, only two writers of distinguished fiction managed to become American household names—Ernest Hemingway and Truman Capote. Each of them succeeded in that dubious distinction by means which hardly included their often distinguished work. Hemingway—strapping, bearded and grinning—reached most households in the pages of *Life, Look* and *Esquire* magazines with a fishing rod or a shotgun in hand or a hapless Spanish bull nearby, on the verge of being killed. After the publication of Capote's nonfiction account of a mass murder in rural Kansas, he (in his tiny frame and high voice) became the instant star of numerous television talk shows—a fame that he maintained even as his consumption of liquor and drugs left him a bloated shadow of his former self. And even now—with Hemingway dead of a self-inflicted gunshot wound since 1961 and Capote of relentless self-abuse since 1984—their best work continues to be gravely denigrated by understandably disaffected critics and readers. Yet many of Hemingway's lucid short stories and at least three of his novels are as near perfection as prose ever manages to be, and Capote left behind not only a riveting crime narrative but also a quantity of early fiction (three brief novels and a handful of short stories) that awaits the close attention and measured admiration he long since earned.

—

Capote's short stories are gathered here; and they range over most of his creative life up until the devastating success of *In Cold Blood,* which was published in 1965 when he was little more than forty years old. With the brilliantly self-managed publicity bonanza of that riveting crime tale, Capote not only landed on millions of American coffee tables and on every TV screen, he further endeared himself to the denizens of café society and the underfed fashion queens whom he'd so bafflingly pursued in earlier years.

Soon he would announce his intention to publish a long novel that would examine the society of rich America as mercilessly as Marcel Proust had portrayed French high society in the late nineteenth and early twentieth centuries. And he may well have gone to work on his plan. Yet one consideration that Capote never seemed to discuss, or even be questioned about in public, was crucial to the eventual collapse of his vision (if he ever had one). Proust's society was one of *blood,* unshakably founded on positions of French social eminence that were reared upon centuries-old money, property and actual power over the lives of other human beings. Capote's society merely teetered upon the unsubstantial and finally inconsequential grounds of financial wealth; fashionable clothes, houses and yachts and occasional physical beauty (the women were frequently beautiful, the men very seldom so). Any long fictional study of such a world was likely to implode upon the ultimate triviality of its subject.

When he surfaced from punishing rounds of frenetic social and sexual activity and began to publish excerpts from his novel— fewer than two hundred pages—Capote found himself abandoned overnight by virtually all his rich friends; and he fled into a nightmare tunnel of drugs, drink and sexual commitments of the most psychically damaging sort. Despite numerous attempts at recovery, his addictions only deepened; and when he died, a miserable soul well short of old age, he left behind only a few pages of the tall stack of manuscript he claimed to have written on his great novel. If more of the novel ever existed, he'd destroyed the pages before his death (and his closest friends disagreed on the likelihood of the existence of a significant amount of work).

Such a tragic arc tempts any observer to make some guess at its cause, and what we know of Capote's early life provides us a near-perfect graph for any student of Freud who predicts that a disastrous adulthood is the all but inevitable result of a miserable childhood. And Gerald Clarke's careful biography of Capote charts just such a dislocated, lonely and emotionally deprived childhood, youth and early manhood. Young Truman was, in essence, deserted by a too-young and sexually adventurous mother and a bounder of a father who left him in small-town Alabama with a houseful of unmarried cousins (cousins and neighbors who at least rewarded him with a useful supply of good tales).

When his mother eventually remarried and summoned the adolescent Truman to her homes in Connecticut and New York, she changed his legal surname from Persons to the name of her second husband, Joe Capote, a Cuban of considerable charm but slim fidelity. The physically odd boy—whose startlingly obvious effeminacy of voice and manner greatly distressed his mother—attended good Northern schools where he performed poorly in virtually all subjects but reading and writing. Then determined on a writer's career, he decided against a college education, took a small job in the art department at *The New Yorker,* launched himself into a few of the mutually exclusive social circles of big-city writing and nighttime carousing and began serious work on the fiction that would bring him his premature fame.

The earliest stories gathered here clearly reflect his reading in the fiction of his contemporaries, especially in the quite recent stories of his fellow Southerners, Carson McCullers from Georgia and Eudora Welty from Mississippi. Capote's "Miriam," with its perhaps too-easy eeriness, and "Jug of Silver," with its affectionate small-town wit, may suggest McCullers's own early stories. And his "The Shape of Things," "My Side of the Matter" and "Children on Their Birthdays" may be readily seen as not-quite-finished stories from Welty, especially "My Side of the Matter" with its close resemblance to Welty's famous "Why I Live at the P.O."

Yet Capote's childhood, spent in a middle-class white world so close to Welty's and McCullers's own—and in a household uncannily like the one described in Welty's comic monologues—might well have extracted such stories from a talented young writer, even if he had never encountered a Welty or McCullers story (Welty told me that when she was undergoing her *Paris Review* interview in 1972, George Plimpton suggested that the interviewer raise the question of her influence on Capote's early work; and she declined to discuss the matter, having no desire to entertain any claim of another writer's dependence upon her).

In general, however, by the late 1940s, Capote's fictional voice was clearly his own. His weirdly potent first novel—*Other Voices, Other Rooms* in 1948—erected as it is upon the conventional grounds of modern Southern Gothic ends as an unquestionably original structure that, even now, is a powerful assertion of the pain of his own early solitude and his bafflement in the face of the sexual and familial mysteries that had begun to impinge upon his confidence and would ultimately contribute heavily to his eventual collapse in agonized shame, even in the midst of so much later artistic, social and financial success. The same dilemmas are on partial display in short stories like "The Headless Hawk," "Shut a Final Door" and "A Tree of Night."

But given the fact that homosexuality was then a troubling daily reality for Capote, and given that American magazines were still averse to candid portrayals of the problem, perhaps we can comprehend now why such early stories lack a clear emotional center. Had he written short stories as candid in their views of homosexuality as his first novel managed to be, they would have almost certainly gone unpublished, certainly not in the widely read women's magazines which were the centers of much of the best short fiction of the time. It was in his second novel—*The Grass Harp* of 1951—that he discovered a mature means of employing important areas of his own past to empower fiction that would ring with convincing personal truth. Those areas centered around, not sexuality but the deeply encouraging devotion he received in childhood from a particular cousin and from the places he and that friend frequented in their games and devotions. The cousin was Miss Sook Faulk, a woman so slender in her concerns and affections that many thought her simple-minded, though she was only (and admirably) simple; and in the years that she and the young Truman shared a home, she gave him the enormous gift of a dignified love—a gift he'd received from no closer kin.

Among these stories, that depth of feeling and its masterful delivery in the memorably clear prose which would mark the remainder of Capote's work, is visible above all in his famous story "A Christmas Memory," and in the less well-known "The Thanksgiving Visitor" and "One Christmas," the last of which may be a little sweet for contemporary tastes but, true as it is, is almost as moving in its revelation of yet another early wound—this one administered by a feckless and distant father. It's likely that more Americans know "A Christmas Memory" through an excellent television film, with an extraordinary performance by Geraldine Page; but anyone who reads the actual tale has encountered a feat rarer than any screen performance. By the sheer clarity of his prose and a brilliant economy of ongoing narrative rhythm, Capote cleanses of any possible sentimentality a small array of characters, actions and emotions that might have gone foully sweet in less watchful and skillful hands. Only Chekhov comes to mind as sufficiently gifted in the treatment of similar matter.

But once possessed of the skills to deliver the width of emotion he wished for, Capote was not limited to the recounting of childhood memory, more or less real or entirely invented. Like many fiction writers, he wrote fewer and fewer short stories as he grew—life often becomes more intricate than brief forms can easily contain. But one story, "Mojave" from 1975, embodies brilliantly and terribly the insights acquired in his years among the rich. Had he lived to write more such angled quick glimpses of their hateful world, he would never have left us with the sense of incompletion that the baffled rumors of a long novel have done.

And had his decades away from the Southern source of all his best fiction—long and short—not left him uninterested, or incapable, of writing more about that primal world, we would likewise have more cause for gratitude for his work. In fact, however, if we lay Capote's fiction atop the stack that includes *In Cold Blood* and a sturdy handful of nonfiction essays, we will have assembled a varied body of work that's equaled by only a very few of his contemporaries in the United States of the second half of the twentieth century.

This man who impersonated an exotic clown in the early, more private years of his career and then—pressed by the heavy weight of his past—became the demented public clown of his ending, left us nonetheless sufficient first-class work to stand him now—cool decades after his death—far taller than his small and despised body ever foretold. In 1966 when he'd begun to announce his work on a long novel—and to take huge publisher's advances for it—he said he'd entitle the book *Answered Prayers*. And he claimed that *Answered Prayers* was a phrase he'd found among the sayings of St. Teresa of Avila—*More tears are shed over answered prayers than unanswered ones*. There are few signs that prayers to God or to some intercessory saint—say a seizure-ridden Spanish mystic or his simple cousin Sook—were ever a steady concern of Truman Capote's life, but his lifelong pursuit of wide attention and wealth was appallingly successful. Before he was forty, he'd achieved both aims, in tidal profusion and utter heartbreak.

In his final wreckage, this slender collection of short stories may well have seemed to Capote the least of his fulfillments; but in the arena of expressed human feeling, they represent his most impressive victory. From the torment of a life willed on him, first, by a viciously neglectful father and a mother who should never have borne a child and, then, by his own refusal to conquer his personal hungers, he nonetheless won on the battlefield of English prose these stories that, at their best, should stand for long years to come as calm enduring prayers and accomplished blessings—free for every reader to use.

THE WALLS ARE COLD

(1943)

". . . so Grant just said to them come on along to a wonderful party, and, well it was as easy as that. Really, I think it was just genius to pick them up, God only knows they might resurrect us from the grave." The girl who was talking tapped her cigarette ash on the Persian throw rug and looked apologetically at her hostess.

The hostess straightened her trim, black dress and pursed her lips nervously. She was very young and small and perfect. Her face was pale and framed with sleek black hair, and her lipstick was a trifle too dark. It was after two and she was tired and wished they would all go, but it was no small task to rid yourself of some thirty people, particularly when the majority were full of her father's scotch. The elevator man had been up twice to complain about the noise; so she gave him a highball, which is all he is after anyway. And now the sailors . . . oh, the hell with it.

"It's all right, Mildred, really. What are a few sailors more or less? God, I hope they don't break anything. Would you go back in the kitchen and see about ice, please? I'll see what I can do with your new-found friends."

"Really, darling, I don't think it's at all necessary. From what I understand, they acclimate themselves very easily."

3

The hostess went toward her sudden guests. They were knotted together in one corner of the drawing-room, just staring and not looking very much at home.

The best looking of the sextet turned his cap nervously and said, "We didn't know it was any kind of party like this, Miss. I mean, you don't want us, do you?"

"Of course you're welcome. What on earth would you be doing here if I didn't want you?"

The sailor was embarrassed.

"That girl, that Mildred and her friend just picked us up in some bar or other and we didn't have any idea we was comin' to no house like this."

"How ridiculous, how utterly ridiculous," the hostess said. "You are from the South, aren't you?"

He tucked his cap under his arm and looked more at ease. "I'm from Mississippi. Don't suppose you've ever been there, have you, Miss?"

She looked away toward the window and ran her tongue across her lips. She was tired of this, terribly tired of it. "Oh, yes," she lied. "A beautiful state."

He grinned. "You must be mixed up with some other place, Miss. There sure's not a lot to catch the eye in Mississippi, 'cept maybe around Natchez way."

"Of course, Natchez. I went to school with a girl from Natchez. Elizabeth Kimberly, do you know her?"

"No, can't say as I do."

Suddenly she realized that she and the sailor were alone; all of his mates had wandered over to the piano where Les was playing Porter. Mildred was right about the acclimation.

"Come on," she said, "I'll fix you a drink. They can shift for themselves. My name's Louise, so please don't call me Miss."

"My sister's name's Louise, I'm Jake."

"Really, isn't that charming? I mean the coincidence." She smoothed her hair and smiled with her too dark lips.

They went into the den and she knew the sailor was watching the way her dress swung around her hips. She stooped through the door behind the bar.

"Well," she said, "what will it be? I forgot, we have scotch and rye and rum; how about a nice rum and coke?"

"If you say so," he grinned, sliding his hand along the mirrored bar's surface, "you know, I never saw a place like this before. It's something right out of a movie."

She whirled ice swiftly around in a glass with a swizzle stick. "I'll take you on a forty-cent tour if you like. It's quite large, for an apartment, that is. We have a country house that's much, much bigger."

That didn't sound right. It was too supercilious. She turned and put the bottle of rum back in its niche. She could see in the mirror that he was staring at her, perhaps through her.

"How old are you?" he asked.

She had to think for a minute, really think. She lied so constantly about her age she sometimes forgot the truth herself. What difference did it make whether he knew her real age or not? So she told him.

"Sixteen."

"And never been kissed . . . ?"

She laughed, not at the cliché but her answer.

"Raped, you mean."

She was facing him and saw that he was shocked and then amused and then something else.

"Oh, for God's sake, don't look at me that way, I'm not a bad girl." He blushed and she climbed back through the door and took his hand. "Come on, I'll show you around."

She led him down a long corridor intermittently lined with mirrors, and showed him room after room. He admired the soft, pastel rugs and the smooth blend of modernistic with period furniture.

"This is my room," she said, holding the door open for him, "you mustn't mind the mess, it isn't all mine, most of the girls have been fixing in here."

There was nothing for him to mind, the room was in perfect order. The bed, the tables, the lamp were all white but the walls and the rug were a dark, cold green.

"Well, Jake . . . what do you think, suit me?"

"I never saw anything like it, my sister wouldn't believe me if I told her . . . but I don't like the walls, if you'll pardon me for saying so . . . that green . . . they look so cold."

She looked puzzled and not knowing quite why, she reached out her hand and touched the wall beside her dressing-table.

"You're right, the walls I mean, they are cold." She looked up at him and for a moment her face was molded in such an expression he was not quite sure whether she was going to laugh or cry.

"I didn't mean it that way. Hell, I don't rightly know what I mean!"

"Don't you, or are we just being euphemistic?" It drew a blank so she sat down on the side of her white bed.

"Here," she said, "sit down and have a cigarette, what ever happened to your drink?"

He sat down beside her. "I left it out in the bar. It sure seems quiet back here after all that racket in front."

"How long have you been in the navy?"

"Eight months."

"Like it?"

"It isn't much concern whether you like it or not. . . . I've seen a lot of places that I wouldn't otherwise."

"Why did you enlist then?"

"Oh, I was going to be drafted and the navy seemed more to my likin'."

"Is it?"

"Well, I tell you, I don't take to this kind of life, I don't like other men bossin' me around. Would you?"

She didn't answer but put a cigarette in her mouth instead. He held the match for her and she let her hand brush against his. His hand was trembling and the light was not very steady. She inhaled and said, "You want to kiss me, don't you?"

She watched him intently and saw the slow, red spread over his face.

"Why don't you?"

"You're not that kind of girl. I'd be scared to kiss a girl like you, 'sides, you're only making fun out of me."

She laughed and blew the smoke in a cloud toward the ceiling. "Stop it, you sound like something out of a gaslight melodrama. What is 'that kind of girl,' anyway? Just an idea. Whether you kiss me or not isn't of the slightest importance. I could explain, but why bother? You'd probably end up thinking I'm a nymphomaniac."

"I don't even know what that is."

"Hell, that's what I mean. You're a man, a real man and I'm so sick of these weak, effeminate boys like Les. I just wanted to know what it would be like, that's all."

He bent over her. "You're a funny kid," he said, and she was in his arms. He kissed her and his hand slid down along her shoulder and pressed against her breast.

She twisted and gave him a violent shove and he went sprawling across the cold, green rug.

She got up and stood over him and they stared at each other. "You dirt," she said. Then she slapped his bewildered face.

She opened the door, paused, and straightened her dress and went back to the party. He sat on the floor for a moment, then he got up and found his way to the foyer and then remembered that he had left his cap in the white room, but he didn't care, all he wanted was to get out of here.

The hostess looked inside the drawing-room and motioned for Mildred to come out.

"For God's sake, Mildred, get these people out of here; those sailors, what do they think this is . . . the USO?"

"What's the matter, was that guy bothering you?"

"No, no, he's just a small town moron who's never seen anything like this before and it's gone to his head in a funny kind of way. It's just one awful bore and I have a headache. Will you get them out for me please . . . everybody?"

She nodded and the hostess turned back down the corridor and went into her mother's room. She lay down on the velvet chaise lounge and stared at the Picasso abstract. She picked up a tiny lace pillow and pushed it against her face as hard as she could. She was going to sleep here tonight, here where the walls were pale rose and warm.

A MINK OF ONE'S OWN

(1944)

Mrs. Munson finished twisting a linen rose in her auburn hair and stepped back from her mirror to judge the effect. Then she ran her hands down her hips . . . the dress was just too tight and that's all there was to it. "Alteration won't save it again," she thought angrily. With one last disparaging glance at her reflection she turned and went into the livingroom.

The windows were open and the room was filled with loud, unearthly shrieks. Mrs. Munson lived on the third floor, and across the street was a public school playground. In the late afternoon the noise was almost unbearable. God, if she'd only known about this before she signed the lease! With a little grunt she closed both windows and as far as she was concerned they could stay that way for the next two years.

But Mrs. Munson was far too excited to be really annoyed. Vini Rondo was coming to see her, imagine, Vini Rondo . . . and this very afternoon! When she thought about it she felt fluttering wings in her stomach. It had been almost five years, and Vini had been in Europe all this time. Whenever Mrs. Munson found herself in a group discussing the war she invariably announced, "Well, you know I have a very dear friend in Paris this very minute, Vini Rondo, she was right there when the Germans marched in! I have positive nightmares when I think what she must be going through!" Mrs. Munson said it as if it were she whose fate lay in the balance.

If there was anyone in the party who hadn't heard the story before she would hasten to explain about her friend. "You see," she would begin, "Vini was just the most talented girl, interested in art and all that sort of thing. Well, she had quite a bit of money, so she went to Europe at least once a year. Finally, when her father died she packed up her things and went for good. My, but she had a fling, and then she married some Count or Baron or something. Maybe you've heard of her . . . Vini Rondo . . . Cholly Knickerbocker used to mention her all the time." And it went on and on, like some historical lecture.

"Vini, back in America," she thought, never ceasing to revel in the wonder of it. She puffed up the small green pillows on the couch and sat down. With piercing eyes she examined her room. Funny you never really see your surroundings until a visitor is expected. Well, Mrs. Munson sighed contentedly, that new girl had, for a rarity, restored pre-war standards.

The door-bell rang abruptly. It buzzed twice before Mrs. Munson could move, she was that excited. Finally she composed herself and went to answer.

At first Mrs. Munson didn't recognize her. The woman who confronted her had no chic up-swept coiffure . . . indeed her hair hung rather limply and had an uncombed look. A print dress in January? Mrs. Munson tried to keep the disappointment out of her voice when she said, "Vini, darling, I should have known you anywhere."

The woman still stood in the threshold. Under her arm she carried a large pink box and her gray eyes looked out at Mrs. Munson curiously.

"Would you, Bertha?" Her voice was a queer whisper. "That's nice, very nice. I should have recognized you, too, although you've gotten rather fat, haven't you?" Then she accepted Mrs. Munson's extended hand and came in.

Mrs. Munson was embarrassed and she didn't know quite what to say. Arm-in-arm they went into the livingroom and sat down.

"How about some sherry?"

Vini shook her dark little head, "No, thank you."

"Well, how about a scotch or something?" Mrs. Munson asked desperately. The figurine clock on the sham mantelpiece chimed softly. Mrs. Munson had never noticed how loud it could sound.

"No," said Vini firmly, "nothing, thank you."

Resignedly Mrs. Munson settled back on the couch. "Now, darling, tell me all about it. When did you get back in the States?" She liked the sound of that. "The States."

Vini placed the big pink box down between her legs and folded her hands. "I've been here for almost a year," she paused, then hurried on, realizing the startled expression of her hostess, "but I haven't been in New York. Naturally I would have gotten in touch with you sooner, but I was out in California."

"Oh, California, I love California!" Mrs. Munson exclaimed, though in point of fact, she had never been further west than Chicago.

Vini smiled and Mrs. Munson noticed how irregular her teeth were and decided they could do with a good brushing.

"So," Vini continued, "when I got back in New York last week I thought of you at once. I had an awful time trying to find you because I couldn't remember your husband's first name. . . ."

"Albert," Mrs. Munson put in unnecessarily.

". . . but I finally did and here I am. You know, Bertha, I really started thinking about you when I decided to get rid of my mink coat."

Mrs. Munson saw a sudden blush on Vini's face.

"Your mink coat?"

"Yes," Vini said, lifting up the pink box. "You remember my mink coat. You always admired it so. You always said it was the loveliest coat you'd ever seen." She started to undo the frayed silk ribbon that held the box together.

"Of course, yes of course," Mrs. Munson said, letting the "course" trill down softly.

"I said to myself, 'Vini Rondo, what on earth do you need that coat for? Why not let Bertha have it?' You see, Bertha, I bought the most gorgeous sable in Paris and you can understand that I really don't need two fur coats. Besides I have my silver-fox jacket."

Mrs. Munson watched her parting the tissue paper in the box, saw the chipped enamel on her nails, saw that her fingers were jewel-less, and suddenly realized a great many other things.

"So I thought of you and unless you want it I'll just keep it because I couldn't bear to think of anyone else having it." She held the coat and stood turning it this way and that. It was a beautiful coat; the fur shone rich and very smooth. Mrs. Munson reached out and ran her fingers across it, ruffling the tiny hairs the wrong way. Without thinking she said: "How much?"

Mrs. Munson brought back her hand quickly, as though she had touched fire, and then she heard Vini's voice, small and tired.

"I paid almost a thousand for it. Is a thousand too much?"

Down in the street Mrs. Munson could hear the deafening roar of the playground and for once she was grateful. It gave her something else to concentrate on, something to lessen the intensity of her own feelings.

"I'm afraid that's too much. I really can't afford it," Mrs. Munson said distractedly, still staring at the coat, afraid to lift her eyes and see the other woman's face.

Vini tossed the coat on the couch. "Well, I want you to have it. It's not so much the money, but I feel I should get something back on my investment. . . . How much could you afford?"

Mrs. Munson closed her eyes. Oh, God, this was awful! Just plain damned awful!

"Maybe four hundred," she answered weakly.

Vini picked up the coat again and said brightly, "Let's see how it fits then."

They went into the bedroom and Mrs. Munson tried on the coat in front of her full-length closet mirror. Just a few alterations, the sleeves shortened, and maybe she would have it re-glazed. Yes, it certainly did things for her.

"Oh, I think it's beautiful, Vini. It was so sweet of you to think of me."

Vini leaned against the wall, her pale face looking hard in the magnified sunlight of the big bedroom windows.

"You can make out the check to me," she said disinterestedly.

"Yes, of course," Mrs. Munson said, suddenly coming back to earth. Imagine Bertha Munson with a mink of her own!

They went back into the livingroom and she wrote the check for Vini. Carefully folding it, Vini deposited it in her small beaded purse.

Mrs. Munson tried hard to make conversation but she came up against a cold wall at each new channel. Once she asked, "Where is your husband, Vini? You must bring him around for Albert to talk to." And Vini answered, "Oh, him! I haven't seen him for aeons. He's still in Lisbon for all I know." And so that was that.

Finally, after promising to phone the next day, Vini left. When she had gone Mrs. Munson thought, "Why, poor Vini, she's nothing but a refugee!" Then she took her new coat and went into the bedroom. She couldn't tell Albert how she got it, that was definite. My, but he would be mad about the money! She decided to hide it in the furthest reaches of her closet and then one day she'd bring it out and say, "Albert, look at the divine mink I bought at an auction. I got it for next to nothing."

Groping in the darkness of her closet she caught the coat on a hook. She gave a little yank and was terrified to hear the sound of ripping. Quickly she snapped on the light and saw that the sleeve was torn. She held the tear apart and pulled slightly. It ripped more and then some more. With a sick emptiness she knew the whole thing was rotten. "Oh, my God," she said, clutching at the linen rose in her hair. "Oh, my God, I've been taken and taken good, and there's nothing in the world I can do about it, nothing in the world!" For suddenly Mrs. Munson realized Vini wouldn't phone tomorrow or ever again.

THE SHAPE OF THINGS

(1944)

A wispish-sized, white pompadoured woman swayed down the dining-car aisle and inched into a seat next to a window. She finished penciling her order and squinted near-sightedly across the table at a ruddy-cheeked Marine and a heart-faced girl. In one sweep she noted a gold band on the girl's finger, a string of red cloth twisted in her hair and decided she was cheap; mentally labeled her war bride. She smiled faintly, inviting conversation.

The girl beamed back, "You was lucky you come so early on account of it's so crowded. We didn't get no lunch 'cause there was Russian soldiers eatin' . . . or somethin'. Gosh you should've seen them, looked just like Boris Karloff, honest!"

It was a voice like a chirping teakettle and caused the woman to clear her throat. "Yes, I'm sure," she said. "Before this trip I never dreamt there were so many in the world, soldiers, I mean. You just never realize until you get on a train. I keep asking myself, where do they all come from?"

"Draft boards," the girl said, and then giggled foolishly.

Her husband blushed apologetically. "You goin' all the way, ma'am?"

"Presumably, but this train's as slow as . . . as . . ."

"Molasses!" the girl exclaimed and followed breathlessly with, "Gee, I'm so excited, you can't imagine. All day I've been just glued to the scenery. Where I come from in Arkansas it's all kinda flat, so I get an extra thrill right from my toes when I see these mountains." And turning to her husband, "Honey, d'ya suppose we're in Carolina?"

He looked out the window where the dusk was thickening on the pane. Gathering swiftly the blue light and the hill humps blending and echoing one another. He blinked back into the diner's brightness. "Must be Virginia," he guessed and shrugged his shoulders.

From the direction of the coaches a soldier suddenly lurched awkwardly toward them and collapsed in the table's empty seat like a rag doll. He was small and his uniform spilled over him in crumpled folds. His face, lean and sharp featured, contrasted palely with the Marine's and his black, crew-cropped hair shone under the light like a cap of sealskin. With tired eyes foggily studying the three as though there were a screen flung between them, he picked nervously at two chevrons sewn on his sleeve.

The woman shifted uncomfortably and pressed nearer the window. She thoughtfully tagged him drunk, and seeing the girl wrinkle up her nose knew she shared the verdict.

While the white-aproned negro unloaded his tray the Corporal said, "What I want is coffee, a big pot of it and a double jigger of cream."

The girl dipped her fork into the creamed chicken. "Dontcha think what these folks charge for their stuff is awful, dear?"

And then it began. The Corporal's head started to bob in short uncontrollable jerks. A lolling pause with his head bent grotesquely forward; a muscle convulsion snapping his neck sideways. His mouth stretched nastily and the neck veins tautened.

"Oh my God," the girl cried and the woman dropped her butter knife and automatically shaded a sensitive hand over her eyes. The Marine stared vacantly for a moment, then quickly recovering he pulled out a pack of cigarettes.

"Here, fella," he said, "you better have one."

"Please, thanks . . . very kind," the soldier muttered and then beat a knuckle-white fist against the table. Silverware trembled, water wasted over the glass tops. A stillness paused in the air and a distant burst of laughter sliced evenly through the car.

Then the girl, aware of attention, smoothed a lock of hair behind her ear. The woman looked up and bit her lip when she saw the Corporal trying to light his cigarette.

"Here, let me," she volunteered.

Her hand shook so badly that the first match went out. When the second attempt connected she managed a trite smile. After a while he quieted. "I'm so ashamed . . . please forgive me."

"Oh, we understand," the woman said. "We understand perfectly."

"Did it hurt?" the girl asked.

"No, no, it doesn't hurt."

"I was scared 'cause I thought it hurt. It sure looks that way. 'Spose it's sorta like hiccups?" She gave a sudden start as though someone had kicked her.

The Corporal traced his finger along the table rim and presently he said, "I was all right till I got on the train. They said I'd be fine. Said, 'You're o.k., soldier.' But it's the excitement, the knowing you're in the States and free and the goddamned waiting's over." He brushed at his eye.

"I'm sorry," he said.

The waiter set the coffee down and the woman tried to help him. With a little angry push he shoved her hand away. "Now please don't. I know how!" Embarrassingly confused she turned to the window and met her face mirrored there. The face was calm and it surprised her because she felt a dizzy unreality as if she were swinging between two dream points. Channeling her thoughts elsewhere she followed the solemn trip of the Marine's fork from plate to mouth. The girl was eating now very voraciously but her own food was growing cold.

Then it began again, not violently as before. In the rawish glare of an oncoming train's searchlight distorted reflection blurred and the woman sighed.

He was swearing softly and it sounded more as though he were praying. Then he frantically clutched the sides of his head in a strong hand vise.

"Listen, fella, you betta get a doctor," the Marine suggested.

The woman reached out and rested her hand on his upraised arm. "Is there anything I can do?" she said.

"What they used to do to stop it was look in my eyes . . . as long as I'm looking in somebody's eyes it'll quit."

She leaned her face close to his. "There," he said, quieting instantly, "there, now. You're a sweetheart."

"Where was it?" she said.

He frowned and said, "There was lots of places . . . it's my nerves. They're all torn up."

"And where are you going now?"

"Virginia."

"And that's home, isn't it?"

"Yeah, that's where home is."

The woman felt an ache in her fingers and loosened her suddenly intense grip on his arm. "That's where home is and you must remember that the other is unimportant."

"You know something," he whispered. "I love you. I love you because you're very silly and very innocent and 'cause you'll never know anything but what you see in pictures. I love you 'cause we're in Virginia and I'm almost home." Abruptly the woman looked away. An offended tenseness embroidered on the silence.

"So you think that's all?" he said. He leaned on the table and pawed his face sleepily. "There's that but then there's dignity. When it happens with people I've always known what then? D'ya think I want to sit down at a table with them or someone like you and make 'em sick? D'ya think I want to scare a kid like this one over here and put ideas in her head about her own guy! I've been waiting for months, and they tell me I'm well but the first time . . ." He stopped and his eyebrows concentrated.

The woman slipped two bills on top of her check and pushed her chair back. "Would you let me through now, please?" she said.

The Corporal heaved up and stood there looking down at the woman's untouched plate. "Go on an' eat, damn you," he said. "You've got to eat!" And then, without looking back he disappeared in the direction of the coaches.

The woman paid for the coffee.

JUG OF SILVER

(1945)

After school I used to work in the Valhalla drugstore. It was owned by my uncle, Mr. Ed Marshall. I call him Mr. Marshall because everybody, including his wife, called him Mr. Marshall. Nevertheless he was a nice man.

This drugstore was maybe old-fashioned, but it was large and dark and cool: during summer months there was no pleasanter place in town. At the left, as you entered, was a tobacco-magazine counter behind which, as a rule, sat Mr. Marshall: a squat, square-faced, pink-fleshed man with looping, manly, white mustaches. Beyond this counter stood the beautiful soda fountain. It was very antique and made of fine, yellowed marble, smooth to the touch but without a trace of cheap glaze. Mr. Marshall bought it at an auction in New Orleans in 1910 and was plainly proud of it. When you sat on the high, delicate stools and looked across the fountain you could see yourself reflected softly, as though by candlelight, in a row of ancient mahogany-framed mirrors. All general merchandise was displayed in glass-doored, curio-like cabinets that were locked with brass keys. There was always in the air the smell of syrup and nutmeg and other delicacies.

The Valhalla was the gathering place of Wachata County till a certain Rufus McPherson came to town and opened a second drugstore directly across the courthouse square. This old Rufus McPherson was a villain; that is, he took away my uncle's trade. He installed fancy equipment such as electric fans and colored lights; he provided curb service and made grilled-cheese sandwiches to order. Naturally, though some remained devoted to Mr. Marshall, most folks couldn't resist Rufus McPherson.

For a while, Mr. Marshall chose to ignore him: if you were to mention McPherson's name, he would sort of snort, finger his mustaches and look the other way. But you could tell he was mad. And getting madder. Then one day toward the middle of October I strolled into the Valhalla to find him sitting at the fountain playing dominoes and drinking wine with Hamurabi.

Hamurabi was an Egyptian and some kind of dentist, though he didn't do much business, as the people hereabouts have unusually strong teeth, due to an element in the water. He spent a great deal of his time loafing around the Valhalla and was my uncle's chief buddy. He was a handsome figure of a man, this Hamurabi, being dark-skinned and nearly seven feet tall; the matrons of the town kept their daughters under lock and key and gave him the eye themselves. He had no foreign accent whatsoever, and it was always my opinion that he wasn't any more Egyptian than the man in the moon.

Anyway, there they were swigging red Italian wine from a gallon jug. It was a troubling sight, for Mr. Marshall was a renowned teeto-taler. So naturally, I thought: Oh, golly, Rufus McPherson has finally got his goat. That was not the case, however.

"Here, son," said Mr. Marshall, "come have a glass of wine."

"Sure," said Hamurabi, "help us finish it up. It's store-bought, so we can't waste it."

Much later, when the jug was dry, Mr. Marshall picked it up and said, "Now we shall see!" And with that disappeared out into the afternoon.

"Where's he off to?" I asked.

"Ah," was all Hamurabi would say. He liked to devil me.

A half-hour passed before my uncle returned. He was stooped and grunting under the load he carried. He set the jug atop the fountain and stepped back, smiling and rubbing his hands together. "Well, what do you think?"

"Ah," purred Hamurabi.

"Gee . . ." I said.

It was the same wine jug, God knows, but there was a wonderful difference; for now it was crammed to the brim with nickels and dimes that shone dully through the thick glass.

"Pretty, eh?" said my uncle. "Had it done over at the First National. Couldn't get in anything bigger-sized than a nickel. Still, there's lotsa money in there, let me tell you."

"But what's the point, Mr. Marshall?" I said. "I mean, what's the idea?"

Mr. Marshall's smile deepened to a grin. "This here's a jug of silver, you might say . . ."

"The pot at the end of the rainbow," interrupted Hamurabi.

". . . and the idea, as you call it, is for folks to guess how much money is in there. For instance, say you buy a quarter's worth of stuff—well, then you get to take a chance. The more you buy, the more chances you get. And I'll keep all guesses in a ledger till Christmas Eve, at which time whoever comes closest to the right amount will get the whole shebang."

Hamurabi nodded solemnly. "He's playing Santa Claus—a mighty crafty Santa Claus," he said. "I'm going home and write a book: *The Skillful Murder of Rufus McPherson.*" To tell the truth, he sometimes did write stories and send them out to the magazines. They always came back.

It was surprising, really like a miracle, how Wachata County took to the jug. Why, the Valhalla hadn't done so much business since Station Master Tully, poor soul, went stark raving mad and claimed to have discovered oil back of the depot, causing the town to be overrun with wildcat prospectors. Even the poolhall bums who never spent a cent on anything not connected with whiskey or women took to investing their spare cash in milk shakes. A few elderly ladies publicly disapproved of Mr. Marshall's enterprise as a kind of gambling, but they didn't start any trouble and some even found occasion to visit us and hazard a guess. The schoolkids were crazy about the whole thing, and I was very popular because they figured I knew the answer.

"I'll tell you why all this is," said Hamurabi, lighting one of the Egyptian cigarettes he bought by mail from a concern in New York City. "It's not for the reason you may imagine; not, in other words, avidity. No. It's the mystery that's enchanting. Now you look at those nickels and dimes and what do you think: ah, so much! No, no. You think: ah, *how* much? And that's a profound question, indeed. It can mean different things to different people. Understand?"

And oh, was Rufus McPherson wild! When you're in trade, you count on Christmas to make up a large share of your yearly profit, and he was hard pressed to find a customer. So he tried to imitate the jug; but being such a stingy man he filled his with pennies. He also wrote a letter to the editor of the *Banner,* our weekly paper, in which he said that Mr. Marshall ought to be "tarred and feathered and strung up for turning innocent little children into confirmed gamblers and sending them down the path to Hell!" You can imagine what kind of laughingstock he was. Nobody had anything for McPherson but scorn. And so by the middle of November he just stood on the sidewalk outside his store and gazed bitterly at the festivities across the square.

At about this time Appleseed and sister made their first appearance.

He was a stranger in town. At least no one could recall ever having seen him before. He said he lived on a farm a mile past Indian Branches; told us his mother weighed only seventy-four pounds and that he had an older brother who would play the fiddle at anybody's wedding for fifty cents. He claimed that Appleseed was the only name he had and that he was twelve years old. But his sister, Middy, said he was eight. His hair was straight and dark yellow. He had a tight, weather-tanned little face with anxious green eyes that had a very wise and knowing look. He was small and puny and high-strung; and he wore always the same outfit: a red sweater, blue denim britches and a pair of man-sized boots that went clop-clop with every step.

It was raining that first time he came into the Valhalla; his hair was plastered round his head like a cap and his boots were caked with red mud from the country roads. Middy trailed behind as he swaggered like a cowboy up to the fountain, where I was wiping some glasses.

"I hear you folks got a bottle fulla money you fixin' to give 'way," he said, looking me square in the eye. "Seein' as you-all are givin' it away, we'd be obliged iffen you'd give it to us. Name's Appleseed, and this here's my sister, Middy."

Middy was a sad, sad-looking kid. She was a good bit taller and older-looking than her brother: a regular bean pole. She had tow-colored hair that was chopped short, and a pale pitiful little face. She wore a faded cotton dress that came way up above her bony knees. There was something wrong with her teeth, and she tried to conceal this by keeping her lips primly pursed like an old lady.

"Sorry," I said, "but you'll have to talk with Mr. Marshall."

So sure enough he did. I could hear my uncle explaining what he would have to do to win the jug. Appleseed listened attentively, nodding now and then. Presently he came back and stood in front of the jug and, touching it lightly with his hand, said, "Ain't it a pretty thing, Middy?"

Middy said, "Is they gonna give it to us?"

"Naw. What you gotta do, you gotta guess how much money's inside there. And you gotta buy two bits' worth so's even to get a chance."

"Huh, we ain't got no two bits. Where you 'spec we gonna get us two bits?"

Appleseed frowned and rubbed his chin. "That'll be the easy part, just leave it to me. The only worrisome thing is: I can't just take a chance and guess . . . I gotta *know*."

Well, a few days later they showed up again. Appleseed perched on a stool at the fountain and boldly asked for two glasses of water, one for him and one for Middy. It was on this occasion that he gave out the information about his family: ". . . then there's Papa Daddy, that's my mama's papa, who's a Cajun, an' on accounta that he don't speak English good. My brother, the one what plays the fiddle, he's been in jail three times. . . . It's on accounta him we had to pick up and leave Louisiana. He cut a fella bad in a razor fight over a woman ten years older'n him. She had yellow hair."

Middy, lingering in the background, said nervously, "You oughtn't to be tellin' our personal private fam'ly business thataway, Appleseed."

"Hush now, Middy," he said, and she hushed. "She's a good little gal," he added, turning to pat her head, "but you can't let her get away with much. You go look at the picture books, honey, and stop frettin' with your teeth. Appleseed here's got some figurin' to do."

This figuring meant staring hard at the jug, as if his eyes were trying to eat it up. With his chin cupped in his hand, he studied it for a long period, not batting his eyelids once. "A lady in Louisiana told me I could see things other folks couldn't see 'cause I was born with a caul on my head."

"It's a cinch you aren't going to see how much there is," I told him. "Why don't you just let a number pop into your head, and maybe that'll be the right one."

"Uh, uh," he said, "too darn risky. Me, I can't take no sucha chance. Now, the way I got it figured, there ain't but one sure-fire thing and that's to count every nickel and dime."

"Count!"

"Count what?" asked Hamurabi, who had just moseyed inside and was settling himself at the fountain.

"This kid says he's going to count how much is in the jug," I explained.

Hamurabi looked at Appleseed with interest. "How do you plan to do that, son?"

"Oh, by countin'," said Appleseed matter-of-factly.

Hamurabi laughed. "You better have X-ray eyes, son, that's all I can say."

"Oh, no. All you gotta do is be born with a caul on your head. A lady in Louisiana told me so. She was a witch; she loved me and when my ma wouldn't give me to her she put a hex on her and now my ma don't weigh but seventy-four pounds."

"Ve-ry in-ter-esting," was Hamurabi's comment as he gave Appleseed a queer glance.

Middy sauntered up, clutching a copy of *Screen Secrets*. She pointed out a certain photo to Appleseed and said: "Ain't she the nicest-lookin' lady? Now you see, Appleseed, you see how pretty her teeth are? Not a one outa joint."

"Well, don't you fret none," he said.

After they left, Hamurabi ordered a bottle of orange Nehi and drank it slowly, while smoking a cigarette. "Do you think maybe that kid's okay upstairs?" he asked presently in a puzzled voice.

Small towns are best for spending Christmas, I think. They catch the mood quicker and change and come alive under its spell. By the first week in December house doors were decorated with wreaths, and store windows were flashy with red paper bells and snowflakes of glittering isinglass. The kids hiked out into the woods and came back dragging spicy evergreen trees. Already the women were busy baking fruit cakes, unsealing jars of mincemeat and opening bottles of blackberry and scuppernong wine. In the courthouse square a huge tree was trimmed with silver tinsel and colored electric bulbs that were lighted up at sunset. Late of an afternoon you could hear the choir in the Presbyterian church practicing carols for their annual pageant. All over town the japonicas were in full bloom.

The only person who appeared not the least touched by this heart-warming atmosphere was Appleseed. He went about his declared business of counting the jug-money with great, persistent care. Every day now he came to the Valhalla and concentrated on the jug, scowling and mumbling to himself. At first we were all fascinated, but after a while, it got tiresome and nobody paid him any mind whatsoever. He never bought anything, apparently having never been able to raise the two bits. Sometimes he'd talk to Hamurabi, who had taken a tender interest in him and occasionally stood treat to a jawbreaker or a penny's worth of licorice.

"Do you still think he's nuts?" I asked.

"I'm not so sure," said Hamurabi. "But I'll let you know. He doesn't eat enough. I'm going to take him over to the Rainbow Café and buy him a plate of barbecue."

"He'd appreciate it more if you'd give him a quarter."

"No. A dish of barbecue is what he needs. Besides, it would be better if he never was to make a guess. A high-strung kid like that, so unusual, I wouldn't want to be the one responsible if he lost. Say, it would be pitiful."

I'll admit that at the time, Appleseed struck me as being just funny. Mr. Marshall felt sorry for him, and the kids tried to tease him, but had to give it up when he refused to respond. There you could see him plain as day sitting at the fountain with his forehead puckered and his eyes fixed forever on that jug. Yet he was so withdrawn you sometimes had this awful creepy feeling that, well, maybe he didn't exist. And when you were pretty much convinced of this he'd wake up and say something like, "You know, I hope a 1913 buffalo nickel's in there. A fella was tellin' me he saw where a 1913 buffalo nickel's worth fifty dollars." Or, "Middy's gonna be a big lady in the picture shows. They make lotsa money, the ladies in the picture shows do, and then we ain't gonna never eat another collard green as long as we live. Only Middy says she can't be in the picture shows 'less her teeth look good."

Middy didn't always tag along with her brother. On those occasions when she didn't come, Appleseed wasn't himself; he acted shy and left soon.

Hamurabi kept his promise and stood treat to a dish of barbecue at the café. "Mr. Hamurabi's nice, all right," said Appleseed afterward, "but he's got peculiar notions: has a notion that if he lived in this place named Egypt, he'd be a king or somethin'."

And Hamurabi said, "That kid has the most touching faith. It's a beautiful thing to see. But I'm beginning to despise the whole business." He gestured toward the jug. "Hope of this kind is a cruel thing to give anybody, and I'm damned sorry I was ever a party to it."

Around the Valhalla the most popular pastime was deciding what you would buy if you won the jug. Among those who participated were: Solomon Katz, Phoebe Jones, Carl Kuhnhardt, Puly Simmons, Addie Foxcroft, Marvin Finkle, Trudy Edwards and a colored man named Erskine Washington. And these were some of their answers: a trip to and a permanent wave in Birmingham, a second-hand piano, a Shetland pony, a gold bracelet, a set of *Rover Boys* books and a life insurance policy.

Once Mr. Marshall asked Appleseed what he would get. "It's a secret," was the reply, and no amount of prying could make him tell. We took it for granted that whatever it was, he wanted it real bad.

Honest winter, as a rule, doesn't settle on our part of the country till late January, and then is mild, lasting only a short time. But in the year of which I write we were blessed with a singular cold spell the week before Christmas. Some still talk of it, for it was so terrible: water pipes froze solid; many folks had to spend the days in bed snuggled under their quilts, having neglected to lay in enough kindling for the fireplace; the sky turned that strange dull gray as it does just before a storm, and the sun was pale as a waning moon. There was a sharp wind: the old dried-up leaves of last fall fell on the icy ground, and the evergreen tree in the courthouse square was twice stripped of its Christmas finery. When you breathed, your breath made smoky clouds. Down by the silk mill where the very poor people lived, the families huddled together in the dark at night and told tales to keep their minds off the cold. Out in the country the farmers covered their delicate plants with gunnysacks and prayed; some took advantage of the weather to slaughter their hogs and bring the fresh sausage to town. Mr. R. C. Judkins, our town drunk, outfitted himself in a red cheesecloth suit and played Santa Claus at the five 'n' dime. Mr. R. C. Judkins was the father of a big family, so everybody was happy to see him sober enough to earn a dollar. There were several church socials, at one of which Mr. Marshall came face to face with Rufus McPherson: bitter words were passed but not a blow was struck.

Now, as has been mentioned, Appleseed lived on a farm a mile below Indian Branches; this would be approximately three miles from town; a mighty long and lonesome walk. Still, despite the cold, he came every day to the Valhalla and stayed till closing time, which, as the days had grown short, was after nightfall. Once in a while he'd catch a ride partway home with the foreman from the silk mill, but not often. He looked tired, and there were worry lines about his mouth. He was always cold and shivered a lot. I don't think he wore any warm drawers underneath his red sweater and blue britches.

It was three days before Christmas when out of the clear sky, he announced: "Well, I'm finished. I mean I know how much is in the bottle." He claimed this with such grave, solemn sureness it was hard to doubt him.

"Why, say now, son, hold on," said Hamurabi, who was present. "You can't know anything of the sort. It's wrong to think so: you're just heading to get yourself hurt."

"You don't need to preach to me, Mr. Hamurabi. I know what I'm up to. A lady in Louisiana, she told me . . ."

"Yes yes yes—but you got to forget that. If it were me, I'd go home and stay put and forget about this goddamned jug."

"My brother's gonna play the fiddle at a wedding over in Cherokee City tonight and he's gonna give me the two bits," said Appleseed stubbornly. "Tomorrow I'll take my chance."

So the next day I felt kind of excited when Appleseed and Middy arrived. Sure enough, he had his quarter: it was tied for safekeeping in the corner of a red bandanna.

The two of them wandered hand in hand among the showcases, holding a whispery consultation as to what to purchase. They decided finally on a thimble-sized bottle of gardenia cologne, which Middy promptly opened and partly emptied on her hair. "I smells like . . . Oh, darlin' Mary, I ain't never smelled nothin' as sweet. Here, Appleseed, honey, let me douse some on your hair." But he wouldn't let her.

Mr. Marshall got out the ledger in which he kept his records, while Appleseed strolled over to the fountain and cupped the jug between his hands, stroking it gently. His eyes were bright and his cheeks flushed from excitement. Several persons who were in the drugstore at that moment crowded close. Middy stood in the background quietly scratching her leg and smelling the cologne. Hamurabi wasn't there.

Mr. Marshall licked the point of his pencil and smiled. "Okay, son, what do you say?"

Appleseed took a deep breath. "Seventy-seven dollars and thirty-five cents," he blurted.

In picking such an uneven sum, he showed originality, for the run-of-the-mill guess was a plain round figure. Mr. Marshall repeated the amount solemnly as he copied it down.

"When'll I know if I won?"

"Christmas Eve," someone said.

"That's tomorrow, huh?"

"Why, so it is," said Mr. Marshall, not surprised. "Come at four o'clock."

During the night the thermometer dropped even lower, and toward dawn there was one of those swift, summerlike rainstorms, so that the following day was bright and frozen. The town was like a picture postcard of a Northern scene, what with icicles sparkling whitely on the trees and frost flowers coating all windowpanes. Mr. R. C. Judkins rose early and, for no clear reason, tramped the streets ringing a supper bell, stopping now and then to take a swig of whiskey from a pint which he kept in his hip pocket. As the day was windless, smoke climbed lazily from various chimneys straightway to the still, frozen sky. By mid-morning the Presbyterian choir was in full swing; and the town kids (wearing horror masks, as at Halloween) were chasing one another round and round the square, kicking up an awful fuss.

Hamurabi dropped by at noon to help us fix up the Valhalla. He brought along a fat sack of Satsumas, and together we ate every last one, tossing the hulls into a newly installed potbellied stove (a present from Mr. Marshall to himself) which stood in the middle of the room. Then my uncle took the jug off the fountain, polished and placed it on a prominently situated table. He was no help after that whatsoever, for he squatted in a chair and spent his time tying and retying a tacky green ribbon around the jug. So Hamurabi and I had the rest to do alone: we swept the floor and washed the mirrors and dusted the cabinets and strung streamers of red and green crepe paper from wall to wall. When we were finished it looked very fine and elegant.

But Hamurabi gazed sadly at our work, and said: "Well, I think I better be getting along now."

"Aren't you going to stay?" asked Mr. Marshall, shocked.

"No, oh, no," said Hamurabi, shaking his head slowly. "I don't want to see that kid's face. This is Christmas and I mean to have a rip-roaring time. And I couldn't, not with something like that on my conscience. Hell, I wouldn't sleep."

"Suit yourself," said Mr. Marshall. And he shrugged, but you could see he was really hurt. "Life's like that—and besides, who knows, he might win."

Hamurabi sighed gloomily. "What's his guess?"

"Seventy-seven dollars and thirty-five cents," I said.

"Now I ask you, isn't that fantastic?" said Hamurabi. He slumped in a chair next to Mr. Marshall and crossed his legs and lit a cigarette. "If you got any Baby Ruths, I think I'd like one; my mouth tastes sour."

As the afternoon wore on, the three of us sat around the table feeling terribly blue. No one said hardly a word and, as the kids had deserted the square, the only sound was the clock tolling the hour in the courthouse steeple. The Valhalla was closed to business, but people kept passing by and peeking in the window. At three o'clock Mr. Marshall told me to unlock the door.

Within twenty minutes the place was jam full; everyone was wearing his Sunday best, and the air smelled sweet, for most of the little silk-mill girls had scented themselves with vanilla flavoring. They scrunched up against the walls, perched on the fountain, squeezed in wherever they could; soon the crowd had spread to the sidewalk and stretched into the road. The square was lined with team-drawn wagons and Model T Fords that had carted farmers and their families into town. There was much laughter and shouting and joking—several outraged ladies complained of the cursing and the rough, shoving ways of the younger men, but nobody left. At the side entrance a gang of colored folks had formed and were having the most fun of all. Everybody was making the best of a good thing. It's usually so quiet around here: nothing much ever happens. It's safe to say that nearly all of Wachata County was present, but invalids and Rufus McPherson. I looked around for Appleseed but didn't see him anywhere.

Mr. Marshall harrumphed, and clapped for attention. When things quieted down and the atmosphere was properly tense, he raised his voice like an auctioneer, and called: "Now listen, everybody, in this here envelope you see in my hand"—he held a manila envelope above his head—"well, in it's the *answer*—which nobody but God and the First National Bank knows up to now, ha, ha. And in this book"—he held up the ledger with his free hand—"I've got written down what you folks guessed. Are there any questions?" All was silence. "Fine. Now, if we could have a volunteer . . ."

Not a living soul budged an inch: it was as if an awful shyness had overcome the crowd, and even those who were ordinarily natural-born show-offs shuffled their feet, ashamed. Then a voice, Appleseed's, hollered, "Lemme by . . . Outa the way, please, ma'am." Trotting along behind as he pushed forward were Middy and a lanky, sleepy-eyed fellow who was evidently the fiddling brother. Appleseed was dressed the same as usual, but his face was scrubbed rosy clean, his boots polished and his hair slicked back skintight with Stacomb. "Did we get here in time?" he panted.

But Mr. Marshall said, "So you want to be our volunteer?"

Appleseed looked bewildered, then nodded vigorously.

"Does anybody have an objection to this young man?"

Still there was dead quiet. Mr. Marshall handed the envelope to Appleseed, who accepted it calmly. He chewed his under lip while studying it a moment before ripping the flap.

In all that congregation there was no sound except an occasional cough and the soft tinkling of Mr. R. C. Judkins' supper bell. Hamurabi was leaning against the fountain, staring up at the ceiling; Middy was gazing blankly over her brother's shoulder, and when he started to tear open the envelope she let out a pained little gasp.

Appleseed withdrew a slip of pink paper and, holding it as though it was very fragile, muttered to himself whatever was written there. Suddenly his face paled and tears glistened in his eyes.

"Hey, speak up, boy," someone hollered.

Hamurabi stepped forward and all but snatched the slip away. He cleared his throat and commenced to read when his expression changed most comically. "Well, Mother o' God . . ." he said.

"Louder! Louder!" an angry chorus demanded.

"Buncha crooks!" yelled Mr. R. C. Judkins, who had a snootful by this time. "I smell a rat and he smells to high heaven!" Whereupon a cyclone of catcalls and whistling rent the air.

Appleseed's brother whirled round and shook his fist. "Shuddup, shuddup 'fore I bust every one of your goddamn heads together so's you got knots the size a musk melons, hear me?"

"Citizens," cried Mayor Mawes, "citizens—I say, this is Christmas . . . I say . . ."

And Mr. Marshall hopped up on a chair and clapped and stamped till a minimum of order was restored. It might as well be noted here that we later found out Rufus McPherson had paid Mr. R. C. Judkins to start the rumpus. Anyway, when the outbreak was quelled, who should be in possession of the slip but me . . . don't ask how.

Without thinking, I shouted, "Seventy-seven dollars and thirty-five cents." Naturally, due to the excitement, I didn't at first catch the meaning; it was just a number. Then Appleseed's brother let forth with his whooping yell, and so I understood. The name of the winner spread quickly, and the awed, murmuring whispers were like a rainstorm.

Oh, Appleseed himself was a sorry sight. He was crying as though he was mortally wounded, but when Hamurabi lifted him onto his shoulders so the crowd could get a gander, he dried his eyes with the cuffs of his sweater and began grinning. Mr. R. C. Judkins yelled, "Gyp! Lousy gyp!" but was drowned out by a deafening round of applause.

Middy grabbed my arm. "My teeth," she squealed. "Now I'm gonna get my teeth."

"Teeth?" said I, kind of dazed.

"The false kind," says she. "That's what we're gonna get us with the money—a lovely set of white false teeth."

But at that moment my sole interest was in how Appleseed had known. "Hey, tell me," I said desperately, "tell me, how in God's name did he know there was just exactly seventy-seven dollars and thirty-five cents?"

Middy gave me this *look*. "Why, I thought he told you," she said, real serious. "He counted."

"Yes, but how—how?"

"Gee, don't you even know how to count?"

"But is that all he did?"

"Well," she said, following a thoughtful pause, "he did do a little praying, too." She started to dart off, then turned back and called, "Besides, he was born with a caul on his head."

And that's the nearest anybody ever came to solving the mystery. Thereafter, if you were to ask Appleseed "How come?" he would smile strangely and change the subject. Many years later he and his family moved to somewhere in Florida and were never heard from again.

But in our town his legend flourishes still; and, till his death a year ago last April, Mr. Marshall was invited each Christmas Day to tell the story of Appleseed to the Baptist Bible class. Hamurabi once typed up an account and mailed it around to various magazines. It was never printed. One editor wrote back and said that "If the little girl really turned out to be a movie star, then there might be something to your story." But that's not what happened, so why should you lie?

MIRIAM

(1945)

For several years, Mrs. H. T. Miller had lived alone in a pleasant apartment (two rooms with kitchenette) in a remodeled brownstone near the East River. She was a widow: Mr. H. T. Miller had left a reasonable amount of insurance. Her interests were narrow, she had no friends to speak of, and she rarely journeyed farther than the corner grocery. The other people in the house never seemed to notice her: her clothes were matter-of-fact, her hair iron-gray, clipped and casually waved; she did not use cosmetics, her features were plain and inconspicuous, and on her last birthday she was sixty-one. Her activities were seldom spontaneous: she kept the two rooms immaculate, smoked an occasional cigarette, prepared her own meals and tended a canary.

Then she met Miriam. It was snowing that night. Mrs. Miller had finished drying the supper dishes and was thumbing through an afternoon paper when she saw an advertisement of a picture playing at a neighborhood theatre. The title sounded good, so she struggled into her beaver coat, laced her galoshes and left the apartment, leaving one light burning in the foyer: she found nothing more disturbing than a sensation of darkness.

The snow was fine, falling gently, not yet making an impression on the pavement. The wind from the river cut only at street crossings. Mrs. Miller hurried, her head bowed, oblivious as a mole burrowing a blind path. She stopped at a drugstore and bought a package of peppermints.

A long line stretched in front of the box office; she took her place at the end. There would be (a tired voice groaned) a short wait for all seats. Mrs. Miller rummaged in her leather handbag till she collected exactly the correct change for admission. The line seemed to be taking its own time and, looking around for some distraction, she suddenly became conscious of a little girl standing under the edge of the marquee.

Her hair was the longest and strangest Mrs. Miller had ever seen: absolutely silver-white, like an albino's. It flowed waist-length in smooth, loose lines. She was thin and fragilely constructed. There was a simple, special elegance in the way she stood with her thumbs in the pockets of a tailored plum-velvet coat.

Mrs. Miller felt oddly excited, and when the little girl glanced toward her, she smiled warmly. The little girl walked over and said, "Would you care to do me a favor?"

"I'd be glad to, if I can," said Mrs. Miller.

"Oh, it's quite easy. I merely want you to buy a ticket for me; they won't let me in otherwise. Here, I have the money." And gracefully she handed Mrs. Miller two dimes and a nickel.

They went over to the theatre together. An usherette directed them to a lounge; in twenty minutes the picture would be over.

"I feel just like a genuine criminal," said Mrs. Miller gaily, as she sat down. "I mean that sort of thing's against the law, isn't it? I do hope I haven't done the wrong thing. Your mother knows where you are, dear? I mean she does, doesn't she?"

The little girl said nothing. She unbuttoned her coat and folded it across her lap. Her dress underneath was prim and dark blue. A gold chain dangled about her neck, and her fingers, sensitive and musical-looking, toyed with it. Examining her more attentively, Mrs. Miller decided the truly distinctive feature was not her hair, but her eyes; they were hazel, steady, lacking any childlike quality whatsoever and, because of their size, seemed to consume her small face.

Mrs. Miller offered a peppermint. "What's your name, dear?"

"Miriam," she said, as though, in some curious way, it were information already familiar.

"Why, isn't that funny—my name's Miriam, too. And it's not a terribly common name either. Now, don't tell me your last name's Miller!"

"Just Miriam."

"But isn't that funny?"

"Moderately," said Miriam, and rolled the peppermint on her tongue.

Mrs. Miller flushed and shifted uncomfortably. "You have such a large vocabulary for such a little girl."

"Do I?"

"Well, yes," said Mrs. Miller, hastily changing the topic to: "Do you like the movies?"

"I really wouldn't know," said Miriam. "I've never been before."

Women began filling the lounge; the rumble of the newsreel bombs exploded in the distance. Mrs. Miller rose, tucking her purse under her arm. "I guess I'd better be running now if I want to get a seat," she said. "It was nice to have met you."

Miriam nodded ever so slightly.

It snowed all week. Wheels and footsteps moved soundlessly on the street, as if the business of living continued secretly behind a pale but impenetrable curtain. In the falling quiet there was no sky or earth, only snow lifting in the wind, frosting the window glass, chilling the rooms, deadening and hushing the city. At all hours it was necessary to keep a lamp lighted, and Mrs. Miller lost track of the days: Friday was no different from Saturday and on Sunday she went to the grocery: closed, of course.

That evening she scrambled eggs and fixed a bowl of tomato soup. Then, after putting on a flannel robe and cold-creaming her face, she propped herself up in bed with a hot-water bottle under her feet. She was reading the *Times* when the doorbell rang. At first she thought it must be a mistake and whoever it was would go away. But it rang and rang and settled to a persistent buzz. She looked at the clock: a little after eleven; it did not seem possible, she was always asleep by ten.

Climbing out of bed, she trotted barefoot across the living room. "I'm coming, please be patient." The latch was caught; she turned it this way and that way and the bell never paused an instant. "Stop it," she cried. The bolt gave way and she opened the door an inch. "What in heaven's name?"

"Hello," said Miriam.

"Oh . . . why, hello," said Mrs. Miller, stepping hesitantly into the hall. "You're that little girl."

"I thought you'd never answer, but I kept my finger on the button; I knew you were home. Aren't you glad to see me?"

Mrs. Miller did not know what to say. Miriam, she saw, wore the same plum-velvet coat and now she had also a beret to match; her white hair was braided in two shining plaits and looped at the ends with enormous white ribbons.

"Since I've waited so long, you could at least let me in," she said.

"It's awfully late. . . ."

Miriam regarded her blankly. "What difference does that make? Let me in. It's cold out here and I have on a silk dress." Then, with a gentle gesture, she urged Mrs. Miller aside and passed into the apartment.

She dropped her coat and beret on a chair. She was indeed wearing a silk dress. White silk. White silk in February. The skirt was beautifully pleated and the sleeves long; it made a faint rustle as she strolled about the room. "I like your place," she said. "I like the rug, blue's my favorite color." She touched a paper rose in a vase on the coffee table. "Imitation," she commented wanly. "How sad. Aren't imitations sad?" She seated herself on the sofa, daintily spreading her skirt.

"What do you want?" asked Mrs. Miller.

"Sit down," said Miriam. "It makes me nervous to see people stand."

Mrs. Miller sank to a hassock. "What do you want?" she repeated.

"You know, I don't think you're glad I came."

For a second time Mrs. Miller was without an answer; her hand motioned vaguely. Miriam giggled and pressed back on a mound of chintz pillows. Mrs. Miller observed that the girl was less pale than she remembered; her cheeks were flushed.

"How did you know where I lived?"

Miriam frowned. "That's no question at all. What's your name? What's mine?"

"But I'm not listed in the phone book."

"Oh, let's talk about something else."

Mrs. Miller said, "Your mother must be insane to let a child like you wander around at all hours of the night—and in such ridiculous clothes. She must be out of her mind."

Miriam got up and moved to a corner where a covered bird cage hung from a ceiling chain. She peeked beneath the cover. "It's a canary," she said. "Would you mind if I woke him? I'd like to hear him sing."

"Leave Tommy alone," said Mrs. Miller, anxiously. "Don't you dare wake him."

"Certainly," said Miriam. "But I don't see why I can't hear him sing." And then, "Have you anything to eat? I'm starving! Even milk and a jam sandwich would be fine."

"Look," said Mrs. Miller, arising from the hassock, "look—if I make some nice sandwiches will you be a good child and run along home? It's past midnight, I'm sure."

"It's snowing," reproached Miriam. "And cold and dark."

"Well, you shouldn't have come here to begin with," said Mrs.

Miller, struggling to control her voice. "I can't help the weather. If you want anything to eat you'll have to promise to leave."

Miriam brushed a braid against her cheek. Her eyes were thoughtful, as if weighing the proposition. She turned toward the bird cage. "Very well," she said, "I promise."

How old is she? Ten? Eleven? Mrs. Miller, in the kitchen, unsealed a jar of strawberry preserves and cut four slices of bread. She poured a glass of milk and paused to light a cigarette. *And why has she come?* Her hand shook as she held the match, fascinated, till it burned her finger. The canary was singing; singing as he did in the morning and at no other time. "Miriam," she called, "Miriam, I told you not to disturb Tommy." There was no answer. She called again; all she heard was the canary. She inhaled the cigarette and discovered she had lighted the cork-tip end and—oh, really, she mustn't lose her temper.

She carried the food in on a tray and set it on the coffee table. She saw first that the bird cage still wore its night cover. And Tommy was singing. It gave her a queer sensation. And no one was in the room. Mrs. Miller went through an alcove leading to her bedroom; at the door she caught her breath.

"What are you doing?" she asked.

Miriam glanced up and in her eyes there was a look that was not ordinary. She was standing by the bureau, a jewel case opened before her. For a minute she studied Mrs. Miller, forcing their eyes to meet, and she smiled. "There's nothing good here," she said. "But I like this." Her hand held a cameo brooch. "It's charming."

"Suppose—perhaps you'd better put it back," said Mrs. Miller, feeling suddenly the need of some support. She leaned against the door frame; her head was unbearably heavy; a pressure weighted the rhythm of her heartbeat. The light seemed to flutter defectively. "Please, child—a gift from my husband . . ."

"But it's beautiful and I want it," said Miriam. *"Give it to me."*

As she stood, striving to shape a sentence which would somehow save the brooch, it came to Mrs. Miller there was no one to whom she might turn; she was alone; a fact that had not been among her thoughts for a long time. Its sheer emphasis was stunning. But here in her own room in the hushed snow-city were evidences she could not ignore or, she knew with startling clarity, resist.

Miriam ate ravenously, and when the sandwiches and milk were gone, her fingers made cobweb movements over the plate, gathering crumbs. The cameo gleamed on her blouse, the blond profile like a trick reflection of its wearer. "That was very nice," she sighed, "though now an almond cake or a cherry would be ideal. Sweets are lovely, don't you think?"

Mrs. Miller was perched precariously on the hassock, smoking a cigarette. Her hair net had slipped lopsided and loose strands straggled down her face. Her eyes were stupidly concentrated on nothing and her cheeks were mottled in red patches, as though a fierce slap had left permanent marks.

"Is there a candy—a cake?"

Mrs. Miller tapped ash on the rug. Her head swayed slightly as she tried to focus her eyes. "You promised to leave if I made the sandwiches," she said.

"Dear me, did I?"

"It was a promise and I'm tired and I don't feel well at all."

"Mustn't fret," said Miriam. "I'm only teasing."

She picked up her coat, slung it over her arm, and arranged her beret in front of a mirror. Presently she bent close to Mrs. Miller and whispered, "Kiss me good night."

"Please—I'd rather not," said Mrs. Miller.

Miriam lifted a shoulder, arched an eyebrow. "As you like," she said, and went directly to the coffee table, seized the vase containing the paper roses, carried it to where the hard surface of the floor lay bare, and hurled it downward. Glass sprayed in all directions and she stamped her foot on the bouquet.

Then slowly she walked to the door, but before closing it she looked back at Mrs. Miller with a slyly innocent curiosity.

Mrs. Miller spent the next day in bed, rising once to feed the canary and drink a cup of tea; she took her temperature and had none, yet her dreams were feverishly agitated; their unbalanced mood lingered even as she lay staring wide-eyed at the ceiling. One dream threaded through the others like an elusively mysterious theme in a complicated symphony, and the scenes it depicted were sharply outlined, as though sketched by a hand of gifted intensity: a small girl, wearing a bridal gown and a wreath of leaves, led a gray procession down a mountain path, and among them there was unusual silence till a woman at the rear asked, "Where is she taking us?" "No one knows," said an old man marching in front. "But isn't she pretty?" volunteered a third voice. "Isn't she like a frost flower . . . so shining and white?"

Tuesday morning she woke up feeling better; harsh slats of sunlight, slanting through Venetian blinds, shed a disrupting light on her unwholesome fancies. She opened the window to discover a thawed, mild-as-spring day; a sweep of clean new clouds crumpled against a vastly blue, out-of-season sky; and across the low line of rooftops she could see the river and smoke curving from tugboat stacks in a warm wind. A great silver truck plowed the snow-banked street, its machine sound humming on the air.

After straightening the apartment, she went to the grocer's, cashed a check and continued to Schrafft's where she ate breakfast and chatted happily with the waitress. Oh, it was a wonderful day—more like a holiday—and it would be so foolish to go home.

She boarded a Lexington Avenue bus and rode up to Eighty-sixth Street; it was here that she had decided to do a little shopping.

She had no idea what she wanted or needed, but she idled along, intent only upon the passers-by, brisk and preoccupied, who gave her a disturbing sense of separateness.

It was while waiting at the corner of Third Avenue that she saw the man: an old man, bowlegged and stooped under an armload of bulging packages; he wore a shabby brown coat and a checkered cap. Suddenly she realized they were exchanging a smile: there was nothing friendly about this smile, it was merely two cold flickers of recognition. But she was certain she had never seen him before.

He was standing next to an El pillar, and as she crossed the street he turned and followed. He kept quite close; from the corner of her eye she watched his reflection wavering on the shopwindows.

Then in the middle of the block she stopped and faced him. He stopped also and cocked his head, grinning. But what could she say? Do? Here, in broad daylight, on Eighty-sixth Street? It was useless and, despising her own helplessness, she quickened her steps.

Now Second Avenue is a dismal street, made from scraps and ends; part cobblestone, part asphalt, part cement; and its atmosphere of desertion is permanent. Mrs. Miller walked five blocks without meeting anyone, and all the while the steady crunch of his footfalls in the snow stayed near. And when she came to a florist's shop, the sound was still with her. She hurried inside and watched through the glass door as the old man passed; he kept his eyes straight ahead and didn't slow his pace, but he did one strange, telling thing: he tipped his cap.

"Six white ones, did you say?" asked the florist. "Yes," she told him, "white roses." From there she went to a glassware store and selected a vase, presumably a replacement for the one Miriam had broken, though the price was intolerable and the vase itself (she thought) grotesquely vulgar. But a series of unaccountable purchases had begun, as if by prearranged plan: a plan of which she had not the least knowledge or control.

She bought a bag of glazed cherries, and at a place called the Knickerbocker Bakery she paid forty cents for six almond cakes.

Within the last hour the weather had turned cold again; like blurred lenses, winter clouds cast a shade over the sun, and the skeleton of an early dusk colored the sky; a damp mist mixed with the wind and the voices of a few children who romped high on mountains of gutter snow seemed lonely and cheerless. Soon the first flake fell, and when Mrs. Miller reached the brownstone house, snow was falling in a swift screen and foot tracks vanished as they were printed.

The white roses were arranged decoratively in the vase. The glazed cherries shone on a ceramic plate. The almond cakes, dusted with sugar, awaited a hand. The canary fluttered on its swing and picked at a bar of seed.

At precisely five the doorbell rang. Mrs. Miller *knew* who it was. The hem of her housecoat trailed as she crossed the floor. "Is that you?" she called.

"Naturally," said Miriam, the word resounding shrilly from the hall. "Open this door."

"Go away," said Mrs. Miller.

"Please hurry . . . I have a heavy package."

"Go away," said Mrs. Miller. She returned to the living room, lighted a cigarette, sat down and calmly listened to the buzzer; on and on and on. "You might as well leave. I have no intention of letting you in."

Shortly the bell stopped. For possibly ten minutes Mrs. Miller did not move. Then, hearing no sound, she concluded Miriam had gone. She tiptoed to the door and opened it a sliver; Miriam was half-reclining atop a cardboard box with a beautiful French doll cradled in her arms.

"Really, I thought you were never coming," she said peevishly. "Here, help me get this in, it's awfully heavy."

It was not spell-like compulsion that Mrs. Miller felt, but rather a curious passivity; she brought in the box, Miriam the doll. Miriam curled up on the sofa, not troubling to remove her coat or beret, and watched disinterestedly as Mrs. Miller dropped the box and stood trembling, trying to catch her breath.

"Thank you," she said. In the daylight she looked pinched and drawn, her hair less luminous. The French doll she was loving wore an exquisite powdered wig and its idiot glass eyes sought solace in Miriam's. "I have a surprise," she continued. "Look into my box."

Kneeling, Mrs. Miller parted the flaps and lifted out another doll; then a blue dress which she recalled as the one Miriam had worn that first night at the theatre; and of the remainder she said, "It's all clothes. Why?"

"Because I've come to live with you," said Miriam, twisting a cherry stem. "Wasn't it nice of you to buy me the cherries . . . ?"

"But you can't! For God's sake go away—go away and leave me alone!"

". . . and the roses and the almond cakes? How really wonderfully generous. You know, these cherries are delicious. The last place I lived was with an old man; he was terribly poor and we never had good things to eat. But I think I'll be happy here." She paused to snuggle her doll closer. "Now, if you'll just show me where to put my things . . ."

Mrs. Miller's face dissolved into a mask of ugly red lines; she began to cry, and it was an unnatural, tearless sort of weeping, as though, not having wept for a long time, she had forgotten how. Carefully she edged backward till she touched the door.

She fumbled through the hall and down the stairs to a landing below. She pounded frantically on the door of the first apartment she came to; a short, redheaded man answered and she pushed past him. "Say, what the hell is this?" he said. "Anything wrong, lover?" asked a young woman who appeared from the kitchen, drying her hands. And it was to her that Mrs. Miller turned.

"Listen," she cried, "I'm ashamed behaving this way but—well, I'm Mrs. H. T. Miller and I live upstairs and . . ." She pressed her hands over her face. "It sounds so absurd. . . ."

The woman guided her to a chair, while the man excitedly rattled pocket change. "Yeah?"

"I live upstairs and there's a little girl visiting me, and I suppose that I'm afraid of her. She won't leave and I can't make her and—she's going to do something terrible. She's already stolen my cameo, but she's about to do something worse—something terrible!"

The man asked, "Is she a relative, huh?"

Mrs. Miller shook her head. "I don't know who she is. Her name's Miriam, but I don't know for certain who she is."

"You gotta calm down, honey," said the woman, stroking Mrs. Miller's arm. "Harry here'll tend to this kid. Go on, lover." And Mrs. Miller said, "The door's open—5A."

After the man left, the woman brought a towel and bathed Mrs. Miller's face. "You're very kind," Mrs. Miller said. "I'm sorry to act like such a fool, only this wicked child . . ."

"Sure honey," consoled the woman. "Now, you better take it easy."

Mrs. Miller rested her head in the crook of her arm; she was quiet enough to be asleep. The woman turned a radio dial; a piano and a husky voice filled the silence and the woman, tapping her foot, kept excellent time. "Maybe we oughta go up too," she said.

"I don't want to see her again. I don't want to be anywhere near her."

"Uh-huh, but what you shoulda done, you shoulda called a cop."

Presently they heard the man on the stairs. He strode into the room frowning and scratching the back of his neck. "Nobody there," he said, honestly embarrassed. "She musta beat it."

"Harry, you're a jerk," announced the woman. "We been sitting here the whole time and we woulda seen . . ." she stopped abruptly, for the man's glance was sharp.

"I looked all over," he said, "and there just ain't nobody there. Nobody, understand?"

"Tell me," said Mrs. Miller, rising, "tell me, did you see a large box? Or a doll?"

"No, ma'am, I didn't."

And the woman, as if delivering a verdict, said, "Well, for cryinout-loud. . . ."

Mrs. Miller entered her apartment softly; she walked to the center of the room and stood quite still. No, in a sense it had not changed: the roses, the cakes, and the cherries were in place. But this was an empty room, emptier than if the furnishings and familiars were not present, lifeless and petrified as a funeral parlor. The sofa loomed before her with a new strangeness: its vacancy had a meaning that would have been less penetrating and terrible had Miriam been curled on it. She gazed fixedly at the space where she remembered setting the box and, for a moment, the hassock spun desperately. And she looked through the window; surely the river was real, surely snow was falling—but then, one could not be certain witness to anything: Miriam, so vividly there—and yet, where was she? Where, where?

As though moving in a dream, she sank to a chair. The room was losing shape; it was dark and getting darker and there was nothing to be done about it; she could not lift her hand to light a lamp.

Suddenly, closing her eyes, she felt an upward surge, like a diver emerging from some deeper, greener depth. In times of terror or immense distress, there are moments when the mind waits, as though for a revelation, while a skein of calm is woven over thought; it is like a sleep, or a supernatural trance; and during this lull one is aware of a force of quiet reasoning: well, what if she had never really known a girl named Miriam? that she had been foolishly frightened on the street? In the end, like everything else, it was of no importance. For the only thing she had lost to Miriam was her identity, but now she knew she had found again the person who lived in this room, who cooked her own meals, who owned a canary, who was someone she could trust and believe in: Mrs. H. T. Miller.

Listening in contentment, she became aware of a double sound: a bureau drawer opening and closing; she seemed to hear it long after completion—opening and closing. Then gradually, the harshness of it was replaced by the murmur of a silk dress and this, delicately faint, was moving nearer and swelling in intensity till the walls trembled with the vibration and the room was caving under a wave of whispers. Mrs. Miller stiffened and opened her eyes to a dull, direct stare.

"Hello," said Miriam.

MY SIDE OF THE MATTER

(1945)

I know what is being said about me and you can take my side or theirs, that's your own business. It's my word against Eunice's and Olivia-Ann's, and it should be plain enough to anyone with two good eyes which one of us has their wits about them. I just want the citizens of the U.S.A. to know the facts, that's all.

The facts: On Sunday, August 12, this year of our Lord, Eunice tried to kill me with her papa's Civil War sword and Olivia-Ann cut up all over the place with a fourteen-inch hog knife. This is not even to mention lots of other things.

It began six months ago when I married Marge. That was the first thing I did wrong. We were married in Mobile after an acquaintance of only four days. We were both sixteen and she was visiting my cousin Georgia. Now that I've had plenty of time to think it over, I can't for the life of me figure how I fell for the likes of her. She has no looks, no body and no brains whatsoever. But Marge is a natural blonde and maybe that's the answer. Well, we were married going on three months when Marge ups and gets pregnant; the second thing I did wrong. Then she starts hollering that she's got to go home to Mama—only she hasn't got no mama, just these two aunts. Eunice and Olivia-Ann. So she makes me quit my perfectly swell position clerking at the Cash 'n' Carry and move here to Admiral's Mill, which is nothing but a damn gap in the road any way you care to consider it.

The day Marge and I got off the train at the L&N depot it was raining cats and dogs and do you think anyone came to meet us? I'd shelled out forty-one cents for a telegram, too! Here my wife's pregnant and we have to tramp seven miles in a downpour. It was bad on Marge, as I couldn't carry hardly any of our stuff on account of I have terrible trouble with my back. When I first caught sight of this house I must say I was impressed. It's big and yellow and has real columns out in front and japonica trees, both red and white, lining the yard.

Eunice and Olivia-Ann had seen us coming and were waiting in the hall. I swear I wish you could get a look at these two. Honest, you'd die! Eunice is this big old fat thing with a behind that must weigh a tenth of a ton. She troops around the house, rain or shine, in this real old-fashioned nightie, calls it a kimono, but it isn't anything in this world but a dirty flannel nightie. Furthermore she chews tobacco and tries to pretend so ladylike, spitting on the sly. She keeps gabbing about what a fine education she had, which is her way of attempting to make me feel bad, although, personally, it never bothers me so much as one whit, as I know for a fact she can't even read the funnies without she spells out every single, solitary word. You've got to hand her one thing, though—she can add and subtract money so fast that there's no doubt but what she could be up in Washington, D.C., working where they make the stuff. Not that she hasn't got plenty of money! Naturally she says she hasn't but I know she has because one day, accidentally, I happened to find close to a thousand dollars hidden in a flowerpot on the side porch. I didn't touch one cent, only Eunice says I stole a hundred-dollar bill, which is a venomous lie from start to finish. Of course anything Eunice says is an order from headquarters, as not a breathing soul in Admiral's Mill can stand up and say he doesn't owe her money and if she said Charlie Carson (a blind ninety-year-old invalid who hasn't taken a step since 1896) threw her on her back and raped her, everybody in this county would swear the same on a stack of Bibles.

Now, Olivia-Ann is worse, and that's the truth! Only she's not so bad on the nerves as Eunice, for she is a natural-born half-wit and ought really to be kept in somebody's attic. She's real pale and skinny and has a mustache. She squats around most of the time whittling on a stick with her fourteen-inch hog knife, otherwise she's up to some devilment, like what she did to Mrs. Harry Steller Smith. I swore not ever to tell anyone that, but when a vicious attempt has been made on a person's life, I say the hell with promises.

Mrs. Harry Steller Smith was Eunice's canary named after a woman from Pensacola who makes home-made cure-all that Eunice takes for the gout. One day I heard this terrible racket in the parlor and upon investigating, what did I find but Olivia-Ann shooing Mrs. Harry Steller Smith out an open window with a broom and the door to the birdcage wide. If I hadn't walked in at exactly that moment, she might never have been caught. She got scared that I would tell Eunice and blurted out the whole thing, said it wasn't fair to keep one of God's creatures locked up that way, besides which she couldn't stand Mrs. Harry Steller Smith's singing. Well, I felt kind of sorry for her and she gave me two dollars, so I helped her cook up a story for Eunice. Of course I wouldn't have taken the money except I thought it would ease her conscience.

The very *first* words Eunice said when I stepped inside this house were, "So this is what you ran off behind our back and married, Marge?"

Marge says, "Isn't he the best-looking thing, Aunt Eunice?"

Eunice eyes me u-p and d-o-w-n and says, "Tell him to turn around."

While my back is turned, Eunice says, "You sure must've picked the runt of the litter. Why, this isn't any sort of man at all."

I've never been so taken back in my life! True, I'm slightly stocky, but then, I haven't got my full growth yet.

"He is too," says Marge.

Olivia-Ann, who's been standing there with her mouth so wide the flies could buzz in and out, says, "You heard what Sister said. He's not any sort of a man whatsoever. The very idea of this little runt running around claiming to be a man! Why, he isn't even of the male sex!"

Marge says, "You seem to forget, Aunt Olivia-Ann, that this is my husband, the father of my unborn child."

Eunice made a nasty sound like only she can and said, "Well, all I can say is I most certainly wouldn't be bragging about it."

Isn't that a nice welcome? And after I gave up my perfectly swell position clerking at the Cash 'n' Carry.

But it's not a drop in the bucket to what came later that same evening. After Bluebell cleared away the supper dishes, Marge asked, just as nice as she could, if we could borrow the car and drive over to the picture show at Phoenix City.

"You must be clear out of your head," says Eunice, and, honest, you'd think we'd asked for the kimono off her back.

"You must be clear out of your head," says Olivia-Ann.

"It's six o'clock," says Eunice, "and if you think I'd let that runt drive my just-as-good-as-brand-new 1934 Chevrolet as far as the privy and back, you must've gone clear out of your head."

Naturally such language makes Marge cry.

"Never you mind, honey," I said, "I've driven pulenty of Cadillacs in my time."

"Humf," says Eunice.

"Yeah," says I.

Eunice says, "If he's ever so much as driven a plow, I'll eat a dozen gophers fried in turpentine."

"I won't have you refer to my husband in any such manner," says Marge. "You're acting simply outlandish! Why, you'd think I'd picked up some absolutely strange man in some absolutely strange place."

"If the shoe fits, wear it!" says Eunice.

"Don't think you can pull the sheep over our eyes," says Olivia-

Ann in that braying voice of hers so much like the mating call of a jackass you can't rightly tell the difference.

"We weren't born just around the corner, you know," says Eunice.

Marge says, "I'll give you to understand that I'm legally wed till death do us part to this man by a certified justice of the peace as of three and one-half months ago. Ask anybody. Furthermore, Aunt Eunice, he is free, white and sixteen. Furthermore, George Far Sylvester does not appreciate hearing his father referred to in any such manner."

George Far Sylvester is the name we've planned for the baby. Has a strong sound, don't you think? Only the way things stand I have positively no feelings in the matter now whatsoever.

"How can a girl have a baby with a girl?" says Olivia-Ann, which was a calculated attack on my manhood. "I do declare there's something new every day."

"Oh, shush up," says Eunice. "Let us hear no more about the picture show in Phoenix City."

Marge sobs, "Oh-h-h, but it's Judy Garland."

"Never mind, honey," I said, "I most likely saw the show in Mobile ten years ago."

"That's a deliberate falsehood," shouts Olivia-Ann. "Oh, you are a scoundrel, you are. Judy hasn't been in the pictures ten years." Olivia-Ann's never seen not even one picture show in her entire fifty-two years (she won't tell anybody how old she is but I dropped a card to the capitol in Montgomery and they were very nice about answering), but she subscribes to eight movie books. According to Postmistress Delancey, it's the only mail she ever gets outside of the Sears & Roebuck. She has this positively morbid crush on Gary Cooper and has one trunk and two suitcases full of his photos.

So we got up from the table and Eunice lumbers over to the window and looks out to the chinaberry tree and says, "Birds settling in their roost—time we went to bed. You have your old room, Marge, and I've fixed a cot for this gentleman on the back porch."

It took a solid minute for that to sink in.

I said, "And what, if I'm not too bold to ask, is the objection to my sleeping with my lawful wife?"

Then they both started yelling at me.

So Marge threw a conniption fit right then and there. "Stop it, stop it, stop it! I can't stand any more. Go on, babydoll—go on and sleep wherever they say. Tomorrow we'll see. . . ."

Eunice says, "I swanee if the child hasn't got a grain of sense, after all."

"Poor dear," says Olivia-Ann, wrapping her arm around Marge's waist and herding her off, "poor dear, so young, so innocent. Let's us just go and have a good cry on Olivia-Ann's shoulder."

May, June and July and the best part of August I've squatted and sweltered on that damn back porch without an ounce of screening. And Marge—she hasn't opened her mouth in protest, not once! This part of Alabama is swampy, with mosquitoes that could murder a buffalo, given half a chance, not to mention dangerous flying roaches and a posse of local rats big enough to haul a wagon train from here to Timbuctoo. Oh, if it wasn't for that little unborn George, I would've been making dust tracks on the road, way before now. I mean to say I haven't had five seconds alone with Marge since that first night. One or the other is always chaperoning and last week they like to have blown their tops when Marge locked herself in her room and they couldn't find me nowhere. The truth is I'd been down watching the niggers bale cotton but just for spite I let on to Eunice like Marge and I'd been up to no good. After that they added Blue-bell to the shift.

And all this time I haven't even had cigarette change.

Eunice has hounded me day in and day out about getting a job. "Why don't the little heathen go out and get some honest work?" says she. As you've probably noticed, she never speaks to me directly, though more often than not I am the only one in her royal presence. "If he was any sort of man you could call a man, he'd be trying to put a crust of bread in that girl's mouth instead of stuffing his own off my vittles." I think you should know that I've been living almost exclusively on cold yams and leftover grits for three months and thirteen days and I've been down to consult Dr. A. N. Carter twice. He's not exactly sure whether I have the scurvy or not.

And as for my not working, I'd like to know what a man of my abilities, a man who held a perfectly swell position with the Cash 'n' Carry, would find to do in a fleabag like Admiral's Mill? There is all of one store here and Mr. Tubberville, the proprietor, is actually so lazy it's painful for him to have to sell anything. Then we have the Morning Star Baptist Church but they already have a preacher, an awful old turd named Shell whom Eunice drug over one day to see about the salvation of my soul. I heard him with my own ears tell her I was too far gone.

But it's what Eunice has done to Marge that really takes the cake. She has turned that girl against me in the most villainous fashion that words could not describe. Why, she even reached the point when she was sassing me back, but I provided her with a couple of good slaps and put a stop to that. No wife of mine is ever going to be disrespectful to me, not on your life!

The enemy lines are stretched tight: Bluebell, Olivia-Ann, Eunice, Marge and the whole rest of Admiral's Mill (pop. 342). Allies: none. Such was the situation as of Sunday, August 12, when the attempt was made upon my very life.

Yesterday was quiet and hot enough to melt rock. The trouble began at exactly two o'clock. I know because Eunice has one of those fool cuckoo contraptions and it scares the daylights out of me. I was minding my own personal business in the parlor, composing a song on the upright piano, which Eunice bought for Olivia-Ann and hired her a teacher to come all the way from Columbus, Georgia, once a week. Postmistress Delancey, who was my friend till she decided that it was maybe not so wise, says that the fancy teacher tore out of this house one afternoon like old Adolf Hitler was on his tail and leaped in his Ford coupé, never to be heard from again. Like I say, I'm trying to keep cool in the parlor not bothering a living soul when Olivia-Ann trots in with her hair all twisted up in curlers and shrieks, "Cease that infernal racket this very instant! Can't you give a body a minute's rest? And get off my piano right smart. It's not your piano, it's my piano, and if you don't get off it right smart, I'll have you in court like a shot the first Monday in September."

She's not anything in this world but jealous on account of I'm a natural-born musician and the songs I make up out of my own head are absolutely marvelous.

"And just look what you've done to my genuine ivory keys, Mr. Sylvester," says she, trotting over to the piano, "torn nearly every one of them off right at the roots for purentee meanness, that's what you've done."

She knows good and well that the piano was ready for the junk heap the moment I entered this house.

I said, "Seeing as you're such a know-it-all, Miss Olivia-Ann, maybe it would interest you to know that I'm in the possession of a few interesting tales myself. A few things that maybe other people would be very grateful to know. Like what happened to Mrs. Harry Steller Smith, as for instance."

Remember Mrs. Harry Steller Smith?

She paused and looked at the empty birdcage. "You gave me your oath," says she and turned the most terrifying shade of purple.

"Maybe I did and again maybe I didn't," says I. "You did an evil thing when you betrayed Eunice that way but if some people will leave other people alone, then maybe I can overlook it."

Well, sir, she walked out of there just as *nice* and *quiet* as you please. So I went and stretched out on the sofa, which is the most horrible piece of furniture I've ever seen and is part of a matched set Eunice bought in Atlanta in 1912 and paid two thousand dollars for, cash— or so she claims. This set is black and olive plush and smells like wet chicken feathers on a damp day. There is a big table in one corner of the parlor which supports two pictures of Miss E and O-A's mama and papa. Papa is kind of handsome but just between you and me I'm convinced he has black blood in him from somewhere. He was a captain in the Civil War and that is one thing I'll never forget on account of his sword, which is displayed over the mantel and figures prominently in the action yet to come. Mama has that hang-dog, half-wit look like Olivia-Ann, though I must say Mama carries it better.

So I had just dozed off when I heard Eunice bellowing, "Where is he? Where is he?" And the next thing I know she's framed in the doorway with her hands planted plumb on those hippo hips and the whole pack scrunched up behind her: Bluebell, Olivia-Ann and Marge.

Several seconds passed with Eunice tapping her big old bare foot just as fast and furious as she could and fanning her fat face with this cardboard picture of Niagara Falls.

"Where is it?" says she. "Where's my hundred dollars that he made away with while my trusting back was turned?"

"*This* is the straw that broke the camel's back," says I, but I was too hot and tired to get up.

"That's not the only back that's going to be broke," says she, her bug eyes about to pop clear out of their sockets. "That was my funeral money and I want it back. Wouldn't you know he'd steal from the dead?"

"Maybe he didn't take it," says Marge.

"You keep your mouth out of this, missy," says Olivia-Ann.

"He stole my money sure as shooting," says Eunice. "Why, look at his eyes—black with guilt!"

I yawned and said, "Like they say in the courts—if the party of the first part falsely accuses the party of the second part, then the party of the first part can be locked away in jail even if the State Home is where they rightfully belong for the protection of all concerned."

"God will punish him," says Eunice.

"Oh, Sister," says Olivia-Ann, "let us not wait for God."

Whereupon Eunice advances on me with this most peculiar look, her dirty flannel nightie jerking along the floor. And Olivia-Ann leeches after her and Bluebell lets forth this moan that must have been heard clear to Eufala and back while Marge stands there wringing her hands and whimpering.

"Oh-h-h," sobs Marge, "please give her back that money, baby-doll."

I said, "Et tu Brute?" which is from William Shakespeare.

"Look at the likes of him," says Eunice, "lying around all day not doing so much as licking a postage stamp."

"Pitiful," clucks Olivia-Ann.

"You'd think he was having a baby instead of that poor child." Eunice speaking.

Bluebell tosses in her two cents, "Ain't it the truth?"

"Well, if it isn't the old pots calling the kettle black," says I.

"After loafing here for three months, does this runt have the audacity to cast aspersions in my direction?" says Eunice.

I merely flicked a bit of ash from my sleeve and not the least bit fazed said, "Dr. A. N. Carter has informed me that I am in a dangerous scurvy condition and can't stand the least excitement whatsoever—otherwise I'm liable to foam at the mouth and bite somebody."

Then Bluebell says, "Why don't he go back to that trash in Mobile, Miss Eunice? I'se sick and tired of carryin' his ol' slop jar."

Naturally that coal-black nigger made me so mad I couldn't see straight.

So just as calm as a cucumber I arose and picked up this umbrella off the hat tree and rapped her across the head with it until it cracked smack in two.

"My real Japanese silk parasol!" shrieks Olivia-Ann.

Marge cries, "You've killed Bluebell, you've killed poor old Bluebell!"

Eunice shoves Olivia-Ann and says, "He's gone clear out of his head, Sister! Run! Run and get Mr. Tubberville!"

"I don't like Mr. Tubberville," says Olivia-Ann staunchly. "I'll go get my hog knife." And she makes a dash for the door, but seeing as I care nothing for death, I brought her down with a sort of tackle. It wrenched my back something terrible.

"He's going to kill her!" hollers Eunice loud enough to bring the house down. "He's going to murder us all! I warned you, Marge. Quick, child, get Papa's sword!"

So Marge gets Papa's sword and hands it to Eunice. Talk about wifely devotion! And, if that's not bad enough, Olivia-Ann gives me this terrific knee punch and I had to let go. The next thing you know we hear her out in the yard bellowing hymns.

> *Mine eyes have seen the glory of the*
> *coming of the Lord;*
> *He is trampling out the vintage where*
> *the grapes of wrath are stored. . . .*

Meanwhile, Eunice is sashaying all over the place, wildly thrashing Papa's sword, and somehow I've managed to clamber atop the piano. Then Eunice climbs up on the piano stool and how that rickety contraption survived a monster like her I'll never be the one to tell.

"Come down from there, you yellow coward, before I run you through," says she and takes a whack and I've got a half-inch cut to prove it.

By this time Bluebell has recovered and skittered away to join Olivia-Ann holding services in the front yard. I guess they were expecting my body and God knows it would've been theirs if Marge hadn't passed out cold.

That's the only good thing I've got to say for Marge.

What happened after that I can't rightly remember except for Olivia-Ann reappearing with her fourteen-inch hog knife and a bunch of the neighbors. But suddenly Marge was the star attraction and I suppose they carried her to her room. Anyway, as soon as they left I barricaded the parlor door.

I've got all those black and olive plush chairs pushed against it and that big mahogany table that must weigh a couple of tons and the hat tree and lots of other stuff. I've locked the windows and pulled down the shades. Also I've found a five-pound box of Sweet Love candy and this very minute I'm munching a juicy, creamy, chocolate cherry. Sometimes they come to the door and knock and yell and plead. Oh, yes, they've started singing a song of a very different color. But as for me—I give them a tune on the piano every now and then just to let them know I'm cheerful.

Preacher's Legend

(1945)

A south-moving cloud slipped over the sun and a patch of dark, an island of shadow, crept down the field, drifted over the ridge. Presently it began to rain: summer rain with sun in it, lasting only a short time; long enough for settling dust, polishing leaves. When the rain ended, an old colored man—his name was Preacher—opened his cabin door and gazed at the field where weeds grew profusely in the rich earth; at a rocky yard shaded by peach trees and dogwood and chinaberry; at a gutted red-clay road that seldom saw car, wagon, or human; and at a ring of green hills that spread, perhaps, to the edge of the world.

Preacher was a small man, a mite, and his face was a million wrinkles. Tufts of gray wool sprouted from his bluish skull and his eyes were sorrowful. He was so bent that he resembled a rusty sickle and his skin was the yellow of superior leather. As he studied what remained of his farm, his hand pestered his chin wisely but, to tell the truth, he was thinking nothing.

It was quiet, of course, and the coolness made him shiver so that he went inside and sat in a rocker and wrapped his legs in a beautiful scrap quilt of green-rose and red-leaf design and fell asleep in the still house with all the windows wide while the wind stirred bright calendars and comic strips he had plastered over the walls.

—

In a quarter of an hour he was awake, for he never slept long and the days passed in a series of naps and wakings, sleep and light, one hardly different from the other. Although it was not cold he lit the fire, filled his pipe and began to rock, his glance wandering over the room. The double iron bed was a hopeless confusion of quilts and pillows and scaly with flecks of pink paint; an arm flapped desolately from the very chair in which he sat; a wonderful poster-picture of a golden-haired girl holding a bottle of NE-HI was torn at the mouth so that her smile was wicked and leering. His eyes paused on a sooty, charred stove, squatting in the corner. He was hungry, but the stove, piled high with dirty pans, made Preacher tired even to consider it. "Can't do nothin' 'bout it," he said, the way certain old people quarrel with themselves; "sick to death of collards an' whatevahelse. Just sit here an' stahve, that be my fate. . . . Bet yo' bottom dollah ain't nobody gonna grieve on dat account, nawsuh." Evelina had always been so clean and neat and good, but she was dead and buried two springs ago. And of their children there was left only Anna-Jo, who had a job in Cypress City where she lived-in and went cavorting every night. Or, at least, Preacher believed this to be the case.

He was very religious and as the afternoon wore on he took his Bible from the mantel and traced the print with a palsied finger. He enjoyed pretending he could read and continued for some time: plotting his own tales and poring over the illustrations. This habit had always been of great concern to Evelina. "Why you all de time studyin' ovah de Good Book, Preacher? I declare you ain't got no sense. . . . Can't no mo' read than I kin."

"Why, honey," he explained, "ever'body kin read de Good Book. He fixed it so'se dey could." It was a claim he had heard made by the Pastor in Cypress City and it satisfied him completely.

When the sunlight made an exact impression from window to door he closed the Bible over his finger and hobbled onto the porch. Blue and white pots of fern swung from the ceiling on wire cords and flowered to the floor, trailing like peacock tails. Slowly, and with great care, he limped down the steps, fashioned from tree trunks, and stood, frail and humped in his overalls and khaki shirt, in the middle of the yard. "Here I is. Didn't spec I'd do it. . . . Didn't spec I had de stren'th in me today."

A smell of damp earth hung on the air and the wind turned the chinaberry leaves. A rooster crowed, and its scarlet comb went darting through the high weeds and disappeared under the house. "You best run, ol' crow, else I git me a hatchet and den you bettah watch out. Bet you taste mighty fine!" The weeds swept up at his bare feet and he stopped and tugged at a handful. "Ain't no use. You just grow right smack back agin, nasty mess."

Near the road the dogwood was in bloom and the rain had scattered petals that were soft under his feet and stuck between his toes. He walked with the aid of a sycamore cane. After crossing the road and passing through a wild pecan grove, he chose the path, as was his custom, that led through the forest down to the creek and *The Place*.

The same journey, the same way, and at the same time: late afternoon because, that way, it gave him something to look forward to. The walks had begun one November day when he had reached his *Decision* and continued all winter when the earth frosted and pine needles clung frozen to his feet.

Now it was May. Six months were gone, and Preacher, born in May and married in May, thought surely here was the month that would see the end of his mission. It was his superstition that a sign marked this day in particular; so he followed the path more rapidly than usual.

Sun pooled in shafts, caught in his hair, changed the color of the Spanish moss, flung limp and long like whiskers across the waterbay branches, from gray to pearl to blue to gray. A cicada called. Another answered. "Shut up, bettle-bugs! Whut you wanna be makin' so much racket fer? You lonesome?"

The path was tricky, and sometimes, because it was really no more than a thread of trampled ground, difficult to maintain. At one point it sloped downward into a hollow that smelled of sweet gum and here began a thickly-vined stretch where it was night black and the brush trembled with who-knows-what. "Git out o' there, all you devils! Ain't nary a one of you kin scare Preacher. Ol' buzzards and ghosts, bettah watch out! Preacher . . . he'll bust you side de haid an' skin off yo' hide an' gouge out yo' eyes an' stomp de whole caboodle down to de pit of fire!" But all the same his heart beat faster, his cane rapped searchingly before him; the beast lurked behind; terrible eyes, shining in hell, watched from their lair!

Evelina, he recalled, had never believed in the Spirits and this made him angry. "Hush now, Preacher," she would say, "I ain't gonna listen to no mo' of dat spook talk. Why, man, dey ain't no spooks 'cept in yo' haid." Oh, she had been unwise, for now, sure as there was a God in heaven, she belonged among the hunters and the hungry-eyed waiting there in the dark. He paused, called, "Evelina? Evelina . . . answuh me, honey." And he hurried on, suddenly fearful that someday she would hear and, not recognizing, devour him whole.

Soon the sound of the creek; from there *The Place* was only a few steps. He pushed aside a thorny nettle and, with anguished grunts, lowered himself down the bank and crossed the stream, stone by stone, with studied precision. Nervous minnow schools made finicky forays along the clear and shallow edge and emerald-winged dragons plucked at the surface. On the opposite bank, a humming bird, whirring its invisible wings, ate the heart of a giant tiger lily.

So the trees thinned and the path broadened into a small, cubic clearing. Preacher's place. Once, before the lumber mill closed, it had been a washing center for the women, but that was long ago. A flow of swallows swept overhead and from somewhere nearby an unfamiliar bird sang a strange, persistent song.

He was tired and out of breath, and he dropped to his knees, leaning his cane against a rotted oak stump on which clusters of devil's snuff grew. Then, unfolding his Bible to where a silver ribbon lay pressed between the pages, he clasped his hands and lifted his head.

Several moments of silence, his eyes pinched narrow, intent upon the ring of sky, the smoky strands of cloud, like stray loops of tow hair, that seemed scarcely to move over the blue screen, paler than milk glass.

Then, in just a whisper:

"Mistuh Jesus? Mistuh Jesus?"

The wind whispered back, uprooting winter-buried leaves that turned furtive cart wheels across the moss-green floor.

"I'se back agin, Mistuh Jesus, faithful to de minute. Please, suh, pay 'tention to ol' Preacher."

Certain of his audience, he smiled sadly and waved. It was time to speak his piece. He said he was old; he didn't know how old, ninety or a hundred, maybe. And his business finished and all his people gone. If there was still the family, then things might be different. Hosanna! But Evelina had passed away and what had become of the children? Billy Boy and Jasmine and Landis and Le Roy and Anna-Jo and Beautiful Love? Some to Memphis and Mobile and Birmingham, some to their graves. Anyway they weren't with him; they had left the land he had worked so hard, and the fields were ruined and he was frightened in the old house at night with nothing for company but the whippoorwill. And so it was very unkind to keep him here when he longed to be with the others wherever they were. "Glory be, Mistuh Jesus, I'se ancient as de ancientess turtle an' ancientuh than dat. . . ."

Lately he had fallen into a habit of pleading his case many times, and the longer he carried on the shriller and more urgent his voice became till it swelled fierce and demanding, and the bluejays, watching from the pine branches, flew away in rage and terror.

He stopped abruptly and cocked his head and listened. It repeated itself: an odd, disturbing sound. He looked this way and that way and then he saw a miracle: A flaming head, bobbing above the brush, was floating towards him; its hair was curled and red; a brilliant beard streamed down its face. Worse yet, another apparition, paler and more luminous, drifted after it.

Intense panic and confusion stiffened Preacher's face and he moaned. Never in the history of Calupa County had such a miserable sound been heard. A crop-eared black-and-tan charged into the clearing, glared and growled with ropes of saliva dangling from its mouth. And two men, two strangers, stepped out of the shade, green shirts open at their throats, snakeskin galluses supporting their corduroy breeches. Both were short but magnificently built and one was curly-headed and sported an orange-red beard, the other yellow-haired and smooth-cheeked. A slain wildcat was slung between them on a bamboo pole and tall rifles stood at their sides.

This was all Preacher needed, and he moaned again and jumped to his feet and bounded like a jack rabbit into the forest and onto the path. So great was his haste that he left his cane resting against the oak stump and his Bible open on the moss. The hound wagged forward, sniffed at the pages and started chase.

"What in all fired hell?" said Curly Head, picking up the book and cane.

"Damnedest thing I ever saw," said Yellow Hair.

They settled the cateymount, swinging on the pole where its paws were secured with hemp, over their broad shoulders, and Curly Head said, "Guess we better get after that dog; cuss him anyway."

"Spec we had," said Yellow Hair. "Only I'd give a pretty penny to rest a spell. . . . Got a blister the size of a half dollar about to kill me."

Swaying under their weight of rifle and game, they struck up a song and moved towards the darkening pines and the cateymount's glazed, golden eyes, fixed wide, caught and reflected the late sun, kicked back its fire.

—

In the meantime Preacher had covered considerable distance. Truly he hadn't run so fast since the day the hoop snake had chased him from here to Kingdom Come. He was no longer decrepit but a sprinter stepping along spry as you please. His legs shot sturdy and sure over the path and it is to be noted that a wretched kink in his back, from which he had suffered twenty years, dissolved that afternoon never to reappear. The dark hollow flew past without his being aware, and, as he waded across the creek, his overalls flapped crazily. Oh, he was wounded with fear and the pad of his racing feet was a raging drum.

Then, just as he reached the dogwood tree, he had a tremendous thought. It was so severe and stunning that he stumbled and fell against the tree, which scattered rain and scared him badly. He rubbed his hurt elbow, flicked his tongue over his lips and nodded. "Lord above," he said, "what has done been did to me?" Yes. Yes, he knew. He knew who the strangers were—knew it from the Good Book—but it was less comfort than might be supposed.

So he crawled to his feet and fled through the yard and up the steps.

On the porch he turned and glanced backward. Quiet, still: nothing stirring but shadows. Dusk was spreading fanwise over the ridge; fields and trees, bush and vine, were webbed in gathering color; purple and rose and the little peach trees were silver-green. And, not far off, the hound was baying. Momentarily, Preacher considered running the miles to Cypress City but that, he knew, would never save him. "Nevuh in dis world."

Shut the door, bolt it good; there, that's fine! Now the windows. But, oh, the shutters are broken and gone!

And he stood helpless and defeated, staring at the hollow squares where moon vine crept over the sill. What was that? "Evelina? Evelina! Evelina!" Mice claws in the walls, only wind flirting a calendar leaf.

So, muttering violently, he shuffled about the cabin arranging, dusting, threatening. "Spiduhs an' widduhs, hide yo' self fo' shame. . . . Pow'ful big comp'ny comin' to call." He lit a brass kerosene lamp (a gift to Evelina, Christmas 1918) and when the flame quickened he placed it on the mantel beside a blurred photograph (taken by the Pose-Yourself man who traveled through once a year) of a cheeky, beverage-colored face, Evelina, smiling, with a twist of white net in her hair. Next he puffed a satin pillow (Grand Prize in Scrap Quilt, awarded to Beautiful Love, Cypress Frolics Fair 1910) and dropped it proudly in the rocker. There was nothing left to do; so he prodded the fire, added a chunk of kindling and sat down to wait.

Not long. For presently there was singing; deep voices chanting airs that echoed and echoed with immense and rollicking power: "I've been workin' on the RAIL-road, *All* the livelong day. . . ."

Preacher, his eyes closed, his hands folded solemnly, measured their merry path: in the pecan grove, on the road, under the chinaberry. . . .

(On the eve of his Pappy's death, it was said, a great red-winged bird with a fearsome beak had sailed into the room from nowhere, twice circled the old man's bed and, before the watcher's very eyes, disappeared.)

Preacher half expected such a symbol now.

Up the steps they tramped and onto the porch, their boots heavy on the sagging boards. He sighed when they knocked; he would have to let them in. So he smiled at Evelina, thought briefly of his outrageous offspring and, moving ever so slowly, reached the door, removed the plank and opened it wide.

Curly Head, the one with the long, orange-red beard, stepped forward first, mopping his square, burned face with a throat bandanna. He saluted as if he were touching an invisible hat.

"Evenin', Mistuh Jesus," said Preacher, bowing low as he could.

"Evening," said Curly Head.

Yellow Hair followed, jaunty and whistling, a cocky swing to his gait and his hands dug deep in the pockets of his corduroys. He gave Preacher a head-to-toe scowl.

"Evenin', Mistuh Saint," said Preacher, distinguishing them arbitrarily.

"Hi."

And Preacher trotted anxiously after them till they were all knotted before the fire. "How you gent'mens feelin'?" he said.

"Can't complain," said Curly Head, admiring the comic-strip papering and calendar-girl display. "You sure got an eye for the gals, Gran'pa."

"Nawsuh," said Preacher gravely, "I ain't studyin' 'bout nona them ol' gals, nawsuh!" And he shook his head for emphasis. "I'se a Christian, Mistuh Jesus: an upstandin' Baptist, paid-in-full membuh of de Cypress City Mornin' Star."

"No offense meant," said Curly Head. "What's your name, Gran'pa?"

"Name? Why, Mistuh Jesus, you knows I'm Preacher. Preacher what's been conversin' wid you nigh on six months?"

"Why, sure I do," said Curly Head and slapped him heartily on the back; "course I do."

"What *is* this?" said Yellow Hair. "What in hell are you talking about?"

"Got me," said Curly Head, and shrugged. "Look, Preacher, we've had a hard day and we're kind of thirsty.... Think you could help us out?"

Preacher smiled craftily, raised his arm, said, "Ain't nevuh touched a drap in my life, dat's de truth."

"We mean water, Gran'pa. Plain old drinking water."

"And make sure the dipper's clean," said Yellow Hair. He was a very particular fellow and a bit sour for all his jaunty ways. "What you have this fire blazing away for, Gran'pa?"

"It be on accounta my health, Mistuh Saint. I gits de chills mighty easy."

Yellow Hair said, "It's just like these colored folks come out of a machine, all of them all the time sick and all the time got funny notions."

"I ain't sick," said Preacher, beaming. "I'se fine! Ain't nevuh felt no bettuh 'n whut I feels right now, nawsuh!" He fondled the arm of the rocker. "Come sits yo'self here in my nice rockah, Mistuh Jesus. See de pretty pillow? Mistuh Saint . . . hims welcome to de baid."

"Much obliged."

"Could do with a sit-down, thanks."

Curly Head was the older and more handsome: head finely set, eyes a kind deep blue, face full and strong and wearing a rather earnest expression. The beard lent a touch of real magnificence. He spread his legs wide and swung one over the rocker's arm. Yellow Hair, sharper featured and paler complexioned, collapsed on the bed and scowled at this and that. The fire made a drowsy sound; the lamp sputtered softly.

"Spec I best git my belongin's?" said Preacher, his voice quite wan.

When no answer was forthcoming he spread his quilt in a far corner, and silently, a little secretively, began gathering Evelina's picture, his pipe, a green bottle that once had held his anniversary scuppernong wine and now contained seven good-luck pink pebbles and a net of dust and spider threads, an empty box of Paradise candy and other objects, equally precious, which he piled on the quilt. Then he rummaged through a cedar chest, smelling of years, and found a shining squirrel-skin cap and pulled it on. It was good and warm; the journey might prove very cold.

While he did this Curly Head methodically picked his teeth with a hen quill he had borrowed from a jar and watched the old man's proceedings with a puzzled frown. Yellow Hair was whistling again; the tune he whistled was completely flat.

After Preacher had been about his business for a great while, Curly

Head cleared his throat and said, "Hope you haven't forgot that drink of water, Gran'pa. Surely would appreciate it."

Preacher hobbled to the well bucket hid among the stove's litter. "Seems lak I can't remembuh nothin', Mistuh Jesus. Seems lak I leaves my haid outside when I come in." He had two gourds and filled them to the brim. When Curly Head finished, he wiped his mouth and said, "Fine and dandy," and began to rock, letting his boots drag the hearth with a sleepy rhythm.

Preacher's hands trembled as he tied his quilt, and it required five tries. Then he perched himself on an upended log between the two men, his small legs barely scraping the floor. The torn lips of the golden girl holding the bottle of NE-HI smiled down and the firelight flared an appealing mural on the walls. Through the open windows could be heard crocheting insects in the weeds and sundry night cadences, familiar in all Preacher's lifetime. Oh, how beautiful his cabin seemed, how wonderful what he had grown to despise. He had been so wrong! What a doggone fool! He could never leave, now or ever. But there, before him, were four feet wearing four boots and the door well behind them.

"Mistuh Jesus," he said, careful of his tone, "I'se been turnin' de whole mattah ovah an' I'se come to conclude I don't wants to go wid y' all."

Curly Head and Yellow Hair exchanged strange glances and Yellow Hair, rising from the bed, hunched himself above Preacher and said, "What's the matter, Gran'pa? You got a fever?"

Mortally ashamed, Preacher said, "Please, suh, beggin' pardon . . . I don't wants to go nowhere."

"Look here, Gran'pa, talk sense," said Curly Head kindly. "If you're sick we'll be glad to get a doctor from town."

"Ain't no use," said Preacher. "If de time's up, de time's up. . . . But I'd be tickled iffen y'all 'ud leave me be."

"All we want to do is help," said Yellow Hair.

"Sure is," said Curly Head and squirted a fat spit into the fire.

"You're being purentee cussed, that's what I say. It's not everybody we'd take so much pains to do them a favor, not by a long shot."

"Thank ya all de same, Mistuh Jesus. I knows I done put y'all to a lota extry trouble."

"Come on now, Gran'pa," said Yellow Hair, his voice dropping several notches, "what's wrong? You in trouble with some gal."

Curly Head said, "Now don't joke with Gran'pa. He's just been sitting in the sun too long, that's all. Else I never saw a case like it."

"Me either," said Yellow Hair. "But you never can tell about these old coons; liable to go off the deep end before you can bat your eyes."

Preacher sank lower and lower till he was almost curved double and his chin had begun twitching.

"First he runs off like he'd seen the devil himself," said Yellow Hair, "and now he acts like I don't know what."

"Dat ain't so," cried Preacher, his eyes alarmingly wide. "I recognize y'all from de Good Book. An' I'se a *good* man. I'se as good a man as evah lived . . . ain't nevah done wrong to nobody. . . ."

"Ahhh," hummed Yellow Hair, "I give up! Gran'pa . . . you ain't worth trifling with."

"That's a fact," said Curly Head.

Preacher bowed his head and brushed a squirrel tail away from his cheek. "I knows," he said. "Yassuh, I does. I'se been a pow'ful big fool and dats de Gospel. But if you leaves me stay put, I'll yank out all dem weeds in de yard and de field and git back to farmin' an' whup dat Anna-Jo 'til she come home an' care fo' her Pappy lak she ought."

Curly Head pulled at his beard and snapped his suspenders. His eyes, very blank and blue, imprisoned Preacher's face exactly. At length he said, "Can't seem to figure it out."

"That's mighty easy," said Yellow Hair. "He's got the devil rattling around inside him."

"I'se an upstandin' Baptist," Preacher reminded, "membuh of de Cypress City Mornin' Star. An' I ain't but seventy yars old."

"Now, Gran'pa," said Yellow Hair. "You're a hundred if you're a day. Oughtn't to tell whoppers like that. It all goes down in that big black book upstairs, remember."

"Miserable sinnuh," said Preacher; "ain't I de most miserablest sinnuh?"

"Well," said Curly Head, "I don't know." Then he smiled and stood up and yawned. "Tell you what," he said, "I speculates I'm hungry enough to eat toadstools. Come on, Jesse, we better get home before the women throw our supper to the hogs."

Yellow Hair said, "Christamighty, I don't know whether I can take a step or not; that blister's on fire," and to Preacher, "Guess we'll have to leave you in your misery too, Gran'pa."

And Preacher grinned so that his four upper teeth and three lower (including the gold cap from Evelina, Christmas 1922) showed. His eyes blinked furiously. Like a wizened and rather peculiar child he fairly danced to the door and insisted upon kissing the men's hands as they trudged past.

Curly Head bounced down the steps and back and handed Preacher his Bible and cane while Yellow Hair waited in the yard where evening had drawn pale curtains.

"Hang onto these now, Gran'pa," said Curly Head, "and don't let us catch you over in the piney woods anymore. An old fellow like you can get into all kinds of trouble. You be good now."

"Hee hee hee," giggled Preacher, "I sure 'nuf will an' thank ya, Mistuh Jesus, an' you too, Mistuh Saint . . . thank ya. Even if ain't nobody gonna believes me iffen I tells 'em."

They shouldered their rifles and lifted the cateymount. "Best of luck," said Curly Head; "we'll be back some other time, for a drink of water, maybe."

"Long life and a merry one, you old goat," said Yellow Hair as they moved across the yard towards the road.

Preacher, watching from the porch, suddenly remembered and he called, "Mistuh Jesus . . . Mistuh Jesus! If you kin see yo' way clear to do me one mo' favuh, I'd 'preciate it if you evah gits de time iffen you'd find my ol' woman . . . name's Evelina . . . an' say hello from Preacher an' tells her what a good happy man I is."

"First thing in the morning, Gran'pa," said Curly Head, and Yellow Hair burst out laughing.

And their shadows turned up the road and the black-and-tan crept from a gully and trotted after them. Preacher called and waved good-bye. But they were laughing too hard to hear and their laughter drifted back on the wind long after they passed over the ridge where fireflies embroidered small moons on the blue air.

A TREE OF NIGHT

(1945)

It was winter. A string of naked light bulbs, from which it seemed all warmth had been drained, illuminated the little depot's cold, windy platform. Earlier in the evening it had rained, and now icicles hung along the station-house eaves like some crystal monster's vicious teeth. Except for a girl, young and rather tall, the platform was deserted. The girl wore a gray flannel suit, a raincoat, and a plaid scarf. Her hair, parted in the middle and rolled up neatly on the sides, was rich blondish-brown; and, while her face tended to be too thin and narrow, she was, though not extraordinarily so, attractive. In addition to an assortment of magazines and a gray suede purse on which elaborate brass letters spelled Kay, she carried conspicuously a green Western guitar.

When the train, spouting steam and glaring with light, came out of the darkness and rumbled to a halt, Kay assembled her paraphernalia and climbed up into the last coach.

The coach was a relic with a decaying interior of ancient red-plush seats, bald in spots, and peeling iodine-colored woodwork. An old-time copper lamp, attached to the ceiling, looked romantic and out of place. Gloomy dead smoke sailed the air; and the car's heated closeness accentuated the stale odor of discarded sandwiches, apple cores, and orange hulls: this garbage, including Lily cups, soda-pop bottles, and mangled newspapers, littered the long aisle. From a water cooler, embedded in the wall, a steady stream trickled to the floor. The passengers, who glanced up wearily when Kay entered, were not, it seemed, at all conscious of any discomfort.

Kay resisted a temptation to hold her nose and threaded her way carefully down the aisle, tripping once, without disaster, over a dozing fat man's protruding leg. Two nondescript men turned an interested eye as she passed; and a kid stood up in his seat squalling, "Hey, Mama, look at de banjo! Hey, lady, lemme play ya banjo!" till a slap from Mama quelled him.

There was only one empty place. She found it at the end of the car in an isolated alcove occupied already by a man and woman who were sitting with their feet settled lazily on the vacant seat opposite. Kay hesitated a second then said, "Would you mind if I sat here?"

The woman's head snapped up as if she had not been asked a simple question, but stabbed with a needle, too. Nevertheless, she managed a smile. "Can't say as I see what's to stop you, honey," she said, taking her feet down and also, with a curious impersonality, removing the feet of the man who was staring out the window, paying no attention whatsoever.

Thanking the woman, Kay took off her coat, sat down, and arranged herself with purse and guitar at her side, magazines in her lap: comfortable enough, though she wished she had a pillow for her back.

The train lurched; a ghost of steam hissed against the window; slowly the dingy lights of the lonesome depot faded past.

"Boy, what a jerkwater dump," said the woman. "No town, no nothin'."

Kay said, "The town's a few miles away."

"That so? Live there?"

No. Kay explained she had been at the funeral of an uncle. An uncle who, though she did not of course mention it, had left her nothing in his will but the green guitar. Where was she going? Oh, back to college.

After mulling this over, the woman concluded, "What'll you ever learn in a place like that? Let me tell you, honey, I'm plenty educated and I never saw the inside of no college."

"You didn't?" murmured Kay politely and dismissed the matter by opening one of her magazines. The light was dim for reading and none of the stories looked in the least compelling. However, not wanting to become involved in a conversational marathon, she continued gazing at it stupidly till she felt a furtive tap on her knee.

"Don't read," said the woman. "I need somebody to talk to. Naturally, it's no fun talking to *him*." She jerked a thumb toward the silent man. "He's afflicted: deaf and dumb, know what I mean?"

Kay closed the magazine and looked at her more or less for the first time. She was short; her feet barely scraped the floor. And like many undersized people she had a freak of structure, in her case an enormous, really huge head. Rouge so brightened her sagging, flesh-featured face it was difficult even to guess at her age: perhaps fifty, fifty-five. Her big sheep eyes squinted, as if distrustful of what they saw. Her hair was an obviously dyed red, and twisted into parched, fat corkscrew curls. A once-elegant lavender hat of impressive size flopped crazily on the side of her head, and she was kept busy brushing back a drooping cluster of celluloid cherries sewed to the brim. She wore a plain, somewhat shabby blue dress. Her breath had a vividly sweetish gin smell.

"You do wanna talk to me, don't you honey?"

"Sure," said Kay, moderately amused.

"Course you do. You bet you do. That's what I like about a train. Bus people are a close-mouthed buncha dopes. But a train's the place for putting your cards on the table, that's what I always say." Her voice was cheerful and booming, husky as a man's. "But on accounta *him,* I always try to get us this here seat; it's more private, like a swell compartment, see?"

"It's very pleasant," Kay agreed. "Thanks for letting me join you."

"Only too glad to. We don't have much company; it makes some folks nervous to be around him."

As if to deny it, the man made a queer, furry sound deep in his throat and plucked the woman's sleeve. "Leave me alone, dearheart," she said, as if she were talking to an inattentive child. "I'm O.K. We're just having us a nice little ol' talk. Now behave yourself or this pretty girl will go away. She's very rich; she goes to college." And winking, she added, "He thinks I'm drunk."

The man slumped in the seat, swung his head sideways, and studied Kay intently from the corners of his eyes. These eyes, like a pair of clouded milky-blue marbles, were thickly lashed and oddly beautiful. Now, except for a certain remoteness, his wide, hairless face had no real expression. It was as if he were incapable of experiencing or reflecting the slightest emotion. His gray hair was clipped close and combed forward into uneven bangs. He looked like a child aged abruptly by some uncanny method. He wore a frayed blue serge suit, and he had anointed himself with a cheap, vile perfume. Around his wrist was strapped a Mickey Mouse watch.

"He thinks I'm drunk," the woman repeated. "And the real funny part is, I am. Oh shoot—you gotta do something, ain't that right?" She bent closer. "Say, ain't it?"

Kay was still gawking at the man; the way he was looking at her made her squeamish, but she could not take her eyes off him. "I guess so," she said.

"Then let's us have us a drink," suggested the woman. She plunged her hand into an oilcloth satchel and pulled out a partially filled gin bottle. She began to unscrew the cap, but, seeming to think better of this, handed the bottle to Kay. "Gee, I forgot about you being company," she said. "I'll go get us some nice paper cups."

So, before Kay could protest that she did not want a drink, the woman had risen and started none too steadily down the aisle toward the water cooler.

Kay yawned and rested her forehead against the windowpane, her fingers idly strumming the guitar: the strings sang a hollow, lulling tune, as monotonously soothing as the Southern landscape, smudged in darkness, flowing past the window. An icy winter moon rolled above the train across the night sky like a thin white wheel.

And then, without warning, a strange thing happened: the man reached out and gently stroked Kay's cheek. Despite the breathtaking delicacy of this movement, it was such a bold gesture Kay was at first too startled to know what to make of it: her thoughts shot in three or four fantastic directions. He leaned forward till his queer eyes were very near her own; the reek of his perfume was sickening. The guitar was silent while they exchanged a searching gaze. Suddenly, from some spring of compassion, she felt for him a keen sense of pity; but also, and this she could not suppress, an overpowering disgust, an absolute loathing: something about him, an elusive quality she could not quite put a finger on, reminded her of—of what?

After a little, he lowered his hand solemnly and sank back in the seat, an asinine grin transfiguring his face, as if he had performed a clever stunt for which he wished applause.

"Giddyup! Giddyup! my little bucker-ROOS . . ." shouted the woman. And she sat down, loudly proclaiming to be, "Dizzy as a witch! Dog tired! Whew!" From a handful of Lily cups she separated two and casually thrust the rest down her blouse. "Keep 'em safe and dry, ha ha ha. . . ." A coughing spasm seized her, but when it was over she appeared calmer. "Has my boy friend been entertaining?" she asked, patting her bosom reverently. "Ah, he's so sweet." She looked as if she might pass out. Kay rather wished she would.

"I don't want a drink," Kay said, returning the bottle. "I never drink: I hate the taste."

"Mustn't be a kill-joy," said the woman firmly. "Here now, hold your cup like a good girl."

"No, please . . ."

"Formercysake, hold it still. Imagine, nerves at your age! Me, I can shake like a leaf, I've got reasons. Oh, Lordy, have I got 'em."

"But . . ."

A dangerous smile tipped the woman's face hideously awry. "What's the matter? Don't you think I'm good enough to drink with?"

"Please, don't misunderstand," said Kay, a tremor in her voice. "It's just that I don't like being forced to do something I don't want to. So look, couldn't I give this to the gentleman?"

"Him? No sirree: he needs what little sense he's got. Come on, honey, down the hatch."

Kay, seeing it was useless, decided to succumb and avoid a possible scene. She sipped and shuddered. It was terrible gin. It burned her throat till her eyes watered. Quickly, when the woman was not watching, she emptied the cup out into the sound hole of the guitar. It happened, however, that the man saw; and Kay, realizing it, recklessly signaled to him with her eyes a plea not to give her away. But she could not tell from his clear-blank expression how much he understood.

"Where you from, kid?" resumed the woman presently.

For a bewildered moment, Kay was unable to provide an answer. The names of several cities came to her all at once. Finally, from this confusion, she extracted: "New Orleans. My home is in New Orleans."

The woman beamed. "N.O.'s where I wanna go when I kick off. One time, oh, say 1923, I ran me a sweet little fortune-teller parlor there. Let's see, that was on St. Peter Street." Pausing, she stooped and set the empty gin bottle on the floor. It rolled into the aisle and rocked back and forth with a drowsy sound. "I was raised in Texas— on a big ranch—my papa was rich. Us kids always had the best; even Paris, France, clothes. I'll bet you've got a big swell house, too. Do you have a garden? Do you grow flowers?"

"Just lilacs."

A conductor entered the coach, preceded by a cold gust of wind that rattled the trash in the aisle and briefly livened the dull air. He lumbered along, stopping now and then to punch a ticket or talk with a passenger. It was after midnight. Someone was expertly playing a harmonica. Someone else was arguing the merits of a certain politician. A child cried out in his sleep.

"Maybe you wouldn't be so snotty if you knew who we was," said the woman, bobbing her tremendous head. "We ain't nobodies, not by a long shot."

Embarrassed, Kay nervously opened a pack of cigarettes and lighted one. She wondered if there might not be a seat in a car up ahead. She could not bear the woman, or, for that matter, the man, another minute. But she had never before been in a remotely comparable situation. "If you'll excuse me now," she said, "I have to be leaving. It's been very pleasant, but I promised to meet a friend on the train. . . ."

With almost invisible swiftness the woman grasped the girl's wrist. "Didn't your mama ever tell you it was sinful to lie?" she stage-whispered. The lavender hat tumbled off her head but she made no effort to retrieve it. Her tongue flicked out and wetted her lips. And, as Kay stood up, she increased the pressure of her grip. "Sit down, dear . . . there ain't any friend . . . Why, we're your only friends and we wouldn't have you leave us for the world."

"Honestly, I wouldn't lie."

"Sit down, dear."

Kay dropped her cigarette and the man picked it up. He slouched in the corner and became absorbed in blowing a chain of lush smoke rings that mounted upward like hollow eyes and expanded into nothing.

"Why, you wouldn't want to hurt his feelings by leaving us, now, would you, dear?" crooned the woman softly. "Sit down—down—now, that's a good girl. My, what a pretty guitar. What a pretty, pretty guitar . . ." Her voice faded before the sudden whooshing, static noise of a second train. And for an instant the lights in the coach went off; in the darkness the passing train's golden windows winked black-yellow-black-yellow-black-yellow. The man's cigarette pulsed like the glow of a firefly, and his smoke rings continued rising tranquilly. Outside, a bell pealed wildly.

When the lights came on again, Kay was massaging her wrist where the woman's strong fingers had left a painful bracelet mark. She was more puzzled than angry. She determined to ask the conductor if he would find her a different seat. But when he arrived to take her ticket, the request stuttered on her lips incoherently.

"Yes, miss?"

"Nothing," she said.

And he was gone.

The trio in the alcove regarded one another in mysterious silence till the woman said, "I've got something here I wanna show you, honey." She rummaged once more in the oilcloth satchel. "You won't be so snotty after you get a gander at this."

What she passed to Kay was a handbill, published on such yellowed, antique paper it looked as if it must be centuries old. In fragile, overly fancy lettering, it read:

LAZARUS

THE MAN WHO IS BURIED ALIVE

A MIRACLE

SEE FOR YOURSELF

Adults, 25¢—Children, 10¢

"I always sing a hymn and read a sermon," said the woman. "It's awful sad: some folks cry, especially the old ones. And I've got me a perfectly elegant costume: a black veil and a black dress, oh, very becoming. *He* wears a gorgeous made-to-order bridegroom suit and a turban and lotsa talcum on his face. See, we try to make it as much like a bonafide funeral as we can. But shoot, nowadays you're likely to get just a buncha smart alecks come for laughs—so sometimes I'm real glad he's afflicted like he is on accounta otherwise his feelings would be hurt, maybe."

Kay said, "You mean you're with a circus or a side-show or something like that?"

"Nope, us alone," said the woman as she reclaimed the fallen hat. "We've been doing it for years and years—played every tank town in the South: Singasong, Mississippi—Spunky, Louisiana—Eureka, Alabama . . ." These and other names rolled off her tongue musically, running together like rain. "After the hymn, after the sermon, we bury him."

"In a coffin?"

"Sort of. It's gorgeous, it's got silver stars painted all over the lid."

"I should think he would suffocate," said Kay, amazed. "How long does he stay buried?"

"All told it takes maybe an hour—course that's not counting the lure."

"The lure?"

"Uh huh. It's what we do the night before the show. See, we hunt up a store, any ol' store with a big glass window'll do, and get the owner to let *him* sit inside this window, and, well, hypnotize himself. Stays there all night stiff as a poker and people come and look: scares the livin' hell out of 'em. . . ." While she talked she jiggled a finger in her ear, withdrawing it occasionally to examine her find. "And one time this ol' bindle-stiff Mississippi sheriff tried to . . ."

The tale that followed was baffling and pointless: Kay did not bother to listen. Nevertheless, what she had heard already inspired a reverie, a vague recapitulation of her uncle's funeral; an event which, to tell the truth, had not much affected her since she had scarcely known him. And so, while gazing abstractedly at the man, an image of her uncle's face, white next the pale silk casket pillow, appeared in her mind's eye. Observing their faces simultaneously, both the man's and uncle's, as it were, she thought she recognized an odd parallel: there was about the man's face the same kind of shocking, embalmed, secret stillness, as though, in a sense, he were truly an exhibit in a glass cage, complacent to be seen, uninterested in seeing.

"I'm sorry, what did you say?"

"I said: I sure wish they'd lend us the use of a regular cemetery. Like it is now we have to put on the show wherever we can . . . mostly in empty lots that are nine times outa ten smack up against some smelly fillin' station, which ain't exactly a big help. But like I say, we got us a swell act, the best. You oughta come see it if you get a chance."

"Oh, I should love to," Kay said, absently.

"Oh, I should love to," mimicked the woman. "Well, who asked you? Anybody ask you?" She hoisted up her skirt and enthusiastically blew her nose on the ragged hem of a petticoat. "Bu-leeve me, it's a hard way to turn a dollar. Know what our take was last month? Fifty-three bucks! Honey, you try living on that sometime." She sniffed and rearranged her skirt with considerable primness. "Well, one of these days my sweet boy's sure enough going to die down there; and even then somebody'll say it was a gyp."

At this point the man took from his pocket what seemed to be a finely shellacked peach seed and balanced it on the palm of his hand. He looked across at Kay and, certain of her attention, opened his eyelids wide and began to squeeze and caress the seed in an undefinably obscene manner.

Kay frowned. "What does he want?"

"He wants you to buy it."

"But what is it?"

"A charm," said the woman. "A love charm."

Whoever was playing the harmonica stopped. Other sounds, less unique, became at once prominent: someone snoring, the gin bottle seesaw rolling, voices in sleepy argument, the train wheels' distant hum.

"Where could you get love cheaper, honey?"

"It's nice. I mean it's cute. . . ." Kay said, stalling for time. The man rubbed and polished the seed on his trouser leg. His head was lowered at a supplicating, mournful angle, and presently he stuck the seed between his teeth and bit it, as if it were a suspicious piece of silver. "Charms always bring me bad luck. And besides . . . please, can't you make him stop acting that way?"

"Don't look so scared," said the woman, more flat-voiced than ever. "He ain't gonna hurt you."

"Make him stop, damn it!"

"What can I do?" asked the woman, shrugging her shoulders. "You're the one that's got money. You're rich. All he wants is a dollar, one dollar."

Kay tucked her purse under her arm. "I have just enough to get back to school," she lied, quickly rising and stepping out into the aisle. She stood there a moment, expecting trouble. But nothing happened.

The woman, with rather deliberate indifference, heaved a sigh and closed her eyes; gradually the man subsided and stuck the charm back in his pocket. Then his hand crawled across the seat to join the woman's in a lax embrace.

Kay shut the door and moved to the front of the observation platform. It was bitterly cold in the open air, and she had left her raincoat in the alcove. She loosened her scarf and draped it over her head.

Although she had never made this trip before, the train was traveling through an area strangely familiar: tall trees, misty, painted pale by malicious moonshine, towered steep on either side without a break or clearing. Above, the sky was a stark, unexplorable blue thronged with stars that faded here and there. She could see streamers of smoke trailing from the train's engine like long clouds of ectoplasm. In one corner of the platform a red kerosene lantern cast a colorful shadow.

She found a cigarette and tried to light it: the wind snuffed match after match till only one was left. She walked to the corner where the lantern burned and cupped her hands to protect the last match: the flame caught, sputtered, died. Angrily she tossed away the cigarette and empty folder; all the tension in her tightened to an exasperating pitch and she slammed the wall with her fist and began to whimper softly, like an irritable child.

The intense cold made her head ache, and she longed to go back inside the warm coach and fall asleep. But she couldn't, at least not yet; and there was no sense in wondering why, for she knew the answer very well. Aloud, partly to keep her teeth from chattering and partly because she needed the reassurance of her own voice, she said: "We're in Alabama now, I think, and tomorrow we'll be in Atlanta and I'm nineteen and I'll be twenty in August and I'm a sophomore. . . ." She glanced around at the darkness, hoping to see a sign of dawn, and finding the same endless wall of trees, the same frosty moon. "I hate him, he's horrible and I hate him. . . ." She stopped, ashamed of her foolishness and too tired to evade the truth: she was afraid.

Suddenly she felt an eerie compulsion to kneel down and touch the lantern. Its graceful glass funnel was warm, and the red glow seeped through her hands, making them luminous. The heat thawed her fingers and tingled along her arms.

She was so preoccupied she did not hear the door open. The train wheels roaring clickety-clack-clackety-click hushed the sound of the man's footsteps.

It was a subtle zero sensation that warned her finally; but some seconds passed before she dared look behind.

He was standing there with mute detachment, his head tilted, his arms dangling at his sides. Staring up into his harmless, vapid face, flushed brilliant by the lantern light, Kay knew of what she was afraid: it was a memory, a childish memory of terrors that once, long ago, had hovered above her like haunted limbs on a tree of night. Aunts, cooks, strangers—each eager to spin a tale or teach a rhyme of spooks and death, omens, spirits, demons. And always there had been the unfailing threat of the wizard man: stay close to the house, child, else a wizard man'll snatch you and eat you alive! He lived everywhere, the wizard man, and everywhere was danger. At night, in bed, hear him tapping at the window? Listen!

Holding onto the railing, she inched upward till she was standing erect. The man nodded and waved his hand toward the door. Kay took a deep breath and stepped forward. Together they went inside.

The air in the coach was numb with sleep: a solitary light now illuminated the car, creating a kind of artificial dusk. There was no motion but the train's sluggish sway, and the stealthy rattle of discarded newspapers.

The woman alone was wide awake. You could see she was greatly excited: she fidgeted with her curls and celluloid cherries, and her plump little legs, crossed at the ankles, swung agitatedly back and forth. She paid no attention when Kay sat down. The man settled in the seat with one leg tucked beneath him and his arms folded across his chest.

In an effort to be casual, Kay picked up a magazine. She realized the man was watching her, not removing his gaze an instant: she knew this though she was afraid to confirm it, and she wanted to cry out and waken everyone in the coach. But suppose they did not hear? What if they were not really *asleep*? Tears started in her eyes, magnifying and distorting the print on a page till it became a hazy blur. She shut the magazine with fierce abruptness and looked at the woman.

"I'll buy it," she said. "The charm, I mean. I'll buy it, if that's all—just all you want."

The woman made no response. She smiled apathetically as she turned toward the man.

As Kay watched, the man's face seemed to change form and recede before her like a moon-shaped rock sliding downward under a surface of water. A warm laziness relaxed her. She was dimly conscious of it when the woman took away her purse, and when she gently pulled the raincoat like a shroud above her head.

THE HEADLESS HAWK

(1946)

*They are of those that rebel against the light; they know not the
ways thereof, nor abide in the paths thereof. In the dark they dig
through houses, which they had marked for themselves in the daytime: they know not the light. For the morning is to them as the
shadow of death: if one know them, they are in the terrors of the
shadow of death.*

—JOB 24: 13, 16, 17

1

Vincent switched off the lights in the gallery. Outside, after locking
the door, he smoothed the brim of an elegant Panama, and started
toward Third Avenue, his umbrella-cane tap-tap-tapping along the
pavement. A promise of rain had darkened the day since dawn, and a
sky of bloated clouds blurred the five o'clock sun; it was hot, though,
humid as tropical mist, and voices, sounding along the gray July
street, sounding muffled and strange, carried a fretful undertone.
Vincent felt as though he moved below the sea. Buses, cruising

crosstown through Fifty-seventh Street, seemed like green-bellied fish, and faces loomed and rocked like wave-riding masks. He studied each passer-by, hunting one, and presently he saw her, a girl in a green raincoat. She was standing on the downtown corner of Fifty-seventh and Third, just standing there smoking a cigarette, and giving somehow the impression she hummed a tune. The raincoat was transparent. She wore dark slacks, no socks, a pair of huaraches, a man's white shirt. Her hair was fawn-colored, and cut like a boy's. When she noticed Vincent crossing toward her, she dropped the cigarette and hurried down the block to the doorway of an antique store.

Vincent slowed his step. He pulled out a handkerchief and dabbed his forehead; if only he could get away, go up to the Cape, lie in the sun. He bought an afternoon paper, and fumbled his change. It rolled in the gutter, dropped silently out of sight down a sewer grating. "Ain't but a nickel, bub," said the newsdealer, for Vincent, though actually unaware of his loss, looked heartbroken. And it was like that often now, never quite in contact, never sure whether a step would take him backward or forward, up or down. Very casually, with the handle of the umbrella hooked over an arm, and his eyes concentrated on the paper's headlines—but what did the damn thing say?—he continued downtown. A swarthy woman carrying a shopping bag jostled him, glared, muttered in coarsely vehement Italian. The ragged cut of her voice seemed to come through layers of wool. As he approached the antique store where the girl in the green raincoat waited, he walked slower still, counting one, two, three, four, five, six—at six he halted before the window.

The window was like a corner of an attic; a lifetime's discardings rose in a pyramid of no particular worth: vacant picture frames, a lavender wig, Gothic shaving mugs, beaded lamps. There was an Oriental mask suspended on a ceiling cord, and wind from an electric fan whirring inside the shop revolved it slowly round and round. Vincent, by degrees, lifted his gaze, and looked at the girl directly.

She was hovering in the doorway so that he saw her greenness distorted wavy through double glass; the elevated pounded overhead and the window trembled. Her image spread like a reflection on silverware, then gradually hardened again: she was watching him.

He hung an Old Gold between his lips, rummaged for a match and, finding none, sighed. The girl stepped from the doorway. She held out a cheap little lighter; as the flame pulsed up, her eyes, pale, shallow, cat-green, fixed him with alarming intensity. Her eyes had an astonished, a shocked look, as though, having at one time witnessed a terrible incident, they'd locked wide open. Carefree bangs fringed her forehead; this boy haircut emphasized the childish and rather poetic quality of her narrow, hollow-cheeked face. It was the kind of face one sometimes sees in paintings of medieval youths.

Letting the smoke pour out his nose, Vincent, knowing it was useless to ask, wondered, as always, what she was living on and where. He flipped away the cigarette, for he had not wanted it to begin with, and then, pivoting, crossed rapidly under the El; as he approached the curb he heard a crash of brakes, and suddenly, as if cotton plugs had been blasted from his ears, city noises crowded in. A cab driver hollered: "Fa crissake, sistuh, get the lead outa yuh pants!" but the girl did not even bother turning her head; trance-eyed, undisturbed as a sleepwalker, and staring straight at Vincent, who watched dumbly, she moved across the street. A colored boy wearing a jazzy purple suit took her elbow. "You sick, Miss?" he said, guiding her forward, and she did not answer. "You look mighty funny, Miss. If you sick, I . . ." then, following the direction of her eyes, he released his hold. There was something here which made him all still inside. "Uh—yeah," he muttered, backing off with a grinning display of tartar-coated teeth.

So Vincent began walking in earnest, and his umbrella tapped codelike block after block. His shirt was soaked through with itchy sweat, and the noises, now so harsh, banged in his head: a trick car horn hooting "My Country 'Tis of Thee," electric spray of sparks crackling bluely off thundering rails, whiskey laughter hiccuping through gaunt doors of beer-stale bars where orchid juke machines manufactured U.S.A. music—"I got spurs that jingle jangle jingle. . . ." Occasionally he caught a glimpse of her, once mirrored in the window of Paul's Seafood Palace, where scarlet lobsters basked on a beach of flaked ice. She followed close with her hands shoved into the pockets of her raincoat. The brassy lights of a movie marquee blinked, and he remembered how she loved movies: murder films, spy chillers, Wild West shows. He turned into a side street leading toward the East River; it was quiet here, hushed like Sunday: a sailor-stroller munching an Eskimo Pie, energetic twins skipping rope, an old velvet lady with gardenia-white hair lifting aside lace curtains and peering listlessly into rain-dark space—a city landscape in July. And behind him the soft insistent slap of sandals. Traffic lights on Second Avenue turned red; at the corner a bearded midget, Ruby the Popcorn Man, wailed, "Hot buttered popcorn, big bag, yah?" Vincent shook his head, and the midget looked very put out, then: "Yuh see?" he jeered, pushing a shovel inside the candlelit cage, where bursting kernels bounced like crazy moths. "Yuh see, de girlie knows popcorn's nourishin'." She bought a dime's worth, and it was in a green sack matching her raincoat, matching her eyes.

This is my neighborhood, my street, the house with the gateway is where I live. To remind himself of this was necessary, inasmuch as he'd substituted for a sense of reality a knowledge of time, and place. He glanced gratefully at sour-faced, faded ladies, at the pipe-puffing males squatting on the surrounding steps of brownstone stoops. Nine pale little girls shrieked round a corner flower cart begging daisies to pin in their hair, but the peddler said "Shoo!" and, fleeing like beads of a broken bracelet, they circled in the street, the wild ones leaping with laughter, and the shy ones, silent and isolated, lifting summer-wilted faces skyward: the rain, would it never come?

Vincent, who lived in a basement apartment, descended several steps and took out his keycase; then, pausing behind the hallway door, he looked back through a peephole in the paneling. The girl was waiting on the sidewalk above; she leaned against a brownstone banister, and her arms fell limp—and popcorn spilled snowlike round her feet. A grimy little boy crept slyly up to pick among it like a squirrel.

2

For Vincent it was a holiday. No one had come by the gallery all morning, which, considering the arctic weather, was not unusual. He sat at his desk devouring tangerines, and enjoying immensely a Thurber story in an old *New Yorker.* Laughing loudly, he did not hear the girl enter, see her cross the dark carpet, notice her at all, in fact, until the telephone rang. "Garland Gallery, hello." She was odd, most certainly, that indecent haircut, those depthless eyes—"Oh, Paul. *Comme ci, comme ça* and you?"—and dressed like a freak: no coat, just a lumberjack's shirt, navy-blue slacks and—was it a joke?—pink ankle socks, a pair of huaraches. "The ballet? Who's dancing? Oh, her!" Under an arm she carried a flat parcel wrapped in sheets of funny-paper—"Look, Paul, what say I call back? There's someone here . . ." and, anchoring the receiver, assuming a commercial smile, he stood up. "Yes?"

Her lips, crusty with chap, trembled with unrealized words as though she had possibly a defect of speech, and her eyes rolled in their sockets like loose marbles. It was the kind of disturbed shyness one associates with children. "I've a picture," she said. "You buy pictures?"

At this, Vincent's smile became fixed. "We exhibit."

"I painted it myself," she said, and her voice, hoarse and slurred, was Southern. "My picture—I painted it. A lady told me there were places around here that bought pictures."

Vincent said, "Yes, of course, but the truth is"—and he made a helpless gesture—"the truth is I've no authority whatever. Mr. Garland—this is his gallery, you know—*is* out of town." Standing there on the expanse of fine carpet, her body sagging sideways with the weight of her package, she looked like a sad rag doll. "Maybe," he began, "maybe Henry Krueger up the street at Sixty-five . . ." but she was not listening.

"I did it myself," she insisted softly. "Tuesdays and Thursdays were our painting days, and a whole year I worked. The others, they kept messing it up, and Mr. Destronelli . . ." Suddenly, as though aware of an indiscretion, she stopped and bit her lip. Her eyes narrowed. "He's not a friend of yours?"

"Who?" said Vincent, confused.

"Mr. Destronelli."

He shook his head, and wondered why it was that eccentricity always excited in him such curious admiration. It was the feeling he'd had as a child toward carnival freaks. And it was true that about those whom he'd loved there was always a little something wrong, broken. Strange, though, that this quality, having stimulated an attraction, should, in his case, regularly end it by destroying it. "Of course I haven't any authority," he repeated, sweeping tangerine hulls into a wastebasket, "but, if you like, I suppose I could look at your work."

A pause; then, kneeling on the floor, she commenced stripping off the funny-paper wrapping. It originally had been, Vincent noticed, part of the New Orleans *Times-Picayune*. "From the South, aren't you?" he said. She did not look up, but he saw her shoulders stiffen. "No," she said. Smiling, he considered a moment, decided it would be tactless to challenge so transparent a lie. Or could she have misunderstood? And all at once he felt an intense longing to touch her head, finger the boyish hair. He shoved his hands in his pockets and glanced at the window. It was spangled with February frost, and some passer-by had scratched on the glass an obscenity. "There," she said.

A headless figure in a monklike robe reclined complacently on top a tacky vaudeville trunk; in one hand she held a fuming blue candle, in the other a miniature gold cage, and her severed head lay bleeding at her feet: it was the girl's, this head, but here her hair was long, very long, and a snowball kitten with crystal spitfire eyes playfully pawed, as it would a spool of yarn, the sprawling ends. The wings of a hawk, headless, scarlet-breasted, copper-clawed, curtained the background like a nightfall sky. It was a crude painting, the hard pure colors molded with male brutality, and, while there was no technical merit evident, it had that power often seen in something deeply felt, though primitively conveyed. Vincent reacted as he did when occasionally a phrase of music surprised a note of inward recognition, or a cluster of words in a poem revealed to him a secret concerning himself: he felt a powerful chill of pleasure run down his spine. "Mr. Garland is in Florida," he said cautiously, "but I think he should see it; you couldn't leave it for, say, a week?"

"I had a ring and I sold it," she said, and he had the feeling she was talking in a trance. "It was a nice ring, a wedding ring—not mine— with writing on it. I had an overcoat, too." She twisted one of her shirt buttons, pulled till it popped off and rolled on the carpet like a pearl eye. "I don't want much—fifty dollars; is that unfair?"

"Too much," said Vincent, more curtly than he intended. Now he wanted her painting, not for the gallery, but for himself. There are certain works of art which excite more interest in their creators than in what they have created, usually because in this kind of work one is able to identify something which has until that instant seemed a private inexpressible perception, and you wonder: who is this that knows me, and how? "I'll give thirty."

For a moment she gaped at him stupidly, and then, sucking her breath, held out her hand, palm up. This directness, too innocent to be offensive, caught him off guard. Somewhat embarrassed, he said, "I'm most awfully afraid I'll have to mail a check. Could you . . . ?" The telephone interrupted, and, as he went to answer, she followed, her hand outstretched, a frantic look pinching her face. "Oh, Paul, may I call back? Oh, I see. Well, hold on a sec." Cupping the mouthpiece against his shoulder, he pushed a pad and pencil across the desk. "Here, write your name and address."

But she shook her head, the dazed, anxious expression deepening.

"Check," said Vincent, "I have to mail a check. Please, your name and address." He grinned encouragingly when at last she began to write.

"Sorry, Paul . . . Whose party? Why, the little bitch, she didn't invite . . . Hey!" he called, for the girl was moving toward the door. "Please, hey!" Cold air chilled the gallery, and the door slammed with a glassy rattle. Hellohellohello. Vincent did not answer; he stood puzzling over the curious information she'd left printed on his pad: D.J.—Y.W.C.A. Hellohellohello.

It hung above his mantel, the painting, and on those nights when he could not sleep he would pour a glass of whiskey and talk to the headless hawk, tell it the stuff of his life: he was, he said, a poet who had never written poetry, a painter who had never painted, a lover who had never loved (absolutely)—someone, in short, without direction, and quite headless. Oh, it wasn't that he hadn't tried—good beginnings, always, bad endings, always. Vincent, white, male, age thirty-six, college graduate: a man in the sea, fifty miles from shore; a victim, born to be murdered, either by himself or another; an actor unemployed. It was there, all of it, in the painting, everything disconnected and cockeyed, and who was she that she should know so much? Inquiries, those he'd made had led nowhere; not another dealer knew of her, and to search for a D.J. living in, presumably, a Y.W.C.A. seemed absurd. Then, too, he'd quite expected she would reappear, but February passed, and March. One evening, crossing the square which fronts the Plaza, he had a queer thing happen. The archaic hansom drivers who line that location were lighting their carriage lamps, for it was dusk, and lamplight traced through moving leaves. A hansom pulled from the curb and rolled past in the twilight. There was a single occupant, and this passenger, whose face he

could not see, was a girl with chopped fawn-colored hair. So he settled on a bench, and whiled away time talking with a soldier, and a
fairy colored boy who quoted poetry, and a man out airing a dachs-
hund: night characters with whom he waited—but the carriage, with
the one for whom he waited, never came back. Again he saw her (or
supposed he did) descending subway stairs, and this time lost her in
the tiled tunnels of painted arrows and Spearmint machines. It was
as if her face were imposed upon his mind; he could no more dispos-
sess it than could, for example, a dead man rid his legendary eyes of
the last image seen. Around the middle of April he went up to Connecticut to spend a weekend with his married sister; keyed-up, caus-
tic, he wasn't, as she complained, at all like himself. "What is it,
Vinny darling—if you need money . . ." "Oh, shut up!" he said. "Must
be love," teased his brother-in-law. "Come on, Vinny, 'fess up; what's
she like?" And all this so annoyed him he caught the next train
home. From a booth in Grand Central he called to apologize, but a
sick nervousness hummed inside him, and he hung up while the operator was still trying to make a connection. He wanted a drink. At
the Commodore Bar he spent an hour or so downing four daiquiris—
it was Saturday, it was nine, there was nothing to do unless he did it
alone, he was feeling sad for himself. Now in the park behind the
Public Library sweethearts moved whisperingly under trees, and
drinking-fountain water bubbled softly, like their voices, but for all
the white April evening meant to him, Vincent, drunk a little and
wandering, might as well have been old, like the old bench-sitters
rasping phlegm.

In the country, spring is a time of small happenings happening
quietly, hyacinth shoots thrusting in a garden, willows burning with
a sudden frosty fire of green, lengthening afternoons of long flowing
dusk, and midnight rain opening lilac; but in the city there is the
fanfare of organ-grinders, and odors, undiluted by winter wind, clog
the air; windows long closed go up, and conversation, drifting beyond a room, collides with the jangle of a peddler's bell. It is the

crazy season of toy balloons and roller skates, of courtyard baritones and men of freakish enterprise, like the one who jumped up now like a jack-in-the-box. He was old, he had a telescope and a sign: 25¢ See the Moon! See the Stars! 25¢. No stars could penetrate a city's glare, but Vincent saw the moon, a round, shadowed whiteness, and then a blaze of electric bulbs: Four Roses, Bing Cro——. He was moving through caramel-scented staleness, swimming through oceans of cheese-pale faces, neon and darkness. Above the blasting of a juke-box, bullet-fire boomed, a cardboard duck fell plop, and somebody screeched: "Yay Iggy!" It was a Broadway funhouse, a penny arcade, and jammed from wall to wall with Saturday splurgers. He watched a penny movie (*What the Bootblack Saw*), and had his fortune told by a wax witch leering behind glass: "Yours is an affectionate nature" . . . but he read no further, for up near the jukebox there was an attractive commotion. A crowd of kids, clapping in time to jazz music, had formed a circle around two dancers. These dancers were both colored, both girls. They swayed together slow and easy, like lovers, rocked and stamped and rolled serious savage eyes, their muscles rhythmically attuned to the ripple of a clarinet, the rising harangue of a drum. Vincent's gaze traveled round the audience, and when he saw her a bright shiver went through him, for something of the dance's violence was reflected in her face. Standing there beside a tall ugly boy, it was as if she were the sleeper and the Negroes a dream. Trumpet-drum-piano, bawling on behind a black girl's froggy voice, wailed toward a rocking finale. The clapping ended, the dancers parted. She was alone now; though Vincent's instinct was to leave before she noticed, he advanced, and, as one would gently waken a sleeper, lightly touched her shoulder. "Hello," he said, his voice too loud. Turning, she stared at him, and her eyes were clear-blank. First terror, then puzzlement replaced the dead lost look. She took a step backward, and, just as the jukebox commenced hollering again, he seized her wrist: "You remember me," he prompted, "the gallery? Your painting?" She blinked, let the lids sink sleepily over those eyes, and he could feel the slow relaxing of tension in her arm. She was thinner than he recalled, prettier, too, and her hair, grown out somewhat, hung in casual disorder. A little Christmas ribbon dangled sadly from a stray lock. He started to say, "Can I buy you a drink?" but she leaned against him, her head resting on his chest like a child's, and he said: "Will you come home with me?" She lifted her face; the answer, when it came, was a breath, a whisper: "Please," she said.

Vincent stripped off his clothes, arranged them neatly in the closet, and admired his nakedness before a mirrored door. He was not so handsome as he supposed, but handsome all the same. For his moderate height he was excellently proportioned; his hair was dark yellow, and his delicate, rather snub-nosed face had a fine, ruddy coloring. The rumble of running water broke the quiet; she was in the bathroom preparing to bathe. He dressed in loose-fitting flannel pajamas, lit a cigarette, said, "Everything all right?" The water went off, a long silence, then: "Yes, thank you." On the way home in a cab he'd made an attempt at conversation, but she had said nothing, not even when they entered the apartment—and this last offended him, for, taking rather female pride in his quarters, he'd expected a complimentary remark. It was one enormously high-ceilinged room, a bath and kitchenette, a backyard garden. In the furnishings he'd combined modern with antique and produced a distinguished result. Decorating the walls were a trio of Toulouse-Lautrec prints, a framed circus poster, D.J.'s painting, photographs of Rilke, Nijinsky and Duse. A candelabra of lean blue candles burned on a desk; the room, washed in their delirious light, wavered. French doors led into the yard. He never used it much, for it was a place impossible to keep clean. There were a few dead tulip stalks dark in the moonshine, a puny heaven tree, and an old weather-worn chair left by the last tenant. He paced back and forth over the cold flagstones, hoping that in the cool air the drugged drunk sensation he felt would wear off.

Nearby a piano was being badly mauled, and in a window above there was a child's face. He was thumbing a blade of grass when her shadow fell long across the yard. She was in the doorway. "You mustn't come out," he said, moving toward her. "It's turned a little cold."

There was about her now an appealing softness; she seemed somehow less angular, less out of tune with the average, and Vincent, offering a glass of sherry, was delighted at the delicacy with which she touched it to her lips. She was wearing his terry-cloth robe; it was by yards too large. Her feet were bare, and she tucked them up beside her on the couch. "It's like Glass Hill, the candlelight," she said, and smiled. "My Granny lived at Glass Hill. We had lovely times, sometimes; do you know what she used to say? She used to say, 'Candles are magic wands; light one and the world is a story book.'"

"What a dreary old lady she must've been," said Vincent, quite drunk. "We should probably have hated each other."

"Granny would've loved you," she said. "She loved any kind of man, every man she ever met, even Mr. Destronelli."

"Destronelli?" It was a name he'd heard before.

Her eyes slid slyly sideways, and this look seemed to say: There must be no subterfuge between us, we who understand each other have no need of it. "Oh, you know," she said with a conviction that, under more commonplace circumstances, would have been surprising. It was, however, as if he'd abandoned temporarily the faculty of surprise. "Everybody knows him."

He curved an arm around her, and brought her nearer. "Not me, I don't," he said, kissing her mouth, neck; she was not responsive especially, but he said—and his voice had gone adolescently shaky— "Never met Mr. Whoozits." He slipped a hand inside her robe, loosening it away from her shoulders. Above one breast she had a birthmark, small and star-shaped. He glanced at the mirrored door, where uncertain light rippled their reflections, made them pale and incomplete. She was smiling. "Mr. Whoozits," he said, "what does he look like?" The suggestion of a smile faded, a small monkeylike frown flickered on her face. She looked above the mantel at her painting, and he realized that this was the first notice she'd shown it; she appeared to study in the picture a particular object, but whether hawk or head he could not say. "Well," she said quietly, pressing closer to him, "he looks like you, like me, like most anybody."

It was raining; in the wet noon light two nubs of candle still burned, and at an open window gray curtains tossed forlornly. Vincent extricated his arm; it was numb from the weight of her body. Careful not to make a noise, he eased out of bed, blew out the candles, tiptoed into the bathroom, and doused his face with cold water. On the way to the kitchenette he flexed his arms, feeling, as he hadn't for a long time, an intensely male pleasure in his strength, a healthy wholeness of person. He made and put on a tray orange juice, raisin-bread toast, a pot of tea; then, so inexpertly that everything on the tray rattled, he brought the breakfast in and placed it on a table beside the bed.

She had not moved; her ruffled hair spread fanwise across the pillow, and one hand rested in the hollow where his head had lain. He leaned over and kissed her lips, and her eyelids, blue with sleep, trembled. "Yes, yes, I'm awake," she murmured, and rain, lifting in the wind, sprayed against the window like surf. He somehow knew that with her, there would be none of the usual artifice: no avoidance of eyes, no shame-faced, accusing pause. She raised herself on her elbow; she looked at him, Vincent thought, as if he were her husband, and, handing her the orange juice, he smiled his gratitude.

"What is today?"

"Sunday," he told her, bundling under the quilt, and settling the tray across his legs.

"But there are no church bells," she said. "And it's raining."

Vincent divided a piece of toast. "You don't mind that, do you? Rain—such a peaceful sound." He poured tea. "Sugar? Cream?"

She disregarded this, and said, "Today is Sunday what? What month, I mean?"

"Where have you been living, in the subway?" he said, grinning. And it puzzled him to think she was serious. "Oh, April . . . April something-or-other."

"April," she repeated. "Have I been here long?"

"Only since last night."

"Oh."

Vincent stirred his tea, the spoon tinkling in the cup like a bell. Toast crumbs spilled among the sheets, and he thought of the *Tribune* and the *Times* waiting outside the door, but they, this morning, held no charms; it was best lying here beside her in the warm bed, sipping tea, listening to the rain. Odd, when you stopped to consider, certainly very odd. She did not know his name, nor he hers. And so he said, "I still owe you thirty dollars, do you realize that? Your own fault, of course—leaving such a damn-fool address. And D.J., what is that supposed to mean?"

"I don't think I'd better tell you my name," she said. "I could make up one easy enough: Dorothy Jordan, Delilah Johnson; see? There are all kinds of names I could make up, and if it wasn't for him, I'd tell you right."

Vincent lowered the tray to the floor. He rolled over on his side, and, facing her, his heartbeat quickened. "Who's him?" Though her expression was calm, anger muddied her voice when she said, "If you don't know him, then tell me, why am I here?"

Silence, and outside the rain seemed suddenly suspended. A ship's horn moaned in the river. Holding her close, he combed his fingers through her hair, and, wanting so much to be believed, said, "Because I love you."

She closed her eyes. "What became of them?"

"Who?"

"The others you've said that to."

It commenced again, the rain spattering grayly at the window, falling on hushed Sunday streets; listening, Vincent remembered. He remembered his cousin, Lucille, poor, beautiful, stupid Lucille, who sat all day embroidering silk flowers on scraps of linen. And Allen T. Baker—there was the winter they'd spent in Havana, the house they'd lived in, crumbling rooms of rose-colored rock; poor Allen, he'd thought it was to be forever. Gordon too. Gordon, with the kinky yellow hair, and a head full of old Elizabethan ballads. Was it true he'd shot himself? And Connie Silver, the deaf girl, the one who had wanted to be an actress—what had become of her? Or Helen, Louise, Laura? "There was just one," he said, and to his own ears this had a truthful ring. "Only one, and she's dead."

Tenderly, as if in sympathy, she touched his cheek. "I suppose he killed her," she said, her eyes so close he could see the outline of his face imprisoned in their greenness. "He killed Miss Hall, you know. The dearest woman in the world, Miss Hall, and so pretty your breath went away. I had piano lessons with her, and when she played the piano, when she said hello and when she said good-bye—it was like my heart would stop." Her voice had taken on an impersonal tone, as though she were talking of matters belonging to another age, and in which she was not concerned directly. "It was the end of summer when she married him—September, I think. She went to Atlanta, and they were married there, and she never came back. It was just that sudden." She snapped her fingers. "Just like that. I saw a picture of him in the paper. Sometimes I think if she'd known how much I loved her—why are there some you can't ever tell?—I think maybe she wouldn't have married; maybe it would've all been different, like I wanted it." She turned her face into the pillow, and if she cried, there was no sound.

On May twentieth she was eighteen; it seemed incredible—Vincent had thought her many years older. He wanted to introduce her at a surprise party, but had finally to admit that this was an unsuitable plan. First off, though the subject was always there on the tip of his tongue, not once had he ever mentioned D.J. to any of his friends; secondly, he could visualize discouragingly well the entertainment provided them at meeting a girl about whom, while they openly shared an apartment, he knew nothing, not even her name. Still the birthday called for some kind of treat. Dinner and the theater were hopeless. She hadn't, through no fault of his, a dress of any sort. He'd given her forty-odd dollars to buy clothes, and here is what she spent it on: a leather windbreaker, a set of military brushes, a raincoat, a cigarette lighter. Also, her suitcase, which she'd brought to the apartment, had contained nothing but hotel soap, a pair of scissors she used for pruning her hair, two Bibles and an appalling color-tinted photograph. The photograph showed a simpering middle-aged woman with dumpy features. There was an inscription: Best Wishes and Good Luck from Martha Lovejoy Hall.

Because she could not cook they had their meals out; his salary and the limitations of her wardrobe confined them mostly to the Automat—her favorite: the macaroni was so delicious!—or one of the bar-grills along Third. And so the birthday dinner was eaten in an Automat. She'd scrubbed her face until the skin shone red, trimmed and shampooed her hair, and with the messy skill of a six-year-old playing grown-up, varnished her nails. She wore the leather windbreaker, and on it pinned a sheaf of violets he'd given her; it must have looked amusing, for two rowdy girls sharing their table giggled frantically. Vincent said if they didn't shut up . . .

"Oh, yeah, who you think you are?"

"Superman. Jerk thinks he's superman."

It was too much, and Vincent lost his temper. He shoved back from the table, upsetting a ketchup jar. "Let's get the hell out of here," he said, but D.J., who had paid the fracas no attention whatever, went right on spooning blackberry cobbler; furious as he was, he waited quietly until she finished, for he respected her remoteness, and yet wondered in what period of time she lived. It was futile, he'd discovered, to question her past; still, she seemed only now and then aware of the present, and it was likely the future didn't mean much to her. Her mind was like a mirror reflecting blue space in a barren room.

"What would you like now?" he said, as they came into the street. "We could ride in a cab through the park."

She wiped off with her jacket-cuff flecks of blackberry staining the corners of her mouth, and said, "I want to go to a picture show."

The movies. Again. In the last month he'd seen so many films, snatches of Hollywood dialogue rumbled in his dreams. One Saturday at her insistence they'd bought tickets to three different theaters, cheap places where smells of latrine disinfectant poisoned the air. And each morning before leaving for work he left on the mantel fifty cents—rain or shine, she went to a picture show. But Vincent was sensitive enough to see why; there had been in his own life a certain time of limbo when he'd gone to movies every day, often sitting through several repeats of the same film; it was in its way like religion, for there, watching the shifting patterns of black and white, he knew a release of conscience similar to the kind a man must find confessing to his father.

"Handcuffs," she said, referring to an incident in *The Thirty-Nine Steps,* which they'd seen at the Beverly in a program of Hitchcock revivals. "That blond woman and the man handcuffed together—well, it made me think of something else." She stepped into a pair of his pajamas, pinned the corsage of violets to the edge of her pillow, and folded up on the bed. "People getting caught like that, locked together."

Vincent yawned. "Uh-huh," he said, and turned off the lights. "Again, happy birthday, darling, it *was* a happy birthday?"

She said, "Once I was in this place, and there were two girls dancing; they were so free—there was just them and nobody else, and it was beautiful like a sunset." She was silent a long while; then, her slow Southern voice dragging over the words: "It was mighty nice of you to bring me violets."

"Glad—like them," he answered sleepily.

"It's a shame they have to die."

"Yes, well, good night."

"Good night."

Close-up. Oh, but John, it isn't for my sake after all we've the children to consider a divorce would ruin their lives! Fadeout. The screen trembles; rattle of drums, flourish trumpets: R.K.O. presents . . .

Here is a hall without exit, a tunnel without end. Overhead, chandeliers sparkle, and wind-bent candles float on currents of air. Before him is an old man rocking in a rocking chair, an old man with yellow-dyed hair, powdered cheeks, kewpie-doll lips: Vincent recognizes Vincent. Go away, screams Vincent, the young and handsome, but Vincent, the old and horrid, creeps forward on all fours, and climbs spiderlike onto his back. Threats, pleas, blows, nothing will dislodge him. And so he races with his shadow, his rider jogging up and down. A serpent of lightning blazes, and all at once the tunnel seethes with men wearing white tie and tails, women costumed in brocaded gowns. He is humiliated; how gauche they must think him appearing at so elegant a gathering carrying on his back, like Sinbad, a sordid old man. The guests stand about in petrified pairs, and there is no conversation. He notices then that many are also saddled with malevolent semblances of themselves, outward embodiments of inner decay. Just beside him a lizardlike man rides an albino-eyed Negro. A man is coming toward him, the host; short, florid, bald, he steps lightly, precisely in glacé shoes; one arm, held stiffly crooked, supports a massive headless hawk whose talons, latched to the wrist, draw blood. The hawk's wings unfurl as its master struts by. On a pedestal there is perched an old-time phonograph. Winding the handle, the host supplies a record: a tinny worn-out waltz vibrates the morning-glory horn. He lifts a hand, and in a soprano voice announces: "Attention! The dancing will commence." The host with his hawk weaves in and out as round and round they dip, they turn.

The walls widen, the ceiling grows tall. A girl glides into Vincent's arms, and a cracked, cruel imitation of his voice says: "Lucille, how divine; that exquisite scent, is it violet?" This is Cousin Lucille, and then, as they circle the room, her face changes. Now he waltzes with another. "Why, Connie, Connie Silver! How marvelous to see you," shrieks the voice, for Connie is quite deaf. Suddenly a gentleman with a bullet-bashed head cuts in: "Gordon, forgive me, I never meant . . ." but they are gone, Gordon and Connie, dancing together. Again, a new partner. It is D.J., and she too has a figure barnacled to her back, an enchanting auburn-haired child; like an emblem of innocence, the child cuddles to her chest a snowball kitten. "I am heavier than I look," says the child, and the terrible voice retorts, "But I am heaviest of all." The instant their hands meet he begins to feel the weight upon him diminish; the old Vincent is fading. His feet lift off the floor, he floats upward from her embrace. The victrola grinds away loud as ever, but he is rising high, and the white receding faces gleam below like mushrooms on a dark meadow.

The host releases his hawk, sends it soaring. Vincent thinks, no matter, it is a blind thing, and the wicked are safe among the blind. But the hawk wheels above him, swoops down, claws foremost; at last he knows there is to be no freedom.

And the blackness of the room filled his eyes. One arm lolled over the bed's edge, his pillow had fallen to the floor. Instinctively he reached out, asking mother-comfort of the girl beside him. Sheets smooth and cold; emptiness, and the tawdry fragrance of drying violets. He snapped up straight: "You, where are you?"

The French doors were open. An ashy trace of moon swayed on the threshold, for it was not yet light, and in the kitchen the refrigerator purred like a giant cat. A stack of paper rustled on the desk. Vincent called again, softly this time, as if he wished himself unheard. Rising, he stumbled forward on dizzy legs, and looked into the yard. She was there, leaning, half-kneeling, against the heaven tree. "What?" and she whirled around. He could not see her well, only a dark substantial shape. She came closer. A finger pressed her lips.

"What is it?" he whispered.

She rose on tiptoe, and her breath tingled in his ear. "I warn you, go inside."

"Stop this foolishness," he said in a normal voice. "Out here barefooted, you'll catch . . ." but she clamped a hand over his mouth.

"I saw him," she whispered. "He's here."

Vincent knocked her hand away. It was hard not to slap her. "Him! Him! Him! What's the matter with you? Are you"—he tried too late to prevent the word—"crazy?" There, the acknowledgment of something he'd known, but had not allowed his conscious mind to crystallize. And he thought: Why should this make a difference? A man cannot be held to account for those he loves. Untrue. Feeble-witted Lucille weaving mosaics on silk, embroidering his name on scarves; Connie, in her hushed deaf world, listening for his footstep, a sound she would surely hear; Allen T. Baker thumbing his photograph, still needing love, but old now, and lost—all betrayed. And he'd betrayed himself with talents unexploited, voyages never taken, promises unfulfilled. There had seemed nothing left him until—oh, why in his lovers must he always find the broken image of himself? Now, as he looked at her in the aging dawn, his heart was cold with the death of love.

She moved away, and under the tree. "Leave me here," she said, her eyes scanning tenement windows. "Only a moment."

Vincent waited, waited. On all sides windows looked down like the doors of dreams, and overhead, four flights up, a family's laundry whipped a washline. The setting moon was like the early moon of dusk, a vaporish cartwheel, and the sky, draining of dark, was washed with gray. Sunrise wind shook the leaves of the heaven tree, and in the paling light the yard assumed a pattern, objects a position, and from the roofs came the throaty morning rumble of pigeons. A light went on. Another.

And at last she lowered her head; whatever she was looking for, she had not found it. Or, he wondered as she turned to him with tilted lips, had she?

"Well, you're home kinda early, aren't you, Mr. Waters?" It was Mrs. Brennan, the super's bowlegged wife. "And, well, Mr. Waters—lovely weather, ain't it?—you and me got sumpin' to talk about."

"Mrs. Brennan"—how hard it was to breathe, to speak; the words grated his hurting throat, sounded loud as thunderclaps—"I'm rather ill, so if you don't mind . . ." and he tried to brush past her.

"Say, that's a pity. Ptomaine, must be ptomaine. Yessir, I tell you a person can't be too careful. It's them Jews, you know. They run all them delicatessens. Uh uh, none of that Jew food for me." She stepped before the gate, blocking his path, and pointed an admonishing finger: "Trouble with you, Mr. Waters, is you don't lead no kinda *normal* life."

A knot of pain was set like a malignant jewel in the core of his head; each aching motion made jeweled pinpoints of color flare out. The super's wife babbled on, but there were blank moments when, fortunately, he could not hear at all. It was like a radio—the volume turned low, then full blast. "Now I know she's a decent Christian lady, Mr. Waters, or else what would a gentleman like you be doing with—hm. Still, the fact is, Mr. Cooper don't tell lies, and he's a real calm man, besides. Been gas meter man for this district I don't know how long." A truck rolled down the street spraying water, and her voice, submerged below its roar, came up again like a shark. "Mr. Cooper had every reason to believe she meant to kill him—well, you can imagine, her standin' there with them scissors, and shoutin'. She called him an Eyetalian name. Now all you got to do is look at Mr. Cooper to know he ain't no Eyetalian. Well, you can see, Mr. Waters, such carryings-on are bound to give the house a bad . . ."

Brittle sunshine plundering the depths of his eyes made tears, and the super's wife, wagging her finger, seemed to break into separate pieces: a nose, a chin, a red, red eye. "Mr. Destronelli," he said. "Excuse me, Mrs. Brennan, I mean excuse me." She thinks I'm drunk, and I'm sick, and can't she see I'm sick? "My guest is leaving. She's leaving today, and she won't be back."

"Well, now, you don't say," said Mrs. Brennan, clucking her tongue. "Looks like she needs a rest, poor little thing. So pale, sorta. Course I don't want no more to do with them Eyetalians than the next one, but imagine thinking Mr. Cooper was an Eyetalian. Why, he's white as you or me." She tapped his shoulder solicitously. "Sorry you feel so sick, Mr. Waters; ptomaine, I tell you. A person can't be too care . . ."

The hall smelled of cooking and incinerator ashes. There was a stairway which he never used, his apartment being on the first floor, straight ahead. A match snapped fire, and Vincent, groping his way, saw a small boy—he was not more than three or four—squatting under the stairwell; he was playing with a big box of kitchen matches, and Vincent's presence appeared not to interest him. He simply struck another match. Vincent could not make his mind work well enough to phrase a reprimand, and as he waited there, tongue-tied, a door, his door, opened.

Hide. For if she saw him, she would know something was wrong, suspect something. And if she spoke, if their eyes met, then he would never be able to go through with it. So he pressed into a dark corner behind the little boy, and the little boy said, "Whatcha doin', Mister?" She was coming—he heard the slap of her sandals, the green whisper of her raincoat. "Whatcha doin', Mister?" Quickly, his heart banging in his chest, Vincent stooped and, squeezing the child against him, pressed his hand over its mouth so it could not make a sound. He did not see her pass; it was later, after the front door clicked, that he realized she was gone. The little boy sank back on the floor. "Whatcha doin', Mister?"

Four aspirins, one right after the other, and he came back into the room; the bed had not been tidied for a week, a spilt ashtray messed the floor, odds and ends of clothing decorated improbable places, lampshades and such. But tomorrow, if he felt better, there would be a general cleaning; perhaps he'd have the walls repainted, maybe fix up the yard. Tomorrow he could begin thinking about his friends again, accept invitations, entertain. And yet this prospect, tasted in advance, was without flavor: all he'd known before seemed to him now sterile and spurious. Footsteps in the hall; could she return this soon, the movie over, the afternoon gone? Fever can make time pass so queerly, and for an instant he felt as though his bones were floating loose inside him. Clop-clop, a child's sloppy shoefall, the footsteps passed up the stairs, and Vincent moved, floated toward the mirrored closet. He longed to hurry, knowing he must, but the air seemed thick with gummy fluid. He brought her suitcase from the closet, and put it on the bed, a sad cheap suitcase with rusty locks and a warped hide. He eyed it with guilt. Where would she go? How would she live? When he'd broken with Connie, Gordon, all the others, there had been about it at least a certain dignity. Really, though— and he'd thought it out—there was no other way. So he gathered her belongings. Miss Martha Lovejoy Hall peeked out from under the leather windbreaker, her music-teacher's face smiling an oblique reproach. Vincent turned her over, face down, and tucked in the frame an envelope containing twenty dollars. That would buy a ticket back to Glass Hill, or wherever it was she came from. Now he tried to close the case, and, too weak with fever, collapsed on the bed. Quick yellow wings glided through the window. A butterfly. He'd never seen a butterfly in this city, and it was like a floating mysterious flower, like a sign of some sort, and he watched with a kind of horror as it waltzed in the air. Outside, somewhere, the razzledazzle of a beggar's grindorgan started up; it sounded like a broken-down pianola, and it played *La Marseillaise*. The butterfly lighted on her painting, crept across crystal eyes and flattened its wings like a ribbon bow over the loose head. He fished about in the suitcase until he found her scissors. He first purposed to slash the butterfly's wings, but it spiraled to the ceiling and hung there like a star. The scissors stabbed the hawk's heart, ate through canvas like a ravening steel mouth, scraps of picture flaking the floor like cuttings of stiff hair. He went on his knees, pushed the pieces into a pile, put them in the suitcase, and slammed the lid shut. He was crying. And through the tears the butterfly magnified on the ceiling, huge as a bird, and there were more: a flock of lilting, winking yellow; whispering lonesomely, like surf sucking a shore. The wind from their wings blew the room into space. He heaved forward, the suitcase banging his leg, and threw open the door. A match flared. The little boy said: "Whatcha doin', Mister?" And Vincent, setting the suitcase in the hall, grinned sheepishly. He closed the door like a thief, bolted the safety lock and, pulling up a chair, tilted it under the knob. In the still room there was only the subtlety of shifting sunlight and a crawling butterfly; it drifted downward like a tricky scrap of crayon paper, and landed on a candlestick. *Sometimes he is not a man at all*—she'd told him that, huddling here on the bed, talking swiftly in the minutes before dawn—*sometimes he is something very different: a hawk, a child, a butterfly.* And then she'd said: *At the place where they took me there were hundreds of old ladies, and young men, and one of the young men said he was a pirate, and one of the old ladies—she was near ninety—used to make me feel her stomach. "Feel," she'd say, "feel how strong he kicks?" This old lady took painting class, too, and her paintings looked like crazy quilts. And naturally he was in this place. Mr. Destronelli. Only he called himself Gum. Doctor Gum. Oh, he didn't fool me, even though he wore a gray wig, and made himself up to look real old and kind, I knew. And then one day I left, ran clear away, and hid under a lilac bush, and a man came along in a little red car, and he had a little mouse-haired mustache, and little cruel eyes. But it was him. And when I told him who he was he made me get out of his car. And then another man, that was in Philadelphia, picked me up in a café and took me into an alley. He talked Italian, and had tattoo pictures all over. But it was him. And the next man, he was the one who painted his toenails, sat down beside me in a movie because he thought I was a boy, and when he found out I wasn't he didn't get mad but let me live in his room, and cooked pretty things for me to eat. But he wore a silver locket and one day I looked inside and there was a picture of Miss Hall. So I knew it was him, so I had this feeling she was dead, so I knew he was going to murder me. And he will. He will.* Dusk, and nightfall, and the fibers of sound called silence wove a shiny blue mask. Waking, he peered through eyeslits, heard the frenzied pulse-beat of his watch, the scratch of a key in a lock. Somewhere in this hour of dusk a murderer separates himself from shadow and with a rope follows the flash of silk legs up doomed stairs. And here the dreamer staring through his mask dreams of deceit. Without investigating, he knows the suitcase is missing, that she has come, that she has gone; why, then, does he feel so little the pleasure of safety, and only cheated, and small—small as the night when he searched the moon through an old man's telescope?

3

Like fragments of an old letter, scattered popcorn lay trampled flat, and she, leaning back in a watchman's attitude, allowed her gaze to hunt among it, as if deciphering here and there a word, an answer. Her eyes shifted discreetly to the man mounting the steps, Vincent. There was about him the freshness of a shower, shave, cologne, but dreary blue circled his eyes, and the crisp seersucker into which he'd changed had been made for a heavier man: a long month of pneumonia, and wakeful burning nights had lightened his weight a dozen pounds, and more. Each morning, evening, meeting her here at his gate, or near the gallery, or outside the restaurant where he lunched, a nameless disorder took hold, a paralysis of time and identity. The wordless pantomime of her pursuit contracted his heart, and there were comalike days when she seemed not one, but all, a multiple person, and her shadow in the street every shadow, following and followed. And once they'd been alone together in an automatic elevator, and he'd screamed: "I am not him! Only me, only me!" But she smiled as she'd smiled telling of the man with painted toenails, because after all, she knew.

It was suppertime, and, not knowing where to eat, he paused under a street lamp that, blooming abruptly, fanned complex light over stone; while he waited there came a clap of thunder, and all along the street every face but two, his and the girl's, tilted upward. A blast of river breeze tossed the children's laughter as they, linking arms, pranced like carousel ponies, and carried the mama's voice who, leaning from a window, howled: rain, Rachel, rain—gonna rain gonna rain! And the gladiola, ivy-filled flower cart jerked crazily as the peddler, one eye slanted skyward, raced for shelter. A potted geranium fell off, and the little girls gathered the blooms and tucked them behind their ears. The blending spatter of running feet and raindrops tinkled on the xylophone sidewalks—the slamming of doors, the lowering of windows, then nothing but silence, and rain. Presently, with slow scraping steps, she came below the lamp to stand beside him, and it was as if the sky were a thunder-cracked mirror, for the rain fell between them like a curtain of splintered glass.

SHUT A FINAL DOOR

(1947)

1

"Walter, listen to me: if everyone dislikes you, works against you, don't believe they do so arbitrarily; you create these situations for yourself."

Anna had said that, and, though his healthier side told him she intended nothing malicious (if Anna was not a friend, then who was?), he'd despised her for it, had gone around telling everybody how much he despised Anna, what a bitch she was. That woman! he said, don't trust that Anna. This plainspoken act of hers—nothing but a cover-up for all her repressed hostility; terrible liar, too, can't believe a word she says: dangerous, my God! And naturally all he said went back to Anna, so that when he called about a play-opening they'd planned attending together, she told him: "Sorry, Walter, I can't afford you any longer. I understand you very well, and I have a certain amount of sympathy. It's very compulsive, your malice, and you aren't too much to blame, but I don't want ever to see you again because I'm not so well myself that I can afford it." But why? And what had he done? Well, sure, he'd gossiped about her, but it wasn't as though he'd meant it, and after all, as he said to Jimmy Bergman (now there was a two-face if ever there was one), what was the use of having friends if you couldn't discuss them objectively?

He said you said they said we said round and round. Round and round, like the paddle-bladed ceiling fan wheeling above; turning and turning, stirring stale air ineffectively, it made a watch-tick sound, counted seconds in the silence. Walter inched to a cooler part of the bed and closed his eyes against the dark little room. At seven that evening he'd arrived in New Orleans, at seven-thirty he'd registered in this hotel, an anonymous, side-street place. It was August, and it was as though bonfires burned in the red night sky, and the unnatural Southern landscape, observed so assiduously from the train, and which, trying to sublimate all else, he retraced in memory, intensified a feeling of having traveled to the end, the falling off.

But why he was here in this stifling hotel in this faraway town he could not say. There was a window in the room, but he could not seem to get it open, and he was afraid to call the bellboy (what queer eyes that kid had!), and he was afraid to leave the hotel, for what if he got lost? and if he got lost, even a little, then he would be lost altogether. He was hungry; he hadn't eaten since breakfast, so he found some peanut-butter crackers left over from a package he'd bought in Saratoga, and washed them down with a finger of Four Roses, the last. It made him sick. He vomited in the wastebasket, collapsed back on the bed, and cried until the pillow was wet. After a while he just lay there in the hot room, shivering, just lay there and watched the slow-turning fan; there was no beginning to its action, and no end; it was a circle.

An eye, the earth, the rings of a tree, everything is a circle, and all circles, Walter said, have a center. It was crazy for Anna to say what had happened was his own doing. If there was anything wrong with him really, then it had been made so by circumstances beyond his control, by, say, his churchly mother, or his father, an insurance official in Hartford, or his older sister, Cecile, who'd married a man forty years her senior. "I just wanted to get out of the house." That was her excuse, and, to tell the truth, Walter had thought it reasonable enough.

But he did not know where to begin thinking about himself, did not know where to find the center. The first telephone call? No, that had been only three days ago and, properly speaking, was the end, not the beginning. Well, he could start with Irving, for Irving was the first person he'd known in New York.

Now Irving was a sweet little Jewish boy with a remarkable talent for chess and not much else: he had silky hair, and pink baby cheeks, and looked about sixteen. Actually he was twenty-three, Walter's age, and they'd met at a bar in the Village. Walter was alone and very lonesome in New York, and so when this sweet little Irving was friendly he decided maybe it would be a good idea to be friendly, too—because you never can tell. Irving knew a great many people, and everyone was very fond of him, and he introduced Walter to all his friends.

And there was Margaret. Margaret was more or less Irving's girl friend. She was only so-so-looking (her eyes bulged, there was always a little lipstick on her teeth, she dressed like a child of ten), but she had a hectic brightness which Walter found attractive. He could not understand why she bothered with Irving at all. "Why do you?" he said, on one of the long walks they'd begun taking together in Central Park.

"Irving is sweet," she said, "and he loves me very purely, and who knows: I might just as well marry him."

"A damn-fool thing to do," he said. "Irving could never be your husband because he's really your little brother. Irving is everyone's little brother."

Margaret was too bright not to see the truth in this. So one day when Walter asked if he might not make love to her she said, all right, she didn't mind if he did. They made love often after that.

Eventually, Irving heard about it, and one Monday there was a nasty scene in, curiously enough, the same bar where they'd met.

There had been that evening a party in honor of Kurt Kuhnhardt (Kuhnhardt Advertising), Margaret's boss, and she and Walter had gone together, afterward stopping by this bar for a nightcap. Except for Irving and a couple of girls in slacks the place was empty. Irving was sitting at the bar, his cheeks quite pink, his eyes rather glazed. He looked like a little boy playing grown-up, for his legs were too short to reach the stool's footrest; they dangled doll-like. The instant Margaret recognized him she tried to turn around and walk out, but Walter wouldn't let her. And anyway, Irving had seen them: never taking his eyes from them, he put down his whiskey, slowly climbed off the stool, and, with a kind of sad, ersatz toughness, strutted forward.

"Irving, dear," said Margaret, and stopped, for he'd given her a terrible look.

His chin was trembling. "You go away," he said, and it was as though he were denouncing some childhood tormentor, "I hate you." Then, almost in slow motion, he swung out and, as if he clutched a knife, struck Walter's chest. It was not much of a blow, and when Walter did nothing but smile, Irving slumped against a jukebox, screaming: "Fight me, you damned coward; come on, and I'll kill you, I swear before God I will." So that was how they left him.

Walking home, Margaret began to cry in a soft tired way. "He'll never be sweet again," she said.

And Walter said, "I don't know what you mean."

"Oh, yes, you do," she told him, her voice a whisper. "Yes, you do; the two of us, we've taught him how to hate. Somehow I don't think he ever knew before."

Walter had been in New York now four months. His original capital of five hundred dollars had fallen to fifteen, and Margaret lent him money to pay his January rent at the Brevoort. Why, she wanted to know, didn't he move someplace cheaper? Well, he told her, it was better to have a good address. And what about a job? When was he going to start working? Or was he? Sure, he said, sure, as a matter of fact he thought about it a good deal. But he didn't intend fooling around with just any little jerkwater thing that came along. He wanted something good, something with a future, something in, say, advertising. All right, said Margaret, maybe she could help him; at any rate, she'd speak with her boss, Mr. Kuhnhardt.

2

The K.K.A., so-called, was a middle-sized agency, but, as such things go, very good, the best. Kurt Kuhnhardt, who'd founded it in 1925, was a curious man with a curious reputation: a lean, fastidious German, a bachelor, he lived in an elegant black house on Sutton Place, a house interestingly furnished with, among other things, three Picassos, a superb music box, South Sea Island masks and a burly Danish youngster, the houseboy. He invited occasionally some one of his staff in to dinner, whoever was favorite at the moment, for he was continually selecting protégés. It was a dangerous position, these alliances being, as they were, whimsical and uncertain: the protégé found himself checking the want ads when, just the evening previous, he'd dined most enjoyably with his benefactor. During his second week at the K.K.A., Walter, who had been hired as Margaret's assistant, received a memorandum from Mr. Kuhnhardt asking him to lunch, and this, of course, excited him unspeakably.

"Kill-joy?" said Margaret, straightening his tie, plucking lint off a lapel. "Nothing of the sort. It's just that—well, Kuhnhardt's wonderful to work for so long as you don't get too involved—or you're likely not to be working—period."

Walter knew what she was up to; she didn't fool him a minute; he felt like telling her so, too, but restrained himself; it wasn't time yet. One of these days, though, he was going to have to get rid of her, and soon. It was degrading, his working for Margaret. And besides, the tendency from now on would be to keep him down. But nobody could do that, he thought, looking into Mr. Kuhnhardt's sea-blue eyes, nobody could keep Walter down.

"You're an idiot," Margaret told him. "My God, I've seen these little friendships of K.K.'s a dozen times, and they don't mean a damn. He used to palsy-walsy around with the switchboard operator. All K.K. wants is someone to play the fool. Take my word, Walter, there aren't any shortcuts: what matters is how you do your job."

He said: "And have you complaints on that score? I'm doing as well as could be expected."

"It depends on what you mean by expected," she said.

One Saturday not long afterward he made a date to meet her in Grand Central. They were going up to Hartford to spend the afternoon with his family, and for this she'd bought a new dress, new hat and shoes. But he did not show up. Instead, he drove out on Long Island with Mr. Kuhnhardt, and was the most awed of three hundred guests at Rosa Cooper's debut ball. Rosa Cooper (née Kuppermann) was heiress to the Cooper Dairy Products: a dark, plump, pleasant child with an unnatural British accent, the result of four years at Miss Jewett's. She wrote a letter to a friend named Anna Stimson, who subsequently showed it to Walter: "Met the divinest man. Danced with him six times, a divine dancer. He is an Advertising Executive, and is terribly divinely good-looking. We have a date—dinner and the theater!"

Margaret did not mention the episode, nor did Walter. It was as though nothing had happened, except that now, unless there was office business to discuss, they never spoke, never saw each other. One afternoon, knowing she would not be at home, he went to her apartment and used a passkey given him long ago; there were things he'd left here, clothes, some books, his pipe; rummaging around collecting all this, he discovered a photograph of himself scrawled red with lipstick: it gave him for an instant the sensation of falling in a dream. He also came across the only gift he'd ever given her, a bottle of

L'Heure Bleue, still unopened. He sat down on the bed, and, smoking a cigarette, stroked his hand over the cool pillow, remembering the way her head had lain there, remembering, too, how they used to lie here Sunday mornings reading the funnies aloud, Barney Google and Dick Tracy and Joe Palooka.

He looked at the radio, a little green box; they'd always made love to music, any kind, jazz, symphonies, choir programs: it had been their signal, for whenever she'd wanted him, she'd said, "Shall we listen to the radio, darling?" Anyway, it was finished, and he hated her, and that was what he needed to remember. He found the bottle of perfume again, and put it in his pocket: Rosa might like a surprise.

In the office the next day he stopped by the water cooler and Margaret was standing there. She smiled at him fixedly, and said: "Well, I didn't know you were a thief." It was the first overt disclosure of the hostility between them. And suddenly it occurred to Walter he hadn't in all the office a single ally. Kuhnhardt? He could never count on him. And everyone else was an enemy: Jackson, Einstein, Fischer, Porter, Capehart, Ritter, Villa, Byrd. Oh, sure, they were all smart enough not to tell him point-blank, not so long as K.K.'s enthusiasm continued.

Well, dislike was at least positive, and the one thing he could not tolerate was vague relations, possibly because his own feelings were so indecisive, ambiguous. He was never certain whether he liked X or not. He needed X's love, but was incapable of loving. He could never be sincere with X, never tell him more than fifty percent of the truth. On the other hand, it was impossible for him to permit X these same imperfections: somewhere along the line Walter was sure he'd be betrayed. He was afraid of X, terrified. Once in high school he'd plagiarized a poem, and printed it in the school magazine; he could not forget its final line, *All our acts are acts of fear.* And when his teacher caught him out, had anything ever seemed to him more unjust?

3

He spent most of the early summer weekends at Rosa Cooper's Long Island place. The house was, as a rule, well staffed with hearty Yale and Princeton undergraduates, which was irritating, for they were the sort of boys who, around Hartford, made green birds fly in his stomach, and seldom allowed him to meet them on their own ground. As for Rosa herself, she was a darling; everyone said so, even Walter.

But darlings are rarely serious, and Rosa was not serious about Walter. He didn't mind too much. He was able on these weekends to make a good many contacts: Taylor Ovington, Joyce Randolph (the starlet), E. L. McEvoy, a dozen or so people whose names cast considerable glare in his address book. One evening he went with Anna Stimson to see a film featuring the Randolph girl, and before they were scarcely seated everyone for aisles around knew she was a Friend of his, knew she drank too much, was immoral, and not nearly so pretty as Hollywood made her out to be. Anna told him he was an adolescent female. "You're a man in only one respect, sweetie," she said.

It was through Rosa that he'd met Anna Stimson. An editor on a fashion magazine, she was almost six feet tall, wore black suits, affected a monocle, a walking cane and pounds of jingling Mexican silver. She'd been married twice, once to Buck Strong, the horse-opera idol, and she had a child, a fourteen-year-old son who'd had to be put away in what she called a "corrective academy."

"He was a nasty child," she said. "He liked to take potshots out the window with a .22, and throw things, and steal from Woolworth's: awful brat, just like you."

Anna was good to him, though, and in her less depressed, less malevolent moments listened kindly while he groaned out his problems, while he explained why he was the way he was. All his life some cheat had been dealing him the wrong cards. Attributing to Anna every vice but stupidity, he liked to use her as a kind of confessor: there was nothing he could tell her of which she might legitimately disapprove. He would say: "I've told Kuhnhardt a lot of lies about Margaret; I suppose that's pretty rotten, but she would do the same for me; and anyway, my idea is not for him to fire her, but maybe transfer her to the Chicago office."

Or, "I was in a bookshop, and a man was standing there and we began talking: a middle-aged man, rather nice, very intelligent. When I went outside he followed, a little ways behind: I crossed the street, he crossed the street, I walked fast, he walked fast. This kept up six or seven blocks, and when I finally figured out what was going on I felt tickled, I felt like kidding him on. So I stopped at the corner and hailed a cab; then I turned around and gave this guy a long, long look, and he came rushing up, all smiles. And I jumped in the cab, and slammed the door and leaned out the window and laughed out loud: the look on his face, it was awful, it was like Christ. I can't forget it. And tell me, Anna, why did I do this crazy thing? It was like paying back all the people who've ever hurt me, but it was something else, too." He would tell Anna these stories, go home and go to sleep. His dreams were clear blue.

Now the problem of love concerned him, mainly because he did not consider it a problem. Nevertheless, he was conscious of being unloved. This knowledge was like an extra heart beating inside him. But there was no one. Anna, perhaps. Did Anna love him? "Oh," said Anna, "when was anything ever what it seemed to be? Now it's a tadpole, now it's a frog. It looks like gold but you put it on your finger and it leaves a green ring. Take my second husband: he looked like a nice guy, and turned out to be just another heel. Look around this very room: why, you couldn't burn incense in that fireplace, and those mirrors, they give space, they tell a lie. Nothing, Walter, is ever what it seems to be. Christmas trees are cellophane, and snow is only soap chips. Flying around inside us is something called the Soul, and when you die you're never dead; yes, and when we're alive we're never alive. And so you want to know if I love you? Don't be dumb, Walter, we're not even friends. . . ."

4

Listen, the fan: turning wheels of whisper: he said you said they said we said round and round fast and slow while time recalled itself in endless chatter. Old broken fan breaking silence: August the third the third the third!

August the third, a Friday, and it was there, right in Winchell's column, his own name: "Big shot Ad exec Walter Ranney and dairy heiress Rosa Cooper are telling intimates to start buying rice." Walter himself had given the item to a friend of a friend of Winchell's. He showed it to the counter boy at the Whelan's where he ate breakfast. "That's me," he said, "I'm the guy," and the look on the boy's face was good for his digestion.

It was late when he reached the office that morning, and as he walked down the aisle of desks a small gratifying flurry among the typists preceded him. No one said anything, however. Around eleven, after a pleasant hour of doing nothing but feel exhilarated, he went to the drugstore downstairs for a cup of coffee. Three men from the office, Jackson, Ritter and Byrd, were there, and when Walter came in, Jackson poked Byrd, and Byrd poked Ritter, and all of them turned around. "Whatcha say, big shot?" said Jackson, a pink man prematurely bald, and the other two laughed. Acting as if he hadn't heard, Walter stepped quickly into a phone booth. "Bastards," he said, pretending to dial a number. And finally, after waiting a long while for them to leave, he made a real call. "Rosa, hello, did I wake you up?"

"No."

"Say, did you see Winchell?"

"Yes."

Walter laughed. "Where do you suppose he gets that stuff?"

Silence.

"What's the matter? You sound kind of funny."

"Do I?"

"Are you mad or something?"

"Just disappointed."

"About what?"

Silence. And then: "It was a cheap thing to do, Walter, pretty cheap."

"I don't know what you mean."

"Good-bye, Walter."

On the way out he paid the cashier for a cup of coffee he'd forgotten to have. There was a barbershop in the building. He said he wanted a shave; no—make it a haircut; no—a manicure; and suddenly, seeing himself in the mirror, where his face reflected as pale almost as the barber's bib, he knew he did not know what he wanted. Rosa had been right, he was cheap. He'd always been willing to confess his faults, for, by admitting them, it was as if he made them no longer to exist. He went back upstairs, and sat at his desk, and felt as though he were bleeding inside, and wished very much to believe in God. A pigeon strutted on the ledge outside his window. For some time he watched the shimmering sunlit feathers, the wobbly sedateness of its movements; then, before realizing it, he'd picked up and thrown a glass paperweight: the pigeon climbed calmly upward, the paperweight careened like a giant raindrop: suppose, he thought, listening for a faraway scream, suppose it hits someone, kills them? But there was nothing. Only the ticking fingers of typists, a knocking at the door! "Hey, Ranney, K.K. wants to see you."

"I'm sorry," said Mr. Kuhnhardt, doodling with a gold pen. "And I'll write a letter for you, Walter. Any time."

Now in the elevator the enemy, all submerging with him, crushed Walter between them; Margaret was there wearing a blue hair-ribbon.

She looked at him, and her face was different from other faces, not vacant as theirs were, and sterile: here still was compassion. But as she looked at him, she looked through him, too. This is my dream: he must not allow himself to believe otherwise; and yet under his own arm he carried the dream's contradiction, a manila envelope stuffed with all the personals saved from his desk. When the elevator emptied into the lobby, he knew he must speak with Margaret, ask her to forgive him, beg her protection, but she was slipping swiftly toward an exit, losing herself among the enemy. I love you, he said, running after her, I love you, he said, saying nothing.

"Margaret! Margaret!"

She turned around. The blue hair-ribbon matched her eyes, and her eyes, gazing up at him, softened, became rather friendly. Or pity-ing.

"Please," he said, "I thought we could have a drink together, go over to Benny's, maybe. We used to like Benny's, remember?"

She shook her head. "I've got a date, and I'm late already."

"Oh."

"Yes—well, I'm late," she said, and began to run. He stood watching as she raced down the street, her ribbon streaming, shining in the darkening summer light. And then she was gone.

His apartment, a one-room walk-up near Gramercy Park, needed an airing, a cleaning, but Walter, after pouring a drink, said to hell with it and stretched out on the couch. What was the use? No matter what you did or how hard you tried, it all came finally to zero; every-day everywhere everyone was being cheated, and who was there to blame? It was strange, though; lying here sipping whiskey in the dusk-graying room, he felt calmer than he had for God knows how long. It was like the time he'd failed algebra and felt so relieved, so free: failure was definite, a certainty, and there is always peace in cer-tainties. Now he would leave New York, take a vacation trip; he had a few hundred dollars, enough to last until fall.

And, wondering where he should go, he all at once saw, as if a film had commenced running in his head, silk caps, cherry-colored and lemon, and little wise-faced men wearing exquisite polka-dot shirts. Closing his eyes, he was suddenly five years old, and it was delicious remembering the cheers, the hot dogs, his father's big pair of binoculars. Saratoga! Shadows masked his face in the sinking light. He turned on a lamp, fixed another drink, put a rumba record on the phonograph, and began to dance, the soles of his shoes whispering on the carpet: he'd often thought that with a little training he could've been a professional.

Just as the music ended, the telephone rang. He simply stood there, afraid somehow to answer, and the lamplight, the furniture, everything in the room went quite dead. When at last he thought it had stopped, it commenced again; louder, it seemed, and more insistent. He tripped over a footstool, picked up the receiver, dropped and recovered it, said: "Yes?"

Long-distance: a call from some town in Pennsylvania, the name of which he didn't catch. Following a series of spasmic rattlings, a voice, dry and sexless and altogether unlike any he'd ever heard before, came through: "Hello, Walter."

"Who is this?"

No answer from the other end, only a sound of strong orderly breathing; the connection was so good it seemed as though whoever it was was standing beside him with lips pressed against his ear. "I don't like jokes. Who is this?"

"Oh, you know me, Walter. You've known me a long time." A click, and nothing.

5

It was night and raining when the train reached Saratoga. He'd slept most of the trip, sweating in the hot dampness of the car, and dreamed of an old castle where only old turkeys lived, and dreamed a dream involving his father, Kurt Kuhnhardt, someone no-faced, Margaret and Rosa, Anna Stimson and a queer fat lady with diamond eyes. He was standing on a long, deserted street; except for an approaching procession of slow, black, funeral-like cars there was no sign of life. Still, he knew, eyes unseen observed his nakedness from every window, and he hailed frantically the first of the limousines; it stopped and a man, his father, invitingly held open the door. Daddy, he yelled, running forward, and the door slammed shut, mashing off his fingers, and his father, with a great belly laugh, leaned out the window to toss an enormous wreath of roses. In the second car was Margaret, in the third the lady with the diamond eyes (wasn't this Miss Casey, his old algebra teacher?), in the fourth Mr. Kuhnhardt and a new protégé, the no-faced creature. Each door opened, each closed, all laughed, all threw roses. The procession rolled smoothly away down the silent street. And with a terrible scream Walter fell among the mountain of roses: thorns tore wounds, and a sudden rain, a gray cloudburst, shattered the blooms, and washed pale blood bleeding over the leaves.

By the fixed stare of a woman sitting opposite, he realized at once he'd yelled aloud in his sleep. He smiled at her sheepishly, and she looked away with, he imagined, some embarrassment. She was a cripple; on her left foot she wore a giant shoe. Later, in the Saratoga station, he helped with her luggage, and they shared a taxi; there was no conversation: each sat in his corner looking at the rain, the blurred lights. In New York a few hours before, he'd withdrawn from the bank all his savings, locked the door of his apartment, and left no messages; furthermore, there was in this town not a soul who knew him. It was a good feeling.

The hotel was filled: not to mention the racing crowd, there was, the desk clerk told him, a medical convention. No, sorry, he didn't know of a room anywhere. Maybe tomorrow.

So Walter found the bar. As long as he was going to stay up all night, he might as well do it drunk. The bar, very large, very hot and noisy, was brilliant with summer-season grotesques: sagging silver-fox ladies, and little stunted jockeys, and pale loud-voiced men wearing cheap fantastic checks. After a couple of drinks, though, the noise seemed faraway. Then, glancing around, he saw the cripple. She was alone at a table, where she sat primly sipping a crème de menthe. They exchanged a smile. Rising, Walter went to join her. "It's not like we were strangers," she said, as he sat down. "Here for the races, I suppose?"

"No," he said, "just a rest. And you?"

She pursed her lips. "Maybe you noticed I've got a clubfoot. Oh, sure now, don't look surprised: you noticed, everybody does. Well, see," she said, twisting the straw in her glass, "see, my doctor's going to give a talk at this convention, going to talk about me and my foot on account of I'm pretty special. Gee, I'm scared. I mean I'm going to have to show off my foot."

Walter said he was sorry, and she said, oh, there was nothing to be sorry about; after all, she was getting a little vacation out of it, wasn't she? "And I haven't been out of the city in six years. It was six years ago I spent a week at the Bear Mountain Inn." Her cheeks were red, rather mottled, and her eyes, set too closely together, were lavender-colored, intense: they seemed never to blink. She wore a gold band on her wedding finger; play-acting, to be sure: it would not have fooled anybody.

"I'm a domestic," she said, answering a question. "And there's nothing wrong with that. It's honest and I like it. The people I work for have the cutest kid, Ronnie. I'm better to him than his mother, and he loves me more; he's told me so. That one, she stays drunk all the time."

It was depressing to listen to, but Walter, afraid suddenly to be alone, stayed and drank and talked in the way he'd once talked to Anna Stimson. Shh! she said at one point, for his voice had risen too high, and a good many people were staring. Walter said the hell with them, he didn't care; it was as if his brain were made of glass, and all the whiskey he'd drunk had turned into a hammer; he could feel the shattered pieces rattling in his head, distorting focus, falsifying shape; the cripple, for instance, seemed not one person, but several: Irving, his mother, a man named Bonaparte, Margaret, all those and others: more and more he came to understand experience is a circle of which no moment can be isolated, forgotten.

6

The bar was closing. They went Dutch on the check and, while waiting for change, neither spoke. Watching him with her unblinking lavender eyes, she seemed quite controlled, but there was going on inside, he could tell, some subtle agitation. When the waiter returned they divided the change, and she said: "If you want to, you can come to my room." A rashlike blush covered her face. "I mean, you said you didn't have any place to sleep. . . ." Walter reached out and took her hand: the smile she gave him was touchingly shy.

Reeking with dime-store perfume, she came out of the bathroom wearing only a sleazy flesh-colored kimono, and the monstrous black shoe. It was then that he realized he could never go through with it. And he'd never felt so sorry for himself: not even Anna Stimson would ever have forgiven him this. "Don't look," she said, and there was a trembling in her voice, "I'm funny about anybody seeing my foot."

He turned to the window, where pressing elm leaves rustled in the rain, and lightning, too far off for sound, winked whitely. "All right," she said. Walter did not move.

"All right," she repeated anxiously. "Shall I put out the light? I mean, maybe you like to get ready—in the dark."

He came to the edge of the bed, and, bending down, kissed her cheek. "I think you're so very sweet, but . . ."

The telephone interrupted. She looked at him dumbly. "Jesus God," she said, and covered the mouthpiece with her hand, "it's long-distance! I'll bet it's about Ronnie! I'll bet he's sick, or—hello—what?—Ranney? Gee, no. You've got the wrong . . ."

"Wait," said Walter, taking the receiver. "This is me, this is Walter Ranney."

"Hello, Walter."

The voice, dull and sexless and remote, went straight to the pit of his stomach. The room seemed to seesaw, to buckle. A mustache of sweat sprouted on his upper lip. "Who is this?" he said so slowly the words did not connect coherently.

"Oh, you know me, Walter. You've known me a long time." Then silence: whoever it was had hung up.

"Gee," said the woman, "now how do you suppose they knew you were in my room? I mean—say, was it bad news? You look kind of . . ."

Walter fell across her, clutching her to him, pressing his wet cheek against hers. "Hold me," he said, discovering he could still cry. "Hold me, please."

"Poor little boy," she said, patting his back. "My poor little boy: we're awfully alone in this world, aren't we?" And presently he went to sleep in her arms.

But he had not slept since, nor could he now, not even listening to the lazy lull of the fan; in its turning he could hear train wheels: Saratoga to New York, New York to New Orleans. And New Orleans he'd chosen for no special reason, except that it was a town of strangers, and a long way off. Four spinning fan blades, wheels and voices, round and round; and after all, as he saw it now, there was to this network of malice no ending, none whatever.

Water flushed down wall pipes, steps passed overhead, keys jangled in the hall, a news commentator rumbled somewhere beyond, next door a little girl said, why? Why? WHY? Yet in the room there was a sense of silence. His feet shining in the transom-light looked like amputated stone: the gleaming toenails were ten small mirrors, all reflecting greenly. Sitting up, he rubbed sweat off with a towel; now more than anything the heat frightened him, for it made him know tangibly his own helplessness. He threw the towel across the room, where, landing on a lampshade, it swung back and forth. At this moment the telephone rang. And rang. And it was ringing so loud he was sure all the hotel could hear. An army would be pounding at his door. So he pushed his face into the pillow, covered his ears with his hands, and thought: Think of nothing things, think of wind.

Children on Their Birthdays

(1948)

(This story is for Andrew Lyndon.)

Yesterday afternoon the six-o'clock bus ran over Miss Bobbit. I'm not sure what there is to be said about it; after all, she was only ten years old, still I know no one of us in this town will forget her. For one thing, nothing she ever did was ordinary, not from the first time that we saw her, and that was a year ago. Miss Bobbit and her mother, they arrived on that same six-o'clock bus, the one that comes through from Mobile. It happened to be my cousin Billy Bob's birthday, and so most of the children in town were here at our house. We were sprawled on the front porch having tutti-frutti and devil cake when the bus stormed around Deadman's Curve. It was the summer that never rained; rusted dryness coated everything; sometimes when a car passed on the road, raised dust would hang in the still air an hour or more. Aunt El said if they didn't pave the highway soon she was going to move down to the seacoast; but she'd said that for such a long time. Anway, we were sitting on the porch, tutti-frutti melting on our plates, when suddenly, just as we were wishing that something would happen, something did; for out of the red road dust appeared Miss Bobbit. A wiry little girl in a starched, lemon-colored party dress, she sassed along with a grown-up mince, one hand on her hip, the other supporting a spinsterish umbrella. Her mother, lugging two cardboard valises and a wind-up victrola, trailed in the background. She was a gaunt shaggy woman with silent eyes and a hungry smile.

All the children on the porch had grown so still that when a cone of wasps started humming the girls did not set up their usual holler. Their attention was too fixed upon the approach of Miss Bobbit and her mother, who had by now reached the gate. "Begging your pardon," called Miss Bobbit in a voice that was at once silky and childlike, like a pretty piece of ribbon, and immaculately exact, like a movie star or a schoolmarm, "but might we speak with the grown-up persons of the house?" This, of course, meant Aunt El; and, at least to some degree, myself. But Billy Bob and all the other boys, no one of whom was over thirteen, followed down to the gate after us. From their faces you would have thought they'd never seen a girl before. Certainly not like Miss Bobbit. As Aunt El said, whoever heard tell of a child wearing makeup? Tangee gave her lips an orange glow, her hair, rather like a costume wig, was a mass of rosy curls, and her eyes had a knowing, penciled tilt; even so, she had a skinny dignity, she was a lady, and, what is more, she looked you in the eye with manlike directness. "I'm Miss Lily Jane Bobbit, Miss Bobbit from Memphis, Tennessee," she said solemnly. The boys looked down at their toes, and, on the porch, Cora McCall, who Billy Bob was courting at the time, led the girls into a fanfare of giggles. "*Country* children," said Miss Bobbit with an understanding smile, and gave her parasol a saucy whirl. "My mother," and this homely woman allowed an abrupt nod to acknowledge herself, "my mother and I have taken rooms here. Would you be so kind as to point out the house? It belongs to a Mrs. Sawyer." Why, sure, said Aunt El, that's Mrs. Sawyer's, right there across the street. The only boarding house around here, it is an old tall dark place with about two dozen lightning rods scattered on the roof: Mrs. Sawyer is scared to death in a thunderstorm.

Coloring like an apple, Billy Bob said, please ma'am, it being such a hot day and all, wouldn't they rest a spell and have some tutti-frutti? and Aunt El said yes, by all means, but Miss Bobbit shook her head. "Very fattening, tutti-frutti; but *merci* you kindly," and they started across the road, the mother half-dragging her parcels in the dust. Then, and with an earnest expression, Miss Bobbit turned back; the sunflower yellow of her eyes darkened, and she rolled them slightly sideways, as if trying to remember a poem. "My mother has a disorder of the tongue, so it is necessary that I speak for her," she announced rapidly and heaved a sigh. "My mother is a very fine seamstress; she has made dresses for the society of many cities and towns, including Memphis and Tallahassee. No doubt you have noticed and admired the dress I am wearing. Every stitch of it was hand-sewn by my mother. My mother can copy any pattern, and just recently she won a twenty-five-dollar prize from the *Ladies' Home Journal*. My mother can also crochet, knit and embroider. If you want any kind of sewing done, please come to my mother. Please advise your friends and family. Thank you." And then, with a rustle and a swish, she was gone.

Cora McCall and the girls pulled their hair-ribbons nervously, suspiciously, and looked very put out and prune-faced. I'm *Miss* Bobbit, said Cora, twisting her face into an evil imitation, and I'm Princess Elizabeth, that's who I am, ha, ha, ha. Furthermore, said Cora, that dress was just as tacky as could be; personally, Cora said, all my clothes come from Atlanta; plus a pair of shoes from New York, which is not even to mention my silver turquoise ring all the way from Mexico City, Mexico. Aunt El said they ought not to behave that way about a fellow child, a stranger in the town, but the girls went on like a huddle of witches, and certain boys, the sillier ones that liked to be with the girls, joined in and said things that made Aunt El go red and declare she was going to send them all home and tell their daddies, to boot. But before she could carry forward this threat Miss Bobbit herself intervened by traipsing across the Sawyer porch, costumed in a new and startling manner.

The older boys, like Billy Bob and Preacher Star, who had sat quiet while the girls razzed Miss Bobbit, and who had watched the house into which she'd disappeared with misty, ambitious faces, they now straightened up and ambled down to the gate. Cora McCall sniffed and poked out her lower lip, but the rest of us went and sat on the steps. Miss Bobbit paid us no mind whatever. The Sawyer yard is dark with mulberry trees and it is planted with grass and sweet shrub. Sometimes after a rain you can smell the sweet shrub all the way into our house; and in the center of this yard there is a sundial which Mrs. Sawyer installed in 1912 as a memorial to her Boston bull, Sunny, who died after having lapped up a bucket of paint. Miss Bobbit pranced into the yard toting the victrola, which she put on the sundial; she wound it up, and started a record playing, and it played the Court of Luxemborg. By now it was almost nightfall, a firefly hour, blue as milkglass; and birds like arrows swooped together and swept into the folds of trees. Before storms, leaves and flowers appear to burn with a private light, color, and Miss Bobbit, got up in a little white skirt like a powderpuff and with strips of gold-glittering tinsel ribboning her hair, seemed, set against the darkening all around, to contain this illuminated quality. She held her arms arched over her head, her hands lily-limp, and stood straight up on the tips of her toes. She stood that way for a good long while, and Aunt El said it was right smart of her. Then she began to waltz around and around, and around and around she went until Aunt El said, why, she was plain dizzy from the sight. She stopped only when it was time to rewind the victrola; and when the moon came rolling down the ridge, and the last supper bell had sounded, and all the children had gone home, and the night iris was beginning to bloom, Miss Bobbit was still there in the dark turning like a top.

We did not see her again for some time. Preacher Star came every morning to our house and stayed straight through to supper. Preacher is a rail-thin boy with a butchy shock of red hair; he has eleven brothers and sisters, and even they are afraid of him, for he has a terrible temper, and is famous in these parts for his green-eyed meanness: last fourth of July he whipped Ollie Overton so bad that Ollie's family had to send him to the hospital in Pensacola; and there was another time he bit off half a mule's ear, chewed it and spit it on the ground. Before Billy Bob got his growth, Preacher played the devil with him, too. He used to drop cockleburrs down his collar, and rub pepper in his eyes, and tear up his homework. But now they are the biggest friends in town: talk alike, walk alike; and occasionally they disappear together for whole days, Lord knows where to. But during these days when Miss Bobbit did not appear they stayed close to the house. They would stand around in the yard trying to sling-shot sparrows off telephone poles; or sometimes Billy Bob would play his ukulele, and they would sing so loud Uncle Billy Bob, who is Judge for this county, claimed he could hear them all the way to the courthouse: *send me a letter, send it by mail, send it in care of the Birmingham jail.* Miss Bobbit did not hear them; at least she never poked her head out the door. Then one day Mrs. Sawyer, coming over to borrow a cup of sugar, rattled on a good deal about her new boarders. You know, she said, squinting her chicken-bright eyes, the husband was a crook, uh huh, the child told me herself. Hasn't an ounce of shame, not a mite. Said her daddy was the dearest daddy and the sweetest singing man in the whole of Tennessee. . . . And I said, honey, where is he? and just as off-hand as you please she says, Oh, he's in the penitentiary and we don't hear from him no more. Say, now, does that make your blood run cold? Uh huh, and I been thinking, her mama, I been thinking she's some kinda foreigner: never says a word, and sometimes it looks like she don't understand what nobody says to her. And you know, they eat everything *raw*. *Raw* eggs, *raw* turnips, carrots—no meat whatsoever. For reasons of health, the child says, but ho! she's been straight out on the bed running a fever since last Tuesday.

That same afternoon Aunt El went out to water her roses, only to discover them gone. These were special roses, ones she'd planned to send to the flower show in Mobile, and so naturally she got a little hysterical. She rang up the Sheriff, and said, listen here, Sheriff, you come over here right fast. I mean somebody's got off with all my Lady Anne's that I've devoted myself to heart and soul since early spring. When the Sheriff's car pulled up outside our house, all the neighbors along the street came out on their porches, and Mrs. Sawyer, layers of cold cream whitening her face, trotted across the road. Oh shoot, she said, very disappointed to find no one had been murdered, oh shoot, she said, nobody's stole them roses. Your Billy Bob brought them roses over and left them for little Bobbit. Aunt El did not say one word. She just marched over to the peach tree, and cut herself a switch. Ohhh, Billy Bob, she stalked along the street calling his name, and then she found him down at Speedy's garage where he and Preacher were watching Speedy take a motor apart. She simply lifted him by the hair and, switching blueblazes, towed him home. But she couldn't make him say he was sorry and she couldn't make him cry. And when she was finished with him he ran into the backyard and climbed high into the tower of a pecan tree and swore he wasn't ever going to come down. Then his daddy stood at the window and called to him: Son, we aren't mad with you, so come down and eat your supper. But Billy Bob wouldn't budge. Aunt El went and leaned against the tree. She spoke in a voice soft as the gathering light. I'm sorry, son, she said, I didn't mean whipping you so hard like that. I've fixed a nice supper, son, potato salad and boiled ham and deviled eggs. Go away, said Billy Bob, I don't want no supper, and I hate you like all-fire. His daddy said he ought not to talk like that to his mother, and she began to cry. She stood there under the tree and cried, raising the hem of her skirt to dab at her eyes. I don't hate you, son. . . . If I didn't love you I wouldn't whip you. The pecan leaves began to rattle; Billy Bob slid slowly to the ground, and Aunt El, rushing her fingers through his hair, pulled him against her. Aw, Ma, he said, Aw, Ma.

After supper Billy Bob came and flung himself on the foot of my bed. He smelled all sour and sweet, the way boys do, and I felt very sorry for him, especially because he looked so worried. His eyes were almost shut with worry. You're s'posed to send sick folks flowers, he said righteously. About this time we heard the victrola, a lilting far-away sound, and a night moth flew through the window, drifting in the air delicate as the music. But it was dark now, and we couldn't tell if Miss Bobbit was dancing. Billy Bob, as though he were in pain, doubled up on the bed like a jackknife; but his face was suddenly clear, his grubby boy-eyes twitching like candles. She's so cute, he whispered, she's the cutest dickens I ever saw, gee, to hell with it, I don't care, I'd pick all the roses in China.

Preacher would have picked all the roses in China, too. He was as crazy about her as Billy Bob. But Miss Bobbit did not notice them. The sole communication we had with her was a note to Aunt El thanking her for the flowers. Day after day she sat on her porch, always dressed to beat the band, and doing a piece of embroidery, or combing curls in her hair, or reading a Webster's dictionary—formal, but friendly enough; if you said good-day to her she said good-day to you. Even so, the boys never could seem to get up the nerve to go over and talk with her, and most of the time she simply looked through them, even when they tomcatted up and down the street trying to get her eye. They wrestled, played Tarzan, did foolheaded bicycle tricks. It was a sorry business. A great many girls in town strolled by the Sawyer house two and three times within an hour just on the chance of getting a look. Some of the girls who did this were: Cora McCall, Mary Murphy Jones, Janice Ackerman. Miss Bobbit did not show any interest in them either. Cora would not speak to Billy Bob any more. The same was true with Janice and Preacher. As a matter of fact, Janice wrote Preacher a letter in red ink on lace-trimmed paper in which she told him he was vile beyond all human beings and words, that she considered their engagement broken, that he could have back the stuffed squirrel he'd given her. Preacher, saying he wanted to act nice, stopped her the next time she passed our house, and said, well, hell, she could keep that old squirrel if she wanted to. Afterwards, he couldn't understand why Janice ran away bawling the way she did.

Then one day the boys were being crazier than usual; Billy Bob was sagging around in his daddy's World War khakis, and Preacher, stripped to the waist, had a naked woman drawn on his chest with one of Aunt El's old lipsticks. They looked like perfect fools, but Miss Bobbit, reclining in a swing, merely yawned. It was noon, and there was no one passing in the street, except a colored girl, baby-fat and sugar-plum shaped, who hummed along carrying a pail of blackberries. But the boys, teasing at her like gnats, joined hands and wouldn't let her go by, not until she paid a tariff. I ain't studyin' no tariff, she said, what kinda tariff you talkin' about, mister? A party in the barn, said Preacher, between clenched teeth, mighty nice party in the barn. And she, with a sulky shrug, said, huh, she intended studyin' no barn parties. Whereupon Billy Bob capsized her berry pail, and when she, with despairing, piglike shrieks, bent down in futile gestures of rescue, Preacher, who can be mean as the devil, gave her behind a kick which sent her sprawling jellylike among the blackberries and the dust. Miss Bobbit came tearing across the road, her finger wagging like a metronome; like a schoolteacher she clapped her hands, stamped her foot, said: "It is a well-known fact that gentlemen are put on the face of this earth for the protection of ladies. Do you suppose boys behave this way in towns like Memphis, New York, London, Hollywood or Paris?" The boys hung back, and shoved their hands in their pockets. Miss Bobbit helped the colored girl to her feet; she dusted her off, dried her eyes, held out a handkerchief and told her to blow. "A pretty pass," she said, "a fine situation when a lady can't walk safely in the public daylight."

Then the two of them went back and sat on Mrs. Sawyer's porch; and for the next year they were never far apart, Miss Bobbit and this baby elephant, whose name was Rosalba Cat. At first, Mrs. Sawyer raised a fuss about Rosalba being so much at her house. She told Aunt El that it went against the grain to have a nigger lolling smack there in plain sight on her front porch. But Miss Bobbit had a certain magic, whatever she did she did it with completeness, and so directly, so solemnly, that there was nothing to do but accept it. For instance, the tradespeople in town used to snicker when they called her *Miss* Bobbit; but by and by she was Miss Bobbit, and they gave her stiff little bows as she whirled by spinning her parasol. Miss Bobbit told everyone that Rosalba was her sister, which caused a good many jokes; but like most of her ideas, it gradually seemed natural, and when we would overhear them calling each other Sister Rosalba and Sister Bobbit none of us cracked a smile. But Sister Rosalba and Sister Bobbit did some queer things. There was the business about the dogs. Now there are a great many dogs in this town, rat terriers, bird dogs, bloodhounds; they trail along the forlorn noon-hot streets in sleepy herds of six to a dozen, all waiting only for dark and the moon, when straight through the lonesome hours you can hear them howling: someone is dying, someone is dead. Miss Bobbit complained to the Sheriff; she said that certain of the dogs always planted themselves under her window, and that she was a light sleeper to begin with; what is more, and as Sister Rosalba said, she did not believe they were dogs at all, but some kind of devil. Naturally the Sheriff did nothing; and so she took the matter into her own hands. One morning, after an especially loud night, she was seen stalking through the town with Rosalba at her side, Rosalba carrying a flower basket filled with rocks; whenever they saw a dog they paused while Miss Bobbit scrutinized him. Sometimes she would shake her head, but more often she said, "Yes, that's one of them, Sister Rosalba," and Sister Rosalba, with ferocious aim, would take a rock from her basket and crack the dog between the eyes.

Another thing that happened concerns Mr. Henderson. Mr. Henderson has a back room in the Sawyer house; a tough runt of a man who formerly was a wildcat oil prospector in Oklahoma, he is about seventy years old and, like a lot of old men, obsessed by functions of the body. Also, he is a terrible drunk. One time he had been drunk for two weeks; whenever he heard Miss Bobbit and Sister Rosalba moving around the house, he would charge to the top of the stairs and bellow down to Mrs. Sawyer that there were midgets in the walls trying to get at his supply of toilet paper. They've already stolen fifteen cents' worth, he said. One evening, when the two girls were sitting under a tree in the yard, Mr. Henderson, sporting nothing more than a nightshirt, stamped out after them. Steal all my toilet paper, will you? he hollered, I'll show you midgets. . . . Somebody come help me, else these midget bitches are liable to make off with every sheet in town. It was Billy Bob and Preacher who caught Mr. Henderson and held him until some grown men arrived and began to tie him up. Miss Bobbit, who had behaved with admirable calm, told the men they did not know how to tie a proper knot, and undertook to do so herself. She did such a good job that all the circulation stopped in Mr. Henderson's hands and feet and it was a month before he could walk again.

It was shortly afterwards that Miss Bobbit paid us a call. She came on Sunday and I was there alone, the family having gone to church. "The odors of a church are so offensive," she said, leaning forward and with her hands folded primly before her. "I don't want you to think I'm a heathen, Mr. C.; I've had enough experience to know that there is a God and that there is a Devil. But the way to tame the Devil is not to go down there to church and listen to what a sinful mean fool he is. No, love the Devil like you love Jesus: because he is a powerful man, and will do you a good turn if he knows you trust him. He has frequently done me good turns, like at dancing school in Memphis. . . . I always called in the Devil to help me get the biggest part in our annual show. That is common sense; you see, I knew Jesus wouldn't have any truck with dancing. Now, as a matter of fact, I have called in the Devil just recently. He is the only one who can help me get out of this town. Not that I live here, not exactly. I think always about somewhere else, somewhere else where everything is dancing, like people dancing in the streets, and everything is pretty, like children on their birthdays. My precious papa said I live in the sky, but if he'd lived more in the sky he'd be rich like he wanted to be. The trouble with my papa was he did not love the Devil, he let the Devil love him. But I am very smart in that respect; I know the next best thing is very often the best. It was the next best thing for us to move to this town; and since I can't pursue my career here, the next best thing for me is to start a little business on the side. Which is what I have done. I am sole subscription agent in this county for an impressive list of magazines, including *Reader's Digest, Popular Mechanics, Dime Detective* and *Child's Life.* To be sure, Mr. C., I'm not here to sell you anything. But I have a thought in mind. I was thinking those two boys that are always hanging around here, it occurred to me that they are men, after all. Do you suppose they would make a pair of likely assistants?"

Billy Bob and Preacher worked hard for Miss Bobbit, and for Sister Rosalba, too. Sister Rosalba carried a line of cosmetics called Dewdrop, and it was part of the boys' job to deliver purchases to her customers. Billy Bob used to be so tired in the evening he could hardly chew his supper. Aunt El said it was a shame and a pity, and finally one day when Billy Bob came down with a touch of sunstroke she said, all right, that settled it, Billy Bob would just have to quit Miss Bobbit. But Billy Bob cussed her out until his daddy had to lock him in his room; whereupon he said he was going to kill himself. Some cook we'd had told him once that if you ate a mess of collards all slopped over with molasses it would kill you sure as shooting; and so that is what he did. I'm dying, he said, rolling back and forth on his bed, I'm dying and nobody cares.

Miss Bobbit came over and told him to hush up. "There's nothing wrong with you, boy," she said. "All you've got is a stomach ache." Then she did something that shocked Aunt El very much: she stripped the covers off Billy Bob and rubbed him down with alcohol from head to toe. When Aunt El told her she did not think that was a nice thing for a little girl to do, Miss Bobbit replied: "I don't know whether it's nice or not, but it's certainly very refreshing." After which Aunt El did all she could to keep Billy Bob from going back to work for her, but his daddy said to leave him alone, they would have to let the boy lead his own life.

Miss Bobbit was very honest about money. She paid Billy Bob and Preacher their exact commission, and she would never let them treat her, as they often tried to do, at the drugstore or to the picture show. "You'd better save your money," she told them. "That is, if you want to go to college. Because neither one of you has got the brains to win a scholarship, not even a football scholarship." But it was over money that Billy Bob and Preacher had a big falling out; that was not the real reason, of course: the real reason was that they had grown cross-eyed jealous over Miss Bobbit. So one day, and he had the gall to do this right in front of Billy Bob, Preacher said to Miss Bobbit that she'd better check her accounts carefully because he had more than a suspicion that Billy Bob wasn't turning over to her *all* the money he collected. That's a damned lie, said Billy Bob, and with a clean left hook he knocked Preacher off the Sawyer porch and jumped after him into a bed of nasturtiums. But once Preacher got a hold on him, Billy Bob didn't stand a chance. Preacher even rubbed dirt in his eyes. During all this, Mrs. Sawyer, leaning out an upper-story window, screamed like an eagle, and Sister Rosalba, fatly cheerful, ambiguously shouted, Kill him! Kill him! Kill him! Only Miss Bobbit seemed to know what she was doing. She plugged in the lawn hose, and gave the boys a close-up, blinding bath. Gasping, Preacher staggered to his feet. Oh, honey, he said, shaking himself like a wet dog, honey, you've got to decide. "Decide *what?*" said Miss Bobbit, right away in a huff. Oh, honey, wheezed Preacher, you don't want us boys killing each other. You got to decide who is your real true sweetheart. "Sweetheart, my eye," said Miss Bobbit. "I should've known better than to get myself involved with a lot of country children. What sort of businessman are you going to make? Now, you listen here, Preacher Star: I don't want a sweetheart, and if I did, it wouldn't be you. As a matter of fact, you don't even get up when a lady enters the room."

Preacher spit on the ground and swaggered over to Billy Bob. Come on, he said, just as though nothing had happened, she's a hard one, she is, she don't want nothing but to make trouble between two good friends. For a moment it looked as if Billy Bob was going to join him in a peaceful togetherness; but suddenly, coming to his senses, he drew back and made a gesture. The boys regarded each other a full minute, all the closeness between them turning an ugly color: you can't hate so much unless you love, too. And Preacher's face showed all of this. But there was nothing for him to do except go away. Oh, yes, Preacher, you looked so lost that day that for the first time I really liked you, so skinny and mean and lost going down the road all by yourself.

They did not make it up, Preacher and Billy Bob; and it was not because they didn't want to, it was only that there did not seem to be any straight way for their friendship to happen again. But they couldn't get rid of this friendship: each was always aware of what the other was up to; and when Preacher found himself a new buddy, Billy Bob moped around for days, picking things up, dropping them again, or doing sudden wild things, like purposely poking his finger in the electric fan. Sometimes in the evenings Preacher would pause by the gate and talk with Aunt El. It was only to torment Billy Bob, I suppose, but he stayed friendly with all of us, and at Christmas time he gave us a huge box of shelled peanuts. He left a present for Billy Bob, too. It turned out to be a book of Sherlock Holmes; and on the flyleaf there was scribbled, "Friends Like Ivy On the Wall Must Fall." That's the corniest thing I ever saw, Billy Bob said. Jesus, what a dope he is! But then, and though it was a cold winter day, he went in the backyard and climbed up into the pecan tree, crouching there all afternoon in the blue December branches.

But most of the time he was happy, because Miss Bobbit was there, and she was always sweet to him now. She and Sister Rosalba treated him like a man; that is to say, they allowed him to do everything for them. On the other hand, they let him win at three-handed bridge, they never questioned his lies, nor discouraged his ambitions. It was a happy while. However, trouble started again when school began. Miss Bobbit refused to go. "It's ridiculous," she said, when one day the principal, Mr. Copland, came around to investigate, "really ridiculous; I can read and write and there are *some* people in this town who have every reason to know that I can count money. No, Mr. Copland, consider for a moment and you will see neither of us has the time nor energy. After all, it would only be a matter of whose spirit broke first, yours or mine. And besides, what is there for you to teach me? Now, if you knew anything about dancing, that would be another matter; but under the circumstances, yes, Mr. Copland, under the circumstances, I suggest we forget the whole thing." Mr. Copland was perfectly willing to. But the rest of the town thought she ought to be whipped. Horace Deasley wrote a piece in the paper which was titled "A Tragic Situation." It was, in his opinion, a tragic situation when a small girl could defy what he, for some reason, termed the Constitution of the United States. The article ended with a question: *Can she get away with it?* She did; and so did Sister Rosalba. Only she was colored, so no one cared. Billy Bob was not as lucky. It was school for him, all right; but he might as well have stayed home for the good it did him. On his first report card he got three F's, a record of some sort. But he is a smart boy. I guess he just couldn't live through those hours without Miss Bobbit; away from her he always seemed half-asleep. He was always in a fight, too; either his eye was black, or his lip was split, or his walk had a limp. He never talked about these fights, but Miss Bobbit was shrewd enough to guess the reason why. "You are a dear, I know, I know. And I appreciate you, Billy Bob. Only don't fight with people because of me. Of course they say mean things about me. But do you know why that is, Billy Bob? It's a compliment, kind of. Because deep down they think I'm absolutely wonderful."

And she was right: if you are not admired no one will take the trouble to disapprove. But actually we had no idea of how wonderful she was until there appeared the man known as Manny Fox. This happened late in February. The first news we had of Manny Fox was a series of jovial placards posted up in the stores around town: Manny Fox Presents the Fan Dancer Without the Fan; then, in smaller print: Also, Sensational Amateur Program Featuring Your Own Neighbors—First Prize, A Genuine Hollywood Screen Test. All this was to take place the following Thursday. The tickets were priced at one dollar each, which around here is a lot of money; but it is not often that we get any kind of flesh entertainment, so everybody shelled out their money and made a great to-do over the whole thing. The drugstore cowboys talked dirty all week, mostly about the fan dancer without the fan, who turned out to be Mrs. Manny Fox. They stayed down the highway at the Chucklewood Tourist Camp; but they were in town all day, driving around in an old Packard which had Manny Fox's full name stenciled on all four doors. His wife was a deadpan pimento-tongued redhead with wet lips and moist eyelids; she was quite large actually, but compared to Manny Fox she seemed rather frail, for he was a fat cigar of a man.

They made the pool hall their headquarters, and every afternoon you could find them there, drinking beer and joking with the town loafs. As it developed, Manny Fox's business affairs were not restricted to theatrics. He also ran a kind of employment bureau: slowly he let it be known that for a fee of $150 he could get for any adventurous boys in the county high-class jobs working on fruit ships sailing from New Orleans to South America. The chance of a lifetime, he called it. There are not two boys around here who readily lay their hands on so much as five dollars; nevertheless, a good dozen managed to raise the money. Ada Willingham took all she'd saved to buy an angel tombstone for her husband and gave it to her son, and Acey Trump's papa sold an option on his cotton crop.

But the night of the show! That was a night when all was forgotten: mortgages, and the dishes in the kitchen sink. Aunt El said you'd think we were going to the opera, everybody so dressed up, so pink and sweet-smelling. The Odeon had not been so full since the night they gave away the matched set of sterling silver. Practically everybody had a relative in the show, so there was a lot of nervousness to contend with. Miss Bobbit was the only contestant we knew real well. Billy Bob couldn't sit still; he kept telling us over and over that we mustn't applaud for anybody but Miss Bobbit; Aunt El said that would be very rude, which sent Billy Bob off into a state again; and when his father bought us all bags of popcorn he wouldn't touch his because it would make his hands greasy, and please, another thing, we mustn't be noisy and eat ours while Miss Bobbit was performing. That she was to be a contestant had come as a last-minute surprise. It was logical enough, and there were signs that should've told us; the fact, for instance, that she had not set foot outside the Sawyer house in how many days? And the victrola going half the night, her shadow whirling on the window shade, and the secret, stuffed look on Sister Rosalba's face whenever asked after Sister Bobbit's health. So there was her name on the program, listed second, in fact, though she did not appear for a long while. First came Manny Fox, greased and leering, who told a lot of peculiar jokes, clapping his hands, ha, ha. Aunt El said if he told another joke like that she was going to walk straight out: he did, and she didn't. Before Miss Bobbit came on there were eleven contestants, including Eustacia Bernstein, who imitated movie stars so that they all sounded like Eustacia, and there was an extraordinary Mr. Buster Riley, a jug-eared old wool-hat from way in the back country who played "Waltzing Matilda" on a saw. Up to that point, he was the hit of the show; not that there was any marked difference in the various receptions, for everybody applauded generously, everybody, that is, except Preacher Star. He was sitting two rows ahead of us, greeting each act with a donkey-loud boo. Aunt El said she was never going to speak to him again. The only person he ever applauded was Miss Bobbit. No doubt the Devil was on her side, but she deserved it. Out she came, tossing her hips, her curls, rolling her eyes. You could tell right away it wasn't going to be one of her classical numbers. She tapped across the stage, daintily holding up the sides of a cloud-blue skirt. That's the cutest thing I ever saw, said Billy Bob, smacking his thigh, and Aunt El had to agree that Miss Bobbit looked real sweet. When she started to twirl the whole audience broke into spontaneous applause; so she did it all over again, hissing, "Faster, faster," at poor Miss Adelaide, who was at the piano doing her Sunday-school best. "I was born in China, and raised in Jay-pan . . ." We had never heard her sing before, and she had a rowdy sandpaper voice. ". . . if you don't like my peaches, stay away from my can, o-ho o-ho!" Aunt El gasped; she gasped again when Miss Bobbit, with a bump, up-ended her skirt to display blue-lace underwear, thereby collecting most of the whistles the boys had been saving for the fan dancer without the fan, which was just as well, as it later turned out, for that lady, to the tune of "An Apple for the Teacher" and cries of gyp gyp, did her routine attired in a bathing suit. But showing off her bottom was not Miss Bobbit's final triumph. Miss Adelaide commenced an ominous thundering in the darker keys, at which point Sister Rosalba, carrying a lighted Roman candle, rushed onstage and handed it to Miss Bobbit, who was in the midst of a full split; she made it, too, and just as she did the Roman candle burst into fiery balls of red, white and blue, and we all had to stand up because she was singing "The Star Spangled Banner" at the top of her lungs. Aunt El said afterwards that it was one of the most gorgeous things she'd ever seen on the American stage.

Well, she surely did deserve a Hollywood screen test and, inasmuch as she won the contest, it looked as though she were going to get it. Manny Fox said she was: honey, he said, you're real star stuff. Only he skipped town the next day, leaving nothing but hearty promises. Watch the mails, my friends, you'll all be hearing from me. That is what he said to the boys whose money he'd taken, and that is what he said to Miss Bobbit. There are three deliveries daily, and this sizable group gathered at the post office for all of them, a jolly crowd growing gradually joyless. How their hands trembled when a letter slid into their mailbox. A terrible hush came over them as the days passed. They all knew what the other was thinking, but no one could bring himself to say it, not even Miss Bobbit. Postmistress Patterson said it plainly, however: the man's a crook, she said, I knew he was a crook to begin with, and if I have to look at your faces one more day I'll shoot myself.

Finally, at the end of two weeks, it was Miss Bobbit who broke the spell. Her eyes had grown more vacant than anyone had ever supposed they might, but one day, after the last mail was up, all her old sizzle came back. "O.K., boys, it's lynch law now," she said, and proceeded to herd the whole troupe home with her. This was the first meeting of the Manny Fox Hangman's Club, an organization which, in a more social form, endures to this day, though Manny Fox has long since been caught and, so to say, hung. Credit for this went quite properly to Miss Bobbit. Within a week she'd written over three hundred descriptions of Manny Fox and dispatched them to Sheriffs throughout the South; she also wrote letters to papers in the larger cities, and these attracted wide attention. As a result, four of the robbed boys were offered good-paying jobs by the United Fruit Company, and late this spring, when Manny Fox was arrested in Uphigh, Arkansas, where he was pulling the same old dodge, Miss Bobbit was presented with a Good Deed Merit award from the Sunbeam Girls of America. For some reason, she made a point of letting the world know that this did not exactly thrill her. "I do not approve of the organization," she said. "All that rowdy bugle blowing. It's neither good-hearted nor truly feminine. And anyway, what is a good deed? Don't let anybody fool you, a good deed is something you do because you want something in return." It would be reassuring to report she was wrong, and that her just reward, when at last it came, was given out of kindness and love. However, this is not the case. About a week ago the boys involved in the swindle all received from Manny Fox checks covering their losses, and Miss Bobbit, with clodhopping determination, stalked into a meeting of the Hangman's Club, which is now an excuse for drinking beer and playing poker every Thursday night. "Look, boys," she said, laying it on the line, "none of you ever thought to see that money again, but now that you have, you ought to invest it in something practical—like me." The proposition was that they should pool their money and finance her trip to Hollywood; in return, they would get ten percent of her life's earnings which, after she was a star, and that would not be very long, would make them all rich men. "At least," as she said, "in this part of the country." Not one of the boys wanted to do it: but when Miss Bobbit looked at you, what was there to say?

Since Monday, it has been raining buoyant summer rain shot through with sun, but dark at night and full of sound, full of dripping leaves, watery chimings, sleepless scuttlings. Billy Bob is wide-awake, dry-eyed, though everything he does is a little frozen and his tongue is as stiff as a bell tongue. It has not been easy for him, Miss Bobbit's going. Because she'd meant more than that. Than what? Than being thirteen years old and crazy in love. She was the queer things in him, like the pecan tree and liking books and caring enough about people to let them hurt him. She was the things he was afraid to show anyone else. And in the dark the music trickled through the rain: won't there be nights when we will hear it just as though it were really there? And afternoons when the shadows will be all at once confused, and she will pass before us, unfurling across the lawn like a pretty piece of ribbon? She laughed to Billy Bob; she held his hand, she even kissed him. "I'm not going to die," she said. "You'll come out there, and we'll climb a mountain, and we'll all live there together, you and me and Sister Rosalba." But Billy Bob knew it would never happen that way, and so when the music came through the dark he would stuff the pillow over his head.

Only there was a strange smile about yesterday, and that was the day she was leaving. Around noon the sun came out, bringing with it into the air all the sweetness of wisteria. Aunt El's yellow Lady Anne's were blooming again, and she did something wonderful, she told Billy Bob he could pick them and give them to Miss Bobbit for good-bye. All afternoon Miss Bobbit sat on the porch surrounded by people who stopped by to wish her well. She looked as though she were going to Communion, dressed in white and with a white parasol. Sister Rosalba had given her a handkerchief, but she had to borrow it back because she couldn't stop blubbering. Another little girl brought a baked chicken, presumably to be eaten on the bus; the only trouble was she'd forgotten to take out the insides before cooking it. Miss Bobbit's mother said that was all right by her, chicken was chicken; which is memorable because it is the single opinion she ever voiced. There was only one sour note. For hours Preacher Star had been hanging around down at the corner, sometimes standing at the curb tossing a coin, and sometimes hiding behind a tree, as if he didn't want anyone to see him. It made everybody nervous. About twenty minutes before bus time he sauntered up and leaned against our gate. Billy Bob was still in the garden picking roses; by now he had enough for a bonfire, and their smell was as heavy as wind. Preacher stared at him until he lifted his head. As they looked at each other the rain began again, falling fine as sea spray and colored by a rainbow. Without a word, Preacher went over and started helping Billy Bob separate the roses into two giant bouquets: together they carried them to the curb. Across the street there were bumblebees of talk, but when Miss Bobbit saw them, two boys whose flower-masked faces were like yellow moons, she rushed down the steps, her arms outstretched. You could see what was going to happen; and we called out, our voices like lightning in the rain, but Miss Bobbit, running toward those moons of roses, did not seem to hear. That is when the six-o'clock bus ran over her.

MASTER MISERY

(1949)

Her high heels, clacking across the marble foyer, made her think of ice cubes rattling in a glass, and the flowers, those autumn chrysanthemums in the urn at the entrance, if touched they would shatter, splinter, she was sure, into frozen dust; yet the house was warm, even somewhat overheated, but cold, and Sylvia shivered, but cold, like the snowy swollen wastes of the secretary's face: Miss Mozart, who dressed all in white, as though she were a nurse. Perhaps she really was; that, of course, could be the answer. Mr. Revercomb, you are mad, and this is your nurse; she thought about it for a moment; well, no. And now the butler brought her scarf. His beauty touched her: slender, so gentle, a Negro with freckled skin and reddish, unreflecting eyes. As he opened the door, Miss Mozart appeared, her starched uniform rustling dryly in the hall. "We hope you will return," she said, and handed Sylvia a sealed envelope. "Mr. Revercomb was most particularly pleased."

Outside, dusk was falling like blue flakes, and Sylvia walked crosstown along the November streets until she reached the lonely upper reaches of Fifth Avenue. It occurred to her then that she might walk home through the park: an act of defiance almost, for Henry and Estelle, always insistent upon their city wisdom, had said over and again, Sylvia, you have no idea how dangerous it is, walking in the park after dark; look what happened to Myrtle Calisher. This isn't Easton, honey. That was the other thing they said. And said. God, she was sick of it. Still, and aside from a few of the other typists at SnugFare, an underwear company for which she worked, who else in New York did she know? Oh, it would be all right if only she did not have to live with them, if she could afford somewhere a small room of her own; but there in that chintz-cramped apartment she sometimes felt she would choke them both. And why had she come to New York? For whatever reason, and it was indeed becoming vague, a principal cause of leaving Easton had been to rid herself of Henry and Estelle; or rather, their counterparts, though in point of fact Estelle was actually from Easton, a town north of Cincinnati. She and Sylvia had grown up together. The real trouble with Henry and Estelle was that they were so excruciatingly married. Namby-pamby, bootsytotsy, and everything had a name: the telephone was Tinkling Tillie, the sofa, Our Nelle, the bed, Big Bear; yes, and what about those His-Her towels, those He-She pillows? Enough to drive you loony. "Loony!" she said aloud, the quiet park erasing her voice. It was lovely now, and she was right to have walked here, with wind moving through the leaves, and globe lamps, freshly aglow, kindling the chalk drawings of children, pink birds, blue arrows, green hearts. But suddenly, like a pair of obscene words, there appeared on the path two boys: pimple-faced, grinning, they loomed in the dusk like menacing flames, and Sylvia, passing them, felt a burning all through her, quite as though she'd brushed fire. They turned and followed her past a deserted playground, one of them bump-bumping a stick along an iron fence, the other whistling: these two sounds accumulated around her like the gathering roar of an oncoming engine, and when one of the boys, with a laugh, called, "Hey, whatsa hurry?" her mouth twisted for breath. Don't, she thought, thinking to throw down her purse and run. At that moment, however, a man walking a dog came up a sidepath, and she followed at his heels to the exit.

Wouldn't they feel gratified, Henry and Estelle, wouldn't they we-told-you-so if she were to tell them? and, what is more, Estelle would write it home and the next thing you knew it would be all over Easton that she'd been raped in Central Park. She spent the rest of the way home despising New York: anonymity, its virtuous terror; and the speaking drainpipe, all-night light, ceaseless footfall, subway corridor, numbered door (3C).

"Shh, honey," Estelle said, sidling out of the kitchen, "Bootsy's doing his homework." Sure enough, Henry, a law student at Columbia, was hunched over his books in the living room, and Sylvia, at Estelle's request, took off her shoes before tiptoeing through. Once inside her room, she threw herself on the bed and put her hands over her eyes. Had today really happened? Miss Mozart and Mr. Revercomb, were they really in the tall house on Seventy-eighth Street?

"So, honey, what happened today?" Estelle had entered without knocking.

Sylvia sat up on her elbow. "Nothing. Except that I typed ninety-seven letters."

"About what, honey?" asked Estelle, using Sylvia's hairbrush.

"Oh, hell, what do you suppose? SnugFare, the shorts that safely support our leaders of Science and Industry."

"Gee, honey, don't sound so cross. I don't know what's wrong with you sometimes. You sound so cross. Ouch! Why don't you get a new brush? This one's just knotted with hair. . . ."

"Mostly yours."

"What did you say?"

"Skip it."

"Oh, I thought you said something. Anyway, like I was saying, I wish you didn't have to go to that office and come home every day feeling cross and out of sorts. Personally, and I said this to Bootsy just last night and he agreed with me one hundred percent, I said, Bootsy, I think Sylvia ought to get married: a girl high-strung like that needs her tensions relaxed. There's no earthly reason why you shouldn't. I mean maybe you're not pretty in the ordinary sense, but you have beautiful eyes, and an intelligent, really sincere look. In fact you're the sort of girl any professional man would be lucky to get. And I should think you would want to . . . Look what a different person I am since I married Henry. Doesn't it make you lonesome seeing how happy we are? I'm here to tell you, honey, that there is nothing like lying in bed at night with a man's arms around you and . . ."

"Estelle! For Christ's sake!" Sylvia sat bolt upright in bed, anger on her cheeks like rouge. But after a moment she bit her lip and lowered her eyelids. "I'm sorry," she said, "I didn't mean to shout. Only I wish you wouldn't talk like that."

"It's all right," said Estelle, smiling in a dumb, puzzled way. Then she went over and gave Sylvia a kiss. "I understand, honey. It's just that you're plain worn out. And I'll bet you haven't had anything to eat either. Come on in the kitchen and I'll scramble you some eggs."

When Estelle set the eggs before her, Sylvia felt quite ashamed; after all, Estelle was trying to be nice; and so then, as though to make it all up, she said: "Something did happen today."

Estelle sat down across from her with a cup of coffee, and Sylvia went on: "I don't know how to tell about it. It's so very odd. But— well, I had lunch at the Automat today, and I had to share the table with these three men. I might as well have been invisible because they talked about the most personal things. One of the men said his girl friend was going to have a baby and he didn't know where he was going to get the money to do anything about it. So one of the other men asked him why didn't he sell something. He said he didn't have anything to sell. Whereupon the third man (he was rather delicate and didn't look as if he belonged with the others) said yes, there was something he could sell: *dreams*. Even I laughed, but the man shook his head and said very seriously: no, it was perfectly true, his wife's aunt, Miss Mozart, worked for a rich man who bought dreams, regular night-time dreams—from anybody. And he wrote down the man's name and address and gave it to his friend; but the man simply left it lying on the table. It was too crazy for him, he said."

"Me, too," Estelle put in a little righteously.

"I don't know," said Sylvia, lighting a cigarette. "But I couldn't get it out of my head. The name written on the paper was A. F. Revercomb and the address was on East Seventy-eighth Street. I only glanced at it for a moment, but it was . . . I don't know, I couldn't seem to forget it. It was beginning to give me a headache. So I left the office early . . ."

Slowly, and with emphasis, Estelle put down her coffee cup. "Honey, listen, you don't mean you went to see him, this Revercomb nut?"

"I didn't mean to," she said, immediately embarrassed. To try and tell about it she now realized was a mistake. Estelle had no imagination, she would never understand. So her eyes narrowed, the way they always did when she composed a lie. "And, as a matter of fact, I didn't," she said flatly. "I started to; but then I realized how silly it was, and went for a walk instead."

"That was sensible of you," said Estelle as she began stacking dishes in the kitchen sink. "Imagine what might have happened. Buying dreams! Whoever heard? Uh uh, honey, this sure isn't Easton."

Before retiring, Sylvia took a Seconal, something she seldom did; but she knew otherwise she would never rest, not with her mind so nimble and somersaulting; then, too, she felt a curious sadness, a sense of loss, as though she'd been the victim of some real or even moral theft, as though, in fact, the boys encountered in the park had snatched (abruptly she switched on the light) her purse. The envelope Miss Mozart had handed her: it was in the purse, and until now she had forgotten it. She tore it open. Inside there was a blue note folded around a bill; on the note there was written: *In payment of one dream, $5*. And now she believed it; it was true, and she had sold Mr. Revercomb a dream. Could it be really so simple as that? She laughed a little as she turned off the light again. If she were to sell a dream only twice a week, think of what she could do: a place somewhere all her own, she thought, deepening toward sleep; ease, like firelight, wavered over her, and there came the moment of twilit lantern slides, deeply deeper. His lips, his arms: telescoped, descending; and distastefully she kicked away the blanket. Were these cold man-arms the arms Estelle had spoken of? Mr. Revercomb's lips brushed her ear as he leaned far into her sleep. Tell me? he whispered.

It was a week before she saw him again, a Sunday afternoon in early December. She'd left the apartment intending to see a movie, but somehow, and as though it had happened without her knowledge, she found herself on Madison Avenue, two blocks from Mr. Revercomb's. It was a cold, silver-skied day, with winds sharp and catching as hollyhock; in store windows icicles of Christmas tinsel twinkled amid mounds of sequined snow: all to Sylvia's distress, for she hated holidays, those times when one is most alone. In one window she saw a spectacle which made her stop still. It was a life-sized, mechanical Santa Claus; slapping his stomach he rocked back and forth in a frenzy of electrical mirth. You could hear beyond the thick glass his squeaky uproarious laughter. The longer she watched the more evil he seemed, until, finally, with a shudder, she turned and made her way into the street of Mr. Revercomb's house. It was, from the outside, an ordinary town house, perhaps a trifle less polished, less imposing than some others, but relatively grand all the same. Winter-withered ivy writhed about the leaded windowpanes and trailed in octopus ropes over the door; at the sides of the door were two small stone lions with blind, chipped eyes. Sylvia took a breath, then rang the bell. Mr. Revercomb's pale and charming Negro recognized her with a courteous smile.

On the previous visit, the parlor in which she had awaited her audience with Mr. Revercomb had been empty except for herself. This time there were others present, women of several appearances, and an excessively nervous, gnat-eyed young man. Had this group been what it resembled, namely, patients in a doctor's anteroom, he would have seemed either an expectant father or a victim of St. Vitus. Sylvia was seated next to him, and his fidgety eyes unbuttoned her rapidly: whatever he saw apparently intrigued him very little, and Sylvia was grateful when he went back to his twitchy preoccupations. Gradually, though, she became conscious of how interested in her the assemblage seemed; in the dim, doubtful light of the plant-filled room their gazes were more rigid than the chairs upon which they sat; one woman was particularly relentless. Ordinarily, her face would have had a soft commonplace sweetness, but now, watching Sylvia, it was ugly with distrust, jealousy. As though trying to tame some creature which might suddenly spring full-fanged, she sat stroking a flea-bitten neck fur, her stare continuing its assault until the earthquake footstep of Miss Mozart was heard in the hall. Immediately, and like frightened students, the group, separating into their individual identities, came to attention. "You, Mr. Pocker," accused Miss Mozart, "you're next!" And Mr. Pocker, wringing his hands, jittering his eyes, followed after her. In the dusk-room the gathering settled again like sun motes.

It began then to rain; melting window reflections quivered on the walls, and Mr. Revercomb's young butler, seeping through the room, stirred a fire in the grate, set tea things upon a table. Sylvia, nearest the fire, felt drowsy with warmth and the noise of rain; her head tilted sideways, she closed her eyes, neither asleep nor really awake. For a long while only the crystal swingings of a clock scratched the polished silence of Mr. Revercomb's house. And then, abruptly, there was an enormous commotion in the hall, capsizing the room into a fury of sound: a bull-deep voice, vulgar as red, roared out: "Stop Oreilly? The ballet butler and who else?" The owner of this voice, a tub-shaped, brick-colored little man, shoved his way to the parlor threshold, where he stood drunkenly seesawing from foot to foot. "Well, well, well," he said, his gin-hoarse voice descending the scale, "and all these ladies before me? But Oreilly is a gentleman, Oreilly waits his turn."

"Not here, he doesn't," said Miss Mozart, stealing up behind him and seizing him sternly by the collar. His face went even redder and his eyes bubbled out: "You're choking me," he gasped, but Miss Mozart, whose green-pale hands were as strong as oak roots, jerked his tie still tighter, and propelled him toward the door, which presently slammed with shattering effect: a tea cup tinkled, and dry dahlia leaves tumbled from their heights. The lady with the fur slipped an aspirin into her mouth. "Dis*gusting*," she said, and the others, all except Sylvia, laughed delicately, admiringly, as Miss Mozart strode past dusting her hands.

It was raining thick and darkly when Sylvia left Mr. Revercomb's. She looked around the desolate street for a taxi; there was nothing, however, and no one; yes, someone, the drunk man who had caused the disturbance. Like a lonely city child, he was leaning against a parked car and bouncing a rubber ball up and down. "Lookit, kid," he said to Sylvia, "lookit, I just found this ball. Do you suppose that means good luck?" Sylvia smiled at him; for all his bravado, she thought him rather harmless, and there was a quality in his face, some grinning sadness suggesting a clown minus makeup. Juggling his ball, he skipped along after her as she headed toward Madison Avenue. "I'll bet I made a fool of myself in there," he said. "When I do things like that I just want to sit down and cry." Standing so long in the rain seemed to have sobered him considerably. "But she ought not to have choked me that way; damn, she's too rough. I've known some rough women: my sister Berenice could brand the wildest bull; but that other one, she's the roughest of the lot. Mark Oreilly's word, she's going to end up in the electric chair," he said, and smacked his lips. "They've got no cause to treat me like that. It's every bit his fault anyhow. I didn't have an awful lot to begin with, but then he took it every bit, and now I've got *niente*, kid, *niente*."

"That's too bad," said Sylvia, though she did not know what she was being sympathetic about. "Are you a clown, Mr. Oreilly?"

"Was," he said.

By this time they had reached the avenue, but Sylvia did not even look for a taxi; she wanted to walk on in the rain with the man who had been a clown. "When I was a little girl I only liked clown dolls," she told him. "My room at home was like a circus."

"I've been other things besides a clown. I have sold insurance also."

"Oh?" said Sylvia, disappointed. "And what do you do now?"

Oreilly chuckled and threw his ball especially high; after the catch his head still remained tilted upward. "I watch the sky," he said. "There I am with my suitcase traveling through the blue. It's where you travel when you've got no place else to go. But what do I do on this planet? I have stolen, begged, and sold my dreams—all for purposes of whiskey. A man cannot travel in the blue without a bottle. Which brings us to a point: how'd you take it, baby, if I asked for the loan of a dollar?"

"I'd take it fine," Sylvia replied, and paused, uncertain of what she'd say next. They wandered along so slowly, the stiff rain enclosing them like an insulating pressure; it was as though she were walking with a childhood doll, one grown miraculous and capable; she reached and held his hand: dear clown traveling in the blue. "But I haven't got a dollar. All I've got is seventy cents."

"No hard feelings," said Oreilly. "But honest, is that the kind of money he's paying nowadays?"

Sylvia knew whom he meant. "No, no—as a matter of fact, I didn't sell him a dream." She made no attempt to explain; she didn't understand it herself. Confronting the graying invisibility of Mr. Revercomb (impeccable, exact as a scale, surrounded in a cologne of clinical odors; flat gray eyes planted like seed in the anonymity of his face and sealed within steel-dull lenses) she could not remember a dream, and so she told of two thieves who had chased her through the park and in and out among the swings of a playground. "Stop, he said for me to stop; there are dreams and dreams, he said, but that is not a real one, that is one you are making up. Now how do you suppose he knew that? So I told him another dream; it was about him, of how he held me in the night with balloons rising and moons falling all around. He said he was not interested in dreams concerning himself." Miss Mozart, who transcribed the dreams in shorthand, was told to call the next person. "I don't think I will go back there again," she said.

"You will," said Oreilly. "Look at me, even I go back, and he has long since finished with me, Master Misery."

"Master Misery? Why do you call him that?"

They had reached the corner where the maniacal Santa Claus rocked and bellowed. His laughter echoed in the rainy squeaking street, and a shadow of him swayed in the rainbow lights of the pavement. Oreilly, turning his back upon the Santa Claus, smiled and said: "I call him Master Misery on account of that's who he is. Master Misery. Only maybe you call him something else; anyway, he is the same fellow, and you must've known him. All mothers tell their kids about him: he lives in hollows of trees, he comes down chimneys late at night, he lurks in graveyards and you can hear his step in the attic. The sonofabitch, he is a thief and a threat: he will take everything you have and end by leaving you nothing, not even a dream. Boo!" he shouted, and laughed louder than Santa Claus. "Now do you know who he is?"

Sylvia nodded. "I know who he is. My family called him something else. But I can't remember what. It was so long ago."

"But you remember him?"

"Yes, I remember him."

"Then call him Master Misery," he said, and, bouncing his ball, walked away from her. "Master Misery," his voice trailed to a mere moth of sound, "Mas-ter Mis-er-y . . ."

It was hard to look at Estelle, for she was in front of a window, and the window was filled with windy sun, which hurt Sylvia's eyes, and the glass rattled, which hurt her head. Also, Estelle was lecturing. Her nasal voice sounded as though her throat were a depository for rusty blades. "I wish you could see yourself," she was saying. Or was that something she'd said a long while back? Never mind. "I don't know what's happened to you: I'll bet you don't weigh a hundred pounds, I can see every bone and vein, and your hair! you look like a poodle."

Sylvia passed a hand over her forehead. "What time is it, Estelle?"

"It's four," she said, interrupting herself long enough to look at her watch. "But where is your watch?"

"I sold it," said Sylvia, too tired to lie. It did not matter. She had sold so many things, including her beaver coat and gold mesh evening bag.

Estelle shook her head. "I give up, honey, I plain give up. And that was the watch your mother gave you for graduation. It's a shame," she said, and made an old-maid noise with her mouth, "a pity and a shame. I'll never understand why you left us. That is your business, I'm sure; only how could you have left us for this . . . this . . . ?"

"Dump," supplied Sylvia, using the word advisedly. It was a furnished room in the East Sixties between Second and Third Avenues. Large enough for a daybed and a splintery old bureau with a mirror like a cataracted eye, it had one window, which looked out on a vast vacant lot (you could hear the tough afternoon voices of desperate running boys) and in the distance, like an exclamation point for the skyline, there was the black smokestack of a factory. This smokestack occurred frequently in her dreams; it never failed to arouse Miss Mozart: "Phallic, phallic," she would mutter, glancing up from her shorthand. The floor of the room was a garbage pail of books begun but never finished, antique newspapers, even orange hulls, fruit cores, underwear, a spilled powder box.

Estelle kicked her way through this trash, and sat down on the daybed. "Honey, you don't know, but I've been worried crazy. I mean I've got pride and all that and if you don't like me, well, o.k.; but you've got no right to stay away like this and not let me hear from you in over a month. So today I said to Bootsy, Bootsy, I've got a feeling something terrible has happened to Sylvia. You can imagine how I felt when I called your office and they told me you hadn't worked there for the last four weeks. What happened, were you fired?"

"Yes, I was fired." Sylvia began to sit up. "Please, Estelle—I've got to get ready; I've got an appointment."

"Be still. You're not going anywhere till I know what's wrong. The landlady downstairs told me you were found sleepwalking. . . ."

"What do you mean talking to her? Why are you spying on me?"

Estelle's eyes puckered, as though she were going to cry. She put her hand over Sylvia's and petted it gently. "Tell me, honey, is it because of a man?"

"It's because of a man, yes," said Sylvia, laughter at the edge of her voice.

"You should have come to me before," Estelle sighed. "I know about men. That is nothing for you to be ashamed of. A man can have a way with a woman that kind of makes her forget everything else. If Henry wasn't the fine upstanding potential lawyer that he is, why, I would still love him, and do things for him that before I knew what it was like to be with a man would have seemed shocking and horrible. But honey, this fellow you're mixed up with, he's taking advantage of you."

"It's not that kind of relationship," said Sylvia, getting up and locating a pair of stockings in the furor of her bureau drawers. "It hasn't got anything to do with love. Forget about it. In fact, go home and forget about me altogether."

Estelle looked at her narrowly. "You scare me, Sylvia; you really scare me." Sylvia laughed and went on getting dressed. "Do you remember a long time ago when I said you ought to get married?"

"Uh huh. And now you listen." Sylvia turned around; there was a row of hairpins spaced across her mouth; she extracted them one at a time all the while she talked. "You talk about getting married as though it were the answer absolute; very well, up to a point I agree. Sure, I want to be loved; who the hell doesn't? But even if I was willing to compromise, where is the man I'm going to marry? Believe me, he must've fallen down a manhole. I mean it seriously when I say there are no men in New York—and even if there were, how do you meet them? Every man I ever met here who seemed the slightest bit attractive was either married, too poor to get married, or queer. And anyway, this is no place to fall in love; this is where you ought to come when you want to get over being in love. Sure, I suppose I could marry somebody; but do I want that? Do I?"

Estelle shrugged. "Then what do you want?"

"More than is coming to me." She poked the last hairpin into place, and smoothed her eyebrows before the mirror. "I have an appointment, Estelle, and it is time for you to go now."

"I can't leave you like this," said Estelle, her hand waving helplessly around the room. "Sylvia, you were my childhood friend."

"That is just the point: we're not children any more; at least, I'm not. No, I want you to go home, and I don't want you to come here again. I just want you to forget about me."

Estelle fluttered at her eyes with a handkerchief, and by the time she reached the door she was weeping quite loudly. Sylvia could not afford remorse: having been mean, there was nothing to be but meaner. "Go on," she said, following Estelle into the hall, "and write home any damn nonsense about me you want to!" Letting out a wail that brought other roomers to their doors, Estelle fled down the stairs.

After this Sylvia went back into her room and sucked a piece of sugar to take the sour taste out of her mouth: it was her grandmother's remedy for bad tempers. Then she got down on her knees and pulled from under the bed a cigar box she kept hidden there. When you opened the box it played a homemade and somewhat disorganized version of "Oh How I Hate to Get Up in the Morning." Her brother had made the music-box and given it to her on her fourteenth birthday. Eating the sugar, she'd thought of her grandmother, and hearing the tune she thought of her brother; the rooms of the house where they had lived rotated before her, all dark and she like a light moving among them: up the stairs, down, out and through, spring sweet and lilac shadows in the air and the creaking of a porch swing. All gone, she thought, calling their names, and now I am absolutely alone. The music stopped. But it went on in her head; she could hear it bugling above the child-cries of the vacant lot. And it interfered with her reading. She was reading a little diary-like book she kept inside the box. In this book she wrote down the essentials of her dreams; they were endless now, and it was so hard to remember. Today she would tell Mr. Revercomb about the three blind children. He would like that. The prices he paid varied, and she was sure this was at least a ten-dollar dream. The cigar-box anthem followed her down the stairs and through the streets and she longed for it to go away.

In the store where the Santa Claus had been there was a new and equally unnerving exhibit. Even when she was late to Mr. Revercomb's, as now, Sylvia was compelled to pause by the window. A plaster girl with intense glass eyes sat astride a bicycle pedaling at the maddest pace; though its wheel spokes spun hypnotically, the bicycle of course never budged: all that effort and the poor girl going nowhere. It was a pitifully human situation, and one that Sylvia could so exactly identify with herself that she always felt a real pang. The music-box rewound in her head: the tune, her brother, the house, a high-school dance, the house, the tune! Couldn't Mr. Revercomb hear it? His penetrating gaze carried such dull suspicion. But he seemed pleased with her dream, and, when she left, Miss Mozart gave her an envelope containing ten dollars.

"I had a ten-dollar dream," she told Oreilly, and Oreilly, rubbing his hands together, said, "Fine! Fine! But that's just my luck, baby—you should've got here sooner 'cause I went and did a terrible thing. I walked into a liquor store up the street, snatched a quart and ran." Sylvia didn't believe him until he produced from his pinned-together overcoat a bottle of bourbon, already half gone. "You're going to get in trouble some day," she said, "and then what would happen to me? I don't know what I would do without you." Oreilly laughed and poured a shot of the whiskey into a water glass. They were sitting in an all-night cafeteria, a great glaring food depot alive with blue mirrors and raw murals. Although to Sylvia it seemed a sordid place, they met there frequently for dinner; but even if she could have afforded it she did not know where else they could go, for together they presented a curious aspect: a young girl and a doddering, drunken man. Even here people often stared at them; if they stared long enough, Oreilly would stiffen with dignity and say: "Hello, hot lips, I remember you from way back. Still working in the men's room?" But usually they were left to themselves, and sometimes they would sit talking until two and three in the morning.

"It's a good thing the rest of Master Misery's crowd don't know he gave you that ten bucks. One of them would say you stole the dream. I had that happen once. Eaten up, all of 'em, never saw such a bunch of sharks, worse than actors or clowns or businessmen. Crazy, if you think about it: you worry whether you're going to go to sleep, if you're going to have a dream, if you're going to remember the dream. Round and round. So you get a couple of bucks, so you rush to the nearest liquor store—or the nearest sleeping-pill machine. And first thing you know, you're roaming your way up outhouse alley. Why, baby, you know what it's like? It's just like life."

"No, Oreilly, that's what it isn't like. It hasn't anything to do with life. It has more to do with being dead. I feel as though everything were being taken from me, as though some thief were stealing me down to the bone. Oreilly, I tell you I haven't an ambition, and there used to be so much. I don't understand it and I don't know what to do."

He grinned. "And you say it isn't like life? Who understands life and who knows what to do?"

"Be serious," she said. "Be serious and put away that whiskey and eat your soup before it gets stone cold." She lighted a cigarette, and the smoke, smarting her eyes, intensified her frown. "If only I knew what he wanted with those dreams, all typed and filed. What does he do with them? You're right when you say he is Master Misery. . . . He can't be simply some silly quack; it can't be so meaningless as that. But why does he want dreams? Help me, Oreilly, think, think: what does it mean?"

Squinting one eye, Oreilly poured himself another drink; the clownlike twist of his mouth hardened into a line of scholarly straightness. "That is a million-dollar question, kid. Why don't you ask something easy, like how to cure the common cold? Yes, kid, what does it mean? I have thought about it a good deal. I have thought about it in the process of making love to a woman, and I have thought about it in the middle of a poker game." He tossed the drink down his throat and shuddered. "Now a sound can start a dream; the noise of one car passing in the night can drop a hundred sleepers into the deep parts of themselves. It's funny to think of that one car racing through the dark, trailing so many dreams. Sex, a sudden change of light, a pickle, these are little keys that can open up our insides, too. But most dreams begin because there are furies inside of us that blow open all the doors. I don't believe in Jesus Christ, but I do believe in people's souls; and I figure it this way, baby: dreams are the mind of the soul and the secret truth about us. Now Master Misery, maybe he hasn't got a soul, so bit by bit he borrows yours, steals it like he would steal your dolls or the chicken wing off your plate. Hundreds of souls have passed through him and gone into a filing case."

"Oreilly, be serious," she said again, annoyed because she thought he was making more jokes. "And look, your soup is . . ." She stopped abruptly, startled by Oreilly's peculiar expression. He was looking toward the entrance. Three men were there, two policemen and a civilian wearing a clerk's cloth jacket. The clerk was pointing toward their table. Oreilly's eyes circled the room with trapped despair; he sighed then, and leaned back in his seat, ostentatiously pouring himself another drink. "Good evening, gentlemen," he said, when the official party confronted him, "will you join us for a drink?"

"You can't arrest him," cried Sylvia, "you can't arrest a clown!" She threw her ten-dollar bill at them, but the policemen did not pay any attention, and she began to pound the table. All the customers in the place were staring, and the manager came running up, wringing his hands. The police said for Oreilly to get to his feet. "Certainly," Oreilly said, "though I do think it shocking you have to trouble yourselves with such petty crimes as mine when everywhere there are master thieves afoot. For instance, this pretty child," he stepped between the officers and pointed to Sylvia, "she is the recent victim of a major theft: poor baby, she has had her soul stolen."

For two days following Oreilly's arrest Sylvia did not leave her room: sun on the window, then dark. By the third day she had run out of cigarettes, so she ventured as far as the corner delicatessen. She bought a package of cupcakes, a can of sardines, a newspaper and cigarettes. In all this time she'd not eaten and it was a light, delicious, sharpening sensation; but the climb back up the stairs, the relief of closing the door, these so exhausted her she could not quite make the daybed. She slid down to the floor and did not move until it was day again. She thought afterwards that she'd been there about twenty minutes. Turning on the radio as loud as it would go, she dragged a chair up to the window and opened the newspaper on her lap: *Lana Denies, Russia Rejects, Miners Conciliate:* of all things this was saddest, that life goes on: if one leaves one's lover, life should stop for him, and if one disappears from the world, then the world should stop, too: and it never did. And that was the real reason for most people getting up in the morning: not because it would matter but because it wouldn't. But if Mr. Revercomb succeeded finally in collecting all the dreams out of every head, perhaps—the idea slipped, became entangled with radio and newspaper. *Falling Temperatures.* A snowstorm moving across Colorado, across the West, falling upon all the small towns, yellowing every light, filling every footfall, falling now and here: but how quickly it had come, the snowstorm: the roofs, the vacant lot, the distance deep in white and deepening, like sleep. She looked at the paper and she looked at the snow. But it must have been snowing all day. It could not have just started. There was no sound of traffic; in the swirling wastes of the vacant lot children circled a bonfire; a car, buried at the curb, winked its headlights: help! help! silent, like the heart's distress. She crumbled a cupcake and sprinkled it on the windowsill: north-birds would come to keep her company. And she left the window open for them; snow-wind scattered flakes that dissolved on the floor like April-fool jewels. *Presents Life Can Be Beautiful:* turn down that radio! The witch of the woods was tapping at her door: Yes, Mrs. Halloran, she said, and turned off the radio altogether. Snow-quiet, sleep-silent, only the fun-fire faraway songsinging of children; and the room was blue with cold, colder than the cold of fairytales: lie down my heart among the igloo flowers of snow. Mr. Revercomb, why do you wait upon the threshold? Ah, do come inside, it is so cold out there.

But her moment of waking was warm and held. The window was closed, and a man's arms were around her. He was singing to her, his voice gentle but jaunty: *cherryberry, moneyberry, happyberry pie, but the best old pie is a loveberry pie* . . .

"Oreilly, is it—is it really you?"

He squeezed her. "Baby's awake now. And how does she feel?"

"I had thought I was dead," she said, and happiness winged around inside her like a bird lamed but still flying. She tried to hug him and she was too weak. "I love you, Oreilly; you are my only friend and I was so frightened. I thought I would never see you again." She paused, remembering. "But why aren't you in jail?"

Oreilly's face got all tickled and pink. "I was never in jail," he said mysteriously. "But first, let's have something to eat. I brought some things up from the delicatessen this morning."

She had a sudden feeling of floating. "How long have you been here?"

"Since yesterday," he said, fussing around with bundles and paper plates. "You let me in yourself."

"That's impossible. I don't remember it at all."

"I know," he said, leaving it at that. "Here, drink your milk like a good kid and I'll tell you a real wicked story. Oh, it's wild," he promised, slapping his sides gladly and looking more than ever like a clown. "Well, like I said, I never was in jail and this bit of fortune came to me because there I was being hustled down the street by those bindlestiffs when who should I see come swinging along but the gorilla woman: you guessed it, Miss Mozart. Hi, I says to her, off to the barber shop for a shave? It's about time you were put under arrest, she says, and smiles at one of the cops. Do your duty, officer. Oh, I says to her, I'm not under arrest. Me, I'm just on my way to the station house to give them the lowdown on you, you dirty communist. You can imagine what sort of holler she set up then; she grabbed hold of me and the cops grabbed hold of her. Can't say I didn't warn them: careful, boys, I said, she's got hair on her chest. And she sure did lay about her. So I just sort of walked off down the street. Never have believed in standing around watching fistfights the way people do in this city."

Oreilly stayed with her in the room over the weekend. It was like the most beautiful party Sylvia could remember; she'd never laughed so much, for one thing, and no one, certainly no one in her family, had ever made her feel so loved. Oreilly was a fine cook, and he fixed delicious dishes on the little electric stove; once he scooped snow off the windowsill and made sherbet flavored with strawberry syrup. By Sunday she was strong enough to dance. They turned on the radio and she danced until she fell to her knees, windless and laughing. "I'll never be afraid again," she said. "I hardly know what I was afraid of to begin with."

"The same things you'll be afraid of the next time," Oreilly told her quietly. "That is a quality of Master Misery: no one ever knows what he is—not even children, and they know mostly everything."

Sylvia went to the window; an arctic whiteness lay over the city, but the snow had stopped, and the night sky was as clear as ice: there, riding above the river, she saw the first star of evening. "I see the first star," she said, crossing her fingers.

"And what do you wish when you see the first star?"

"I wish to see another star," she said. "At least that is what I usually wish."

"But tonight?"

She sat down on the floor and leaned her head against his knee. "Tonight I wished that I could have back my dreams."

"Don't we all?" Oreilly said, stroking her hair. "But then what would you do? I mean what would you do if you could have them back?"

Sylvia was silent a moment; when she spoke her eyes were gravely distant. "I would go home," she said slowly. "And that is a terrible decision, for it would mean giving up most of my other dreams. But if Mr. Revercomb would let me have them back, then I would go home tomorrow."

Saying nothing, Oreilly went to the closet and brought back her coat. "But why?" she asked as he helped her on with it. "Never mind," he said, "just do what I tell you. We're going to pay Mr. Revercomb a call, and you're going to ask him to give you back your dreams. It's a chance."

Sylvia balked at the door. "Please, Oreilly, don't make me go. I can't, please, I'm afraid."

"I thought you said you'd never be afraid again."

But once in the street he hurried her so quickly against the wind she did not have time to be frightened. It was Sunday, stores were closed and the traffic lights seemed to wink only for them, for there were no moving cars along the snow-deep avenue. Sylvia even forgot where they were going, and chattered of trivial oddments: right here at this corner is where she'd seen Garbo, and over there, that is where the old woman was run over. Presently, however, she stopped, out of breath and overwhelmed with sudden realization. "I can't, Oreilly," she said, pulling back. "What can I say to him?"

"Make it like a business deal," said Oreilly. "Tell him straight out that you want your dreams, and if he'll give them to you you'll pay back all the money: on the installment plan, naturally. It's simple enough, kid. Why the hell couldn't he give them back? They are all right there in a filing case."

This speech was somehow convincing and, stamping her frozen feet, Sylvia went ahead with a certain courage. "That's the kid," he said. They separated on Third Avenue, Oreilly being of the opinion that Mr. Revercomb's immediate neighborhood was not for the moment precisely safe. He confined himself in a doorway, now and then lighting a match and singing aloud: *but the best old pie is a whiskeyberry pie!* Like a wolf, a long thin dog came padding over the moon-slats under the elevated, and across the street there were the misty shapes of men ganged around a bar: the idea of maybe cadging a drink in there made him groggy.

Just as he had decided on perhaps trying something of the sort, Sylvia appeared. And she was in his arms before he knew that it was really her. "It can't be so bad, sweetheart," he said softly, holding her as best he could. "Don't cry, baby; it's too cold to cry: you'll chap your face." As she strangled for words, her crying evolved into a tremulous, unnatural laugh. The air was filled with the smoke of her laughter. "Do you know what he said?" she gasped. "Do you know what he said when I asked for my dreams?" Her head fell back, and her laughter rose and carried over the street like an abandoned, wildly colored kite. Oreilly had finally to shake her by the shoulders. "He said—I couldn't have them back because—because he'd used them all up."

She was silent then, her face smoothing into an expressionless calm. She put her arm through Oreilly's, and together they moved down the street; but it was as if they were friends pacing a platform, each waiting for the other's train, and when they reached the corner he cleared his throat and said: "I guess I'd better turn off here. It's as likely a spot as any."

Sylvia held on to his sleeve. "But where will you go, Oreilly?"

"Traveling in the blue," he said, trying a smile that didn't work out very well.

She opened her purse. "A man cannot travel in the blue without a bottle," she said, and, kissing him on the cheek, slipped five dollars in his pocket.

"Bless you, baby."

It did not matter that it was the last of her money, that now she would have to walk home, and alone. The pilings of snow were like the white waves of a white sea, and she rode upon them, carried by winds and tides of the moon. I do not know what I want, and perhaps I shall never know, but my only wish from every star will always be another star; and truly I am not afraid, she thought. Two boys came out of a bar and stared at her; in some park some long time ago she'd seen two boys and they might be the same. Truly I am not afraid, she thought, hearing their snowy footsteps following after her: and anyway, there was nothing left to steal.

THE BARGAIN

(1950)

Several things about her husband irritated Mrs. Chase. For instance, his voice: he sounded always as though he were bidding in a poker game. To hear his unresponsive drawl was exasperating, especially now when, talking to him on the telephone, she herself was strident with excitement. "Of course I already have one, I know that. But you don't understand, dear—it's a bargain," she said, stressing the last word, then pausing to let its magic develop. Simply silence happened. "Well, you could say something. No, I'm not in a shop, I'm at home. Alice Severn is coming for lunch. It's her coat that I'm trying to tell you about. Certainly you remember Alice Severn." His leaky memory was another irritant, and though she reminded him that out in Greenwich they had often seen Arthur and Alice Severn, had, in fact, entertained them, he pretended no knowledge of the name. "It doesn't matter," she sighed. "I'm only going to look at the coat anyway. Have a good lunch, dear."

Later, as she fussed with the precise waves of her touched-up hair, Mrs. Chase admitted that really there was no reason why her husband should have remembered the Severns too clearly. She realized this when, with faulty success, she tried to arouse an image of Alice Severn. There, she almost had it: a rosy, gangling woman, less than thirty, and always riding in a station-wagon accompanied by an Irish setter and two beautiful, gold-red children. It was said that her husband drank; or was it the other way round? Then, too, they were supposed to be a bad credit risk, at least Mrs. Chase recalled once hearing of incredible debts, and someone, was it herself?, had described Alice Severn as just too bohemian.

Before moving into the city, the Chases had kept a house in Greenwich, which was a bore to Mrs. Chase, for she disliked the hint of nature there and preferred the amusement of New York shop windows. In Greenwich, at a cocktail party, at the railway station, they'd now and again encountered the Severns, that was all it had amounted to. We were not even friends, she concluded, somewhat surprised. As so often happens when one hears suddenly from a person of the past, and someone known in a different context, she had been startled into a feeling of intimacy. On second thought, however, it seemed extraordinary of Alice Severn, whom she'd not seen in over a year, to have called offering for sale a mink coat.

Mrs. Chase stopped in the kitchen to order a soup and salad lunch: it never occurred to her that not everyone was on a diet. She filled a sherry decanter and brought it with her into the living room. It was a green glass–bright room, rather like her too-youthful taste in clothes. Wind bustled the windows, for the apartment was high-up with an aeroplane view of downtown Manhattan. She put a linguaphone record on a phonograph, and sat in an unrelaxed position listening to the strained voice pronouncing French phrases. In April the Chases planned to celebrate their twentieth anniversary with a trip to Paris; for this reason she had undertaken the linguaphone lessons, and for this reason, too, she considered Alice Severn's coat: it was more practical, she felt, to travel in a second-hand mink; later on, she might have it made into a stole.

Alice Severn arrived a few minutes early, an accident, certainly, for she was not an anxious person, at least judging from her subdued, ambling manner. She wore sensible shoes, a tweed suit that had seen its best days, and carried a box tied with scrappy cord.

"I was so delighted when you called this morning. Heaven knows, it's been an age, but of course we never get to Greenwich anymore."

Though smiling, her guest remained silent, and Mrs. Chase, keyed to an effusive style, was a little taken aback. As they seated themselves her eyes caught at the younger woman, and it occurred to her that if they had met casually she might not have known her, not because her appearance was so very altered, but because Mrs. Chase realized that she had never before looked closely at her, which seemed odd, for Alice Severn was someone you would notice. If she had been less long, more compact, one might have passed over her, perhaps remarking that she was attractive. As it was, with her red hair, the sense of distance in her eyes, her freckled, autumnal face and gaunt, strong hands, there was a distinction about her not easily disregarded.

"Sherry?"

Alice Severn nodded, and her head, balanced precariously on her thin neck, was like a chrysanthemum too heavy for its stalk.

"Cracker?" offered Mrs. Chase, observing that anyone so lean and stretched-out must eat like a horse. Her soup-and-salad skimpiness gave her a sudden qualm, and she told the following lie: "I don't know what Martha's making for lunch. You know how difficult it is on short notice. But tell me, dear, what is happening in Greenwich?"

"In Greenwich?" she said, her eyelids beating, as though an unexpected light had flared in the room. "I have no idea. We haven't lived there for some while, six months or more."

"Oh?" said Mrs. Chase. "You see how far behind I am. But where are you living, dear?"

Alice Severn lifted one of her bony awkward hands and waved it toward the windows. "Out there," she said, peculiarly. Her voice was plain, but it had an exhausted quality, as though she were coming down with a cold. "In town, I mean. We don't like it much, Fred especially."

With the dimmest inflection, Mrs. Chase said, "Fred?" for she perfectly remembered Arthur as the name of her guest's husband.

"Yes, Fred, my dog, an Irish setter, you must have seen him. He's used to space, and the apartment is so small, a room really."

Hard days indeed must have fallen if all the Severns were living in one room. Curious as she was, Mrs. Chase checked herself and did not inquire into this. She tasted her sherry and said, "Of course I remember your dog; and the children: all three of their red heads hanging out of your station-wagon."

"The kids haven't red hair. They're blondes, like Arthur."

The correction was given so humorlessly that Mrs. Chase was provoked into a puzzled small laugh. "And Arthur, how is he?" she said, preparing to stand and lead the way to lunch. But Alice Severn's answer made her sit down again. Delivered with no change in her placidly undecorated expression, it consisted of only: "Fatter."

"Fatter," she repeated after a moment. "The last time I saw him, I guess it was only a week ago, he was crossing a street, almost waddling. If he had seen me, I would've had to laugh: he was always so finicky about his figure."

Mrs. Chase touched her hips. "You and Arthur. Separated? It's simply remarkable."

"We're not separated." She brushed her hand in the air as though to clear away cobwebs. "I've known him since I was a child, since we both were children: do you think," she said quietly, "that we could ever be separate of each other, Mrs. Chase?"

The exact use of her name seemed to exclude Mrs. Chase; fleetingly she felt herself sealed off, and as they went together toward the dining room she imagined a hostility to move between them. Possibly it was the sight of Alice Severn's gawky hands fumblingly unfolding a napkin that persuaded her this was not true. Except for courteous exchanges they ate in silence, and she was beginning to fear there was not to be a story.

At last, "As a matter of fact," said Alice Severn, blurting it, "we were divorced last August."

Mrs. Chase waited; then, between the dip and rise of her soup spoon, said, "How awful. His drinking, I suppose?"

"Arthur never drank," she answered with a pleasant but astonished smile. "That is, we both did. We drank for fun, not to be mean. It was very nice in the summer. We used to go down to the brook and pick mint and make mint juleps, huge ones in fruitjars. Sometimes, on hot nights when we couldn't sleep, we used to fill the thermos full of cold beer and wake up the kids, then we would drive out to the shore: it's fun to drink beer and swim and sleep on the sand. Those were lovely times; I remember once we stayed till daylight. No," she said, some serious idea tightening her face, "I'll tell you. I'm almost a head taller than Arthur, and I think it worried him. When we were children he always thought he would outgrow me, but then he never did. He hated to dance with me, and he loves to dance. And he liked a lot of people around, tiny little people with high voices. I'm not like that, I wanted just us. In those ways I wasn't a pleasure to him. Now, you remember Jeannie Bjorkman? The one with the round face and the curls, about your height."

"I should say I do," said Mrs. Chase. "She was on the Red Cross committee. Dreadful."

"No," said Alice Severn, pondering, "Jeannie isn't dreadful. We were very good friends. The strange thing is, Arthur used to say he hated her, but then I guess he was always crazy about her, certainly he is now, and the kids, too. Somehow I wish the kids didn't like her, though I should be happy that they do, since they have to live with her."

"It isn't true: your husband married to that awful Bjorkman girl!"

"Since August."

Mrs. Chase, pausing first to suggest that they have coffee in the living room, said, "It's outrageous for you to be living alone in New York. At least you could have the children with you."

"Arthur wanted them," said Alice Severn simply. "But I'm not alone. Fred is one of my closest friends."

Mrs. Chase gestured impatiently: she did not enjoy fantasy. "A dog. It's nonsense. There is nothing to think except that you're a fool: any man that tried to walk over me would get his feet cut to pieces. I suppose you haven't even arranged that he should," she hesitated, "should contribute."

"You don't understand, Arthur hasn't any money," said Alice Severn with the dismay of a child who has discovered that grownups after all are not very logical. "He's even had to sell the car and walks back and forth between the station. But you know, I think he's happy."

"What you need is a good pinch," said Mrs. Chase, as though she were ready to do the job.

"It's Fred that bothers me. He's used to space, and only one person doesn't leave many bones. Do you suppose that when I finish my course I could get a job in California? I'm studying at a business school, but I'm not awfully quick, especially at typing, my fingers seem to hate it so. I guess it's like playing the piano, you should learn when you're very young." She glanced speculatively at her hands, sighing. "I have a lesson at three; would you mind if I showed you the coat now?"

The festiveness of things coming out of a box could usually be counted on to cheer Mrs. Chase, but as she saw the lid taken off, a melancholy uneasiness cornered her.

"It belonged to my mother."

Who must have worn it sixty years, thought Mrs. Chase, facing a mirror. The coat hung to her ankles. She rubbed her hand against the lusterless, balding fur and it was moldy, sour, as though it had lain in an attic by the seashore. It was cold inside the coat, she shivered, at the same time a flush heated her face, for just then she noticed that Alice Severn was gazing over her shoulder, and in her expression there was a drawn, undignified expectancy that had not been there before. Where sympathy was concerned, Mrs. Chase knew thrift: before giving it she took the precaution of attaching a string, so that if necessary it could be yanked back. Looking at Alice Severn, however, it was as though the string had been severed, and for once she was confronted head-on with the obligations of sympathy. She wriggled even so, hunting a loophole, but then her eyes collided with those other eyes, and she saw there was none. The recollection of a word from her linguaphone lessons made a certain question easier: *"Combien?"* she said.

"It isn't worth anything, is it?" There was confusion in the asking, not frankness.

"No, it isn't," she said tiredly, almost testily. "But I may have some use for it." She did not inquire again; it was clear that part of her obligation was to be fulfilled by fixing a price herself.

Still trailing the clumsy coat, she went to a corner of the room where there was a desk and, writing with resentful jabs, made a check on her private account: she did not intend that her husband should know. More than most Mrs. Chase despised the sense of loss; a misplaced key, a dropped coin, quickened her awareness of theft and the cheats of life. Some similar sensation was with her as she handed the check to Alice Severn who, folding it, and without looking at it, put it in her suit pocket. It was for fifty dollars.

"Darling," said Mrs. Chase, grim with spurious concern, "you must ring me and let me know how everything is going. You mustn't feel lonely."

Alice Severn did not thank her, and at the door she did not say goodbye. Instead, she took one of Mrs. Chase's hands in her own and patted it, as though she were gently rewarding an animal, a dog. Closing the door, Mrs. Chase stared at her hand, brought it near her lips. The feel of the other hand was still upon it, and she stood there, waiting while it drained away: presently her hand was again quite cold.

A DIAMOND GUITAR

(1950)

The nearest town to the prison farm is twenty miles away. Many forests of pine trees stand between the farm and the town, and it is in these forests that the convicts work; they tap for turpentine. The prison itself is in a forest. You will find it there at the end of a red rutted road, barbed wire sprawling like a vine over its walls. Inside, there live one hundred and nine white men, ninety-seven Negroes and one Chinese. There are two sleep houses—great green wooden buildings with tar-paper roofs. The white men occupy one, the Negroes and the Chinese the other. In each sleep house there is one large potbellied stove, but the winters are cold here, and at night with the pines waving frostily and a freezing light falling from the moon the men, stretched on their iron cots, lie awake with the fire colors of the stove playing in their eyes.

The men whose cots are nearest the stove are the important men—those who are looked up to or feared. Mr. Schaeffer is one of these. Mr. Schaeffer—for that is what he is called, a mark of special respect—is a lanky, pulled-out man. He has reddish, silvering hair, and his face is attenuated, religious; there is no flesh to him; you can see the workings of his bones, and his eyes are a poor, dull color. He can read and he can write, he can add a column of figures. When another man receives a letter, he brings it to Mr. Schaeffer. Most of these letters are sad and complaining; very often Mr. Schaeffer improvises more cheerful messages and does not read what is written on the page. In the sleep house there are two other men who can read. Even so, one of them brings his letters to Mr. Schaeffer, who obliges by never reading the truth. Mr. Schaeffer himself does not receive mail, not even at Christmas; he seems to have no friends beyond the prison, and actually he has none there—that is, no particular friend. This was not always true.

One winter Sunday some winters ago Mr. Schaeffer was sitting on the steps of the sleep house carving a doll. He is quite talented at this. His dolls are carved in separate sections, then put together with bits of spring wire; the arms and legs move, the head rolls. When he has finished a dozen or so of these dolls, the Captain of the farm takes them into town, and there they are sold in a general store. In this way Mr. Schaeffer earns money for candy and tobacco.

That Sunday, as he sat cutting out the fingers for a little hand, a truck pulled into the prison yard. A young boy, handcuffed to the Captain of the farm, climbed out of the truck and stood blinking at the ghostly winter sun. Mr. Schaeffer only glanced at him. He was then a man of fifty, and seventeen of those years he'd lived at the farm. The arrival of a new prisoner could not arouse him. Sunday is a free day at the farm, and other men who were moping around the yard crowded down to the truck. Afterward, Pick Axe and Goober stopped by to speak with Mr. Schaeffer.

Pick Axe said, "He's a foreigner, the new one is. From Cuba. But with yellow hair."

"A knifer, Cap'n says," said Goober, who was a knifer himself. "Cut up a sailor in Mobile."

"Two sailors," said Pick Axe. "But just a café fight. He didn't hurt them boys none."

"To cut off a man's ear? You call that not hurtin' him? They give him two years, Cap'n says."

Pick Axe said, "He's got a guitar with jewels all over it."

It was getting too dark to work. Mr. Schaeffer fitted the pieces of his doll together and, holding its little hands, set it on his knee. He rolled a cigarette; the pines were blue in the sundown light, and the smoke from his cigarette lingered in the cold, darkening air. He could see the Captain coming across the yard. The new prisoner, a blond young boy, lagged a pace behind. He was carrying a guitar studded with glass diamonds that cast a starry twinkle, and his new uniform was too big for him; it looked like a Halloween suit.

"Somebody for you, Schaeffer," said the Captain, pausing on the steps of the sleep house. The Captain was not a hard man; occasionally he invited Mr. Schaeffer into his office, and they would talk together about things they had read in the newspaper. "Tico Feo," he said as though it were the name of a bird or a song, "this is Mr. Schaeffer. Do like him, and you'll do right."

Mr. Schaeffer glanced up at the boy and smiled. He smiled at him longer than he meant to, for the boy had eyes like strips of sky—blue as the winter evening—and his hair was as gold as the Captain's teeth. He had a fun-loving face, nimble, clever; and, looking at him, Mr. Schaeffer thought of holidays and good times.

"Is like my baby sister," said Tico Feo, touching Mr. Schaeffer's doll. His voice with its Cuban accent was soft and sweet as a banana. "She sit on my knee also."

Mr. Schaeffer was suddenly shy. Bowing to the Captain, he walked off into the shadows of the yard. He stood there whispering the names of the evening stars as they opened in flower above him. The stars were his pleasure, but tonight they did not comfort him; they did not make him remember that what happens to us on earth is lost in the endless shine of eternity. Gazing at them—the stars—he thought of the jeweled guitar and its worldly glitter.

It could be said of Mr. Schaeffer that in his life he'd done only one really bad thing: he'd killed a man. The circumstances of that deed are unimportant, except to say that the man deserved to die and that for it Mr. Schaeffer was sentenced to ninety-nine years and a day. For a long while—for many years, in fact—he had not thought of how it was before he came to the farm. His memory of those times was like a house where no one lives and where the furniture has rotted away. But tonight it was as if lamps had been lighted through all the gloomy dead rooms. It had begun to happen when he saw Tico Feo coming through the dusk with his splendid guitar. Until that moment he had not been lonesome. Now, recognizing his loneliness, he felt alive. He had not wanted to be alive. To be alive was to remember brown rivers where the fish run, and sunlight on a lady's hair.

Mr. Schaeffer hung his head. The glare of the stars had made his eyes water.

The sleep house usually is a glum place, stale with the smell of men and stark in the light of two unshaded electric bulbs. But with the advent of Tico Feo it was as though a tropic occurrence had happened in the cold room, for when Mr. Schaeffer returned from his observance of the stars he came upon a savage and garish scene. Sitting cross-legged on a cot, Tico Feo was picking at his guitar with long swaying fingers and singing a song that sounded as jolly as jingling coins. Though the song was in Spanish, some of the men tried to sing it with him, and Pick Axe and Goober were dancing together. Charlie and Wink were dancing too, but separately. It was nice to hear the men laughing, and when Tico Feo finally put aside his guitar, Mr. Schaeffer was among those who congratulated him.

"You deserve such a fine guitar," he said.

"Is diamond guitar," said Tico Feo, drawing his hand over its vaudeville dazzle. "Once I have a one with rubies. But that one is stole. In Havana my sister work in a, how you say, where make guitar; is how I have this one."

Mr. Schaeffer asked him if he had many sisters, and Tico Feo, grinning, held up four fingers. Then, his blue eyes narrowing greedily, he said, "Please, Mister, you give me doll for my two little sister?"

The next evening Mr. Schaeffer brought him the dolls. After that he was Tico Feo's best friend and they were always together. At all times they considered each other.

Tico Feo was eighteen years old and for two years had worked on a freighter in the Caribbean. As a child he'd gone to school with nuns, and he wore a gold crucifix around his neck. He had a rosary too. The rosary he kept wrapped in a green silk scarf that also held three other treasures: a bottle of Evening in Paris cologne, a pocket mirror and a Rand McNally map of the world. These and the guitar were his only possessions, and he would not allow anyone to touch them. Perhaps he prized his map the most. At night, before the lights were turned off, he would shake out his map and show Mr. Schaeffer the places he'd been—Galveston, Miami, New Orleans, Mobile, Cuba, Haiti, Jamaica, Puerto Rico, the Virgin Islands—and the places he wanted to go to. He wanted to go almost everywhere, especially Madrid, especially the North Pole. This both charmed and frightened Mr. Schaeffer. It hurt him to think of Tico Feo on the seas and in far places. He sometimes looked defensively at his friend and thought, "You are just a lazy dreamer."

It is true that Tico Feo was a lazy fellow. After that first evening he had to be urged even to play his guitar. At daybreak when the guard came to rouse the men, which he did by banging a hammer on the stove, Tico Feo would whimper like a child. Sometimes he pretended to be ill, moaned and rubbed his stomach; but he never got away with this, for the Captain would send him out to work with the rest of the men. He and Mr. Schaeffer were put together on a highway gang. It was hard work, digging at frozen clay and carrying croker sacks filled with broken stone. The guard had always to be shouting at Tico Feo, for he spent most of the time trying to lean on things.

Each noon, when the dinner buckets were passed around, the two friends sat together. There were some good things in Mr. Schaeffer's bucket, as he could afford apples and candy bars from the town. He liked giving these things to his friend, for his friend enjoyed them so much, and he thought, "You are growing; it will be a long time until you are a grown man."

Not all the men liked Tico Feo. Because they were jealous, or for more subtle reasons, some of them told ugly stories about him. Tico Feo himself seemed unaware of this. When the men gathered around him, and he played his guitar and sang his songs, you could see that he felt he was loved. Most of the men did feel a love for him; they waited for and depended upon the hour between supper and lights out. "Tico, play your box," they would say. They did not notice that afterward there was a deeper sadness than there had ever been. Sleep jumped beyond them like a jack rabbit, and their eyes lingered ponderingly on the firelight that creaked behind the grating of the stove. Mr. Schaeffer was the only one who understood their troubled feeling, for he felt it too. It was that his friend had revived the brown rivers where the fish run, and ladies with sunlight in their hair.

Soon Tico Feo was allowed the honor of having a bed near the stove and next to Mr. Schaeffer. Mr. Schaeffer had always known that his friend was a terrible liar. He did not listen for the truth in Tico Feo's tales of adventure, of conquests and encounters with famous people. Rather, he took pleasure in them as plain stories, such as you would read in a magazine, and it warmed him to hear his friend's tropic voice whispering in the dark.

Except that they did not combine their bodies or think to do so, though such things were not unknown at the farm, they were as lovers. Of the seasons, spring is the most shattering: stalks thrusting through the earth's winter-stiffened crust, young leaves cracking out on old left-to-die branches, the falling-asleep wind cruising through all the newborn green. And with Mr. Schaeffer it was the same, a breaking up, a flexing of muscles that had hardened.

It was late January. The friends were sitting on the steps of the sleep house, each with a cigarette in his hand. A moon thin and yellow as a piece of lemon rind curved above them, and under its light, threads of ground frost glistened like silver snail trails. For many days Tico Feo had been drawn into himself—silent as a robber waiting in the shadows. It was no good to say to him, "Tico, play your box." He would only look at you with smooth, under-ether eyes.

"Tell a story," said Mr. Schaeffer, who felt nervous and helpless when he could not reach his friend. "Tell about when you went to the race track in Miami."

"I not ever go to no race track," said Tico Feo, thereby admitting to his wildest lie, one involving hundreds of dollars and a meeting with Bing Crosby. He did not seem to care. He produced a comb and pulled it sulkily through his hair. A few days before this comb had been the cause of a fierce quarrel. One of the men, Wink, claimed that Tico Feo had stolen the comb from him, to which the accused replied by spitting in his face. They had wrestled around until Mr. Schaeffer and another man got them separated. "Is my comb. You tell him!" Tico Feo had demanded of Mr. Schaeffer. But Mr. Schaeffer with quiet firmness had said no, it was not his friend's comb—an answer that seemed to defeat all concerned. "Aw," said Wink, "if he wants it so much, Christ's sake, let the sonofabitch keep it." And later, in a puzzled, uncertain voice, Tico Feo had said, "I thought you was my friend." "I am," Mr. Schaeffer had thought, though he said nothing.

"I not go to no race track, and what I said about the widow woman, that is not true also." He puffed up his cigarette to a furious glow and looked at Mr. Schaeffer with a speculating expression. "Say, you have money, Mister?"

"Maybe twenty dollars," said Mr. Schaeffer hesitantly, afraid of where this was leading.

"Not so good, twenty dollar," Tico said, but without disappointment. "No important, we work our way. In Mobile I have my friend Frederico. He will put us on a boat. There will not be trouble," and it was as though he were saying that the weather had turned colder.

There was a squeezing in Mr. Schaeffer's heart; he could not speak.

"Nobody here can run to catch Tico. He run the fastest."

"Shotguns run faster," said Mr. Schaeffer in a voice hardly alive. "I'm too old," he said, with the knowledge of age churning like nausea inside him.

Tico Feo was not listening. "Then, the world. The world, *el mundo*, my friend." Standing up, he quivered like a young horse; everything seemed to draw close to him—the moon, the callings of screech owls. His breath came quickly and turned to smoke in the air. "Should we go to Madrid? Maybe someone teach me to bullfight. You think so, Mister?"

Mr. Schaeffer was not listening either. "I'm too old," he said. "I'm too damned old."

For the next several weeks Tico Feo kept after him—the world, *el mundo*, my friend; and he wanted to hide. He would shut himself in the toilet and hold his head. Nevertheless, he was excited, tantalized. What if it could come true, the race with Tico across the forests and to the sea? And he imagined himself on a boat, he who had never seen the sea, whose whole life had been land-rooted. During this time one of the convicts died, and in the yard you could hear the coffin being made. As each nail thudded into place, Mr. Schaeffer thought, "This is for me, it is mine."

Tico Feo himself was never in better spirits; he sauntered about with a dancer's snappy, gigolo grace, and had a joke for everyone. In the sleep house after supper his fingers popped at the guitar like firecrackers. He taught the men to cry *olé*, and some of them sailed their caps through the air.

When work on the road was finished, Mr. Schaeffer and Tico Feo were moved back into the forests. On Valentine's Day they ate their lunch under a pine tree. Mr. Schaeffer had ordered a dozen oranges from the town and he peeled them slowly, the skins unraveling in a spiral; the juicier slices he gave to his friend, who was proud of how far he could spit the seeds—a good ten feet.

It was a cold beautiful day, scraps of sunlight blew about them like butterflies, and Mr. Schaeffer, who liked working with the trees, felt dim and happy. Then Tico Feo said, "That one, he no could catch a fly in his mouth." He meant Armstrong, a hog-jowled man sitting with a shotgun propped between his legs. He was the youngest of the guards and new at the farm.

"I don't know," said Mr. Schaeffer. He'd watched Armstrong and noticed that, like many people who are both heavy and vain, the new guard moved with a skimming lightness. "He might could fool you."

"I fool him, maybe," said Tico Feo, and spit an orange seed in Armstrong's direction. The guard scowled at him, then blew a whistle. It was the signal for work to begin.

Sometime during the afternoon the two friends came together again; that is, they were nailing turpentine buckets onto trees that stood next to each other. At a distance below them a shallow bouncing creek branched through the woods. "In water no smell," said Tico Feo meticulously, as though remembering something he'd heard. "We run in the water; until dark we climb a tree. Yes, Mister?"

Mr. Schaeffer went on hammering, but his hand was shaking, and the hammer came down on his thumb. He looked around dazedly at his friend. His face showed no reflection of pain, and he did not put the thumb in his mouth, the way a man ordinarily might.

Tico Feo's blue eyes seemed to swell like bubbles, and when in a voice quieter than the wind sounds in the pinetops he said, "Tomorrow," these eyes were all that Mr. Schaeffer could see.

"Tomorrow, Mister?"

"Tomorrow," said Mr. Schaeffer.

The first colors of morning fell upon the walls of the sleep house, and Mr. Schaeffer, who had rested little, knew that Tico Feo was awake too. With the weary eyes of a crocodile he observed the movements of his friend in the next cot. Tico Feo was unknotting the scarf that contained his treasures. First he took the pocket mirror. Its jellyfish light trembled on his face. For a while he admired himself with serious delight, and combed and slicked his hair as though he were preparing to step out to a party. Then he hung the rosary about his neck. The cologne he never opened, nor the map. The last thing he did was to tune his guitar. While the other men were dressing, he sat on the edge of his cot and tuned the guitar. It was strange, for he must have known he would never play it again.

Bird shrills followed the men through the smoky morning woods. They walked single file, fifteen men to a group, and a guard bringing up the rear of each line. Mr. Schaeffer was sweating as though it were a hot day, and he could not keep in marching step with his friend, who walked ahead, snapping his fingers and whistling at the birds.

A signal had been set. Tico Feo was to call, "Time out," and pretend to go behind a tree. But Mr. Schaeffer did not know when it would happen.

The guard named Armstrong blew a whistle, and his men dropped from the line and separated to their various stations. Mr. Schaeffer, though going about his work as best he could, took care always to be in a position where he could keep an eye on both Tico Feo and the guard. Armstrong sat on a stump, a chew of tobacco lopsiding his face, and his gun pointing into the sun. He had the tricky eyes of a cardsharp; you could not really tell where he was looking.

Once another man gave the signal. Although Mr. Schaeffer had known at once that it was not the voice of his friend, panic had pulled at his throat like a rope. As the morning wore on there was such a drumming in his ears he was afraid he would not hear the signal when it came.

The sun climbed to the center of the sky. "He is just a lazy dreamer. It will never happen," thought Mr. Schaeffer, daring a moment to believe this. But "First we eat," said Tico Feo with a practical air as they set their dinner pails on the bank above the creek. They ate in silence, almost as though each bore the other a grudge, but at the end of it Mr. Schaeffer felt his friend's hand close over his own and hold it with a tender pressure.

"Mister Armstrong, time out . . ."

Near the creek Mr. Schaeffer had seen a sweet gum tree, and he was thinking it would soon be spring and the sweet gum ready to chew. A razory stone ripped open the palm of his hand as he slid off the slippery embankment into the water. He straightened up and began to run; his legs were long, he kept almost abreast of Tico Feo, and icy geysers sprayed around them. Back and forth through the woods the shouts of men boomed hollowly like voices in a cavern, and there were three shots, all highflying, as though the guard were shooting at a cloud of geese.

Mr. Schaeffer did not see the log that lay across the creek. He thought he was still running, and his legs thrashed about him; it was as though he were a turtle stranded on its back.

While he struggled there, it seemed to him that the face of his friend, suspended above him, was part of the white winter sky—it was so distant, judging. It hung there but an instant, like a hummingbird, yet in that time he'd seen that Tico Feo had not wanted him to make it, had never thought he would, and he remembered once thinking that it would be a long time before his friend was a grown man. When they found him, he was still lying in the ankle-deep water as though it were a summer afternoon and he were idly floating on the stream.

Since then three winters have gone by, and each has been said to be the coldest, the longest. Two recent months of rain washed deeper ruts in the clay road leading to the farm, and it is harder than ever to get there, harder to leave. A pair of searchlights has been added to the walls, and they burn there through the night like the eyes of a giant owl. Otherwise, there have not been many changes. Mr. Schaeffer, for instance, looks much the same, except that there is a thicker frost of white in his hair, and as the result of a broken ankle he walks with a limp. It was the Captain himself who said that Mr. Schaeffer had broken his ankle attempting to capture Tico Feo. There was even a picture of Mr. Schaeffer in the newspaper, and under it this caption: "Tried to Prevent Escape." At the time he was deeply mortified, not because he knew the other men were laughing, but because he thought of Tico Feo seeing it. But he cut it out of the paper anyway, and keeps it in an envelope along with several clippings pertaining to his friend: a spinster woman told the authorities he'd entered her home and kissed her, twice he was reported seen in the Mobile vicinity, finally it was believed that he had left the country.

No one has ever disputed Mr. Schaeffer's claim to the guitar. Several months ago a new prisoner was moved into the sleep house. He was said to be a fine player, and Mr. Schaeffer was persuaded to lend him the guitar. But all the man's tunes came out sour, for it was as though Tico Feo, tuning his guitar that last morning, had put a curse upon it. Now it lies under Mr. Schaeffer's cot, where its glass diamonds are turning yellow; in the night his hand sometimes searches it out, and his fingers drift across the strings: then, the world.

HOUSE OF FLOWERS

(1951)

Ottilie should have been the happiest girl in Port-au-Prince. As Baby said to her, look at all the things that can be put to your credit. Like what? said Ottilie, for she was vain and preferred compliments to pork or perfume. Like your looks, said Baby: you have a lovely light color, even almost blue eyes, and such a pretty, sweet face—there is no girl on the road with steadier customers, every one of them ready to buy you all the beer you can drink. Ottilie conceded that this was true, and with a smile continued to total her fortunes: I have five silk dresses and a pair of green satin shoes, I have three gold teeth worth thirty thousand francs, maybe Mr. Jamison or someone will give me another bracelet. But, Baby, she sighed, and could not express her discontent.

Baby was her best friend; she had another friend too: Rosita. Baby was like a wheel, round, rolling; junk rings had left green circles on several of her fat fingers, her teeth were dark as burnt tree stumps, and when she laughed you could hear her at sea, at least so the sailors claimed. Rosita, the other friend, was taller than most men, and stronger; at night, with the customers on hand, she minced about, lisping in a silly doll voice, but in the daytime she took spacious, loping strides and spoke out in a military baritone. Both of

197

Ottilie's friends were from the Dominican Republic, and considered it reason enough to feel themselves a cut above the natives of this darker country. It did not concern them that Ottilie was a native. You have brains, Baby told her, and certainly what Baby doted on was a good brain. Ottilie was often afraid that her friends would discover that she could neither read nor write.

The house where they lived and worked was rickety, thin as a steeple, and frosted with fragile, bougainvillea-vined balconies. Though there was no sign outside, it was called the Champs Elysées. The proprietress, a spinsterish, smothered-looking invalid, ruled from an upstairs room, where she stayed locked away rocking in a rocking chair and drinking ten to twenty Coca-Colas a day. All counted, she had eight ladies working for her; with the exception of Ottilie, no one of them was under thirty. In the evening, when the ladies assembled on the porch, where they chatted and flourished paper fans that beat the air like delirious moths, Ottilie seemed a delightful dreaming child surrounded by older, uglier sisters.

Her mother was dead, her father was a planter who had gone back to France, and she had been brought up in the mountains by a rough peasant family, the sons of whom had each at a young age lain with her in some green and shadowy place. Three years earlier, when she was fourteen, she had come down for the first time to the market in Port-au-Prince. It was a journey of two days and a night, and she'd walked carrying a ten-pound sack of grain; to ease the load she'd let a little of the grain spill out, then a little more, and by the time she had reached the market there was almost none left. Ottilie had cried because she thought of how angry the family would be when she came home without the money for the grain; but these tears were not for long: such a jolly nice man helped her dry them. He bought her a slice of coconut, and took her to see his cousin, who was the proprietress of the Champs Elysées. Ottilie could not believe her good luck; the jukebox music, the satin shoes and joking men were as strange and marvelous as the electric-light bulb in her room, which she never tired of clicking on and off. Soon she had become the most talked-of girl on the road, the proprietress was able to ask double for her, and Ottilie grew vain; she could pose for hours in front of a mirror. It was seldom that she thought of the mountains; and yet, after three years, there was much of the mountains still with her: their winds seemed still to move around her, her hard, high haunches had not softened, nor had the soles of her feet, which were rough as lizard's hide.

When her friends spoke of love, of men they had loved, Ottilie became sulky: How do you feel if you're in love? she asked. Ah, said Rosita with swooning eyes, you feel as though pepper has been sprinkled on your heart, as though tiny fish are swimming in your veins. Ottilie shook her head; if Rosita was telling the truth, then she had never been in love, for she had never felt that way about any of the men who came to the house.

This so troubled her that at last she went to see a *Houngan* who lived in the hills above town. Unlike her friends, Ottilie did not tack Christian pictures on the walls of her room; she did not believe in God, but many gods: of food, light, of death, ruin. The Houngan was in touch with these gods; he kept their secrets on his altar, could hear their voices in the rattle of a gourd, could dispense their power in a potion. Speaking through the gods, the Houngan gave her this message: You must catch a wild bee, he said, and hold it in your closed hand . . . if the bee does not sting, then you will know you have found love.

On the way home she thought of Mr. Jamison. He was a man past fifty, an American connected with an engineering project. The gold bracelets chattering on her wrists were presents from him, and Ottilie, passing a fence snowy with honeysuckle, wondered if after all she was not in love with Mr. Jamison. Black bees festooned the honeysuckle. With a brave thrust of her hand she caught one dozing. Its stab was like a blow that knocked her to her knees; and there she knelt, weeping until it was hard to know whether the bee had stung her hand or her eyes.

—

It was March, and events were leading toward carnival. At the Champs Elysées the ladies were sewing on their costumes; Ottilie's hands were idle, for she had decided not to wear a costume at all. On rah-rah weekends, when drums sounded at the rising moon, she sat at her window and watched with a wandering mind the little bands of singers dancing and drumming their way along the road; she listened to the whistling and the laughter and felt no desire to join in. Somebody would think you were a thousand years old, said Baby, and Rosita said: Ottilie, why don't you come to the cockfight with us?

She was not speaking of an ordinary cockfight. From all parts of the island contestants had arrived bringing their fiercest birds. Ottilie thought she might as well go, and screwed a pair of pearls into her ears. When they arrived the exhibition was already under way; in a great tent a sea-sized crowd sobbed and shouted, while a second crowd, those who could not get in, thronged on the outskirts. Entry was no problem to the ladies from the Champs Elysées: a policeman friend cut a path for them and made room on a bench by the ring. The country people surrounding them seemed embarrassed to find themselves in such stylish company. They looked shyly at Baby's lacquered nails, the rhinestone combs in Rosita's hair, the glow of Ottilie's pearl earrings. However, the fights were exciting, and the ladies were soon forgotten; Baby was annoyed that this should be so, and her eyes rolled about searching for glances in their direction. Suddenly she nudged Ottilie. Ottilie, she said, you've got an admirer: see that boy over there, he's staring at you like you were something cold to drink.

At first she thought he must be someone she knew, for he was looking at her as though she should recognize him; but how could she know him when she'd never known anyone so beautiful, anyone with such long legs, little ears? She could see that he was from the mountains: his straw country hat and the worn-out blue of his thick shirt told her as much. He was a ginger color, his skin shiny as a lemon, smooth as a guava leaf, and the tilt of his head was as arrogant as the black and scarlet bird he held in his hands. Ottilie was used to boldly smiling at men; but now her smile was fragmentary, it clung to her lips like cake crumbs.

Eventually there was an intermission. The arena was cleared, and all who could crowded into it to dance and stamp while an orchestra of drums and strings sang out carnival tunes. It was then that the young man approached Ottilie; she laughed to see his bird perched like a parrot on his shoulder. Off with you, said Baby, outraged that a peasant should ask Ottilie to dance, and Rosita rose menacingly to stand between the young man and her friend. He only smiled, and said: Please, madame, I would like to speak with your daughter. Ottilie felt herself being lifted, felt her hips meet against his to the rhythm of music, and she did not mind at all, she let him lead her into the thickest tangle of dancers. Rosita said: Did you hear that, he thought I was her mother? And Baby, consoling her, grimly said: After all, what do you expect? They're only natives, both of them: when she comes back we'll just pretend we don't know her.

As it happened, Ottilie did not return to her friends. Royal, this was the young man's name, Royal Bonaparte, he told her, had not wanted to dance. We must walk in a quiet place, he said, hold my hand and I will take you. She thought him strange, but did not feel strange with him, for the mountains were still with her, and he was of the mountains. With her hands together, and the iridescent cock swaying on his shoulder, they left the tent and wandered lazily down a white road, then along a soft lane where birds of sunlight fluttered through the greenness of leaning acacia trees.

I have been sad, he said, not looking sad. In my village Juno is a champion, but the birds here are strong and ugly, and if I let him fight I would only have a dead Juno. So I will take him home and say that he won. Ottilie, will you have a dip of snuff?

She sneezed voluptuously. Snuff reminded her of her childhood, and mean as those years had been, nostalgia touched her with its far-reaching wand. Royal, she said, be still a minute, I want to take off my shoes.

Royal himself did not have shoes; his golden feet were slender and airy, and the prints they left were like the track of a delicate animal. He said: How is it that I find you here, in all the world here, where nothing is good, where the rum is bad and the people thieves? Why do I find you here, Ottilie?

Because I must make my way, the same as you, and here there is a place for me. I work in a—oh, kind of hotel.

We have our own place, he said. All the side of a hill, and there at the top of the hill is my cool house. Ottilie, will you come and sit inside it?

Crazy, said Ottilie, teasing him, crazy, and she ran between the trees, and he was after her, his arms out as though he held a net. The bird Juno flared his wings, crowed, flew to the ground. Scratchy leaves and fur of moss thrilled the soles of Ottilie's feet as she lilted through the shade and shadows; abruptly, into a veil of rainbow fern, she fell with a thorn in her heel. She winced when Royal pulled out the thorn; he kissed the place where it had been, his lips moved to her hands, her throat, and it was as though she were among drifting leaves. She breathed the odor of him, the dark, clean smell that was like the roots of things, of geraniums, of heavy trees.

Now that's enough, she pleaded, though she did not feel that this was so: it was only that after an hour of him her heart was about to give out. He was quiet then, his tickly haired head rested above her heart, and shoo she said to the gnats that clustered about his sleeping eyes, shush she said to Juno who pranced around crowing at the sky.

While she lay there, Ottilie saw her old enemy, the bees. Silently, in a line like ants, the bees were crawling in and out of a broken stump that stood not far from her. She loosened herself from Royal's arms, and smoothed a place on the ground for his head. Her hand was trembling as she lay it in the path of the bees, but the first that came along tumbled onto her palm, and when she closed her fingers it made no move to hurt her. She counted ten, just to be sure, then opened her hand, and the bee, in spiraling arcs, climbed the air with a joyful singing.

The proprietress gave Baby and Rosita a piece of advice: Leave her alone, let her go, a few weeks and she will be back. The proprietress spoke in the calm of defeat: to keep Ottilie with her, she'd offered the best room in the house, a new gold tooth, a Kodak, an electric fan, but Ottilie had not wavered, she had gone right on putting her belongings in a cardboard box. Baby tried to help, but she was crying so much that Ottilie had to stop her: it was bound to be bad luck, all those tears falling on a bride's possessions. And to Rosita she said: Rosita, you ought to be glad for me instead of standing there wringing your hands.

It was only two days after the cockfight that Royal shouldered Ottilie's cardboard box and walked her in the dusk toward the mountains. When it was learned that she was no longer at the Champs Elysées many of the customers took their trade elsewhere; others, though remaining loyal to the old place, complained of a gloom in the atmosphere: some evenings there was hardly anyone to buy the ladies a beer. Gradually it began to be felt that Ottilie after all would not come back; at the end of six months the proprietress said: She must be dead.

Royal's house was like a house of flowers; wisteria sheltered the roof, a curtain of vines shaded the windows, lilies bloomed at the door. From the windows one could see far, faint winkings of the sea, as the house was high up a hill; here the sun burned hot but the shadows were cold. Inside, the house was always dark and cool, and the walls rustled with pasted pink and green newspapers. There was only one room; it contained a stove, a teetering mirror on top a marble table, and a brass bed big enough for three fat men.

But Ottilie did not sleep in this grand bed. She was not allowed even to sit upon it, for it was the property of Royal's grandmother, Old Bonaparte. A charred, lumpy creature, bowlegged as a dwarf and bald as a buzzard, Old Bonaparte was much respected for miles around as a maker of spells. There were many who were afraid to have her shadow fall upon them; even Royal was wary of her, and he stuttered when he told her that he'd brought home a wife. Motioning Ottilie to her, the old woman bruised her here and there with vicious little pinches, and informed her grandson that his bride was too skinny: She will die with her first.

Each night the young couple waited to make love until they thought Old Bonaparte had gone to sleep. Sometimes, stretched on the straw moonlit pallet where they slept, Ottilie was sure that Old Bonaparte was awake and watching them. Once she saw a gummy, star-struck eye shining in the dark. There was no use complaining to Royal, he only laughed: What harm was there in an old woman who had seen so much of life wanting to see a little more?

Because she loved Royal, Ottilie put away her grievances and tried not to resent Old Bonaparte. For a long while she was happy; she did not miss her friends or the life in Port-au-Prince; even so, she kept her souvenirs of those days in good repair: with a sewing basket Baby had given her as a wedding gift she mended the silk dresses, the green silk stockings that now she never wore, for there was no place to wear them: only men congregated at the café in the village, at the cockfights. When women wanted to meet they met at the washing stream. But Ottilie was too busy to be lonesome. At daybreak she gathered eucalyptus leaves to start a fire and begin their meals; there were chickens to feed, a goat to be milked, there was Old Bonaparte's whining for attention. Three and four times a day she filled a bucket of drinking water and carried it to where Royal worked in the cane fields a mile below the house. She did not mind that on these visits he was gruff with her: she knew that he was showing off before the other men who worked in the fields, and who grinned at her like split watermelons. But at night, when she had him home, she'd pull his ears and pout that he treated her like a dog until, in the dark of the yard where the fireflies flamed, he would hold her and whisper something to make her smile.

They had been married about five months when Royal began doing the things he'd done before his marriage. Other men went to the café in the evenings, stayed whole Sundays at a cockfight—he couldn't understand why Ottilie should carry on about it; but she said he had no right behaving the way he did, and that if he loved her he wouldn't leave her alone day and night with that mean old woman. I love you, he said, but a man has to have his pleasures too. There were nights when he pleasured himself until the moon was in the middle of the sky; she never knew when he was coming home, and she would lie fretting on the pallet, imagining she could not sleep without his arms around her.

But Old Bonaparte was the real torment. She was about to worry Ottilie out of her mind. If Ottilie was cooking, the terrible old woman was sure to come poking around the stove, and when she did not like what there was to eat she would take a mouthful and spit it on the floor. Every mess she could think of she made: she wet the bed, insisted on having the goat in the room, whatever she touched was soon spilled or broken, and to Royal she complained that a woman who couldn't keep a nice house for her husband was worthless. She was underfoot the whole day, and her red, remorseless eyes were seldom shut; but the worst of it, the thing that finally made Ottilie threaten to kill her, was the old woman's habit of sneaking up from nowhere and pinching her so hard you could see the fingernail marks. If you do that one more time, if you just dare, I'll snatch that knife and cut out your heart! Old Bonaparte knew Ottilie meant it, and though she stopped the pinching, she thought of other jokes: for instance, she made a point of walking all over a certain part of the yard, pretending she did not know that Ottilie had planted a little garden there.

One day two exceptional things happened. A boy came from the village bringing a letter for Ottilie; at the Champs Elysées postcards had once in a while arrived from sailors and other traveling men who had spent pleasant moments with her, but this was the first letter she'd ever received. Since she could not read it, her first impulse was to tear it up: there was no use having it hang around to haunt her. Of course there was a chance that someday she would learn to read; and so she went to hide it in her sewing basket.

When she opened the sewing basket, she made a sinister discovery: there, like a gruesome ball of yarn, was the severed head of a yellow cat. So, the miserable old woman was up to new tricks! She wants to put a spell, thought Ottilie, not in the least frightened. Primly lifting the head by one of its ears, she carried it to the stove and dropped it into a boiling pot: at noon Old Bonaparte sucked her teeth and remarked that the soup Ottilie had made for her was surprisingly tasty.

The next morning, just in time for the midday meal, she found twisting in her basket a small green snake which, chopping fine as sand, she sprinkled into a serving of stew. Each day her ingenuity was tested: there were spiders to bake, a lizard to fry, a buzzard's breast to boil. Old Bonaparte ate several helpings of everything. With a restless glittering her eyes followed Ottilie as she watched for some sign that the spell was taking hold. You don't look well, Ottilie, she said, mixing a little molasses in the vinegar of her voice. You eat like an ant: here now, why don't you have a bowl of this good soup?

Because, answered Ottilie evenly, I don't like buzzard in my soup; or spiders in my bread, snakes in the stew: I have no appetite for such things.

Old Bonaparte understood; with swelling veins and a stricken, powerless tongue, she rose shakily to her feet, then crashed across the table. Before nightfall she was dead.

Royal summoned mourners. They came from the village, from the neighboring hills and, wailing like dogs at midnight, laid siege to the house. Old women beat their heads against the walls, moaning men prostrated themselves: it was the art of sorrow, and those who best mimicked grief were much admired. After the funeral everyone went away, satisfied that they'd done a good job.

Now the house belonged to Ottilie. Without Old Bonaparte's prying and her mess to clean she had more spare time, but she did not know what to do with it. She sprawled on the great brass bed, she loafed in front of the mirror; monotony hummed in her head, and to drive away its fly-buzz sound she would sing the songs she'd learned from the jukebox at the Champs Elysées. Waiting in the twilight for Royal she would remember that at this hour her friends in Port-au-Prince were gossiping on the porch and waiting for the turning headlights of a car; but when she saw Royal ambling up the path, his cane cutter swinging at his side like a crescent moon, she forgot such thoughts and ran with a satisfied heart to meet him.

One night as they lay half-drowsing, Ottilie felt suddenly another presence in the room. Then, gleaming there at the foot of the bed, she saw, as she had seen before, a watching eye; thus she knew what for some time she had suspected: that Old Bonaparte was dead but not gone. Once, when she was alone in the house, she'd heard a laugh, and once again, out in the yard, she'd seen the goat gazing at someone who was not there and twinkling his ears as he did whenever the old woman scratched his skull.

Stop shaking the bed, said Royal, and Ottilie, with a finger raised at the eye, whisperingly asked him if he could not see it. When he replied that she was dreaming, she reached for the eye and screamed at feeling only air. Royal lighted a lamp; he cuddled Ottilie on his lap and smoothed her hair while she told him of the discoveries she'd made in her sewing basket, and of how she had disposed of them. Was it wrong what she'd done? Royal did not know, it was not for him to say, but it was his opinion that she would have to be punished; and why? because the old woman wanted it, because she would otherwise never leave Ottilie in peace: that was the way with haunts.

In accordance with this, Royal fetched a rope the next morning and proposed to tie Ottilie to a tree in the yard: there she was to remain until dark without food or water, and anyone passing would know her to be in a state of disgrace.

But Ottilie crawled under the bed and refused to come out. I'll run away, she whimpered. Royal, if you try to tie me to that old tree I'll run away.

Then I'd have to go and get you, said Royal, and that would be the worse for you.

He gripped her by an ankle and dragged her squealing from under the bed. All the way to the yard she caught at things, the door, a vine, the goat's beard, but none of these would hold her, and Royal was not detained from tying her to the tree. He made three knots in the rope, and went off to work sucking his hand where she had bit him. She hollered to him all the bad words she'd ever heard until he disappeared over the hill. The goat, Juno and the chickens gathered to stare at her humiliation; slumping to the ground, Ottilie stuck out her tongue at them.

Because she was almost asleep, Ottilie thought it was a dream when, in the company of a child from the village, Baby and Rosita, wobbling on high heels and carrying fancy umbrellas, tottered up the path calling her name. Since they were people in a dream, they probably would not be surprised to find her tied to a tree.

My God, are you mad? shrieked Baby, keeping her distance as though she feared that indeed this must be the case. Speak to us, Ottilie!

Blinking, giggling, Ottilie said: I'm just happy to see you. Rosita, please untie me so that I can hug you both.

So this is what the brute does, said Rosita, tearing at the ropes. Wait till I see him, beating you and tying you in the yard like a dog.

Oh no, said Ottilie. Royal never beats me. It's just that today I'm being punished.

You wouldn't listen to us, said Baby. And now you see what's come of it. That man has plenty to answer for, she added, brandishing her umbrella.

Ottilie hugged her friends and kissed them. Isn't it a pretty house? she said, leading them toward it. It's like you picked a wagon of flowers and built a house with them: that is what I think. Come in out of the sun. It's cool inside and smells so sweet.

Rosita sniffed as though what she smelled was nothing sweet, and in her well-bottom voice declared that yes, it was better that they stay out of the sun, as it seemed to be affecting Ottilie's head.

It's a mercy that we've come, said Baby, fishing inside an enormous purse. And you can thank Mr. Jamison for that. Madame said you were dead, and when you never answered our letter we thought it must be so. But Mr. Jamison, that's the loveliest man you'll ever know, he hired a car for me and Rosita, your dearest loving friends, to come up here and find out what had happened to our Ottilie. Ottilie, I've got a bottle of rum here in my purse, so get us a glass and we'll all have a round.

The elegant foreign manners and flashing finery of the city ladies had intoxicated their guide, a little boy whose peeking black eyes bobbed at the window. Ottilie was impressed, too, for it was a long time since she'd seen painted lips or smelled bottle perfume, and while Baby poured the rum she got out her satin shoes, her pearl earrings. Dear, said Rosita when Ottilie had finished dressing up, there's no man alive that wouldn't buy you a whole keg of beer; to think of it, a gorgeous piece like you suffering far away from those who love you.

I haven't been suffering so much, said Ottilie. Just sometimes.

Hush now, said Baby. You don't have to talk about it yet. It's all over anyway. Here, dear, let me see your glass again. A toast to old times, and those to be! Tonight Mr. Jamison is going to buy champagne for everybody: Madame is letting him have it at half-price.

Oh, said Ottilie, envying her friends. Well, she wanted to know, what did people say of her, was she remembered?

Ottilie, you have no idea, said Baby; men nobody ever laid eyes on before have come into the place asking where is Ottilie, because they've heard about you way off in Havana and Miami. As for Mr. Jamison, he doesn't even look at us other girls, just comes and sits on the porch drinking by himself.

Yes, said Ottilie wistfully. He was always sweet to me, Mr. Jamison.

Presently the sun was slanting, and the bottle of rum stood three-quarters empty. A thunderburst of rain had for a moment drenched the hills that now, seen through the windows, shimmered like dragonfly wings, and a breeze, rich with the scent of rained-on flowers, roamed the room rustling the green and pink papers on the walls. Many stories had been told, some of them funny, a few that were sad; it was like any night's talk at the Champs Elysées, and Ottilie was happy to be a part of it again.

But it's getting late, said Baby. And we promised to be back before midnight. Ottilie, can we help you pack?

Although she had not realized that her friends expected her to leave with them, the rum stirring in her made it seem a likely assumption, and with a smile she thought: I told him I would go away. Only, she said aloud, it's not like I would have even a week to enjoy myself: Royal will come right down and get me.

Both her friends laughed at this. You're so silly, said Baby. I'd like to see that Royal when some of our men got through with him.

I wouldn't stand for anybody hurting Royal, said Ottilie. Besides, he'd be even madder when we got home.

Baby said: But, Ottilie, you wouldn't be coming back here with him.

Ottilie giggled, and looked about the room as though she saw something invisible to the others. Why, sure I would, she said.

Rolling her eyes, Baby produced a fan and jerked it in front of her face. That's the craziest thing I've ever heard, she said between hard lips. Isn't that the craziest thing you've ever heard, Rosita?

It's that Ottilie's been through so much, said Rosita. Dear, why don't you lie down on the bed while we pack your things?

Ottilie watched as they commenced piling her possessions. They scooped her combs and pins, they wound up her silk stockings. She took off her pretty clothes, as if she were going to put on something finer still; instead, she slipped back into her old dress; then, working quietly, and as though she were helping her friends, she put everything back where it belonged. Baby stamped her foot when she saw what was happening.

Listen, said Ottilie. If you and Rosita are my friends, please do what I tell you: tie me in the yard just like I was when you came. That way no bee is ever going to sting me.

Stinking drunk, said Baby; but Rosita told her to shut up. I think, said Rosita with a sigh, I think Ottilie is in love. If Royal wanted her back, she would go with him, and this being the way things were they might as well go home and say that Madame was right, that Ottilie was dead.

Yes, said Ottilie, for the drama of it appealed to her. Tell them that I am dead.

So they went into the yard; there, with heaving bosoms and eyes as round as the daytime moon scudding above, Baby said she would have no part in tying Ottilie to the tree, which left Rosita to do it alone. On parting, it was Ottilie who cried the most, though she was glad to see them go, for she knew that as soon as they were gone she would not think of them again. Teetering on their high heels down the dips of the path, they turned to wave, but Ottilie could not wave back, and so she forgot them before they were out of sight.

Chewing eucalyptus leaves to sweeten her breath, she felt the chill of twilight twitch the air. Yellow deepened the daytime moon, and roosting birds sailed into the darkness of the tree. Suddenly, hearing

Royal on the path, she threw her legs akimbo, let her neck go limp, lolled her eyes far back into their sockets. Seen from a distance, it would look as though she had come to some violent, pitiful end; and, listening to Royal's footsteps quicken to a run, she happily thought: This will give him a good scare.

A CHRISTMAS MEMORY

(1956)

Imagine a morning in late November. A coming of winter morning more than twenty years ago. Consider the kitchen of a spreading old house in a country town. A great black stove is its main feature; but there is also a big round table and a fireplace with two rocking chairs placed in front of it. Just today the fireplace commenced its seasonal roar.

A woman with shorn white hair is standing at the kitchen window. She is wearing tennis shoes and a shapeless gray sweater over a summery calico dress. She is small and sprightly, like a bantam hen; but, due to a long youthful illness, her shoulders are pitifully hunched. Her face is remarkable—not unlike Lincoln's, craggy like that, and tinted by sun and wind; but it is delicate too, finely boned, and her eyes are sherry-colored and timid. "Oh my," she exclaims, her breath smoking the windowpane, "it's fruitcake weather!"

The person to whom she is speaking is myself. I am seven; she is sixty-something. We are cousins, very distant ones, and we have lived together—well, as long as I can remember. Other people inhabit the house, relatives; and though they have power over us, and frequently make us cry, we are not, on the whole, too much aware of them. We are each other's best friend. She calls me Buddy, in memory of a boy who was formerly her best friend. The other Buddy died in the 1880's, when she was still a child. She is still a child.

"I knew it before I got out of bed," she says, turning away from the window with a purposeful excitement in her eyes. "The courthouse bell sounded so cold and clear. And there were no birds singing; they've gone to warmer country, yes indeed. Oh, Buddy, stop stuffing biscuit and fetch our buggy. Help me find my hat. We've thirty cakes to bake."

It's always the same: a morning arrives in November, and my friend, as though officially inaugurating the Christmas time of year that exhilarates her imagination and fuels the blaze of her heart, announces: "It's fruitcake weather! Fetch our buggy. Help me find my hat."

The hat is found, a straw cartwheel corsaged with velvet roses out-of-doors has faded: it once belonged to a more fashionable relative. Together, we guide our buggy, a dilapidated baby carriage, out to the garden and into a grove of pecan trees. The buggy is mine; that is, it was bought for me when I was born. It is made of wicker, rather unraveled, and the wheels wobble like a drunkard's legs. But it is a faithful object; springtimes, we take it to the woods and fill it with flowers, herbs, wild fern for our porch pots; in the summer, we pile it with picnic paraphernalia and sugar-cane fishing poles and roll it down to the edge of a creek; it has its winter uses, too: as a truck for hauling firewood from the yard to the kitchen, as a warm bed for Queenie, our tough little orange and white rat terrier who has survived distemper and two rattlesnake bites. Queenie is trotting beside it now.

Three hours later we are back in the kitchen hulling a heaping buggyload of windfall pecans. Our backs hurt from gathering them: how hard they were to find (the main crop having been shaken off the trees and sold by the orchard's owners, who are not us) among the concealing leaves, the frosted, deceiving grass. Caarackle! A cheery crunch, scraps of miniature thunder sound as the shells collapse and the golden mound of sweet oily ivory meat mounts in the milk-glass bowl. Queenie begs to taste, and now and again my friend sneaks her a mite, though insisting we deprive ourselves. "We mustn't, Buddy. If we start, we won't stop. And there's scarcely enough as there is. For thirty cakes." The kitchen is growing dark. Dusk turns the window into a mirror: our reflections mingle with the rising moon as we work by the fireside in the firelight. At last, when the moon is quite high, we toss the final hull into the fire and, with joined sighs, watch it catch flame. The buggy is empty, the bowl is brimful.

We eat our supper (cold biscuits, bacon, blackberry jam) and discuss tomorrow. Tomorrow the kind of work I like best begins: buying. Cherries and citron, ginger and vanilla and canned Hawaiian pineapple, rinds and raisins and walnuts and whiskey and oh, so much flour, butter, so many eggs, spices, flavorings: why, we'll need a pony to pull the buggy home.

But before these purchases can be made, there is the question of money. Neither of us has any. Except for skinflint sums persons in the house occasionally provide (a dime is considered very big money); or what we earn ourselves from various activities: holding rummage sales, selling buckets of hand-picked blackberries, jars of homemade jam and apple jelly and peach preserves, rounding up flowers for funerals and weddings. Once we won seventy-ninth prize, five dollars, in a national football contest. Not that we know a fool thing about football. It's just that we enter any contest we hear about: at the moment our hopes are centered on the fifty-thousand-dollar Grand Prize being offered to name a new brand of coffee (we suggested "A.M."; and, after some hesitation, for my friend thought it perhaps sacrilegious, the slogan "A.M.! Amen!"). To tell the truth, our only *really* profitable enterprise was the Fun and Freak Museum we conducted in a back-yard woodshed two summers ago. The Fun was a stereopticon with slide views of Washington and New York lent us by a relative who had been to those places (she was furious when she discovered why we'd borrowed it); the Freak was a three-legged biddy chicken hatched by one of our own hens. Everybody hereabouts wanted to see that biddy: we charged grownups a nickel, kids two cents. And took in a good twenty dollars before the museum shut down due to the decease of the main attraction.

But one way and another we do each year accumulate Christmas savings, a Fruitcake Fund. These moneys we keep hidden in an ancient bead purse under a loose board under the floor under a chamber pot under my friend's bed. The purse is seldom removed from this safe location except to make a deposit, or, as happens every Saturday, a withdrawal; for on Saturdays I am allowed ten cents to go to the picture show. My friend has never been to a picture show, nor does she intend to: "I'd rather hear you tell the story, Buddy. That way I can imagine it more. Besides, a person my age shouldn't squander their eyes. When the Lord comes, let me see him clear." In addition to never having seen a movie, she has never: eaten in a restaurant, traveled more than five miles from home, received or sent a telegram, read anything except funny papers and the Bible, worn cosmetics, cursed, wished someone harm, told a lie on purpose, let a hungry dog go hungry. Here are a few things she has done, does do: killed with a hoe the biggest rattlesnake ever seen in this county (sixteen rattles), dip snuff (secretly), tame hummingbirds (just try it) till they balance on her finger, tell ghost stories (we both believe in ghosts) so tingling they chill you in July, talk to herself, take walks in the rain, grow the prettiest japonicas in town, know the recipe for every sort of old-time Indian cure, including a magical wart-remover.

Now, with supper finished, we retire to the room in a faraway part of the house where my friend sleeps in a scrap-quilt-covered iron bed painted rose pink, her favorite color. Silently, wallowing in the pleasures of conspiracy, we take the bead purse from its secret place and spill its contents on the scrap quilt. Dollar bills, tightly rolled and green as May buds. Somber fifty-cent pieces, heavy enough to weight a dead man's eyes. Lovely dimes, the liveliest coin, the one that really jingles. Nickels and quarters, worn smooth as creek pebbles. But mostly a hateful heap of bitter-odored pennies. Last summer others in the house contracted to pay us a penny for every twenty-five flies we killed. Oh, the carnage of August: the flies that flew to heaven! Yet it was not work in which we took pride. And, as we sit counting pennies, it is as though we were back tabulating dead flies. Neither of us has a head for figures; we count slowly, lose track, start again. According to her calculations, we have $12.73. According to mine, exactly $13. "I do hope you're wrong, Buddy. We can't mess around with thirteen. The cakes will fall. Or put somebody in the cemetery. Why, I wouldn't dream of getting out of bed on the thirteenth." This is true: she always spends thirteenths in bed. So, to be on the safe side, we subtract a penny and toss it out the window.

Of the ingredients that go into our fruitcakes, whiskey is the most expensive, as well as the hardest to obtain: State laws forbid its sale. But everybody knows you can buy a bottle from Mr. Haha Jones. And the next day, having completed our more prosaic shopping, we set out for Mr. Haha's business address, a "sinful" (to quote public opinion) fish-fry and dancing café down by the river. We've been there before, and on the same errand; but in previous years our dealings have been with Haha's wife, an iodine-dark Indian woman with brazzy peroxided hair and a dead-tired disposition. Actually, we've never laid eyes on her husband, though we've heard that he's an Indian too. A giant with razor scars across his cheeks. They call him Haha because he's so gloomy, a man who never laughs. As we approach his café (a large log cabin festooned inside and out with chains of garish-gay naked lightbulbs and standing by the river's muddy edge under the shade of river trees where moss drifts through the branches like gray mist) our steps slow down. Even Queenie stops prancing and sticks close by. People have been murdered in Haha's café. Cut to pieces. Hit on the head. There's a case coming up in court next month. Naturally these goings-on happen at night when the colored lights cast crazy patterns and the victrola wails. In the daytime

Haha's is shabby and deserted. I knock at the door, Queenie barks, my friend calls: "Mrs. Haha, ma'am? Anyone to home?"

Footsteps. The door opens. Our hearts overturn. It's Mr. Haha Jones himself! And he *is* a giant; he *does* have scars; he *doesn't* smile. No, he glowers at us through Satan-tilted eyes and demands to know: "What you want with Haha?"

For a moment we are too paralyzed to tell. Presently my friend half-finds her voice, a whispery voice at best: "If you please, Mr. Haha, we'd like a quart of your finest whiskey."

His eyes tilt more. Would you believe it? Haha is smiling! Laughing, too. "Which one of you is a drinkin' man?"

"It's for making fruitcakes, Mr. Haha. Cooking."

This sobers him. He frowns. "That's no way to waste good whiskey." Nevertheless, he retreats into the shadowed café and seconds later appears carrying a bottle of daisy yellow unlabeled liquor. He demonstrates its sparkle in the sunlight and says: "Two dollars."

We pay him with nickels and dimes and pennies. Suddenly, jangling the coins in his hand like a fistful of dice, his face softens. "Tell you what," he proposes, pouring the money back into our bead purse, "just send me one of them fruitcakes instead."

"Well," my friend remarks on our way home, "there's a lovely man. We'll put an extra cup of raisins in *his* cake."

The black stove, stoked with coal and firewood, glows like a lighted pumpkin. Eggbeaters whirl, spoons spin round in bowls of butter and sugar, vanilla sweetens the air, ginger spices it; melting, nose-tingling odors saturate the kitchen, suffuse the house, drift out to the world on puffs of chimney smoke. In four days our work is done. Thirty-one cakes, dampened with whiskey, bask on window sills and shelves.

Who are they for?

Friends. Not necessarily neighbor friends: indeed, the larger share are intended for persons we've met maybe once, perhaps not at all. People who've struck our fancy. Like President Roosevelt. Like the

Reverend and Mrs. J. C. Lucey, Baptist missionaries to Borneo who lectured here last winter. Or the little knife grinder who comes through town twice a year. Or Abner Packer, the driver of the six o'clock bus from Mobile, who exchanges waves with us every day as he passes in a dust-cloud whoosh. Or the young Wistons, a California couple whose car one afternoon broke down outside the house and who spent a pleasant hour chatting with us on the porch (young Mr. Wiston snapped our picture, the only one we've ever had taken). Is it because my friend is shy with everyone *except* strangers that these strangers, and merest acquaintances, seem to us our truest friends? I think yes. Also, the scrapbooks we keep of thank-you's on White House stationery, time-to-time communications from California and Borneo, the knife grinder's penny post cards, make us feel connected to eventful worlds beyond the kitchen with its view of a sky that stops.

Now a nude December fig branch grates against the window. The kitchen is empty, the cakes are gone; yesterday we carted the last of them to the post office, where the cost of stamps turned our purse inside out. We're broke. That rather depresses me, but my friend insists on celebrating—with two inches of whiskey left in Haha's bottle. Queenie has a spoonful in a bowl of coffee (she likes her coffee chicory-flavored and strong). The rest we divide between a pair of jelly glasses. We're both quite awed at the prospect of drinking straight whiskey; the taste of it brings screwed-up expressions and sour shudders. But by and by we begin to sing, the two of us singing different songs simultaneously. I don't know the words to mine, just: *Come on along, come on along, to the dark-town strutters' ball.* But I can dance: that's what I mean to be, a tap dancer in the movies. My dancing shadow rollicks on the walls; our voices rock the chinaware; we giggle: as if unseen hands were tickling us. Queenie rolls on her back, her paws plow the air, something like a grin stretches her black lips. Inside myself, I feel warm and sparky as those crumbling logs, carefree as the wind in the chimney. My friend waltzes round the stove, the hem of her poor calico skirt pinched between her fingers as though it were a party dress: *Show me the way to go home,* she sings, her tennis shoes squeaking on the floor. *Show me the way to go home.*

Enter: two relatives. Very angry. Potent with eyes that scold, tongues that scald. Listen to what they have to say, the words tumbling together into a wrathful tune: "A child of seven! whiskey on his breath! are you out of your mind? feeding a child of seven! must be loony! road to ruination! remember Cousin Kate? Uncle Charlie? Uncle Charlie's brother-in-law? shame! scandal! humiliation! kneel, pray, beg the Lord!"

Queenie sneaks under the stove. My friend gazes at her shoes, her chin quivers, she lifts her skirt and blows her nose and runs to her room. Long after the town has gone to sleep and the house is silent except for the chimings of clocks and the sputter of fading fires, she is weeping into a pillow already as wet as a widow's handkerchief.

"Don't cry," I say, sitting at the bottom of her bed and shivering despite my flannel nightgown that smells of last winter's cough syrup, "don't cry," I beg, teasing her toes, tickling her feet, "you're too old for that."

"It's because," she hiccups, "I *am* too old. Old and funny."

"Not funny. Fun. More fun than anybody. Listen. If you don't stop crying you'll be so tired tomorrow we can't go cut a tree."

She straightens up. Queenie jumps on the bed (where Queenie is not allowed) to lick her cheeks. "I know where we'll find pretty trees, Buddy. And holly, too. With berries big as your eyes. It's way off in the woods. Farther than we've ever been. Papa used to bring us Christmas trees from there: carry them on his shoulder. That's fifty years ago. Well, now: I can't wait for morning."

Morning. Frozen rime lusters the grass; the sun, round as an orange and orange as hot-weather moons, balances on the horizon, burnishes the silvered winter woods. A wild turkey calls. A renegade hog grunts in the undergrowth. Soon, by the edge of knee-deep, rapid-running water, we have to abandon the buggy. Queenie wades the stream first, paddles across barking complaints at the swiftness of the current, the pneumonia-making coldness of it. We follow, holding our shoes and equipment (a hatchet, a burlap sack) above our heads. A mile more: of chastising thorns, burs and briers that catch at our clothes; of rusty pine needles brilliant with gaudy fungus and molted feathers. Here, there, a flash, a flutter, an ecstasy of shrillings remind us that not all the birds have flown south. Always, the path unwinds through lemony sun pools and pitch vine tunnels. Another creek to cross: a disturbed armada of speckled trout froths the water round us, and frogs the size of plates practice belly flops; beaver workmen are building a dam. On the farther shore, Queenie shakes herself and trembles. My friend shivers, too: not with cold but enthusiasm. One of her hat's ragged roses sheds a petal as she lifts her head and inhales the pine-heavy air. "We're almost there; can you smell it, Buddy?" she says, as though we were approaching an ocean.

And, indeed, it is a kind of ocean. Scented acres of holiday trees, prickly-leafed holly. Red berries shiny as Chinese bells: black crows swoop upon them screaming. Having stuffed our burlap sacks with enough greenery and crimson to garland a dozen windows, we set about choosing a tree. "It should be," muses my friend, "twice as tall as a boy. So a boy can't steal the star." The one we pick is twice as tall as me. A brave handsome brute that survives thirty hatchet strokes before it keels with a creaking rending cry. Lugging it like a kill, we commence the long trek out. Every few yards we abandon the struggle, sit down and pant. But we have the strength of triumphant huntsmen; that and the tree's virile, icy perfume revive us, goad us on. Many compliments accompany our sunset return along the red clay road to town; but my friend is sly and noncommittal when passers-by praise the treasure perched on our buggy: what a fine tree and where did it come from? "Yonderways," she murmurs vaguely. Once a car stops and the rich mill owner's lazy wife leans out and whines: "Giveya two-bits cash for that ol tree." Ordinarily my friend is afraid of saying no; but on this occasion she promptly shakes her head: "We wouldn't take a dollar." The mill owner's wife persists. "A dollar, my foot! Fifty cents. That's my last offer. Goodness, woman, you can get another one." In answer, my friend gently reflects: "I doubt it. There's never two of anything."

Home: Queenie slumps by the fire and sleeps till tomorrow, snoring loud as a human.

A trunk in the attic contains: a shoebox of ermine tails (off the opera cape of a curious lady who once rented a room in the house), coils of frazzled tinsel gone gold with age, one silver star, a brief rope of dilapidated, undoubtedly dangerous candy-like light bulbs. Excellent decorations, as far as they go, which isn't far enough: my friend wants our tree to blaze "like a Baptist window," droop with weighty snows of ornament. But we can't afford the made-in-Japan splendors at the five-and-dime. So we do what we've always done: sit for days at the kitchen table with scissors and crayons and stacks of colored paper. I make sketches and my friend cuts them out: lots of cats, fish too (because they're easy to draw), some apples, some watermelons, a few winged angels devised from saved-up sheets of Hershey-bar tin foil. We use safety pins to attach these creations to the tree; as a final touch, we sprinkle the branches with shredded cotton (picked in August for this purpose). My friend, surveying the effect, clasps her hands together. "Now honest, Buddy. Doesn't it look good enough to eat?" Queenie tries to eat an angel.

After weaving and ribboning holly wreaths for all the front windows, our next project is the fashioning of family gifts. Tie-dye scarves for the ladies, for the men a home-brewed lemon and licorice and aspirin syrup to be taken "at the first Symptoms of a Cold and after Hunting." But when it comes time for making each other's gift, my friend and I separate to work secretly. I would like to buy her a pearl-handled knife, a radio, a whole pound of chocolate-covered cherries (we tasted some once, and she always swears: "I could live on them, Buddy, Lord yes I could—and that's not taking His name in

vain"). Instead, I am building her a kite. She would like to give me a
bicycle (she's said so on several million occasions: "If only I could,
Buddy. It's bad enough in life to do without something *you* want; but
confound it, what gets my goat is not being able to give somebody
something you want *them* to have. Only one of these days I will,
Buddy. Locate you a bike. Don't ask how. Steal it, maybe"). Instead,
I'm fairly certain that she is building me a kite—the same as last year,
and the year before: the year before that we exchanged slingshots. All
of which is fine by me. For we are champion kite-fliers who study the
wind like sailors; my friend, more accomplished than I, can get a kite
aloft when there isn't enough breeze to carry clouds.

Christmas Eve afternoon we scrape together a nickel and go to the
butcher's to buy Queenie's traditional gift, a good gnawable beef
bone. The bone, wrapped in funny paper, is placed high in the tree
near the silver star. Queenie knows it's there. She squats at the foot
of the tree staring up in a trance of greed: when bedtime arrives she
refuses to budge. Her excitement is equaled by my own. I kick the
covers and turn my pillow as though it were a scorching summer's
night. Somewhere a rooster crows: falsely, for the sun is still on the
other side of the world.

"Buddy, are you awake?" It is my friend, calling from her room,
which is next to mine; and an instant later she is sitting on my bed
holding a candle. "Well, I can't sleep a hoot," she declares. "My
mind's jumping like a jack rabbit. Buddy, do you think Mrs. Roosevelt will serve our cake at dinner?" We huddle in the bed, and she
squeezes my hand I-love-you. "Seems like your hand used to be so
much smaller. I guess I hate to see you grow up. When you're grown
up, will we still be friends?" I say always. "But I feel so bad, Buddy. I
wanted so bad to give you a bike. I tried to sell my cameo Papa gave
me. Buddy"—she hesitates, as though embarrassed—"I made you another kite." Then I confess that I made her one, too; and we laugh.
The candle burns too short to hold. Out it goes, exposing the
starlight, the stars spinning at the window like a visible caroling that

slowly, slowly daybreak silences. Possibly we doze; but the beginnings of dawn splash us like cold water: we're up, wide-eyed and wandering while we wait for others to waken. Quite deliberately my friend drops a kettle on the kitchen floor. I tap-dance in front of closed doors. One by one the household emerges, looking as though they'd like to kill us both; but it's Christmas, so they can't. First, a gorgeous breakfast: just everything you can imagine—from flapjacks and fried squirrel to hominy grits and honey-in-the-comb. Which puts everyone in a good humor except my friend and I. Frankly, we're so impatient to get at the presents we can't eat a mouthful.

Well, I'm disappointed. Who wouldn't be? With socks, a Sunday school shirt, some handkerchiefs, a hand-me-down sweater and a year's subscription to a religious magazine for children. *The Little Shepherd.* It makes me boil. It really does.

My friend has a better haul. A sack of Satsumas, that's her best present. She is proudest, however, of a white wool shawl knitted by her married sister. But she *says* her favorite gift is the kite I built her. And it *is* very beautiful; though not as beautiful as the one she made me, which is blue and scattered with gold and green Good Conduct stars; moreover, my name is painted on it, "Buddy."

"Buddy, the wind is blowing."

The wind is blowing, and nothing will do till we've run to a pasture below the house where Queenie has scooted to bury her bone (and where, a winter hence, Queenie will be buried, too). There, plunging through the healthy waist-high grass, we unreel our kites, feel them twitching at the string like sky fish as they swim into the wind. Satisfied, sun-warmed, we sprawl in the grass and peel Satsumas and watch our kites cavort. Soon I forget the socks and hand-me-down sweater. I'm as happy as if we'd already won the fifty-thousand-dollar Grand Prize in that coffee-naming contest.

"My, how foolish I am!" my friend cries, suddenly alert, like a woman remembering too late she has biscuits in the oven. "You know what I've always thought?" she asks in a tone of discovery, and not smiling at me but a point beyond. "I've always thought a body would have to be sick and dying before they saw the Lord. And I imagined that when He came it would be like looking at the Baptist window: pretty as colored glass with the sun pouring through, such a shine you don't know it's getting dark. And it's been a comfort: to think of that shine taking away all the spooky feeling. But I'll wager it never happens. I'll wager at the very end a body realizes the Lord has already shown Himself. That things as they are"—her hand circles in a gesture that gathers clouds and kites and grass and Queenie pawing earth over her bone—"just what they've always seen, was seeing Him. As for me, I could leave the world with today in my eyes."

This is our last Christmas together.

Life separates us. Those who Know Best decide that I belong in a military school. And so follows a miserable succession of bugle-blowing prisons, grim reveille-ridden summer camps. I have a new home too. But it doesn't count. Home is where my friend is, and there I never go.

And there she remains, puttering around the kitchen. Alone with Queenie. Then alone. ("Buddy dear," she writes in her wild hard-to-read script, "yesterday Jim Macy's horse kicked Queenie bad. Be thankful she didn't feel much. I wrapped her in a Fine Linen sheet and rode her in the buggy down to Simpson's pasture where she can be with all her Bones . . .") For a few Novembers she continues to bake her fruitcakes single-handed; not as many, but some: and, of course, she always sends me "the best of the batch." Also, in every letter she encloses a dime wadded in toilet paper: "See a picture show and write me the story." But gradually in her letters she tends to confuse me with her other friend, the Buddy who died in the 1880's; more and more thirteenths are not the only days she stays in bed: a morning arrives in November, a leafless birdless coming of winter morning, when she cannot rouse herself to exclaim: "Oh my, it's fruitcake weather!"

And when that happens, I know it. A message saying so merely confirms a piece of news some secret vein had already received, severing from me an irreplaceable part of myself, letting it loose like a kite on a broken string. That is why, walking across a school campus on this particular December morning, I keep searching the sky. As if I expected to see, rather like hearts, a lost pair of kites hurrying toward heaven.

AMONG THE PATHS TO EDEN

(1960)

One Saturday in March, an occasion of pleasant winds and sailing clouds, Mr. Ivor Belli bought from a Brooklyn florist a fine mass of jonquils and conveyed them, first by subway, then foot, to an immense cemetery in Queens, a site unvisited by him since he had seen his wife buried there the previous autumn. Sentiment could not be credited with returning him today, for Mrs. Belli, to whom he had been married twenty-seven years, during which time she had produced two now-grown and matrimonially-settled daughters, had been a woman of many natures, most of them trying: he had no desire to renew so unsoothing an acquaintance, even in spirit. No; but a hard winter had just passed, and he felt in need of exercise, air, a heart-lifting stroll through the handsome, spring-prophesying weather; of course, rather as an extra dividend, it was nice that he would be able to tell his daughters of a journey to their mother's grave, especially so since it might a little appease the elder girl, who seemed resentful of Mr. Belli's too comfortable acceptance of life as lived alone.

The cemetery was not a reposeful, pretty place; was, in fact, a damned frightening one: acres of fog-colored stone spilled across a sparsely grassed and shadeless plateau. An unhindered view of Manhattan's skyline provided the location with beauty of a stage-prop sort—it loomed beyond the graves like a steep headstone honoring these quiet folk, its used-up and very former citizens: the juxtaposed spectacle made Mr. Belli, who was by profession a tax accountant and therefore equipped to enjoy irony however sadistic, smile, actually chuckle—yet, oh God in heaven, its inferences chilled him, too, deflated the buoyant stride carrying him along the cemetery's rigid, pebbled paths. He slowed until he stopped, thinking: "I ought to have taken Morty to the zoo"; Morty being his grandson, aged three. But it would be churlish not to continue, vengeful: and why waste a bouquet? The combination of thrift and virtue reactivated him; he was breathing hard from hurry when, at last, he stooped to jam the jonquils into a rock urn perched on a rough gray slab engraved with Gothic calligraphy declaring that

SARAH BELLI

1901–1959

had been the

DEVOTED WIFE OF IVOR

BELOVED MOTHER OF IVY AND REBECCA.

Lord, what a relief to know the woman's tongue was finally stilled. But the thought, pacifying as it was, and though supported by visions of his new and silent bachelor's apartment, did not relight the suddenly snuffed-out sense of immortality, of glad-to-be-aliveness, which the day had earlier kindled. He had set forth expecting such good from the air, the walk, the aroma of another spring about to be. Now he wished he had worn a scarf; the sunshine was false, without real warmth, and the wind, it seemed to him, had grown rather wild. As he gave the jonquils a decorative pruning, he regretted he could not delay their doom by supplying them with water; relinquishing the flowers, he turned to leave.

A woman stood in his way. Though there were few other visitors to the cemetery, he had not noticed her before, or heard her approach. She did not step aside. She glanced at the jonquils; presently her eyes, situated behind steel-rimmed glasses, swerved back to Mr. Belli.

"Uh. Relative?"

"My wife," he said, and sighed as though some such noise was obligatory.

She sighed, too; a curious sigh that implied gratification. "Gee, I'm sorry."

Mr. Belli's face lengthened. "Well."

"It's a shame."

"Yes."

"I hope it wasn't a long illness. Anything painful."

"No-o-o," he said, shifting from one foot to the other. "In her sleep." Sensing an unsatisfied silence, he added, "Heart condition."

"Gee. That's how I lost my father. Just recently. Kind of gives us something in common. Something," she said, in a tone alarmingly plaintive, "something to talk about."

"—know how you must feel."

"At least they didn't suffer. That's a comfort."

The fuse attached to Mr. Belli's patience shortened. Until now he had kept his gaze appropriately lowered, observing, after his initial glimpse of her, merely the woman's shoes, which were of the sturdy, so-called sensible type often worn by aged women and nurses. "A great comfort," he said, as he executed three tasks: raised his eyes, tipped his hat, took a step forward.

Again the woman held her ground; it was as though she had been employed to detain him. "Could you give me the time? My old clock," she announced, self-consciously tapping some dainty machinery strapped to her wrist, "I got it for graduating high school. That's why it doesn't run so good any more. I mean, it's pretty old. But it makes a nice appearance."

Mr. Belli was obliged to unbutton his topcoat and plow around for a gold watch embedded in a vest pocket. Meanwhile, he scrutinized the lady, really took her apart. She must have been blond as a child, her general coloring suggested so: the clean shine of her Scandinavian skin, her chunky cheeks, flushed with peasant health, and the blueness of her genial eyes—such honest eyes, attractive despite the thin silver spectacles surrounding them; but the hair itself, what could be discerned of it under a drab felt hat, was poorly permanented frizzle of no particular tint. She was a bit taller than Mr. Belli, who was five-foot-eight with the aid of shoe lifts, and she may have weighed more; at any rate he couldn't imagine that she mounted scales too cheerfully. Her hands: kitchen hands; and the nails: not only nibbled ragged, but painted with a pearly lacquer queerly phosphorescent. She wore a plain brown coat and carried a plain black purse. When the student of these components recomposed them he found they assembled themselves into a very decent-looking person whose looks he liked; the nail polish was discouraging; still he felt that here was someone you could trust. As he trusted Esther Jackson, Miss Jackson, his secretary. Indeed, that was who she reminded him of, Miss Jackson; not that the comparison was fair—to Miss Jackson, who possessed, as he had once in the course of a quarrel informed Mrs. Belli, "intellectual elegance and elegance otherwise." Nevertheless, the woman confronting him seemed imbued with that quality of good-will he appreciated in his secretary, Miss Jackson, Esther (as he'd lately, absent-mindedly, called her). Moreover, he guessed them to be about the same age: rather on the right side of forty.

"Noon. Exactly."

"Think of that! Why, you must be famished," she said, and unclasped her purse, peered into it as though it were a picnic hamper crammed with sufficient treats to furnish a smörgåsbord. She scooped out a fistful of peanuts. "I practically live on peanuts since Pop—since I haven't anyone to cook for. I must say, even if I do say so, I miss my own cooking; Pop always said I was better than any restaurant he ever went to. But it's no pleasure cooking just for yourself, even when you *can* make pastries light as a leaf. Go on. Have some. They're fresh-roasted."

Mr. Belli accepted; he'd always been childish about peanuts and, as he sat down on his wife's grave to eat them, only hoped his friend had more. A gesture of his hand suggested that she sit beside him; he was surprised to see that the invitation seemed to embarrass her; sudden additions of pink saturated her cheeks, as though he'd asked her to transform Mrs. Belli's bier into a love bed.

"It's okay for you. A relative. But me. Would she like a stranger sitting on her—resting place?"

"Please. Be a guest. Sarah won't mind," he told her, grateful the dead cannot hear, for it both awed and amused him to consider what Sarah, that vivacious scene-maker, that energetic searcher for lipstick traces and stray blond strands, would say if she could see him shelling peanuts on her tomb with a woman not entirely unattractive.

And then, as she assumed a prim perch on the rim of the grave, he noticed her leg. Her left leg; it stuck straight out like a stiff piece of mischief with which she planned to trip passers-by. Aware of his interest, she smiled, lifted the leg up and down. "An accident. You know. When I was a kid. I fell off a roller coaster at Coney. Honest. It was in the paper. Nobody knows why I'm alive. The only thing is I can't bend my knee. Otherwise it doesn't make any difference. Except to go dancing. Are you much of a dancer?"

Mr. Belli shook his head; his mouth was full of peanuts.

"So that's something else we have in common. Dancing. I *might* like it. But I don't. I like music, though."

Mr. Belli nodded his agreement.

"And flowers," she added, touching the bouquet of jonquils; then her fingers traveled on and, as though she were reading Braille, brushed across the marble lettering on his name. "Ivor," she said, mispronouncing it. "Ivor Belli. My name is Mary O'Meaghan. But I wish *I* were Italian. My sister is; well, she married one. And oh, he's full of fun; happy-natured and outgoing, like all Italians. He says my spaghetti's the best he's ever had. Especially the kind I make with sea-food sauce. You ought to taste it."

Mr. Belli, having finished the peanuts, swept the hulls off his lap. "You've got a customer. But he's not Italian. Belli sounds like that. Only I'm Jewish."

She frowned, not with disapproval, but as if he had mysteriously daunted her.

"My family came from Russia; I was born there."

This last information restored her enthusiasm, accelerated it. "I don't care what they say in the papers. I'm sure Russians are the same as everybody else. Human. Did you see the Bolshoi Ballet on TV? Now didn't that make you proud to be a Russian?"

He thought: she means well; and was silent.

"Red cabbage soup—hot or cold—with sour cream. Hmnn. See," she said, producing a second helping of peanuts, "you *were* hungry. Poor fellow." She sighed. "How you must miss your wife's cooking."

It was true, he did; and the conversational pressure being applied to his appetite made him realize it. Sarah had set an excellent table: varied, on time, and well flavored. He recalled certain cinnamon-scented feast-days. Afternoons of gravy and wine, starchy linen, the "good" silver; followed by a nap. Moreover, Sarah had never asked him to dry a dish (he could hear her calmly humming in the kitchen), had never complained of housework; and she had contrived to make the raising of two girls a smooth series of thought-out, affectionate events; Mr. Belli's contribution to their upbringing had been to be an admiring witness; if his daughters were a credit to him (Ivy living in Bronxville, and married to a dental surgeon; her sister the wife of A. J. Krakower, junior partner in the law firm of Finnegan, Loeb and Krakower), he had Sarah to thank; they were her accomplishment. There was much to be said for Sarah, and he was glad to discover himself thinking so, to find himself remembering not the long hell of hours she had spent honing her tongue on his habits, supposed poker-playing, woman-chasing vices, but gentler episodes: Sarah showing off her self-made hats, Sarah scattering crumbs on snowy window sills for winter pigeons: a tide of visions that towed to sea the junk of harsher recollections. He felt, was all at once happy to feel, mournful, sorry he had not been sorry sooner; but, though he did genuinely value Sarah suddenly, he could not pretend regret that their life together had terminated, for the current arrangement was, on the whole, preferable by far. However, he wished that, instead of jonquils, he had brought her an orchid, the gala sort she'd always salvaged from her daughters' dates and stored in the icebox until they shriveled.

"—aren't they?" he heard, and wondered who had spoken until, blinking, he recognized Mary O'Meaghan, whose voice had been playing along unlistened to: a shy and lulling voice, a sound strangely small and young to come from so robust a figure.

"I said they must be cute, aren't they?"

"Well," was Mr. Belli's safe reply.

"Be modest. But I'm sure they are. If they favor their father; ha ha, don't take me serious, I'm joking. But, seriously, kids just slay me. I'll trade any kid for any grownup that ever lived. My sister has five, four boys and a girl. Dot, that's my sister, she's always after me to baby-sit now that I've got the time and don't have to look after Pop every minute. She and Frank, he's my brother-in-law, the one I mentioned, they say Mary, nobody can handle kids like *you*. At the same time have fun. But it's so easy; there's nothing like hot cocoa and a mean pillow fight to make kids sleepy. Ivy," she said, reading aloud the tombstone's dour script. "Ivy and Rebecca. Sweet names. And I'm sure you do your best. But two little girls without a mother."

"No, no," said Mr. Belli, at last caught up. "Ivy's a mother herself. And Becky's expecting."

Her face restyled momentary chagrin into an expression of disbelief. "A grandfather? You?"

Mr. Belli had several vanities: for example, he thought he was *saner* than other people; also, he believed himself to be a walking compass; his digestion, and an ability to read upside down, were other ego-enlarging items. But his reflection in a mirror aroused little inner applause; not that he disliked his appearance; he just knew that it was very so-what. The harvesting of his hair had begun decades ago; now his head was an almost barren field. While his nose had character, his chin, though it made a double effort, had none. His shoulders were broad; but so was the rest of him. Of course he was neat: kept his shoes shined, his laundry laundered, twice a day scraped and talcumed his bluish jowls; but such measures failed to camouflage, actually they emphasized, his middle-class, middle-aged ordinariness. Nonetheless, he did not dismiss Mary O'Meaghan's flattery; after all, an undeserved compliment is often the most potent.

"Hell, I'm fifty-one," he said, subtracting four years. "Can't say I feel it." And he didn't; perhaps it was because the wind had subsided, the warmth of the sun grown more authentic. Whatever the reason, his expectations had reignited, he was again immortal, a man planning ahead.

"Fifty-one. That's nothing. The prime. Is if you take care of yourself. A man your age needs tending so. Watching after."

Surely in a cemetery one was safe from husband stalkers? The question, crossing his mind, paused midway while he examined her cozy and gullible face, tested her gaze for guile. Though reassured, he thought it best to remind her of their surroundings. "Your father. Is he"—Mr. Belli gestured awkwardly—"near by?"

"Pop? Oh, no. He was very firm; absolutely refused to be buried. So he's at home." A disquieting image gathered in Mr. Belli's head, one that her next words, "His ashes are," did not fully dispel. "Well," she shrugged, "that's how he wanted it. Or—I see—you wondered why *I'm* here? I don't live too far away. It's somewhere to walk, and the view . . ." They both turned to stare at the skyline where the steeples of certain buildings flew pennants of cloud, and sun-dazzled windows glittered like a million bits of mica. Mary O'Meaghan said, "What a perfect day for a parade!"

Mr. Belli thought, *You're a very nice girl;* then he said it, too, and wished he hadn't, for naturally she asked him why. "Because. Well, that was nice what you said. About parades."

"See? So many things in common! I never miss a parade," she told him triumphantly. "The bugles. I play the bugle myself; used to, when I was at Sacred Heart. You said before—" She lowered her voice, as though approaching a subject that required grave tones. "You indicated you were a music lover. Because I have thousands of old records. Hundreds. Pop was in the business and that was his job. Till he retired. Shellacking records in a record factory. Remember Helen Morgan? She slays me, she really knocks me out."

"*Jesus* Christ," he whispered. Ruby Keeler, Jean Harlow: those had been keen but curable infatuations; but Helen Morgan, albino-pale, a sequinned wraith shimmering beyond Ziegfeld footlights—truly, truly he had loved her.

"Do you believe it? That she drank herself to death? On account of a gangster?"

"It doesn't matter. She was lovely."

"Sometimes, like when I'm alone and sort of fed up, I pretend I'm her. Pretend I'm singing in a night club. It's fun; you know?"

"Yes, I know," said Mr. Belli, whose own favorite fantasy was to imagine the adventures he might have if he were invisible.

"May I ask: would you do me a favor?"

"If I can. Certainly."

She inhaled, held her breath as if she were swimming under a wave of shyness; surfacing, she said: "Would you listen to my imitation? And tell me your honest opinion?" Then she removed her glasses: the silver rims had bitten so deeply their shape was permanently printed on her face. Her eyes, nude and moist and helpless, seemed stunned by freedom; the skimpily lashed lids fluttered like long-captive birds abruptly let loose. "There: everything's soft and smoky. Now you've got to use your imagination. So pretend I'm sitting on a piano—gosh, for*give* me, Mr. Belli."

"Forget it. Okay. You're sitting on a piano."

"I'm sitting on a piano," she said, dreamily drooping her head backward until it assumed a romantic posture. She sucked in her cheeks, parted her lips; at the same moment Mr. Belli bit into his. For it was a tactless visit that glamour made on Mary O'Meaghan's filled-out and rosy face; a visit that should not have been paid at all; it was the wrong address. She waited, as though listening for music to cue her; then, *"Don't ever leave me, now that you're here! Here is where you belong. Everything seems so right when you're near, When you're away it's all wrong."* And Mr. Belli was shocked, for what he was hearing was exactly Helen Morgan's voice, and the voice, with its vulnerable sweetness, refinement, its tender quaver toppling high notes, seemed not to be borrowed, but Mary O'Meaghan's own, a natural expression of some secluded identity. Gradually she abandoned theatrical poses, sat upright singing with her eyes squeezed shut: *"—I'm so dependent, When I need comfort, I always run to you. Don't ever leave me! 'Cause if you do, I'll have no one to run to."* Until too late, neither she nor Mr. Belli noticed the coffin-laden entourage invading their privacy: a black caterpillar composed of sedate Negroes who stared at the white couple as though they had stumbled upon a pair of drunken grave robbers—except one mourner, a dry-eyed little girl who started laughing and couldn't stop; her hiccup-like hilarity resounded long after the procession had disappeared around a distant corner.

"If that kid was mine," said Mr. Belli.

"I feel so ashamed."

"Say, listen. What for? That was beautiful. I mean it; you can sing."

"Thanks," she said; and, as though setting up a barricade against impending tears, clamped on her spectacles.

"Believe me, I was touched. What I'd like is, I'd like an encore."

It was as if she were a child to whom he'd handed a balloon, a unique balloon that kept swelling until it swept her upward, danced her along with just her toes now and then touching ground. She descended to say: "Only not here. Maybe," she began, and once more seemed to be lifted, lilted through the air, "maybe sometime you'll let me cook you dinner. I'll plan it really Russian. And we can play records."

The thought, the apparitional suspicion that had previously

passed on tiptoe, returned with a heavier tread, a creature fat and foursquare that Mr. Belli could not evict. "Thank you, Miss O'Meaghan. That's something to look forward to," he said. Rising, he reset his hat, adjusted his coat. "Sitting on cold stone too long, you can catch something."

"When?"

"Why, never. You should *never* sit on cold stone."

"When will you come to dinner?"

Mr. Belli's livelihood rather depended upon his being a skilled inventor of excuses. "Any time," he answered smoothly. "Except any time soon. I'm a tax man; you know what happens to us fellows in March. Yes sir," he said, again hoisting out his watch, "back to the grind for me." Still he couldn't—could he?—simply saunter off, leave her sitting on Sarah's grave? He owed her courtesy; for the peanuts, if nothing more, though there was more—perhaps it was due to her that he had remembered Sarah's orchids withering in the icebox. And anyway, she *was* nice, as likeable a woman, stranger, as he'd ever met. He thought to take advantage of the weather, but the weather offered none: clouds were fewer, the sun exceedingly visible. "Turned chilly," he observed, rubbing his hands together. "Could be going to rain."

"Mr. Belli. Now I'm going to ask you a very personal question," she said, enunciating each word decisively. "Because I wouldn't want you to think I go about inviting just anybody to dinner. My intentions are—" her eyes wandered, her voice wavered, as though the forthright manner had been a masquerade she could not sustain. "So I'm going to ask you a very personal question. Have you considered marrying again?"

He hummed, like a radio warming up before it speaks; when he did, it amounted to static: "Oh, at *my* age. Don't even want a dog. Just give me TV. Some beer. Poker once a week. Hell. Who the hell would want me?" he said; and, with a twinge, remembered Rebecca's mother-in-law, Mrs. A. J. Krakower, Sr., Dr. Pauline Krakower, a female dentist (retired) who had been an audacious participant in a certain family plot. Or what about Sarah's best friend, the persistent "Brownie" Pollock? Odd, but as long as Sarah lived he had enjoyed, upon occasion taken advantage of, "Brownie's" admiration; afterwards—finally he had *told* her not to telephone him any more (and she had shouted: "Everything Sarah ever said, she was right. You fat little *hairy* little bastard"). Then; and then there was Miss Jackson. Despite Sarah's suspicions, her in fact devout conviction, nothing untoward, very untoward, had transpired between him and the pleasant Esther, whose hobby was bowling. But he had always surmised, and in recent months known, that if one day he suggested drinks, dinner, a workout in some bowling alley . . . He said: "I *was* married. For twenty-seven years. That's enough for any lifetime"; but as he said it, he realized that, in just this moment, he had come to a decision, which was: he *would* ask Esther to dinner, he would take her bowling and buy her an orchid, a gala purple one with a lavender-ribbon bow. And where, he wondered, do couples honeymoon in April? At the latest May. Miami? Bermuda? Bermuda! "No, I've never considered it. Marrying again."

One would have assumed from her attentive posture that Mary O'Meaghan was raptly listening to Mr. Belli—except that her eyes played hookey, roamed as though she were hunting at a party for a different, more promising face. The color had drained from her own face; and with it had gone most of her healthy charm. She coughed.

He coughed. Raising his hat, he said: "It's been very pleasant meeting you, Miss O'Meaghan."

"Same here," she said, and stood up. "Mind if I walk with you to the gate?"

He did, yes; for he wanted to mosey along alone, devouring the tart nourishment of this spring-shiny, parade-weather, be alone with his many thoughts of Esther, his hopeful, zestful, live-forever mood. "A pleasure," he said, adjusting his stride to her slower pace and the slight lurch her stiff leg caused.

"But it *did* seem like a sensible idea," she said argumentatively.

"And there was old Annie Austin: the living proof. Well, nobody had a *better* idea. I mean, everybody was at me: Get married. From the day Pop died, my sister and everybody was saying: Poor Mary, what's to become of her? A girl that can't type. Take shorthand. With her leg and all; can't even wait on table. What happens to a girl—a *grown* woman—that doesn't know anything, never done anything? Except cook and look after her father. All I heard was: Mary, you've got to get married."

"So. Why fight that? A fine person like you, you ought to be married. You'd make some fellow very happy."

"Sure I would. But *who?*" She flung out her arms, extended a hand toward Manhattan, the country, the continents beyond. "So I've looked; I'm not lazy by nature. But honestly, frankly, how does anybody ever find a husband? If they're not very, very pretty; a terrific dancer. If they're just—oh ordinary. Like me."

"No, no, not at all," Mr. Belli mumbled. "Not ordinary, no. Couldn't you make something of your talent? Your voice?"

She stopped, stood clasping and unclasping her purse. "Don't poke fun. Please. My life is at stake." And she insisted: "I *am* ordinary. So is old Annie Austin. And she says the place for me to find a husband—a decent, comfortable man—is in the obituary column."

For a man who believed himself a human compass, Mr. Belli had the anxious experience of feeling he had lost his way; with relief he saw the gates of the cemetery a hundred yards ahead. "She does? She says that? Old Annie Austin?"

"Yes. And she's a very practical woman. She feeds six people on $58.75 a week: food, clothes, everything. And the way she explained it, it certainly *sounded* logical. Because the obituaries are full of un-married men. Widowers. You just go to the funeral and sort of intro-duce yourself: sympathize. Or the cemetery: come here on a nice day, or go to Woodlawn, there are always widowers walking around. Fel-lows thinking how much they miss home life and maybe wishing they were married again."

When Mr. Belli understood that she was in earnest, he was appalled; but he was also entertained: and he laughed, jammed his hands in his pockets and threw back his head. She joined him, spilled a laughter that restored her color, that, in skylarking style, made her rock against him. "Even I—" she said, clutching at his arm, "even *I* can see the humor." But it was not a lengthy vision; suddenly solemn, she said: "But that is how Annie met her husbands. Both of them: Mr. Cruikshank, and then Mr. Austin. So it *must* be a practical idea. Don't you think?"

"Oh, I do think."

She shrugged. "But it hasn't worked out too well. Us, for instance. *We* seemed to have such a lot in common."

"One day," he said, quickening his steps. "With a livelier fellow."

"I don't know. I've met some grand people. But it always ends like this. Like us . . ." she said, and left unsaid something more, for a new pilgrim, just entering through the gates of the cemetery, had attached her interest: an alive little man spouting cheery whistlings and with plenty of snap to his walk. Mr. Belli noticed him, too, observed the black band sewn round the sleeve of the visitor's bright green tweed coat, and commented: "Good luck, Miss O'Meaghan. Thanks for the peanuts."

The Thanksgiving Visitor

(1967)

for Lee

Talk about mean! Odd Henderson was the meanest human creature in my experience.

And I'm speaking of a twelve-year-old boy, not some grownup who has had the time to ripen a naturally evil disposition. At least, Odd was twelve in 1932, when we were both second-graders attending a small-town school in rural Alabama.

Tall for his age, a bony boy with muddy-red hair and narrow yellow eyes, he towered over all his classmates—would have in any event, for the rest of us were only seven or eight years old. Odd had failed first grade twice and was now serving his second term in the second grade. This sorry record wasn't due to dumbness—Odd was intelligent, maybe cunning is a better word—but he took after the rest of the Hendersons. The whole family (there were ten of them, not counting Dad Henderson, who was a bootlegger and usually in jail, all scrunched together in a four-room house next door to a Negro church) was a shiftless, surly bunch, every one of them ready to do you a bad turn; Odd wasn't the worst of the lot, and brother, that is *saying* something.

Many children in our school came from families poorer than the Hendersons; Odd had a pair of shoes, while some boys, girls too, were forced to go barefoot right through the bitterest weather—that's how hard the Depression had hit Alabama. But nobody, I don't care who, looked as down-and-out as Odd—a skinny, freckled scarecrow in sweaty cast-off overalls that would have been a humiliation to a chain-gang convict. You might have felt pity for him if he hadn't been so hateful. All the kids feared him, not just us younger kids, but even boys his own age and older.

Nobody ever picked a fight with him except one time a girl named Ann "Jumbo" Finchburg, who happened to be the other town bully. Jumbo, a sawed-off but solid tomboy with an all-hell-let-loose wrestling technique, jumped Odd from behind during recess one dull morning, and it took three teachers, each of whom must have wished the combatants would kill each other, a good long while to separate them. The result was a sort of draw: Jumbo lost a tooth and half her hair and developed a grayish cloud in her left eye (she never could see clear again); Odd's afflictions included a broken thumb, plus scratch scars that will stay with him to the day they shut his coffin. For months afterward, Odd played every kind of trick to goad Jumbo into a rematch; but Jumbo had gotten her licks and gave him considerable berth. As I would have done if he'd let me; alas, I was the object of Odd's relentless attentions.

Considering the era and locale, I was fairly well off—living, as I did, in a high-ceilinged old country house situated where the town ended and the farms and forests began. The house belonged to distant relatives, elderly cousins, and these cousins, three maiden ladies and their bachelor brother, had taken me under their roof because of a disturbance among my more immediate family, a custody battle that, for involved reasons, had left me stranded in this somewhat eccentric Alabama household. Not that I was unhappy there; indeed, moments of those few years turned out to be the happiest part of an otherwise difficult childhood, mainly because the youngest of the cousins, a woman in her sixties, became my first friend. As she was a child herself (many people thought her less than that, and murmured about her as though she were the twin of poor nice Lester Tucker, who roamed the streets in a sweet daze), she understood children, and understood me absolutely.

Perhaps it was strange for a young boy to have as his best friend an aging spinster, but neither of us had an ordinary outlook or background, and so it was inevitable, in our separate loneliness, that we should come to share a friendship apart. Except for the hours I spent at school, the three of us, me and old Queenie, our feisty little rat terrier, and Miss Sook, as everyone called my friend, were almost always together. We hunted herbs in the woods, went fishing on remote creeks (with dried sugarcane stalks for fishing poles) and gathered curious ferns and greeneries that we transplanted and grew with trailing flourish in tin pails and chamber pots. Mostly, though, our life was lived in the kitchen—a farmhouse kitchen, dominated by a big black wood-burning stove, that was often dark and sunny at the same time.

Miss Sook, sensitive as shy-lady fern, a recluse who had never traveled beyond the county boundaries, was totally unlike her brother and sisters, the latter being down-to-earth, vaguely masculine ladies who operated a dry-goods store and several other business ventures. The brother, Uncle B., owned a number of cotton farms scattered around the countryside; because he refused to drive a car or endure any contact whatever with mobilized machinery, he rode horseback, jogging all day from one property to another. He was a kind man, though a silent one: he grunted yes or no, and really never opened his mouth except to feed it. At every meal he had the appetite of an Alaskan grizzly after a winter's hibernation, and it was Miss Sook's task to fill him up.

Breakfast was our principal meal; midday dinner, except on Sundays, and supper were casual menus, often composed of leftovers from the morning. These breakfasts, served promptly at 5:30 A.M., were regular stomach swellers. To the present day I retain a nostalgic hunger for those cockcrow repasts of ham and fried chicken, fried pork chops, fried catfish, fried squirrel (in season), fried eggs, hominy grits with gravy, black-eyed peas, collards with collard liquor and cornbread to mush it in, biscuits, pound cake, pancakes and molasses, honey in the comb, homemade jams and jellies, sweet milk, buttermilk, coffee chicory-flavored and hot as Hades.

The cook, accompanied by her assistants, Queenie and myself, rose every morning at four to fire the stove and set the table and get everything started. Rising at that hour was not the hardship it may sound; we were used to it, and anyway we always went to bed as soon as the sun dropped and the birds had settled in the trees. Also, my friend was not as frail as she seemed; though she had been sickly as a child and her shoulders were hunched, she had strong hands and sturdy legs. She could move with sprightly, purposeful speed, the frayed tennis shoes she invariably wore squeaking on the waxed kitchen floor, and her distinguished face, with its delicately clumsy features and beautiful, youthful eyes, bespoke a fortitude that suggested it was more the reward of an interior spiritual shine than the visible surface of mere mortal health.

Nevertheless, depending on the season and the number of hands employed on Uncle B.'s farms, there were sometimes as many as fifteen people sitting down to those dawn banquets; the hands were entitled to one hot meal a day—it was part of their wages. Supposedly, a Negro woman came in to help wash the dishes, make the beds, clean the house and do the laundry. She was lazy and unreliable but a lifelong friend of Miss Sook's—which meant that my friend would not consider replacing her and simply did the work herself. She chopped firewood, tended a large menagerie of chickens, turkeys and hogs, scrubbed, dusted, mended all our clothes; yet when I came home from school, she was always eager to keep me company—to play a card game named Rook or rush off on a mushroom hunt or have a pillow fight or, as we sat in the kitchen's waning afternoon light, help me with homework.

She loved to pore over my textbooks, the geography atlas especially ("Oh, Buddy," she would say, because she called me Buddy, "just think of it—a lake named Titicaca. That really exists somewhere in the world"). My education was her education, as well. Due to her childhood illness, she had had almost no schooling; her handwriting was a series of jagged eruptions, the spelling a highly personal and phonetic affair. I could already write and read with a smoother assurance than she was capable of (though she managed to "study" one Bible chapter every day, and never missed "Little Orphan Annie" or "The Katzenjammer Kids," comics carried by the Mobile paper). She took a bristling pride in "our" report cards ("Gosh, Buddy! Five A's. Even arithmetic. I didn't dare to hope we'd get an A in arithmetic"). It was a mystery to her why I hated school, why some mornings I wept and pleaded with Uncle B., the deciding voice in the house, to let me stay home.

Of course it wasn't that I hated school; what I hated was Odd Henderson. The torments he contrived! For instance, he used to wait for me in the shadows under a water oak that darkened an edge of the school grounds; in his hand he held a paper sack stuffed with prickly cockleburs collected on his way to school. There was no sense in trying to outrun him, for he was quick as a coiled snake; like a rattler, he struck, slammed me to the ground and, his slitty eyes gleeful, rubbed the burrs into my scalp. Usually a circle of kids ganged around to titter, or pretend to; they didn't really think it funny; but Odd made them nervous and ready to please. Later, hiding in a toilet in the boys' room, I would untangle the burrs knotting my hair; this took forever and always meant missing the first bell.

Our second-grade teacher, Miss Armstrong, was sympathetic, for she suspected what was happening; but eventually, exasperated by my continual tardiness, she raged at me in front of the whole class: "Little mister big britches. What a big head he has! Waltzing in here twenty minutes after the bell. A half hour." Whereupon I lost control; I pointed at Odd Henderson and shouted: "Yell at him. He's the one to blame. The sonafabitch."

I knew a lot of curse words, yet even I was shocked when I heard what I'd said resounding in an awful silence, and Miss Armstrong, advancing toward me clutching a heavy ruler, said, "Hold out your hands, sir. Palms up, sir." Then, while Odd Henderson watched with a small citric smile, she blistered the palms of my hands with her brass-edged ruler until the room blurred.

It would take a page in small print to list the imaginative punishments Odd inflicted, but what I resented and suffered from most was the sense of dour expectations he induced. Once, when he had me pinned against a wall, I asked him straight out what had I done to make him dislike me so much; suddenly he relaxed, let me loose and said, "You're a sissy. I'm just straightening you out." He was right, I was a sissy of sorts, and the moment he said it, I realized there was nothing I could do to alter his judgment, other than toughen myself to accept and defend the fact.

As soon as I regained the peace of the warm kitchen, where Queenie might be gnawing an old dug-up bone and my friend puttering with a piecrust, the weight of Odd Henderson would blessedly slide from my shoulders. But too often at night, the narrow lion eyes loomed in my dreams while his high, harsh voice, pronouncing cruel promises, hissed in my ears.

My friend's bedroom was next to mine; occasionally cries arising from my nightmare upheavals wakened her; then she would come and shake me out of an Odd Henderson coma. "Look," she'd say, lighting a lamp, "you've even scared Queenie. She's shaking." And, "Is it a fever? You're wringing wet. Maybe we ought to call Doctor Stone." But she knew that it wasn't a fever, she knew that it was because of my troubles at school, for I had told and told her how Odd Henderson treated me.

But now I'd stopped talking about it, never mentioned it any more, because she refused to acknowledge that any human could be as bad as I made him out. Innocence, preserved by the absence of experience that had always isolated Miss Sook, left her incapable of encompassing an evil so complete.

"Oh," she might say, rubbing heat into my chilled hands, "he only picks on you out of jealousy. He's not smart and pretty as you are." Or, less jestingly, "The thing to keep in mind, Buddy, is this boy can't help acting ugly; he doesn't know any different. All those Henderson children have had it hard. And you can lay that at Dad Henderson's door. I don't like to say it, but that man never was anything except a mischief and a fool. Did you know Uncle B. horsewhipped him once? Caught him beating a dog and horsewhipped him on the spot. The best thing that ever happened was when they locked him up at State Farm. But I remember Molly Henderson before she married Dad. Just fifteen or sixteen she was, and fresh from somewhere across the river. She worked for Sade Danvers down the road, learning to be a dressmaker. She used to pass here and see me hoeing in the garden—such a polite girl, with lovely red hair, and so appreciative of everything; sometimes I'd give her a bunch of sweet peas or a japonica, and she was always so appreciative. Then she began strolling by arm in arm with Dad Henderson—and him so much older and a perfect rascal, drunk or sober. Well, the Lord must have His reasons. But it's a shame; Molly can't be more than thirty-five, and there she is without a tooth in her head or a dime to her name. Nothing but a houseful of children to feed. You've got to take all that into account, Buddy, and be patient."

Patient! What was the use of discussing it? Finally, though, my friend did comprehend the seriousness of my despair. The realization arrived in a quiet way and was not the outcome of unhappy midnight wakings or pleading scenes with Uncle B. It happened one rainy November twilight when we were sitting alone in the kitchen close by the dying stove fire; supper was over, the dishes stacked, and Queenie was tucked in a rocker, snoring. I could hear my friend's whispery voice weaving under the skipping noise of rain on the roof, but my mind was on my worries and I was not attending, though I was aware that her subject was Thanksgiving, then a week away.

My cousins had never married (Uncle B. had *almost* married, but his fiancée returned the engagement ring when she saw that sharing a house with three very individual spinsters would be part of the bargain); however, they boasted extensive family connections throughout the vicinity: cousins aplenty, and an aunt, Mrs. Mary Taylor Wheelwright, who was one hundred and three years old. As our house was the largest and the most conveniently located, it was traditional for these relations to aim themselves our way every year at Thanksgiving; though there were seldom fewer than thirty celebrants, it was not an onerous chore, because we provided only the setting and an ample number of stuffed turkeys.

The guests supplied the trimmings, each of them contributing her particular specialty: a cousin twice removed, Harriet Parker from Flomaton, made perfect ambrosia, transparent orange slices combined with freshly ground coconut; Harriet's sister Alice usually arrived carrying a dish of whipped sweet potatoes and raisins; the Conklin tribe, Mr. and Mrs. Bill Conklin and their quartet of handsome daughters, always brought a delicious array of vegetables canned during the summer. My own favorite was a cold banana pudding—a guarded recipe of the ancient aunt who, despite her longevity, was still domestically energetic; to our sorrow she took the secret with her when she died in 1934, age one hundred and five (and it wasn't age that lowered the curtain; she was attacked and trampled by a bull in a pasture).

Miss Sook was ruminating on these matters while my mind wandered through a maze as melancholy as the wet twilight. Suddenly I heard her knuckles rap the kitchen table: "Buddy!"

"What?"

"You haven't listened to one word."

"Sorry."

"I figure we'll need five turkeys this year. When I spoke to Uncle B. about it, he said he wanted you to kill them. Dress them, too."

"But *why*?"

"He says a boy ought to know how to do things like that."

Slaughtering was Uncle B.'s job. It was an ordeal for me to watch him butcher a hog or even wring a chicken's neck. My friend felt the same way; neither of us could abide any violence bloodier than swatting flies, so I was taken aback at her casual relaying of this command.

"Well, I won't."

Now she smiled. "Of course you won't. I'll get Bubber or some other colored boy. Pay him a nickel. But," she said, her tone descending conspiratorially, "we'll let Uncle B. believe it was you. Then he'll be pleased and stop saying it's such a bad thing."

"What's a bad thing?"

"Our always being together. He says you ought to have other friends, boys your own age. Well, he's right."

"I don't want any other friend."

"Hush, Buddy. Now hush. You've been real good to me. I don't know what I'd do without you. Just become an old crab. But I want to see you happy, Buddy. Strong, able to go out in the world. And you're never going to until you come to terms with people like Odd Henderson and turn them into friends."

"Him! He's the last friend in the world I want."

"Please, Buddy—invite that boy here for Thanksgiving dinner."

Though the pair of us occasionally quibbled, we never quarreled. At first I was unable to believe she meant her request as something more than a sample of poor-taste humor; but then, seeing that she was serious, I realized, with bewilderment, that we were edging toward a falling-out.

"I thought you were my *friend*."

"I am, Buddy. Truly."

"If you were, you couldn't think up a thing like that. Odd Henderson hates me. He's my *enemy*."

"He can't hate you. He doesn't know you."

"Well, I hate him."

"Because you don't know him. That's all I ask. The chance for you to know each other a little. Then I think this trouble will stop. And maybe you're right, Buddy, maybe you boys won't ever be friends. But I doubt that he'd pick on you any more."

"You don't understand. You've never hated anybody."

"No, I never have. We're allotted just so much time on earth, and I wouldn't want the Lord to see me wasting mine in any such manner."

"I won't do it. He'd think I was crazy. And I would be."

The rain had let up, leaving a silence that lengthened miserably. My friend's clear eyes contemplated me as though I were a Rook card she was deciding how to play; she maneuvered a salt-pepper lock of hair off her forehead and sighed. "Then I will. Tomorrow," she said, "I'll put on my hat and pay a call on Molly Henderson." This statement certified her determination, for I'd never known Miss Sook to plan a call on anyone, not only because she was entirely without social talent, but also because she was too modest to presume a welcome. "I don't suppose there will be much Thanksgiving in their house. Probably Molly would be very pleased to have Odd sit down with us. Oh, I know Uncle B. would never permit it, but the nice thing to do is invite them all."

My laughter woke Queenie; and after a surprised instant, my friend laughed too. Her cheeks pinked and a light flared in her eyes; rising, she hugged me and said, "Oh, Buddy, I knew you'd forgive me and recognize there was some sense to my notion."

She was mistaken. My merriment had other origins. Two. One was the picture of Uncle B. carving turkey for all those cantankerous Hendersons. The second was: It had occurred to me that I had no cause for alarm; Miss Sook might extend the invitation and Odd's mother might accept it in his behalf; but Odd wouldn't show up in a million years.

He would be too proud. For instance, throughout the Depression years, our school distributed free milk and sandwiches to all children whose families were too poor to provide them with a lunch box. But Odd, emaciated as he was, refused to have anything to do with these handouts; he'd wander off by himself and devour a pocketful of peanuts or gnaw a large raw turnip. This kind of pride was characteristic of the Henderson breed: they might steal, gouge the gold out of a dead man's teeth, but they would never accept a gift offered openly, for anything smacking of charity was offensive to them. Odd was sure to figure Miss Sook's invitation as a charitable gesture; or see it—and not incorrectly—as a blackmailing stunt meant to make him ease up on me.

I went to bed that night with a light heart, for I was certain my Thanksgiving would not be marred by the presence of such an unsuitable visitor.

The next morning I had a bad cold, which was pleasant; it meant no school. It also meant I could have a fire in my room and cream-of-tomato soup and hours alone with Mr. Micawber and David Copperfield: the happiest of stayabeds. It was drizzling again; but true to her promise, my friend fetched her hat, a straw cartwheel decorated with weather-faded velvet roses, and set out for the Henderson home. "I won't be but a minute," she said. In fact, she was gone the better part of two hours. I couldn't imagine Miss Sook sustaining so long a conversation except with me or herself (she talked to herself often, a habit of sane persons of a solitary nature); and when she returned, she did seem drained.

Still wearing her hat and an old loose raincoat, she slipped a thermometer in my mouth, then sat at the foot of the bed. "I like her," she said firmly. "I always have liked Molly Henderson. She does all she can, and the house was clean as Bob Spencer's fingernails"—Bob Spencer being a Baptist minister famed for his hygienic gleam—"but bitter cold. With a tin roof and the wind right in the room and not a scrap of fire in the fireplace. She offered me refreshment, and I surely would have welcomed a cup of coffee, but I said no. Because I don't expect there was any coffee on the premises. Or sugar.

"It made me feel ashamed, Buddy. It hurts me all the way down to see somebody struggling like Molly. Never able to see a clear day. I don't say people should have everything they want. Though, come to think of it, I don't see what's wrong with that, either. You ought to have a bike to ride, and why shouldn't Queenie have a beef bone every day? Yes, now it's come to me, now I understand: We really all of us ought to have everything we want. I'll bet you a dime that's what the Lord intends. And when all around us we see people who can't satisfy the plainest needs, I feel ashamed. Oh, not of myself, because who am I, an old nobody who never owned a mite; if I hadn't had a family to pay my way, I'd have starved or been sent to the County Home. The shame I feel is for all of us who have anything extra when other people have nothing.

"I mentioned to Molly how we had more quilts here than we could ever use—there's a trunk of scrap quilts in the attic, the ones I made when I was a girl and couldn't go outdoors much. But she cut me off, said the Hendersons were doing just fine, thank you, and the only thing they wanted was Dad to be set free and sent home to his people. 'Miss Sook,' she told me, 'Dad is a good husband, no matter what else he might be.' Meanwhile, she has her children to care for.

"And, Buddy, you must be wrong about her boy Odd. At least partially. Molly says he's a great help to her and a great comfort. Never complains, regardless of how many chores she gives him. Says he can sing good as you hear on the radio, and when the younger children start raising a ruckus, he can quiet them down by singing to them. Bless us," she lamented, retrieving the thermometer, "all we can do for people like Molly is respect them and remember them in our prayers."

The thermometer had kept me silent; now I demanded, "But what about the invitation?"

"Sometimes," she said, scowling at the scarlet thread in the glass, "I think these eyes are giving out. At my age, a body starts to look around very closely. So you'll remember how cobwebs really looked. But to answer your question, Molly was happy to hear you thought enough of Odd to ask him over for Thanksgiving. And," she continued, ignoring my groan, "she said she was sure he'd be tickled to come. Your temperature is just over the hundred mark. I guess you can count on staying home tomorrow. That ought to bring smiles! Let's see you smile, Buddy."

As it happened, I was smiling a good deal during the next few days prior to the big feast, for my cold had advanced to croup and I was out of school the entire period. I had no contact with Odd Henderson and therefore could not personally ascertain his reaction to the invitation; but I imagined it must have made him laugh first and spit next. The prospect of his actually appearing didn't worry me; it was as farfetched a possibility as Queenie snarling at me or Miss Sook betraying my trust in her.

Yet Odd remained a presence, a redheaded silhouette on the threshold of my cheerfulness. Still, I was tantalized by the description his mother had provided; I wondered if it was true he had another side, that somewhere underneath the evil a speck of humaneness existed. But that was impossible! Anybody who believed so would leave their house unlocked when the gypsies came to town. All you had to do was look at him.

Miss Sook was aware that my croup was not as severe as I pretended, and so in the mornings, when the others had absented themselves—Uncle B. to his farms and the sisters to their dry-goods store—she tolerated my getting out of bed and even let me assist in the springlike housecleaning that always preceded the Thanksgiving assembly. There was such a lot to do, enough for a dozen hands. We polished the parlor furniture, the piano, the black curio cabinet (which contained only a fragment of Stone Mountain the sisters had brought back from a business trip to Atlanta), the formal walnut rockers and florid Biedermeier pieces—rubbed them with lemon-scented wax until the place was shiny as lemon skin and smelled like a citrus grove. Curtains were laundered and rehung, pillows punched, rugs beaten; wherever one glanced, dust motes and tiny feathers drifted in the sparkling November light sifting through the tall rooms. Poor Queenie was relegated to the kitchen, for fear she might leave a stray hair, perhaps a flea, in the more dignified areas of the house.

The most delicate task was preparing the napkins and tablecloths that would decorate the dining room. The linen had belonged to my friend's mother, who had received it as a wedding gift; though it had been used only once or twice a year, say two hundred times in the past eighty years, nevertheless it was eighty years old, and mended patches and freckled discolorations were apparent. Probably it had not been a fine material to begin with, but Miss Sook treated it as though it had been woven by golden hands on heavenly looms: "My mother said, 'The day may come when all we can offer is well water and cold cornbread, but at least we'll be able to serve it on a table set with proper linen.' "

At night, after the day's dashing about and when the rest of the house was dark, one feeble lamp burned late while my friend, propped in bed with napkins massed on her lap, repaired blemishes and tears with thread and needle, her forehead crumpled, her eyes cruelly squeezed, yet illuminated by the fatigued rapture of a pilgrim approaching an altar at journey's end.

From hour to hour, as the shivery tolls of the faraway courthouse clock numbered ten and eleven and twelve, I would wake up and see her lamp still lit, and would drowsily lurch into her room to reprimand her: "You ought to be asleep!"

"In a minute, Buddy. I can't just now. When I think of all the company coming, it scares me. Starts my head whirling," she said, ceasing to stitch and rubbing her eyes. "Whirling with stars."

Chrysanthemums: some as big as a baby's head. Bundles of curled penny-colored leaves with flickering lavender underhues. "Chrysanthemums," my friend commented as we moved through our garden stalking flower-show blossoms with decapitating shears, "are like lions. Kingly characters. I always expect them to *spring*. To turn on me with a growl and a roar."

It was the kind of remark that caused people to wonder about Miss Sook, though I understand that only in retrospect, for I always knew just what she meant, and in this instance the whole idea of it, the notion of lugging all those growling gorgeous roaring lions into the house and caging them in tacky vases (our final decorative act on Thanksgiving Eve) made us so giggly and giddy and stupid we were soon out of breath.

"Look at Queenie," my friend said, stuttering with mirth. "Look at her ears, Buddy. Standing straight up. She's thinking, Well, what kind of lunatics are these I'm mixed up with? Ah, Queenie. Come here, honey. I'm going to give you a biscuit dipped in hot coffee."

A lively day, that Thanksgiving. Lively with on-and-off showers and abrupt sky clearings accompanied by thrusts of raw sun and sudden bandit winds snatching autumn's leftover leaves.

The noises of the house were lovely, too: pots and pans and Uncle B.'s unused and rusty voice as he stood in the hall in his creaking Sunday suit, greeting our guests as they arrived. A few came by horseback or mule-drawn wagon, the majority in shined-up farm trucks and rackety flivvers. Mr. and Mrs. Conklin and their four beautiful daughters drove up in a mint-green 1932 Chevrolet (Mr. Conklin was well off; he owned several fishing smackers that operated out of Mobile), an object which aroused warm curiosity among the men present; they studied and poked it and all but took it apart.

The first guests to arrive were Mrs. Mary Taylor Wheelwright, escorted by her custodians, a grandson and his wife. She was a pretty little thing, Mrs. Wheelwright; she wore her age as lightly as the tiny red bonnet that, like the cherry on a vanilla sundae, sat perkily atop her milky hair. "Darlin' Bobby," she said, hugging Uncle B., "I realize we're an itty-bit early, but you know me, always punctual to a fault." Which was an apology deserved, for it was not yet nine o'clock and guests weren't expected much before noon.

However, *everybody* arrived earlier than we intended—except the Perk McCloud family, who suffered two blowouts in the space of thirty miles and arrived in such a stomping temper, particularly Mr. McCloud, that we feared for the china. Most of these people lived year-round in lonesome places hard to get away from: isolated farms, whistle-stops and crossroads, empty river hamlets or lumber-camp communities deep in the pine forests; so of course it was eagerness that caused them to be early, primed for an affectionate and memorable gathering.

And so it was. Some while ago, I had a letter from one of the Conklin sisters, now the wife of a naval captain and living in San Diego; she wrote: "I think of you often around this time of year, I suppose because of what happened at one of our Alabama Thanksgivings. It was a few years before Miss Sook died—would it be 1933? Golly, I'll never forget that day."

By noon, not another soul could be accommodated in the parlor, a hive humming with women's tattle and womanly aromas: Mrs. Wheelwright smelled of lilac water and Annabel Conklin like geraniums after rain. The odor of tobacco fanned out across the porch, where most of the men had clustered, despite the wavering weather, the alternations between sprinkles of rain and sunlit wind squalls. Tobacco was a substance alien to the setting; true, Miss Sook now and again secretly dipped snuff, a taste acquired under unknown tutelage and one she refused to discuss; her sisters would have been mortified had they suspected, and Uncle B., too, for he took a harsh stand on all stimulants, condemning them morally and medically.

The virile redolence of cigars, the pungent nip of pipe smoke, the tortoiseshell richness they evoked, constantly lured me out of the parlor onto the porch, though it was the parlor I preferred, due to the presence of the Conklin sisters, who played by turn our untuned piano with a gifted, rollicking lack of airs. "Indian Love Call" was among their repertoire, and also a 1918 war ballad, the lament of a child pleading with a house thief, entitled "Don't Steal Daddy's Medals, He Won Them for Bravery." Annabel played and sang it; she was the oldest of the sisters and the loveliest, though it was a chore to pick among them, for they were like quadruplets of unequal height. One thought of apples, compact and flavorful, sweet but cider-tart; their hair, loosely plaited, had the blue luster of a well-groomed ebony racehorse, and certain features, eyebrows, noses, lips when smiling, tilted in an original style that added humor to their charms. The nicest thing was that they were a bit plump: "pleasingly plump" describes it precisely.

It was while listening to Annabel at the piano, and falling in love with her, that I felt Odd Henderson. I say *felt* because I was aware of him before I saw him: the sense of peril that warns, say, an experienced woodsman of an impending encounter with a rattler or bobcat alerted me.

I turned, and there the fellow stood at the parlor entrance, half in, half out. To others he must have seemed simply a grubby twelve-year-old beanpole who had made some attempt to rise to the event by parting and slicking his difficult hair, the comb grooves were still damply intact. But to me he was as unexpected and sinister as a genie released from a bottle. What a dumbhead I'd been to think he wouldn't show up! Only a dunce wouldn't have guessed that he would come out of spite: the joy of spoiling for me this awaited day.

However, Odd had not yet seen me: Annabel, her firm, acrobatic fingers somersaulting over the warped piano keys, had diverted him, for he was watching her, lips separated, eyes slitted, as though he had come upon her disrobed and cooling herself in the local river. It was as if he were contemplating some wished-for vision; his already red ears had become pimiento. The entrancing scene so dazed him I was able to squeeze directly past him and run along the hall to the kitchen. "He's here!"

My friend had completed her work hours earlier; moreover she had two colored women helping out. Nevertheless she had been hiding in the kitchen since our party started, under a pretense of keeping the exiled Queenie company. In truth, she was afraid of mingling with any group, even one composed of relatives, which was why, despite her reliance on the Bible and its Hero, she rarely went to church. Although she loved all children and was at ease with them, she was not acceptable as a child, yet she could not accept herself as a peer of grownups and in a collection of them behaved like an awkward young lady, silent and rather astonished. But the *idea* of parties exhilarated her; what a pity she couldn't take part invisibly, for then how festive she would have felt.

I noticed that my friend's hands were trembling; so were mine. Her usual outfit consisted of calico dresses, tennis shoes and Uncle B.'s discarded sweaters; she had no clothes appropriate to starchy occasions. Today she was lost inside something borrowed from one of her stout sisters, a creepy navy-blue dress its owner had worn to every funeral in the county since time remembered.

"He's here," I informed her for the third time. "Odd Henderson."

"Then why aren't you with him?" she said admonishingly. "That's not polite, Buddy. He's your particular guest. You ought to be out there seeing he meets everybody and has a good time."

"I *can't*. I can't speak to him."

Queenie was curled on her lap, having a head rub; my friend stood up, dumping Queenie and disclosing a stretch of navy-blue material sprinkled with dog hair, said "*Buddy*. You mean you haven't spoken to that boy!" My rudeness obliterated her timidity; taking me by the hand, she steered me to the parlor.

She need not have fretted over Odd's welfare. The charms of Annabel Conklin had drawn him to the piano. Indeed, he was scrunched up beside her on the piano seat, sitting there studying her delightful profile, his eyes opaque as the orbs of the stuffed whale I'd seen that summer when a touring honky-tonk passed through town (it was advertised as *The Original Moby Dick*, and it cost five cents to view the remains—what a bunch of crooks!). As for Annabel, she would flirt with anything that walked or crawled—no, that's unfair, for it was really a form of generosity, of simply being alive. Still, it gave me a hurt to see her playing cute with that mule skinner.

Hauling me onward, my friend introduced herself to him: "Buddy and I, we're so happy you could come." Odd had the manners of a billy goat: he didn't stand up or offer his hand, hardly looked at her and at me not at all. Daunted but dead game, my friend said: "Maybe Odd will sing us a tune. I know he can; his mother told me so. Annabel, sugar, play something Odd can sing."

Reading back, I see that I haven't thoroughly described Odd Henderson's ears—a major omission, for they were a pair of eye-catchers, like Alfalfa's in the *Our Gang* comedy pictures. Now, because of Annabel's flattering receptivity to my friend's request, his ears became so beet-bright it made your eyes smart. He mumbled, he shook his head hangdog; but Annabel said: "Do you know 'I Have Seen the Light'?" He didn't, but her next suggestion was greeted with a grin of recognition; the biggest fool could tell his modesty was all put on.

Giggling, Annabel struck a rich chord, and Odd, in a voice precociously manly, sang: "When the red, red robin comes bob, bob, bobbin' along." The Adam's apple in his tense throat jumped; Annabel's enthusiasm accelerated; the women's shrill hen chatter slackened as they became aware of the entertainment. Odd was good, he could sing for sure, and the jealousy charging through me had enough power to electrocute a murderer. Murder was what I had in mind; I could have killed him as easily as swat a mosquito. Easier.

Once more, unnoticed even by my friend, who was absorbed in the musicale, I escaped the parlor and sought The Island. That was the name I had given a place in the house where I went when I felt blue or inexplicably exuberant or just when I wanted to think things over. It was a mammoth closet attached to our only bathroom; the bathroom itself, except for its sanitary fixtures, was like a cozy winter parlor, with a horsehair love seat, scatter rugs, a bureau, a fireplace and framed reproductions of "The Doctor's Visit," "September Morn," "The Swan Pool" and calendars galore.

There were two small stained-glass windows in the closet; lozenge-like patterns of rose, amber and green light filtered through the windows, which looked out on the bathroom proper. Here and there patches of color had faded from the glass or been chipped away; by applying an eye to one of these clearings, it was possible to identify the room's visitors. After I'd been secluded there awhile, brooding over my enemy's success, footsteps intruded: Mrs. Mary Taylor Wheelwright, who stopped before a mirror, smacked her face with a powder puff, rouged her antique cheeks and then, perusing the effect, announced: "Very nice, Mary. Even if Mary says so herself."

It is well known that women outlive men; could it merely be superior vanity that keeps them going? Anyway, Mrs. Wheelwright sweetened my mood, so when, following her departure, a heartily rung dinner bell sounded through the house, I decided to quit my refuge and enjoy the feast, regardless of Odd Henderson.

But just then footsteps echoed again. *He* appeared, looking less sullen than I'd ever seen him. Strutty. Whistling. Unbuttoning his trousers and letting go with a forceful splash, he whistled along, jaunty as a jaybird in a field of sunflowers. As he was leaving, an open box on the bureau summoned his attention. It was a cigar box in which my friend kept recipes torn out of newspapers and other junk, as well as a cameo brooch her father had long ago given her. Sentimental value aside, her imagination had conferred upon the object a rare costliness; whenever we had cause for serious grievance against her sisters or Uncle B., she would say, "Never mind, Buddy. We'll sell my cameo and go away. We'll take the bus to New Orleans." Though never discussing what we would do once we arrived in New Orleans, or what we would live on after the cameo money ran out, we both relished this fantasy. Perhaps each of us secretly realized the brooch was only a Sears Roebuck novelty; all the same, it seemed to us a talisman of true, though untested, magic: a charm that promised us our freedom if indeed we did decide to pursue our luck in fabled spheres. So my friend never wore it, for it was too much a treasure to risk its loss or damage.

Now I saw Odd's sacrilegious fingers reach toward it, watched him bounce it in the palm of his hand, drop it back in the box and turn to go. Then return. This time he swiftly retrieved the cameo and sneaked it into his pocket. My boiling first instinct was to rush out of the closet and challenge him; at that moment, I believe I could have pinned Odd to the floor. *But*—Well, do you recall how, in simpler days, funny-paper artists used to illustrate the birth of an idea by sketching an incandescent light bulb above the brow of Mutt or Jeff or whomever? That's how it was with me: a sizzling light bulb suddenly radiated my brain. The shock and brilliance of it made me burn and shiver—laugh, too. Odd had handed me an ideal instrument for revenge, one that would make up for all the cockleburs.

In the dining room, long tables had been joined to shape a T. Uncle B. was at the upper center, Mrs. Mary Taylor Wheelwright at his right and Mrs. Conklin at his left. Odd was seated between two of the Conklin sisters, one of them Annabel, whose compliments kept him in top condition. My friend had put herself at the foot of the table among the youngest children; according to her, she had chosen the position because it provided quicker access to the kitchen, but of course it was because that was where she wished to be. Queenie, who had somehow got loose, was under the table—trembling and wagging with ecstasy as she skittered between the rows of legs—but nobody seemed to object, probably because they were hypnotized by the uncarved, lusciously glazed turkeys and the excellent aromas rising from dishes of okra and corn, onion fritters and hot mince pies.

My own mouth would have watered if it hadn't gone bone-dry at the heart-pounding prospect of total revenge. For a second, glancing at Odd Henderson's suffused face, I experienced a fragmentary regret, but I really had no qualms.

Uncle B. recited grace. Head bowed, eyes shut, calloused hands prayerfully placed, he intoned: "Bless You, O Lord, for the bounty of our table, the varied fruits we can be thankful for on this Thanksgiving Day of a troubled year"—his voice, so infrequently heard, croaked with the hollow imperfections of an old organ in an abandoned church—"Amen."

Then, as chairs were adjusted and napkins rustled, the necessary pause I'd been listening for arrived. "Someone here is a thief." I spoke clearly and repeated the accusation in even more measured tones: "Odd Henderson is a thief. He stole Miss Sook's cameo."

Napkins gleamed in suspended, immobilized hands. Men coughed, the Conklin sisters gasped in quadruplet unison and little Perk McCloud, Jr., began to hiccup, as very young children will when startled.

My friend, in a voice teetering between reproach and anguish, said, "Buddy doesn't mean that. He's only teasing."

"I do mean it. If you don't believe me, go look in your box. The cameo isn't there. Odd Henderson has it in his pocket."

"Buddy's had a bad croup," she murmured. "Don't blame him, Odd. He hasn't a notion what he's saying."

I said, "Go look in your box. I saw him take it."

Uncle B., staring at me with an alarming wintriness, took charge. "Maybe you'd better," he told Miss Sook. "That should settle the matter."

It was not often that my friend disobeyed her brother; she did not now. But her pallor, the mortified angle of her shoulders, revealed with what distaste she accepted the errand. She was gone only a minute, but her absence seemed an eon. Hostility sprouted and surged around the table like a thorn-encrusted vine growing with uncanny speed—and the victim trapped in its tendrils was not the accused, but his accuser. Stomach sickness gripped me; Odd, on the other hand, seemed calm as a corpse.

Miss Sook returned, smiling. "Shame on you, Buddy," she chided, shaking a finger. "Playing that kind of joke. My cameo was exactly where I left it."

Uncle B. said, "Buddy, I want to hear you apologize to our guest."

"No, he don't have to do that," Odd Henderson said, rising. "He was telling the truth." He dug into his pocket and put the cameo on the table. "I wish I had some excuse to give. But I ain't got none."

Starting for the door, he said, "You must be a special lady, Miss Sook, to fib for me like that." And then, damn his soul, he walked right out of there.

So did I. Except I ran. I pushed back my chair, knocking it over. The crash triggered Queenie; she scooted from under the table, barked and bared her teeth. And Miss Sook, as I went past her, tried to stop me: "Buddy!" But I wanted no part of her *or* Queenie. That dog had snarled at me and my friend had taken Odd Henderson's side, she'd lied to save his skin, betrayed our friendship, my love: things I'd thought could never happen.

Simpson's pasture lay below the house, a meadow brilliant with high November gold and russet grass. At the edge of the pasture there were a gray barn, a pig corral, a fenced-in chicken yard and a smokehouse. It was the smokehouse I slipped into, a black chamber cool on even the hottest summer days. It had a dirt floor and a smoke pit that smelled of hickory cinders and creosote; rows of hams hung from rafters. It was a place I'd always been wary of, but now its darkness seemed sheltering. I fell on the ground, my ribs heaving like the gills of a beach-stranded fish; and I didn't care that I was demolishing my one nice suit, the one with long trousers, by thrashing about on the floor in a messy mixture of earth and ashes and pork grease.

One thing I knew: I was going to quit that house, that town, that night. Hit the road. Hop a freight and head for California. Make my living shining shoes in Hollywood. Fred Astaire's shoes. Clark Gable's. Or—maybe I just might become a movie star myself. Look at Jackie Cooper. Oh, they'd be sorry then. When I was rich and famous and refused to answer their letters and even telegrams, probably.

Suddenly I thought of something that would make them even sorrier. The door to the shed was ajar, and a knife of sunshine exposed a shelf supporting several bottles. Dusty bottles with skull-and-crossbone labels. If I drank from one of those, then all of them up there in the dining room, the whole swilling and gobbling caboodle, would know what sorry was. It was worth it, if only to witness

Uncle B.'s remorse when they found me cold and stiff on the smoke-house floor; worth it to hear the human wails and Queenie's howls as my coffin was lowered into cemetery depths.

The only hitch was, I wouldn't actually be able to see or hear any of this: how could I, being dead? And unless one can observe the guilt and regret of the mourners, surely there is nothing satisfactory about being dead?

Uncle B. must have forbidden Miss Sook to go look for me until the last guest had left the table. It was late afternoon before I heard her voice floating across the pasture; she called my name softly, for-lornly as a mourning dove. I stayed where I was and did not answer.

It was Queenie who found me; she came sniffing around the smokehouse and yapped when she caught my scent, then entered and crawled toward me and licked my hand, an ear and a cheek; she knew she had treated me badly.

Presently, the door swung open and the light widened. My friend said, "Come here, Buddy." And I wanted to go to her. When she saw me, she laughed. "Goodness, boy. You look dipped in tar and all ready for feathering." But there were no recriminations or references to my ruined suit.

Queenie trotted off to pester some cows; and trailing after her into the pasture, we sat down on a tree stump. "I saved you a drumstick," she said, handing me a parcel wrapped in waxed paper. "And your favorite piece of turkey. The pulley."

The hunger that direr sensations had numbed now hit me like a belly-punch. I gnawed the drumstick clean, then stripped the pulley, the sweet part of the turkey around the wishbone.

While I was eating, Miss Sook put her arm around my shoulders. "There's just this I want to say, Buddy. Two wrongs never made a right. It was wrong of him to take the cameo. But we don't know why he took it. Maybe he never meant to keep it. Whatever his reason, it can't have been calculated. Which is why what you did was much worse: you *planned* to humiliate him. It was deliberate. Now listen to me, Buddy: there is only one unpardonable sin—*deliberate cruelty*. All else can be forgiven. That, never. Do you understand me, Buddy?"

I did, dimly, and time has taught me that she was right. But at that moment I mainly comprehended that because my revenge had failed, my method must have been wrong. Odd Henderson had emerged—how? why?—as someone superior to me, even more honest.

"Do you, Buddy? Understand?"

"Sort of. Pull," I said, offering her one prong of the wishbone.

We split it; my half was the larger, which entitled me to a wish. She wanted to know what I'd wished.

"That you're still my friend."

"Dumbhead," she said, and hugged me.

"Forever?"

"I won't be here forever, Buddy. Nor will you." Her voice sank like the sun on the pasture's horizon, was silent a second and then climbed with the strength of a new sun. "But yes, forever. The Lord willing, you'll be here long after I've gone. And as long as you remember me, then we'll always be together." . . .

Afterward, Odd Henderson let me alone. He started tussling with a boy his own age, Squirrel McMillan. And the next year, because of Odd's poor grades and general bad conduct, our school principal wouldn't allow him to attend classes, so he spent the winter working as a hand on a dairy farm. The last time I saw him was shortly before he hitchhiked to Mobile, joined the Merchant Marine and disappeared. It must have been the year before I was packed off to a miserable fate in a military academy, and two years prior to my friend's death. That would make it the autumn of 1934.

Miss Sook had summoned me to the garden; she had transplanted a blossoming chrysanthemum bush into a tin washtub and needed help to haul it up the steps onto the front porch, where it would make a fine display. It was heavier than forty fat pirates, and while we were struggling with it ineffectually, Odd Henderson passed along the road. He paused at the garden gate and then opened it, saying, "Let me do that for you, ma'am." Life on a dairy farm had done him a lot of good; he'd thickened, his arms were sinewy and his red coloring had deepened to a ruddy brown. Airily he lifted the big tub and placed it on the porch.

My friend said, "I'm obliged to you, sir. That was neighborly."

"Nothing," he said, still ignoring me.

Miss Sook snapped the stems of her showiest blooms. "Take these to your mother," she told him, handing him the bouquet. "And give her my love."

"Thank you, ma'am. I will."

"Oh, Odd," she called, after he'd regained the road, "be careful! They're lions, you know." But he was already out of hearing. We watched until he turned a bend at the corner, innocent of the menace he carried, the chrysanthemums that burned, that growled and roared against a greenly lowering dusk.

MOJAVE

(1975)

At 5 p.m. that winter afternoon she had an appointment with Dr. Bentsen, formerly her psychoanalyst and currently her lover. When their relationship had changed from the analytical to the emotional, he insisted, on ethical grounds, that she cease to be his patient. Not that it mattered. He had not been of much help as an analyst, and as a lover—well, once she had watched him running to catch a bus, two hundred and twenty pounds of shortish, fiftyish, frizzly-haired, hip-heavy, myopic Manhattan Intellectual, and she had laughed: how was it possible that she could love a man so ill-humored, so ill-favored as Ezra Bentsen? The answer was she didn't; in fact, she disliked him. But at least she didn't associate him with resignation and despair. She feared her husband; she was not afraid of Dr. Bentsen. Still, it was her husband she loved.

She was rich; at any rate, had a substantial allowance from her husband, who was rich, and so could afford the studio-apartment hideaway where she met her lover perhaps once a week, sometimes twice, never more. She could also afford gifts he seemed to expect on these occasions. Not that he appreciated their quality: Verdura cuff links, classic Paul Flato cigarette cases, the obligatory Cartier watch, and (more to the point) occasional specific amounts of cash he asked to "borrow."

He had never given *her* a single present. Well, one: a mother-of-pearl Spanish dress comb that he claimed was an heirloom, a mother-treasure. Of course, it was nothing she could wear, for she wore her own hair, fluffy and tobacco-colored, like a childish aureole around her deceptively naïve and youthful face. Thanks to dieting, private exercises with Joseph Pilatos, and the dermatological attentions of Dr. Orentreich, she looked in her early twenties; she was thirty-six.

The Spanish comb. Her hair. That reminded her of Jaime Sanchez and something that had happened yesterday. Jaime Sanchez was her hairdresser, and though they had known each other scarcely a year, they were, in their own way, good friends. She confided in him somewhat; he confided in her considerably more. Until recently she had judged Jaime to be a happy, almost overly blessed young man. He shared an apartment with an attractive lover, a young dentist named Carlos. Jaime and Carlos had been schoolmates in San Juan; they had left Puerto Rico together, settling first in New Orleans, then New York, and it was Jaime, working as a beautician, a talented one, who had put Carlos through dental school. Now Carlos had his own office and a clientele of prosperous Puerto Ricans and blacks.

However, during her last several visits she had noticed that Jaime Sanchez's usually unclouded eyes were somber, yellowed, as though he had a hangover, and his expertly articulate hands, ordinarily so calm and capable, trembled a little.

Yesterday, while scissor-trimming her hair, he had stopped and stood gasping, gasping—not as though fighting for air, but as if struggling against a scream.

She had said: "What is it? Are you all right?"

"No."

He had stepped to a washbasin and splashed his face with cold water. While drying himself, he said: "I'm going to kill Carlos." He waited, as if expecting her to ask him why; when she merely stared, he continued: "There's no use talking anymore. He understands nothing. My words mean nothing. The only way I can communicate with him is to kill him. Then he will understand."

"I'm not sure that I do, Jaime."

"Have I ever mentioned to you Angelita? My cousin Angelita? She came here six months ago. She has always been in love with Carlos. Since she was, oh, twelve years old. And now Carlos is in love with her. He wants to marry her and have a household of children."

She felt so awkward that all she could think to ask was: "Is she a nice girl?"

"Too nice." He had seized the scissors and resumed clipping. "No, I mean that. She is an excellent girl, very petite, like a pretty parrot, and much too nice; her kindness becomes cruel. Though she doesn't understand that she is being cruel. For example . . ." She glanced at Jaime's face moving in the mirror above the washbasin; it was not the merry face that had often beguiled her, but pain and perplexity exactly reflected. "Angelita and Carlos want me to live with them after they are married, all of us together in one apartment. It was her idea, but Carlos says yes! yes! we must all stay together and from now on he and I will live like brothers. That is the reason I have to kill him. He could never have loved me, not if he could ignore my enduring such hell. He says, 'Yes, I love you, Jaime; but Angelita—this is different.' There is no difference. You love or you do not. You destroy or you do not. But Carlos will never understand that. Nothing reaches him, nothing can—only a bullet or a razor."

She wanted to laugh; at the same time she couldn't because she realized he was serious and also because she well knew how true it was that certain persons could only be made to recognize the truth, be made to *understand,* by subjecting them to extreme punishment.

Nevertheless, she did laugh, but in a manner that Jaime would not interpret as genuine laughter. It was something comparable to a sympathetic shrug. "You could never kill anyone, Jaime."

He began to comb her hair; the tugs were not gentle, but she knew the anger implied was against himself, not her. "Shit!" Then: "No.

And that's the reason for most suicides. Someone is torturing you. You want to kill them, but you can't. All that pain is because you love them, and you can't kill them because you love them. So you kill yourself instead."

Leaving, she considered kissing him on the cheek, but settled for shaking his hand. "I know how trite this is, Jaime. And for the moment certainly no help at all. But remember—there's always somebody else. Just don't look for the same person, that's all."

The rendezvous apartment was on East Sixty-fifth Street; today she walked to it from her home, a small town house on Beekman Place. It was windy, there was leftover snow on the sidewalk and a promise of more in the air, but she was snug enough in the coat her husband had given her for Christmas—a sable-colored suede coat that was lined with sable.

A cousin had rented the apartment for her in his own name. The cousin, who was married to a harridan and lived in Greenwich, sometimes visited the apartment with his secretary, a fat Japanese woman who drenched herself in nose-boggling amounts of Mitsouko. This afternoon the apartment reeked of the lady's perfume, from which she deduced that her cousin had lately been dallying here. That meant she would have to change the sheets.

She did so, then prepared herself. On a table beside the bed she placed a small box wrapped in shiny cerulean paper; it contained a gold toothpick she had bought at Tiffany, a gift for Dr. Bentsen, for one of his unpleasing habits was constantly picking his teeth, and, moreover, picking them with an endless series of paper matches. She had thought the gold pick might make the whole process a little less disagreeable. She put a stack of Lee Wiley and Fred Astaire records on a phonograph, poured herself a glass of cold white wine, undressed entirely, lubricated herself and stretched out on the bed, humming, singing along with the divine Fred and listening for the scratch of her lover's key at the door.

To judge from appearances, orgasms were agonizing events in the life of Ezra Bentsen: he grimaced, he ground his dentures, he whimpered like a frightened mutt. Of course, she was always relieved when she heard the whimper; it meant that soon his lathered carcass would roll off her, for he was not one to linger, whispering tender compliments: he just rolled right off. And today, having done so, he greedily reached for the blue box, knowing it was a present for him. After opening it, he grunted.

She explained: "It's a gold toothpick."

He chuckled, an unusual sound coming from him, for his sense of humor was meager. "That's kind of cute," he said, and began picking his teeth. "You know what happened last night? I slapped Thelma. But good. And I punched her in the stomach, too."

Thelma was his wife; she was a child psychiatrist, and by reputation a fine one.

"The trouble with Thelma is you can't talk to her. She doesn't understand. Sometimes that's the only way you can get the message across. Give her a fat lip."

She thought of Jaime Sanchez.

"Do you know a Mrs. Roger Rhinelander?" Dr. Bentsen said.

"Mary Rhinelander? Her father was my father's best friend. They owned a racing stable together. One of her horses won the Kentucky Derby. Poor Mary, though. She married a real bastard."

"So she tells me."

"Oh? Is Mrs. Rhinelander a new patient?"

"Brand-new. Funny thing. She came to me for more or less the particular reason that brought you; her situation is almost identical."

The particular reason? Actually, she had a number of problems that had contributed to her eventual seduction on Dr. Bentsen's couch, the principal one being that she had not been capable of having a sexual relationship with her husband since the birth of their second child. She had married when she was twenty-four; her husband was fifteen years her senior. Though they had fought a lot, and were jealous of each other, the first five years of their marriage remained in her memory as an unblemished vista. The difficulty started when he asked her to have a child; if she hadn't been so much in love with him, she would never have consented—she had been afraid of children when she herself was a child, and the company of a child still made her uneasy. But she had given him a son, and the experience of pregnancy had traumatized her: when she wasn't actually suffering, she imagined she was, and after the birth she descended into a depression that continued more than a year. Every day she slept fourteen hours of Seconal sleep; as for the other ten, she kept awake by fueling herself with amphetamines. The second child, another boy, had been a drunken accident—though she suspected that really her husband had tricked her. The instant she knew she was pregnant again she had insisted on having an abortion; he had told her that if she went ahead with it, he would divorce her. Well, he had lived to regret that. The child had been born two months prematurely, had nearly died, and because of massive internal hemorrhaging, so had she; they had both hovered above an abyss through months of intensive care. Since then, she had never shared a bed with her husband; she wanted to, but she couldn't, for the naked presence of him, the thought of his body inside hers, summoned intolerable terrors.

Dr. Bentsen wore thick black socks with garters, which he never removed while "making love"; now, as he was sliding his gartered legs into a pair of shiny-seated blue serge trousers, he said: "Let's see. Tomorrow is Tuesday. Wednesday is our anniversary . . ."

"Our anniversary?"

"Thelma's! Our twentieth. I want to take her to . . . Tell me the best restaurant around now?"

"What does it matter? It's very small and very smart and the owner would never give you a table."

His lack of humor asserted itself: "That's a damn strange thing to say. What do you mean, he wouldn't give me a table?"

"Just what I said. One look at you and he'd know you had hairy heels. There are *some* people who won't serve people with hairy heels. He's one of them."

Dr. Bentsen was familiar with her habit of introducing unfamiliar lingo, and he had learned to pretend he knew what it signified; he was as ignorant of her ambience as she was of his, but the shifting instability of his character would not allow him to admit it.

"Well, then," he said, "is Friday all right? Around five?"

She said: "No, thank you." He was tying his tie and stopped; she was still lying on the bed, uncovered, naked; Fred was singing "By Myself." "No, thank you, darling Dr. B. I don't think we'll be meeting here anymore."

She could see he was startled. Of course he would miss her—she was beautiful, she was considerate, it never bothered her when he asked her for money. He knelt beside the bed and fondled her breast. She noticed an icy mustache of sweat on his upper lip. "What is this? Drugs? Drink?"

She laughed and said: "All I drink is white wine, and not much of that. No, my friend. It's simply that you have hairy heels."

Like many analysts, Dr. Bentsen was quite literal-minded; just for a second she thought he was going to strip off his socks and examine his feet. Churlishly, like a child, he said: "I *don't* have hairy heels."

"Oh, yes you do. Just like a horse. All ordinary horses have hairy heels. Thoroughbreds don't. The heels of a well-bred horse are flat and glistening. Give my love to Thelma."

"Smart-ass. Friday?"

The Astaire record ended. She swallowed the last of the wine.

"Maybe. I'll call you," she said.

As it happened, she never called, and she never saw him again—except once, a year later, when she sat on a banquette next to him at La Grenouille; he was lunching with Mary Rhinelander, and she was amused to see that Mrs. Rhinelander signed the check.

—

The promised snow had arrived by the time she returned, again on foot, to the house on Beekman Place. The front door was painted pale yellow and had a brass knocker shaped like a lion's claw. Anna, one of four Irishwomen who staffed the house, answered the door and reported that the children, exhausted from an afternoon of ice-skating at Rockefeller Center, had already had their supper and been put to bed.

Thank God. Now she wouldn't have to undergo the half hour of playtime and tale-telling and kiss-goodnight that customarily concluded her children's day; she may not have been an affectionate mother, but she was a dutiful one—just as her own mother had been. It was seven o'clock, and her husband had phoned to say he would be home at seven-thirty; at eight they were supposed to go to a dinner party with the Sylvester Hales, friends from San Francisco. She bathed, scented herself to remove memories of Dr. Bentsen, remodeled her make-up, of which she wore the most modest quantity, and changed into a gray silk caftan and gray silk slippers with pearl buckles.

She was posing by the fireplace in the library on the second floor when she heard her husband's footsteps on the stairs. It was a graceful pose, inviting as the room itself, an unusual octagonal room with cinnamon lacquered walls, a yellow lacquered floor, brass bookshelves (a notion borrowed from Billy Baldwin), two huge bushes of brown orchids ensconced in yellow Chinese vases, a Marino Marini horse standing in a corner, a South Seas Gauguin over the mantel, and a delicate fire fluttering in the fireplace. French windows offered a view of a darkened garden, drifting snow and lighted tugboats floating like lanterns on the East River. A voluptuous couch, upholstered in mocha velvet, faced the fireplace, and in front of it, on a table lacquered the yellow of the floor, rested an ice-filled silver bucket; embedded in the bucket was a carafe brimming with pepper-flavored red Russian vodka.

Her husband hesitated in the doorway, and nodded at her approvingly: he was one of those men who truly noticed a woman's appearance, gathered at a glance the total atmosphere. He was worth dressing for, and it was one of her lesser reasons for loving him. A more important reason was that he resembled her father, a man who had been, and forever would be, the man in her life; her father had shot himself, though no one ever knew why, for he was a gentleman of almost abnormal discretion. Before this happened, she had terminated three engagements, but two months after her father's death she met George, and married him because in both looks and manners he approximated her great lost love.

She moved across the room to meet her husband halfway. She kissed his cheek, and the flesh against her lips felt as cold as the snowflakes at the window. He was a large man, Irish, black-haired and green-eyed, handsome even though he had lately accumulated considerable poundage and had gotten a bit jowly, too. He projected a superficial vitality; both men and women were drawn to him by that alone. Closely observed, however, one sensed a secret fatigue, a lack of any real optimism. His wife was severely aware of it, and why not? She was its principal cause.

She said: "It's such a rotten night out, and you look so tired. Let's stay home and have supper by the fire."

"Really, darling—you wouldn't mind? It seems a mean thing to do to the Haleses. Even if she is a cunt."

"*George!* Don't use that word. You know I hate it."

"Sorry," he said; he was, too. He was always careful not to offend her, just as she took the same care with him: a consequence of the quiet that simultaneously kept them together and apart.

"I'll call and say you're coming down with a cold."

"Well, it won't be a lie. I think I am."

—

While she called the Haleses, and arranged with Anna for a soup and soufflé supper to be served in an hour's time, he chug-a-lugged a dazzling dose of the scarlet vodka and felt it light a fire in his stomach; before his wife returned, he poured himself a respectable shot and stretched full length on the couch. She knelt on the floor and removed his shoes and began to massage his feet: God knows, *he* didn't have hairy heels.

He groaned. "Hmm. That feels good."

"I love you, George."

"I love you, too."

She thought of putting on a record, but no, the sound of the fire was all the room needed.

"George?"

"Yes, darling."

"What are you thinking about?"

"A woman named Ivory Hunter."

"You really know somebody named Ivory Hunter?"

"Well. That was her stage name. She'd been a burlesque dancer."

She laughed. "What is this, some part of your college adventures?"

"I never knew her. I only heard about her once. It was the summer after I left Yale."

He closed his eyes and drained his vodka. "The summer I hitch-hiked out to New Mexico and California. Remember? That's how I got my nose broke. In a bar fight in Needles, California." She liked his broken nose, it offset the extreme gentleness of his face; he had once spoken of having it rebroken and reset, but she had talked him out of it. "It was early September, and that's always the hottest time of the year in Southern California; over a hundred almost every day. I ought to have treated myself to a bus ride, at least across the desert. But there I was like a fool, deep in the Mojave, hauling a fifty-pound knapsack and sweating until there was no sweat in me. I swear it was a hundred and fifty in the shade. Except there wasn't any shade. Nothing but sand and mesquite and this boiling blue sky. Once a big truck drove by, but it wouldn't stop for me. All it did was kill a rattlesnake that was crawling across the road.

"I kept thinking something was bound to turn up somewhere. A garage. Now and then cars passed, but I might as well have been invisible. I began to feel sorry for myself, to understand what it means to be helpless, and to understand why it's a good thing that Buddhists send out their young monks to beg. It's chastening. It rips off that last layer of baby fat.

"And then I met Mr. Schmidt. I thought maybe it was a mirage. An old white-haired man about a quarter mile up the highway. He was standing by the road with heat waves rippling around him. As I got closer I saw that he carried a cane and wore pitch-black glasses, and he was dressed as if headed for church—white suit, white shirt, black tie, black shoes.

"Without looking at me, and while some distance away, he called out: 'My name is George Schmidt.'

"I said: 'Yes. Good afternoon, sir.'

"He said: '*Is* it afternoon?'

" 'After three.'

" 'Then I must have been standing here two hours or more. Would you mind telling me where I am?'

" 'In the Mojave Desert. About eighteen miles west of Needles.'

" 'Imagine that,' he said. 'Leaving a seventy-year-old blind man stranded alone in the desert. Ten dollars in my pocket, and not another rag to my name. Women are like flies: they settle on sugar or shit. I'm not saying I'm sugar, but she's sure settled for shit now. My name is George Schmidt.'

"I said: 'Yes, sir, you told me. I'm George Whitelaw.' He wanted to know where I was going, what I was up to, and when I said I was hitchhiking, heading for New York, he asked if I would take his hand and help him along a bit, maybe until we could catch a ride. I forgot to mention that he had a German accent and was extremely stout, almost fat; he looked as if he'd been lying in a hammock all his life. But when I held his hand I felt the roughness, the immense strength of it. You wouldn't have wanted a pair of hands like that around your throat. He said: 'Yes, I have strong hands. I've worked as a masseur for fifty years, the last twelve in Palm Springs. You got any water?' I gave him my canteen, which was still half full. And he said: 'She left me here without even a drop of water. The whole thing took me by surprise. Though I can't say it should have, knowing Ivory good as I did. That's my wife. Ivory Hunter, she was. A stripper; she played the Chicago World's Fair, 1932, and she would have been a star if it hadn't been for that Sally Rand. Ivory invented this fan-dance thing and that Rand woman stole it off her. So Ivory said. Probably just more of her bullshit. Uh-oh, watch out for that rattler, he's over there someplace, I can hear him really singing. There's two things I'm scared of. Snakes and women. They have a lot in common. One thing they have in common is: the last thing that dies is their tail.'

"A couple of cars passed and I stuck out my thumb and the old man tried to flag them down with his stick, but we must have looked too peculiar—a dirty kid in dungarees and a blind fat man dressed in his city best. I guess we'd still be out there if it hadn't been for this truck driver. A Mexican. He was parked by the road fixing a flat. He could speak about five words of Tex-Mex, all of them four-letter, but I still remembered a lot of Spanish from the summer with Uncle Alvin in Cuba. So the Mexican told me he was on his way to El Paso, and if that was our direction, we were welcome aboard.

"But Mr. Schmidt wasn't too keen. I had practically to drag him into the caboose. 'I hate Mexicans. Never met a Mexican I liked. If it wasn't for a Mexican . . . Him only nineteen and her I'd say from the touch of her skin, I'd say Ivory was a woman way past sixty. When I married her a couple of years ago, she said she was fifty-two. See, I was living in this trailer camp out on Route 111. One of those trailer camps halfway between Palm Springs and Cathedral City. Cathedral City! Some name for a dump that's nothing but honky-tonks and pool halls and fag bars. The only thing you can say about it is Bing Crosby lives there. If that's saying something. Anyway, living next to me in this other trailer is my friend Hulga. Ever since my wife died— she died the same day Hitler died—Hulga had been driving me to work; she works as a waitress at this Jew club where I'm the masseur.

All the waiters and waitresses at the club are big blond Germans. The Jews like that; they really keep them stepping. So one day Hulga tells me she has a cousin coming to visit. Ivory Hunter. I forget her legal name, it was on the marriage certificate, but I forget. She had about three husbands before; she probably didn't remember the name she was born with. Anyway, Hulga tells me that this cousin of hers, Ivory, used to be a famous dancer, but now she's just come out of the hospital and she's lost her last husband on account of she's spent a year in the hospital with TB. That's why Hulga asked her out to Palm Springs. Because of the air. Also, she didn't have any place else to go. The first night she was there, Hulga invited me over, and I liked her cousin right away; we didn't talk much, we listened to the radio mostly, but I liked Ivory. She had a real nice voice, real slow and gentle, she sounded like nurses ought to sound; she said she didn't smoke or drink and she was a member of the Church of God, same as me. After that, I was over at Hulga's almost every night.' "

George lit a cigarette, and his wife tilted out a jigger more of the pepper vodka for him. To her surprise, she poured one for herself. A number of things about her husband's narrative had accelerated her ever-present but usually Librium-subdued anxiety; she couldn't imagine where his memoir was leading, but she knew there was some destination, for George seldom rambled. He had graduated third in his class at Yale Law School, never practiced law but had gone on to top his class at Harvard Business School; within the past decade he had been offered a presidential Cabinet post, and an ambassadorship to England or France or wherever he wanted. However, what had made her feel the need for red vodka, a ruby bauble burning in the firelight, was the disquieting manner in which George Whitelaw had become Mr. Schmidt; her husband was an exceptional mimic. He could imitate certain of their friends with infuriating accuracy. But this was not casual mimicry; he seemed entranced, a man fixed in another man's mind.

" 'I had an old Chevy nobody had driven since my wife died. But

Ivory got it tuned up, and pretty soon it wasn't Hulga driving me to work and bringing me home, but Ivory. Looking back, I can see it was all a plot between Hulga and Ivory, but I didn't put it together then. Everybody around the trailer park, and everybody that met her, all they said was what a lovely woman she was, big blue eyes and pretty legs. I figured it was just good-heartedness, the Church of God—I figured that was why she was spending her evenings cooking dinner and keeping house for an old blind man. One night we were listening to the *Hit Parade* on the radio, and she kissed me and rubbed her hand along my leg. Pretty soon we were doing it twice a day—once before breakfast and once after dinner, and me a man of sixty-nine. But it seemed like she was as crazy about my cock as I was about her cunt—' "

She tossed her vodka into the fireplace, a splash that made the flames hiss and flourish; but it was an idle protest: Mr. Schmidt would not be reproached.

" 'Yes, sir, Ivory was all cunt. Whatever way you want to use the word. It was exactly one month from the day I met her to the day I married her. She didn't change much, she fed me good, she was always interested to hear about the Jews at the club, and it was me that cut down on the sex—*way* down, what with my blood pressure and all. But she never complained. We read the Bible together, and night after night she would read aloud from magazines, good magazines like *Reader's Digest* and *The Saturday Evening Post,* until I fell asleep. She was always saying she hoped she died before I did because she would be heartbroken and destitute. It was true I didn't have much to leave. No insurance, just some bank-savings that I turned into a joint account, and I had the trailer put in her name. No, I can't say there was a harsh word between us until she had the big fight with Hulga.

" 'For a long time I didn't know what the fight was about. All I knew was that they didn't speak to each other anymore, and when I asked Ivory what was going on, she said: "Nothing." As far as she was concerned, she hadn't had any falling-out with Hulga: "But you know how much she drinks." That was true. Well, like I told you, Hulga was a waitress at the club, and one day she comes barging into the massage room. I had a customer on the table, had him there spread out buck-naked, but a lot she cared—she smelled like a Four Roses factory. She could hardly stand up. She told me she had just got fired, and suddenly she started swearing and pissing. She was hollering at me and pissing all over the floor. She said everybody at the trailer park was laughing at me. She said Ivory was an old whore who had latched on to me because she was down and out and couldn't do any better. And she said what kind of a chowderhead was I? Didn't I know my wife was fucking the balls off Freddy Feo since God knows when?

" 'Now, see, Freddy Feo was an itinerant Tex-Mex kid—he was just out of jail somewhere, and the manager of the trailer park had picked him up in one of those fag bars in Cat City and put him to work as a handyman. I don't guess he could have been one-hundred-percent fag because he was giving plenty of the old girls around there a tickle for their money. One of them was Hulga. She was loop-de-do over him. On hot nights him and Hulga used to sit outside her trailer on her swing-seat drinking straight tequila, forget the lime, and he'd play the guitar and sing spic songs. Ivory described it to me as a green guitar with his name spelled out in rhinestone letters. I'll say this, the spic could sing. But Ivory always claimed she couldn't stand him; she said he was a cheap little greaser out to take Hulga for every nickel she had. Myself, I don't remember exchanging ten words with him, but I didn't like him because of the way he smelled. I have a nose like a bloodhound and I could smell him a hundred yards off, he wore so much brilliantine in his hair, and something else that Ivory said was called Evening in Paris.

" 'Ivory swore up and down it wasn't so. Her? *Her* let a Tex-Mex monkey like Freddy Feo put a finger on her? She said it was because Hulga had been dumped by this kid that she was crazy and jealous and thought he was humping everything from Cat City to Indio. She said she was insulted that I'd listen to such lies, even though Hulga was more to be pitied than reviled. And she took off the wedding ring I'd given her—it had belonged to my first wife, but she said that didn't make any difference because she knew I'd loved Hedda and that made it all the better—and she handed it to me and she said if I didn't believe her, then here was the ring and she'd take the next bus going anywhere. So I put it back on her finger and we knelt on the floor and prayed together.

" 'I did believe her; at least I thought I did; but in some way it was like a seesaw in my head—yes, no, yes, no. And Ivory had lost her looseness; before, she had an easiness in her body that was like the easiness in her voice. But now it was all wire—tense, like those Jews at the club that keep whining and scolding because you can't rub away all their worries. Hulga got a job at the Miramar, but out at the trailer park I always turned away when I smelled her coming. Once she sort of whispered up beside me: "Did you know that sweet wife of yours gave the greaser a pair of gold earrings! But his boyfriend won't let him wear them." I don't know. Ivory prayed every night with me that the Lord would keep us together, healthy in spirit and body. But I noticed . . . Well, on those warm summer nights when Freddy Feo would be out there somewhere in the dark, singing and playing his guitar, she'd turn off the radio right in the middle of Bob Hope or Edgar Bergen or whatever, and go sit outside and listen. She said she was looking at the stars: "I bet there's no place in the world you can see the stars like here." But suddenly it turned out she hated Cat City and the Springs. The whole desert, the sandstorms, summers with temperatures up to a hundred thirty degrees, and nothing to do if you wasn't rich and belonged to the Racquet Club. She just announced this one morning. She said we should pick up the trailer and plant it down anywhere where the air was cool. Wisconsin. Michigan. I felt good about the idea; it set my mind to rest as to what might be going on between her and Freddy Feo.

" 'Well, I had a client there at the club, a fellow from Detroit, and he said he might be able to get me on as a masseur at the Detroit Athletic Club; nothing definite, only one of them maybe deals. But that was enough for Ivory. Twenty-three skidoo, and she's got the trailer uprooted, fifteen years of planting strewn all over the ground, the Chevy ready to roll, and all our savings turned into traveler's checks. Last night she scrubbed me top to bottom and shampooed my hair, and this morning we set off a little after daylight.

" 'I realized something was wrong, and I'd have known what it was if I hadn't dozed off soon as we hit the highway. She must have dumped sleeping pills in my coffee.

" 'But when I woke up, I smelled him. The brilliantine and the dime-store perfume. He was hiding in the trailer. Coiled back there somewhere like a snake. What I thought was: Ivory and the kid are going to kill me and leave me for the buzzards. She said: "You're awake, George." The way she said it, the slight fear, I could tell she knew what was going on in my head. That I'd guessed it all. I told her, *Stop the car.* She wanted to know what for? Because I had to take a leak. She stopped the car, and I could hear she was crying. As I got out, she said: "You been good to me, George, but I didn't know nothing else to do. And you got a profession. There'll always be a place for you somewhere."

" 'I got out of the car, and I really did take a leak, and while I was standing there the motor started up and she drove away. I didn't know where I was until you came along, Mr. . . . ?'

" 'George Whitelaw.' And I told him: 'Jesus, that's just like murder. Leaving a blind man helpless in the middle of nowhere. When we get to El Paso we'll go to the police station.'

"He said: 'Hell, no. She's got enough trouble without the cops. She settled on shit—leave her to it. Ivory's the one out in nowhere. Besides, I love her. A woman can do you like that, and still you love her.' "

—

George refilled his vodka; she placed a small log on the fire, and the new rush of flame was only a little brighter than the furious red suddenly flushing her cheeks.

"That *women* do," she said, her tone aggressive, challenging. "Only a crazy person . . . Do you think I could do something like that?"

The expression in his eyes, a certain visual silence, shocked her and made her avert her eyes, withdrawing the question. "Well, what happened to him?"

"Mr. Schmidt?"

"Mr. Schmidt."

He shrugged. "The last I saw of him he was drinking a glass of milk in a diner, a truck stop outside El Paso. I was lucky; I got a ride with a trucker all the way to Newark. I sort of forgot about it. But for the last few months I find myself wondering about Ivory Hunter and George Schmidt. It must be age; I'm beginning to feel old myself."

She knelt beside him again; she held his hand, interweaving her fingers with his. "Fifty-two? And you feel *old*?"

He had retreated; when he spoke, it was the wondering murmur of a man addressing himself. "I always had such confidence. Just walking the street, I felt such a *swing*. I could feel people looking at me—on the street, in a restaurant, at a party—envying me, wondering who is that guy. Whenever I walked into a party, I knew I could have half the women in the room if I wanted them. But that's all over. Seems as though old George Whitelaw has become the invisible man. Not a head turns. I called Mimi Stewart twice last week, and she never returned the calls. I didn't tell you, but I stopped at Buddy Wilson's yesterday, he was having a little cocktail thing. There must have been twenty fairly attractive girls, and they all looked right through me; to them I was a tired old guy who smiled too much."

She said: "But I thought you were still seeing Christine."

"I'll tell you a secret. Christine is engaged to that Rutherford boy from Philadelphia. I haven't seen her since November. He's okay for her; she's happy and I'm happy for her."

"Christine! Which Rutherford boy? Kenyon or Paul?"

"The older one."

"That's Kenyon. You knew that and didn't tell me?"

"There's so much I haven't told you, my dear."

Yet that was not entirely true. For when they had stopped sleeping together, they had begun discussing together—indeed, collaborating on—each of his affairs. Alice Kent: five months; ended because she'd demanded he divorce and marry her. Sister Jones: terminated after one year when her husband found out about it. Pat Simpson: a *Vogue* model who'd gone to Hollywood, promised to return and never had. Adele O'Hara: beautiful, an alcoholic, a rambunctious scenemaker; he'd broken that one off himself. Mary Campbell, Mary Chester, Jane Vere-Jones. Others. And now Christine.

A few he had discovered himself; the majority were "romances" she herself had stage-managed, friends she'd introduced him to, confidantes she had trusted to provide him with an outlet but not to exceed the mark.

"Well," she sighed. "I suppose we can't blame Christine. Kenyon Rutherford's rather a catch." Still, her mind was running, searching like the flames shivering through the logs: a name to fill the void. Alice Combs: available, but too dull. Charlotte Finch: too rich, and George felt emasculated by women—or men, for that matter—richer than himself. Perhaps the Ellison woman? The soigné Mrs. Harold Ellison, who was in Haiti getting a swift divorce . . .

He said: "Stop frowning."

"I'm not frowning."

"It just means more silicone, more bills from Orentreich. I'd rather see the human wrinkles. It doesn't matter whose fault it is. We all, sometimes, leave each other out there under the skies, and we never understand why."

An echo, caverns resounding: Jaime Sanchez and Carlos and Angelita; Hulga and Freddy Feo and Ivory Hunter and Mr. Schmidt; Dr.

Bentsen and George, George and herself, Dr. Bentsen and Mary
Rhinelander . . .

He gave a slight pressure to their interwoven fingers, and with his
other hand, raised her chin and insisted on their eyes meeting. He
moved her hand up to his lips and kissed its palm.

"I love you, Sarah."

"I love you, too."

But the touch of his lips, the insinuated threat, tautened her.
Below stairs, she heard the rattle of silver on trays: Anna and Margaret were ascending with the fireside supper.

"I love you, too," she repeated with pretended sleepiness, and with
a feigned languor moved to draw the window draperies. Drawn, the
heavy silk concealed the night river and the lighted riverboats, so
snow-misted that they were as muted as the design in a Japanese
scroll of winter night.

"George?" An urgent plea before the supper-laden Irishwomen arrived, expertly balancing their offerings: "*Please,* darling. We'll think
of somebody."

ONE CHRISTMAS

(1982)

for Gloria Dunphy

First, a brief autobiographical prologue. My mother, who was exceptionally intelligent, was the most beautiful girl in Alabama. Everyone said so, and it was true; and when she was sixteen she married a twenty-eight-year-old businessman who came from a good New Orleans family. The marriage lasted a year. My mother was too young to be a mother or a wife; she was also too ambitious—she wanted to go to college and to have a career. So she left her husband; and as for what to do with me, she deposited me in the care of her large Alabama family.

Over the years, I seldom saw either of my parents. My father was occupied in New Orleans, and my mother, after graduating from college, was making a success for herself in New York. So far as I was concerned, this was not an unpleasant situation. I was happy where I was. I had many kindly relatives, aunts and uncles and cousins, particularly *one* cousin, an elderly, white-haired, slightly crippled woman named Sook. Miss Sook Faulk. I had other friends, but she was by far my best friend.

It was Sook who told me about Santa Claus, his flowing beard, his red suit, his jangling present-filled sled, and I believed her, just as I believed that everything was God's will, or the Lord's, as Sook always called Him. If I stubbed my toe, or fell off a horse, or caught a good-sized fish at the creek—well, good or bad, it was all the Lord's will. And that was what Sook said when she received the frightening news from New Orleans: My father wanted me to travel there to spend Christmas with him.

I cried. I didn't want to go. I'd never left this small, isolated Alabama town surrounded by forests and farms and rivers. I'd never gone to sleep without Sook combing her fingers through my hair and kissing me good-night. Then, too, I was afraid of strangers, and my father was a stranger. I had seen him several times, but the memory was a haze; I had no idea what he was like. But, as Sook said: "It's the Lord's will. And who knows, Buddy, maybe you'll see snow."

Snow! Until I could read myself, Sook read me many stories, and it seemed a lot of snow was in almost all of them. Drifting, dazzling fairytale flakes. It was something I dreamed about; something magical and mysterious that I wanted to see and feel and touch. Of course I never had, and neither had Sook; how could we, living in a hot place like Alabama? I don't know why she thought I would see snow in New Orleans, for New Orleans is even hotter. Never mind. She was just trying to give me courage to make the trip.

I had a new suit. It had a card pinned to the lapel with my name and address. That was in case I got lost. You see, I had to make the trip alone. By bus. Well, everybody thought I'd be safe with my tag. Everybody but me. I was scared to death; and angry. Furious at my father, this stranger, who was forcing me to leave home and be away from Sook at Christmastime.

It was a four-hundred-mile trip, something like that. My first stop was in Mobile. I changed buses there, and rode along forever and forever through swampy lands and along seacoasts until we arrived in a loud city tinkling with trolley cars and packed with dangerous foreign-looking people.

That was New Orleans.

And suddenly, as I stepped off the bus, a man swept me in his arms, squeezed the breath out of me; he was laughing, he was crying—a tall, good-looking man, laughing and crying. He said: "Don't you know me? Don't you know your daddy?"

I was speechless. I didn't say a word until at last, while we were riding along in a taxi, I asked: "Where is it?"

"Our house? It's not far—"

"Not the house. The snow."

"What snow?"

"I thought there would be a lot of snow."

He looked at me strangely, but laughed. "There never has been any snow in New Orleans. Not that I heard of. But listen. Hear that thunder? It's sure going to rain!"

I don't know what scared me most, the thunder, the sizzling zigzags of lightning that followed it—or my father. That night, when I went to bed, it was still raining. I said my prayers and prayed that I would soon be home with Sook. I didn't know how I could ever go to sleep without Sook to kiss me good-night. The fact was, I couldn't go to sleep, so I began to wonder what Santa Claus would bring me. I wanted a pearl-handled knife. And a big set of jigsaw puzzles. A cowboy hat with matching lasso. And a B.B. rifle to shoot sparrows. (Years later, when I did have a B.B. gun, I shot a mockingbird and a bobwhite, and I can never forget the regret I felt, the grief; I never killed another thing, and every fish I caught I threw back into the water.) And I wanted a box of crayons. And, most of all, a radio but I knew that was impossible: I didn't know ten people who had radios. Remember, this was the Depression, and in the Deep South houses furnished with radios or refrigerators were rare.

My father had both. He seemed to have everything—a car with a rumble seat, not to mention an old, pink pretty little house in the French Quarter with iron-lace balconies and a secret patio garden colored with flowers and cooled by a fountain shaped like a mermaid. He also had a half-dozen, I'd say full-dozen, lady friends. Like my mother, my father had not remarried; but they both had determined admirers and, willingly or not, eventually walked the path to the altar—in fact, my father walked it six times.

So you can see he must have had charm; and, indeed, he seemed to charm most people—everybody except me. That was because he embarrassed me so, always hauling me around to meet his friends, everybody from his banker to the barber who shaved him every day. And, of course, all his lady friends. And the worst part: All the time he was hugging and kissing me and bragging about me. I felt so ashamed. First of all, there was nothing to brag about. I was a real country boy. I believed in Jesus, and faithfully said my prayers. I knew Santa Claus existed. And at home in Alabama, except to go to church, I never wore shoes; winter or summer.

It was pure torture, being pulled along the streets of New Orleans in those tightly laced, hot as hell, heavy as lead shoes. I don't know what was worse—the shoes or the food. Back home I was used to fried chicken and collard greens and butter beans and corn bread and other comforting things. But these New Orleans restaurants! I will never forget my first oyster, it was like a bad dream sliding down my throat; decades passed before I swallowed another. As for all that spicy Creole cookery—just to think of it gave me heartburn. No sir, I hankered after biscuits right from the stove and milk fresh from the cows and homemade molasses straight from the bucket.

My poor father had no idea how miserable I was, partly because I never let him see it, certainly never told him; and partly because, despite my mother's protest, he had managed to get legal custody of me for this Christmas holiday.

He would say: "Tell the truth. Don't you want to come and live here with me in New Orleans?"

"I can't."

"What do you mean you can't?"

"I miss Sook. I miss Queenie; we have a little rat terrier, a funny little thing. But we both love her."

He said: "Don't you love me?"

I said: "Yes." But the truth was, except for Sook and Queenie and a few cousins and a picture of my beautiful mother beside my bed, I had no real idea of what love meant.

I soon found out. The day before Christmas, as we were walking along Canal Street, I stopped dead still, mesmerized by a magical object that I saw in the window of a big toy store. It was a model airplane large enough to sit in and pedal like a bicycle. It was green and had a red propeller. I was convinced that if you pedaled fast enough it would take off and fly! Now wouldn't that be something! I could just see my cousins standing on the ground while I flew about among the clouds. Talk about green! I laughed; and laughed and laughed. It was the first thing I'd done that made my father look confident, even though he didn't know what I thought was so funny.

That night I prayed that Santa Claus would bring me the airplane.

My father had already bought a Christmas tree, and we spent a great deal of time at the five 'n' dime picking out things to decorate it with. Then I made a mistake. I put a picture of my mother under the tree. The moment my father saw it he turned white and began to tremble. I didn't know what to do. But he did. He went to a cabinet and took out a tall glass and a bottle. I recognized the bottle because all my Alabama uncles had plenty just like it. Prohibition moonshine. He filled the tall glass and drank it with hardly a pause. After that, it was as though the picture had vanished.

And so I awaited Christmas Eve, and the always exciting advent of fat Santa. Of course, I had never seen a weighted, jangling, belly-swollen giant flop down a chimney and gaily dispense his largesse under a Christmas tree. My cousin Billy Bob, who was a mean little runt but had a brain like a fist made of iron, said it was a lot of hooey, there was no such creature.

"My foot!" he said. "Anybody would believe there was any Santa Claus would believe a mule was a horse." This quarrel took place in the tiny courthouse square. I said: *"There is a Santa Claus because what he does is the Lord's will and whatever is the Lord's will is the truth."* And

Billy Bob, spitting on the ground, walked away: "Well, looks like we've got another preacher on our hands."

I always swore I'd never go to sleep on Christmas Eve, I wanted to hear the prancing dance of reindeer on the roof, and to be right there at the foot of the chimney to shake hands with Santa Claus. And on this particular Christmas Eve, nothing, it seemed to me, could be easier than staying awake.

My father's house had three floors and seven rooms, several of them huge, especially the three leading to the patio garden: a parlor, a dining room and a "musical" room for those who liked to dance and play and deal cards. The two floors above were trimmed with lacy balconies whose dark green iron intricacies were delicately entwined with bougainvillea and rippling vines of scarlet spider orchids—a plant that resembles lizards flicking their red tongues. It was the kind of house best displayed by lacquered floors and some wicker here, some velvet there. It could have been mistaken for the house of a rich man; rather, it was the place of a man with an appetite for elegance. To a poor (but happy) barefoot boy from Alabama it was a mystery how he managed to satisfy that desire.

But it was no mystery to my mother, who, having graduated from college, was putting her magnolia delights to full use while struggling to find in New York a truly suitable fiancé who could afford Sutton Place apartments and sable coats. No, my father's resources were familiar to her, though she never mentioned the matter until many years later, long after she had acquired ropes of pearls to glisten around her sable-wrapped throat.

She had come to visit me in a snobbish New England boarding school (where my tuition was paid by her rich and generous husband), when something I said tossed her into a rage; she shouted: "So you don't know how he lives so well? Charters yachts and cruises the Greek Islands? His *wives*! Think of the whole long string of them. All widows. All rich. *Very* rich. And all much older than he. Too old for any sane young man to marry. That's why you are his only child.

And that's why I'll never have another child—I was too young to have any babies, but he was a beast, he wrecked me, he ruined me—"

Just a gigolo, everywhere I go, people stop and stare . . . Moon, moon over Miami . . . This is my first affair, so please be kind . . . Hey, mister, can you spare a dime? . . . Just a gigolo, everywhere I go, people stop and stare . . .

All the while she talked (and I tried not to listen, because by telling me my birth had destroyed her, *she* was destroying me), these tunes ran through my head, or tunes like them. They helped me not to hear her, and they reminded me of the strange haunting party my father had given in New Orleans that Christmas Eve.

The patio was filled with candles, and so were the three rooms leading off it. Most of the guests were gathered in the parlor, where a subdued fire in the fireplace made the Christmas tree glitter; but many others were dancing in the music room and the patio to music from a wind-up Victrola. After I had been introduced to the guests, and been made much of, I had been sent upstairs; but from the terrace outside my French-shuttered bedroom door, I could watch all the party, see all the couples dancing. I watched my father waltz a graceful lady around the pool that surrounded the mermaid fountain. She *was* graceful, and dressed in a wispy silver dress that shimmered in the candlelight; but she was old—at least ten years older than my father, who was then thirty-five.

I suddenly realized my father was by far the youngest person at his party. None of the ladies, charming as they were, were any younger than the willowy waltzer in the floating silver dress. It was the same with the men, so many of whom were smoking sweet-smelling Havana cigars; more than half of them were old enough to be my father's father.

Then I saw something that made me blink. My father and his agile partner had danced themselves into a niche shadowed by scarlet spider orchids; and they were embracing, kissing. I was so startled, I was so *irate*, I ran into my bedroom, jumped into bed and pulled the covers over my head. What would my nice-looking young father want with an old woman like that! And why didn't all those people downstairs go home so Santa Claus could come? I lay awake for hours listening to them leave, and when my father said good-bye for the last time, I heard him climb the stairs and open my door to peek at me; but I pretended to be asleep.

Several things occurred that kept me awake the whole night. First, the footfalls, the noise of my father running up and down the stairs, breathing heavily. I had to see what he was up to. So I hid on the balcony among the bougainvillea. From there, I had a complete view of the parlor and the Christmas tree and the fireplace where a fire still palely burned. Moreover, I could see my father. He was crawling around under the tree arranging a pyramid of packages. Wrapped in purple paper, and red and gold and white and blue, they rustled as he moved them about. I felt dizzy, for what I saw forced me to reconsider everything. If these were presents intended for me, then obviously they had not been ordered by the Lord and delivered by Santa Claus; no, they were gifts bought and wrapped by my father. Which meant that my rotten little cousin Billy Bob and other rotten kids like him weren't lying when they taunted me and told me there was no Santa Claus. The worst thought was: Had Sook known the truth, and lied to me? No, Sook would never lie to me. She *believed*. It was just that—well, though she was sixty-something, in some ways she was at least as much of a child as I was.

I watched until my father had finished his chores and blown out the few candles that still burned. I waited until I was sure he was in bed and sound asleep. Then I crept downstairs to the parlor, which still reeked of gardenias and Havana cigars.

I sat there, thinking: Now I will have to be the one to tell Sook the truth. An anger, a weird malice was spiraling inside me: It was not directed towards my father, though he turned out to be its victim.

When the dawn came, I examined the tags attached to each of the packages. They all said: "For Buddy." All but one, which said: "For Evangeline." Evangeline was an elderly colored woman who drank

Coca-Cola all day long and weighed three hundred pounds; she was my father's housekeeper—she also mothered him. I decided to open the packages: It was Christmas morning, I was awake, so why not? I won't bother to describe what was inside them: just shirts and sweaters and dull stuff like that. The only thing I appreciated was a quite snazzy cap-pistol. Somehow I got the idea it would be fun to waken my father by firing it. So I did. *Bang. Bang. Bang.*

He raced out of his room, wild-eyed.

Bang. Bang. Bang.

"Buddy—what the hell do you think you're doing?"

Bang. Bang. Bang.

"Stop that!"

I laughed. "Look, Daddy. Look at all the wonderful things Santa Claus brought me."

Calm now, he walked into the parlor and hugged me. "You like what Santa Claus brought you?"

I smiled at him. He smiled at me. There was a tender lingering moment, shattered when I said: "Yes. But what are *you* going to give me, Daddy?" His smile evaporated. His eyes narrowed suspiciously—you could see that he thought I was pulling some kind of stunt. But then he blushed, as though he was ashamed to be thinking what he was thinking. He patted my head, and coughed and said: "Well, I thought I'd wait and let you pick out something you wanted. Is there anything particular you want?"

I reminded him of the airplane we had seen in the toy store on Canal Street. His face sagged. Oh, yes, he remembered the airplane and how expensive it was. Nevertheless, the next day I was sitting in that airplane dreaming I was zooming toward heaven while my father wrote out a check for a happy salesman. There had been some argument about shipping the plane to Alabama, but I was adamant—I insisted it should go with me on the bus that I was taking at two o'clock that afternoon. The salesman settled it by calling the bus company, who said that they could handle the matter easily.

But I wasn't free of New Orleans yet. The problem was a large silver flask of moonshine; maybe it was because of my departure, but anyway my father had been swilling it all day, and on the way to the bus station, he scared me by grabbing my wrist and harshly whispering: "I'm not going to let you go. I can't let you go back to that crazy family in that crazy old house. Just look at what they've done to you. A boy six, almost seven, talking about Santa Claus! It's all their fault, all those sour old spinsters with their Bibles and their knitting needles, those drunken uncles. *Listen* to me, Buddy. There is no God! There *is* no Santa Claus." He was squeezing my wrist so hard that it ached. "Sometimes, oh, God, I think your mother and I, the both of us, we ought to kill ourselves to have let this happen—" (He never killed himself, but my mother did: She walked down the Seconal road thirty years ago.) "Kiss me. Please. Please. Kiss me. Tell your daddy that you love him." But I couldn't speak. I was terrified I was going to miss my bus. And I was worried about my plane, which was strapped to the top of the taxi. "Say it: 'I love you.' Say it. Please. Buddy. Say it."

It was lucky for me that our taxi-driver was a good-hearted man. Because if it hadn't been for his help, and the help of some efficient porters and a friendly policeman, I don't know what would have happened when we reached the station. My father was so wobbly he could hardly walk, but the policeman talked to him, quieted him down, helped him to stand straight, and the taxi-man promised to take him safely home. But my father would not leave until he had seen the porters put me on the bus.

Once I was on the bus, I crouched in a seat and shut my eyes. I felt the strangest pain. A crushing pain that hurt everywhere. I thought if I took off my heavy city shoes, those crucifying monsters, the agony would ease. I took them off, but the mysterious pain did not leave me. In a way it never has; never will.

Twelve hours later I was home in bed. The room was dark. Sook was sitting beside me, rocking in a rocking chair, a sound as soothing as ocean waves. I had tried to tell her everything that had happened, and only stopped when I was hoarse as a howling dog. She stroked her fingers through my hair, and said: "Of course there is a Santa Claus. It's just that no single somebody could do all he has to do. So the Lord has spread the task among us all. That's why everybody is Santa Claus. I am. You are. Even your cousin Billy Bob. Now go to sleep. Count stars. Think of the quietest thing. Like snow. I'm sorry you didn't get to see any. But now snow is falling through the stars—" Stars sparkled, snow whirled inside my head; the last thing I remembered was the peaceful voice of the Lord telling me something I must do. And the next day I did it. I went with Sook to the post office and bought a penny postcard. That same postcard exists today. It was found in my father's safety deposit box when he died last year. Here is what I had written him: *Hello pop hope you are well l am and I am lurning to pedel my plain so fast I will soon be in the sky so keep your eyes open and yes I love you Buddy.*

STORY CREDITS

Penguin Modern Classics

OTHER VOICES, OTHER ROOMS
TRUMAN CAPOTE

'Truman Capote is the most perfect writer of my generation' Norman Mailer

After the death of his mother, thirteen-year-old Joel Knox is summoned to live with a father he has never met in a vast decaying mansion in rural Alabama, its baroque splendour now faded and tarnished. But when he arrives, his father is nowhere to be seen and Joel is greeted instead by his prim, sullen new stepmother Miss Amy and his debauched Cousin Randolph – living like spirits in the fragile decadence of a house full of secrets.

Truman Capote's first novel, *Other Voices, Other Rooms* is a story of hallucinatory power, vividly conjuring up the Gothic landscape of the Deep South and a boy's first glimpse into a mysterious adult world.

With an Introduction by John Berendt

PENGUIN MODERN CLASSICS

BREAKFAST AT TIFFANY'S
TRUMAN CAPOTE

'One of the twentieth century's most gorgeously romantic fictions' *Daily Telegraph*

It's New York in the 1940s, where the martinis flow from cocktail hour till breakfast at Tiffany's. And nice girls don't, except, of course, Holly Golightly. Pursued by Mafia gangsters and playboy millionaires, Holly is a fragile eyeful of tawny hair and turned-up nose, a heart-breaker, a perplexer, a traveller, a tease. She is irrepressibly 'top banana in the shock department', and one of the shining flowers of American fiction.

This edition also contains three stories: 'House of Flowers', 'A Diamond Guitar' and 'A Christmas Memory'.

Penguin Modern Classics

N COLD BLOOD
TRUMAN CAPOTE

'The American dream turning into the American nightmare ... a remarkable book'
Tony Tanner, *Spectator*

Controversial and compelling, *In Cold Blood* reconstructs the murder in 1959 of a
Kansas farmer, his wife and both their children. Truman Capote's comprehensive
study of the killings and subsequent investigation explores the circumstances
surrounding this terrible crime and the effect it had on those involved. At the
centre of his study are the amoral young killers Perry Smith and Dick Hickock,
who, vividly drawn by Capote, are shown to be reprehensible, yet entirely and
frighteningly human.

The book that made Capote's name, *In Cold Blood* is a seminal work of modern
prose, a remarkable synthesis of journalistic skill and powerfully evocative
narrative.

Penguin Modern Classics

ANSWERED PRAYERS
TRUMAN CAPOTE

'Brilliant, wicked, entertaining … a shimmering work … delightful' Melvyn Bragg

A brilliantly malicious exposé of the literary jet-set, when *Answered Prayers* first appeared in excerpts in *Esquire* magazine it outraged Capote's society friends, who recognized thinly veiled portraits of themselves in these scandalous fictional 'memoirs'.

P. B. Jones is the amoral, bisexual protagonist of this great, unfinished novel, who discovers that bed-hopping rather than literary ability is the way to get published. Living by his wits and his charm, Jones makes his way through the exotic boudoirs of the glitterati – only to discover that the prayers that are answered cause more pain than those that remain ignored.

'A literary gem … gloriously wicked; wickedly bitchy' *Time Out*
